The Adventure Begins In Fantasma

E.K. BUTENUTH, TYLER D. CABLE

MILK AND HONEY PUBLISHING LLC

In memory of Tyler David Cable.
Thank you for inspiring me. I miss you.

Thank you to my family, and for your love.
You have made me into the creative, hilarious,
and God-fearing woman I am today.

This book is dedicated to my annoying little
cousins, who gave me a lot of funny content.
Even if life takes us on different adventures,
I will love you forever, my Ruth, my Milly, and my Rose.

Contents

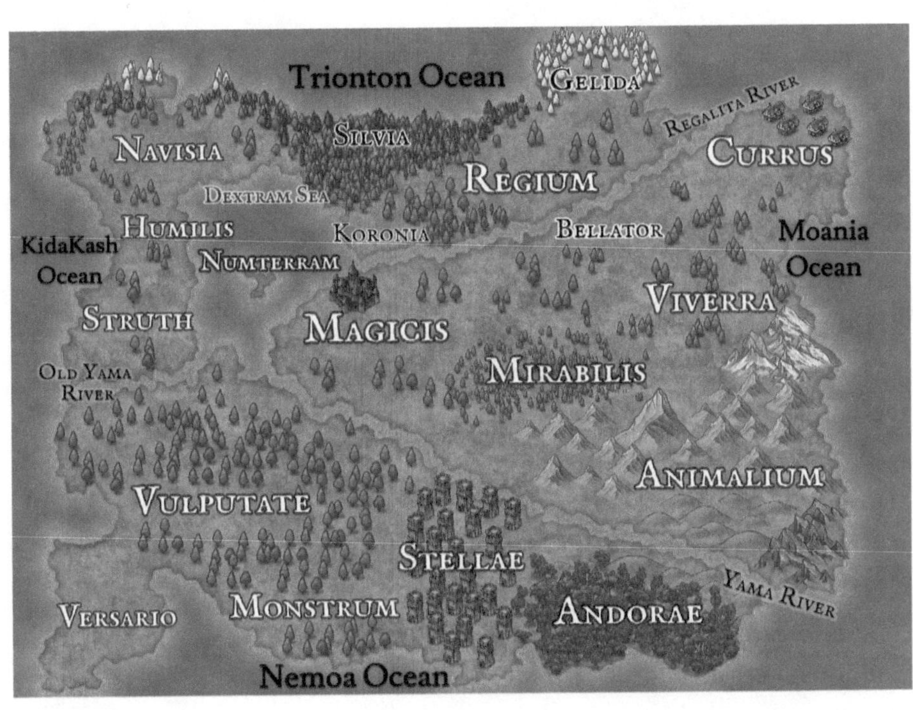

Trionton Ocean
Gelida
Regalita River
Navisia
Silvia
Currus
Regium
Dextram Sea
Moania
Ocean
KidaKash
Ocean
Humilis
Koronia
Bellator
Numterram
Viverra
Struth
Magicis
Old Yama
River
Mirabilis
Animalium
Vulputate
Stellae
Yama River
Versario
Monstrum
Andorae
Nemoa Ocean

Regions of Fantasma

Regions (Districts):

Andorae
Animalium (Conlis, Renosum)
Currus (Chemica, Metalli, Papyru, Technolia, Textila, Transportem)
Humilis
Magicis (Nilrem, Rutrah)
Mirabilis (Tearspool, Glasslook, Croquenti, Doorvis, Roseeloo)
Monstrum (Sulania, Mikan)
Navisia (Aquilo, Auster)
Numterram (Sirenia, Quamnemu, Miermie)
Regium (Bellator, Gelida, Koronia, Silvia)
Stellae
Struth (Pupia, Iwin)
Versario (Callidus, Insanis, Scelus)
Viverra (Rustay, Allwyne)
Vulputate (Ranso, Stanie, Vengera, Taincap)

Prologue: A Letter of Introduction

To My Dearest,

Once upon a time, Fantasma was filled with magic. Fantasma in the year 4000 was not that strange of a place. It was like any other normal land that also had horseless carriages, magic wands, dragons, flying lessons, and an abnormal amount of adventure. But most hardly noticed the magic. It was such a natural part of daily life that the only time people recognized the presence of magic was when it had disappeared completely.

This story you're about to read is not that unique of a tale either. It's about normal girls who lived normal lives- until a few seemingly small decisions changed them forever. Before I spoil the whole story, I'll stop here and leave you to discover the world of Fantasma for yourself.

Please enjoy this story about ordinary girls
going on some not so ordinary adventures.

Chapter 1: No Good Reason To Stay

Breathing usually came easy to Elsif, but in this moment, it did not. "This is-going to be- an amazing- year." Elsif told herself between sniffles as she tried not to cry.

Looking in the mirror, Elsif forced herself to smile. She had to regain her composure so she could face the new reality that she had desperately been trying to run from. It was hard for her to believe she could brave the coming torment when she was face to face with her current state. She did not look good.

Her blue eyes were bloodshot and scary looking. Her blonde hair was all frizz instead of curl, sticking out in different directions. Her glasses remained tear-stained no matter how many times she wiped them. Elsif had never been the prettiest girl, but at that moment she was a complete lost cause.

"You look good today," Elsif said to her sad image, trying and failing to encourage herself.

She forced herself to look away and end her vain pity party. In the past Elsif had never cared about how she looked, so she willed herself to not start now. All she cared about was doing well in school. That's all that mattered at Merlin Academy. Not looking pretty, being popular, or even having a single friend.

Who needed friends anyway? Certainly not Elsif. She was going to be a successful professor at Merlin Academy one day, and her social life before that didn't matter. When she was publishing new historical evidence and winning awards, no one would be asking her about how many friends she had at seventeen. That would be ridiculous.

"Having no friends is *ridiculous*," Elsif muttered, as she shook her head to clear her thoughts.

"This is going to be an amazing year," Elsif repeated the phrase over and over again, determined to echo the words until she believed them. She hoped she wouldn't be muttering the same words in ten years.

Elsif scolded herself for being too dramatic. She shouldn't be *this* worked up when people around Fantasma had much worse problems. People in Versario were starving and being set on fire by dragons! Their life was tragic, not hers. But in the back of Elsif's mind she thought that to most seventeen year old girls, her situation would still be a solid tragedy. Not the worst tragedy, but still a solid one.

Elsif heard her mother call her from downstairs. "The carriage will be here in ten minutes!"

She wanted to scream in response but decided against it so she wouldn't startle her poor mother. "Thank you," she called back, with a forced cheerfulness.

"This is going to be an amazing y-" Elsif couldn't finish the sentence. *It's going to be a different year*, she finally conceded. It may not end up being an amazing or even a great year, but it was undoubtedly going to be different.

"Maybe *different* can be amazing?" Elsif said, once again addressing herself in the mirror, hoping for a confidence boost. It still didn't work.

Taming her hair into a ponytail, Elsif practiced what she would say if her worst fears came true: running into her ex-best friend.

"Hey Libi, how was your August break?" *No, I don't want to talk to her. Just be pleasant and move on.*

"Hello Libi." *Way too forced.*

"How's it going Libi?" *Too friendly.*

"Hey Libi." *Can I just disappear forever?*

Libi probably wasn't practicing her best greeting for Elsif in front of a mirror. She had new friends and new roommates to hang out with that weren't lame like Elsif. Libi probably hadn't given her one thought since they parted ways the night of the Felix Finis Ball. The night Elsif moved out of the chambers, she wasn't invited to live in the next school year. Ten years of friendship thrown away for a reason that Elsif didn't know. There had been no clear reason why Libi had gradually stopped talking to her.

Elsif remembered her first day of Merlin like it was yesterday, likely because she was currently experiencing very similar emotions. At seven years old she stepped into Merlin for the first time with so much fear and uncertainty. Would she make friends? Would she fail her classes? Would she be too homesick and beg her parents to come get her?

But Libi was her hero that day. Elsif didn't even have a room assignment when she first walked up to check in. Libi overheard her, and demanded that they be roommates because she didn't have one either. They had been inseparable since. Best friends and roommates for ten years.

That all crashed and burned last year. Since it was Elsif's second to last year in Merlin's regular program, she decided she needed to put all her focus into her studies. So much so, that by the time Elsif had finally noticed that Libi had made other friends and wasn't around anymore, it was too late.

Libi was always good at making new friends. Elsif always found it tremendously hard so she would piggyback off of Libi's new friendships. But Elsif slowly realized last year that Libi hadn't been inviting her to things anymore.

Maybe Elsif should have said something or fought for the friendship, but in her mind, who was she to stop someone who wanted to leave? She wanted to respect Libi's decision and didn't want to cause drama.

But deep down Elsif knew there was a different reason she didn't fight for the friendship. She was scared. Scared to uncover the ugly truth of why Libi didn't want to be friends anymore. Elsif was fairly self-aware, but she wasn't sure if she wanted all her faults to be put on display for herself.

"We grew apart," Elsif quickly told herself. "Friends grow apart all the time. It's a part of life."

Elsif tried to understand the situation from Libi's perspective, but in her weakest moments she found mountains of anger and hatred growing underneath the surface. She attempted to ignore those developing feelings and focus on the present. Elsif just had to mentally prepare herself for moving into her cousins' chambers and everything would be fine.

Her cousins were alright. They were great. The only hesitation Elsif had about living with them was that they were all absolutely clinically insane. A minor detail. Thinking it through, Elsif actually didn't mind their insanity, she could manage them. What really bugged her is that they were her *cousins*, not her friends. Of course she loved them, they were more like sisters than cousins. But roommates were supposed to be your buddies. Elsif knew the whole year she was going to be trying to protect them from harm and bossing them around out of habit from years of watching them. But she didn't want to feel like a mom at school. She needed to focus on her studies, not their shenanigans.

Now that Elsif had stressed herself to capacity, she was even less ready for the carriage that was about to arrive. Libi was the more pressing matter and as soon as she got the awkward hello out of the way, Elsif could enjoy the rest of her year. It was the last year of regular school before Elsif applied for advanced classes at Merlin so she had to be completely focused.

"How's it hanging Libi?" *Am I the most awkward person alive?*

"Sup Libi." *I'm the worst.*

"Good day Libi." *Why am I using an accent?*

Maybe Elsif could dye her hair, ditch the glasses, use an accent, and convince everyone at Merlin that she was a new student from Andorae or some other weird place that students hardly came from. She had some doubt about it working, she had been attending Merlin for a decade, so someone was bound to recognize her. At the very least her cousins would never allow her to forget who she truly was.

"Seventeen and already pathetic," Elsif laughed at herself.

It was weird to suddenly not be friends with someone that you grew up with. Elsif knew practically everything about Libi. Her favorite animal was a giraffe, she hated how often her parents fought, her go-to nail polish was pale yellow, her backpack had native flowers from Viverra on it, she hated apricots because she ate a moldy one once, and she enjoyed baking cookies but didn't like eating them. Elsif had never gone through a romantic breakup, but she had a feeling that a friendship breakup was worse.

"Elsif, look at me," she said, staring at herself in the mirror. "You may not be the prettiest, or the most social, or the thinnest, or the smartest, and your personality is a little annoying sometimes- but you are very humorous. I'd even go so far to say you are the wittiest person in all of Fantasma. Granted, all your jokes are perfect because you're the target audience, but nonetheless you're hilarious and no one can take that away from you."

"The carriage is here!" Her mother yelled from the front door.

With a deep sigh, Elsif realized that she had spent the last twenty minutes talking to herself in the mirror.

As she moved out the door, Elsif muttered her mantra, "This is going to be an amazing year. An amazing year. Amazing year. Amazing ye-" The more she said it, the stranger it sounded, as if the phrase (and reality) was moving farther and farther out of reach.

In the blink of an eye, the carriage was pulling away from Elsif's home and moving towards Merlin Academy. She couldn't hide from the future any longer. It was time to face the music, but unfortunately Elsif was tone-deaf.

After the first few minutes, there was an announcement about an additional stop. In Koronia.

Everyone in the carriage shared surprised expressions. This was a strange announcement for two reasons. First of all, Elsif memorized the carriage schedule several weeks ago and there were only supposed to be seven stops in the Gelida district. Elsif arranged to be in a carriage with minimal stops and no out of district detours. This way she would get to Merlin in a timely manner and have more time to study in the library.

The other reason this was an alarming announcement was because no one ever left Koronia. People in Koronia kept to themselves and never traveled.

Elsif concluded it must have been a new student who just enrolled. A new student from a new place, who was going to need new friends. Elsif instantly knew this was her chance.

She leaned back in her seat and finally relaxed. "This is going to be an amazing year."

*****

The quiet little village of Mellberg was waking up to a seemingly average day. What the town did not know was that an important visitor was coming from the Magicis region. The visitor was Ms. Princey. She was an ambassador for Merlin Academy, which was only the *most* prestigious school in the whole land of Fantasma. Ms. Princey was old, strict, and looking for only the brightest to let into the school.

One random old lady visiting a town might not seem like big news, but it was to this particular town. Nothing unusual ever happened in Mellberg. Nothing unusual happened in the whole Koronia district. This part of Regium was known for one thing: living in the past. They could not let go of their traditions, welcome new things, or meet new people. Koronia had been left in the past by the rest of Fantasma, doomed to follow the same routines and think the same ideas day after day. Everyone had the same unspoken agreement to follow these rules. Well, everyone except Jazzy.

Jazzy was not by any means a spontaneous, chaotic, adventure-seeking girl, but compared to the rest of Mellberg, she practically was. She was not completely an outsider, but different enough that she never felt completely comfortable. For example, her actual name was Jasmine. That's what her mother called her before she passed away years ago, but Jazzy decided to give herself a nickname. For a place like Mellberg, that was strange. They believed you were given one name, and there was no reason to have a second one. She also enjoyed baking new foods, trying new recipes, sewing outside of patterns, and finding new trails around town. To the average person it may not sound like much, but in this particular community it was monumental.

Sixteen years isn't necessarily a long time to be alive, but it was enough time for Jazzy to realize she wanted a tad more than what her village was willing to offer her. But she had no idea that the opportunity she had been unconsciously waiting for was coming into town that very day.

Ms. Princey placed her stand in the middle of the village, the busiest place in town. Once she had everything neatly arranged, Ms. Princey sat down and waited for the applicants to come rushing up to her table.

But after a few minutes Ms. Princey looked around and noticed that no one was within thirty feet of her. She began to wonder what strange place she had been sent to by her superiors. After half an hour, she came to the conclusion that there was something seriously wrong with the people of this town, since not a single one was interested in interviewing for a potential spot at Merlin Academy.

The Merlin Academy! Did they not know that Merlin was the most prestigious school in all of Fantasma, where millions of students applied every year?

Scoffing, Ms. Princey began to pack hastily, deciding that the measly town had offended her far too much and she could not stay there another minute. She had traveled ten hours that morning to give the pathetic little village a chance, and all she received in return was a rude lack of acknowledgement. Ms. Princey came to the conclusion that the town was far too ignorant to see a great opportunity.

As she was about to leave, a very mediocre looking girl came strolling up to her. "Would you like an apple, miss?"

Ms. Princey crinkled up her nose. "No, I would not."

"I also have a pear or an apricot?" The girl offered with wide-eyed innocence.

With a sigh, Ms. Princey grabbed the apple and stuffed it in her bag, not because she was going to eat it, but because she wanted to leave and didn't want to stand there all day while the annoying girl offered her every fruit in the district.

When Ms. Princey realized the girl had not walked away, but instead stood there with a grin, she turned to the girl and barked, "What do you want?"

"I wanted to say hello," the girl said hesitantly. "I'm Jazzy."

"I'm Ms. Princey, an admission counselor for Merlin Academy," she replied with an air of snobbery.

"Merlin Academy?" Jazzy asked with a tilt of her head.

Ms. Princey's eyes grew wide as her whole worldview shattered. "You don't know about Merlin Academy? I knew that Koronia liked to keep to themselves, but this is a whole other level of isolation. How do you people live with such ignorance of the outside world? The rest of Regium sends students, and the rest of Fantasma certainly does as well. Please tell me, are you, child, particularly uneducated or does your lack of knowledge extend to the surrounding villages?"

Jazzy tried to stifle her giggles at the strange question. "I'm fairly certain that no one in my village or the next would know about Merlin Academy."

Ms. Princey's face began to grow distressed, so Jazzy continued earnestly, "Oh please don't be offended, our village doesn't worry about many things beyond our small borders. We like to keep to ourselves, and don't always take kindly to strangers. Which is the reason no one is coming to your lovely booth. Please tell me more about your Academy, it sounds fascinating."

"Well," Ms. Princey began as she looked down at Jazzy. "It's only the most influential school in the whole fifteen regions. We are sent for only the brightest and most intelligent students in Fantasma."

"Sent?" Jazzy inquired. "Who sent you?"

"My superiors," Ms. Princey said with a vague wave. "It doesn't matter who sent me, what matters is the location. They have specific reasons and specific students in mind when we travel to each location, and I am here to weed out who the *specific* students are." With a shake of her head Ms. Princey sighed. "They must have been wrong this time, I don't have a single application."

"I could apply," Jazzy suggested. "If that will help you."

Ms. Princey frowned, and took a long look around the village. "You might as well not bother yourself. I'll accept you right now so that I can leave this dreadful place."

Jazzy was taken aback. "Accept me? Now? I'm not sure that I would qualify for this school. I'm certainly not the most intelligent or brightest in the village."

"You have no competition," Ms. Princey stated. "Please accept, so *I* can leave."

"Well," Jazzy thought for a moment. "Could I hear a little more about Merlin Academy? Such as where it is, or what is expected of me if I agree?"

"Fine," Ms. Princey muttered, plopping back down in her seat. "As I said before, it is a very influential school," she began her short and fast spiel. "A student can be educated for almost any career they choose in any of the regions in Fantasma. They will receive the highest possible education in the land. We only accept the most exceptional, remarkable, distinct individuals as our pupils. Merlin is classified as a twelve-year school but we also have preschool opportunities and an extensive higher degree program. Thousands of students travel from all four corners of Fantasma to attend our school to receive the finest education. It is by far the most sought out school." Ms. Princey stopped for only a moment to take a breath before she continued, "The school is located in the northwest corner of the Magicis region, right on the Dextram Sea. The school is in official term for six months out of the year: September, November, January, March, May, and July with the first day of the term being September 1st and the last day being July 31st. The school runs six days a week, with Sunday off, and ten hours a day from 7am to 5pm. We offer each of our students a full scholarship for room, board, and all classes. The only 'payment' we ask of the student is that they abide by all 752 rules in our handbook."

Blinking through the whirlwind of words, Jazzy took a deep breath. "That is a lot of information. A lot of absolutely wonderful information, but a lot."

"Are you accepting or not?" Ms. Princey asked with no sympathy.

"Well," Jazzy hesitated, thinking about her reasons to stay and her reasons to go. She came up with several reasons to go but not many to stay. Jazzy always liked trying new things, so why shouldn't she try something like this? "I suppose I could. I mean, why not?" she smiled at Ms. Princey with a tiny shrug.

"Perfect," Ms. Princey plopped a form in front of Jazzy. "I just need a parent's signature."

"Oh, my parents passed away," Jazzy explained. "My father passed before I was born, and my mother right after my fifth birthday."

Ms. Princey rolled her eyes. "Fine, we'll forget the signature. ID number?"

"I don't think I have one of those," Jazzy said with a bit of embarrassment.

"Your government is the most incompetent in all of Fantasma," Ms. Princey groaned. "Even worse than Versario. I'll figure out a way to get you an ID number and you'll find it on your Merlin ID when you check in. Now I think that's everything. Do you have any questions?"

"Uh." Jazzy had a million questions but she didn't think she would be able to verbalize any. "I don't believe so."

This was a big commitment that shouldn't be made lightly, but Jazzy had never been a sensible girl. At least that's what the other villagers always told her. Jazzy liked her village well enough, but she had to admit she never fit in. She was labeled different and odd, and while it had never bothered her before, something about the way the stranger talked made her wonder. Maybe something new was exactly what Jazzy needed.

"I'd love to go to Merlin Academy."

"Alright, sign here," Ms. Princey stated.

Jazzy signed, having no idea what she was in for, but not caring in that moment. There was no turning back from the grand adventure that was about to unfold.

Chapter 2: New Characters Galore

"Do you want to sit here?" Elsif offered a little too loudly as the new student passed her bench in the carriage.

The new girl flinched at the loud question, but smiled once she saw Elsif and the empty seat beside her. "Thank you," she replied and took the seat. "I'm Jazzy."

"I'm Elsif. Are you a new student?"

Jazzy flashed a nervous smile. "I am, yes. How did you know?"

"This carriage doesn't usually stop in Koronia," Elsif explained, trying to sound casual, and not like she had been plotting about how to become friends for two hours. "So it was a lucky guess."

Jazzy nodded. "Oh, Ms. Princey had mentioned that not many of the students were from Koronia."

"Was she your admissions counselor?" Elsif asked. "She can be pretty brutal sometimes."

"She was nice," Jazzy said. "She was a little confused by my village, but it was so nice of her to take the time to talk to me and offer me a spot at Merlin Academy."

Elsif tried to stop herself from laughing. "I don't think I've ever heard someone describe Ms. Princey as *nice*."

Jazzy returned a shy laugh. "I guess I could see that. She had a few interesting words to describe Mellberg. I don't think it was to her liking. Where are you from?"

"I'm from Regium too," Elsif stated, trying to lay down some common ground. "I live in the Gelida district."

"You have all that snow," Jazzy perked up. "I absolutely love snow. We don't get nearly enough in the winter."

"Yeah the north of Gelida gets a ton of snow for like nine months out of the year," Elsif explained. "But I live in the south so it's not as bad."

"That's lovely," Jazzy beamed. "Do you like Merlin?"

"Yeah," Elsif nodded eagerly. "It's a great school. I've been there for a decade if you have any questions."

"I have one," Jazzy admitted. "But it's about the carriage, not the school. I was wondering where the horses were?"

"Horses?"

"The horses to pull the carriage."

Elsif's eyes grew wide as she realized that all the rumors she had heard about Koronia were true, they didn't use any magic! They lived like they were still in the Ancient Age when there was no magic in the land.

"Well, it's magic," Elsif answered.

Jazzy's eyes grew even wider than Elsif's. "Magic is real?" She whispered her question like she didn't dare believe it herself.

"Ms. Princey didn't tell you that Merlin teaches magic?"

Jazzy shook her head, then let a nervous laugh escape her mouth. "I can't believe magic is real. This is the greatest day of my life."

Elsif laughed along with Jazzy as the girls began to form their inseparable bond. Jazzy shared that magic was just a bedtime story in Koronia, and that she had always dreamed of witnessing it in real life. Elsif told her as much as she could about Merlin and magic, but she realized it was a hard thing to describe.

As they switched from the topic of magic, to every other topic in the world, the ten hour carriage ride went by in the blink of an eye. Jazzy was filled with excitement over every new thing she learned, but as the minutes passed, Elsif grew increasingly worried for Jazzy and how she would survive at Merlin

The dreaded announcement that the carriage had arrived finally came, and Elsif was more determined than ever to change her trajectory for the year. She wanted a new friend and also wanted to help Jazzy succeed at Merlin. It was now or never if Elsif was going to take a step out of her well-built comfort zone.

"Hey Jazzy," Elsif forced herself to say. "Do you have a room assignment for this year?"

"Not yet," Jazzy responded while grabbing her bag.

Taking a deep breath Elsif asked, "Would you want to live in my chambers with my cousins and I?"

Jazzy smiled. "Really?"

"Yeah," Elsif relaxed at Jazzy's expression. "We have three rooms, and there's four of us right now. Rose and Milly are sharing a room, and I can share a room with Ruth. She's been begging me to be her roommate for years, so she'll be absolutely thrilled. Then you could have the third bedroom all to yourself. My cousins are really sweet girls too. A little crazy and annoying and a tad overbearing, but sweet!"

"That sounds absolutely wonderful," Jazzy beamed. "I can't believe I'm making so many new friends already."

Elsif's heart pounded at the word *friend*. Elsif had never initiated a friendship in her entire life; she had never needed to. She had never been the outgoing type or a great conversationalist, so the fact that she seemed to be making a friend was impressive. Elsif finally began to believe that maybe it could be an amazing year.

As Jazzy stepped out of the carriage her mouth fell open as she looked around. It was by far the grandest building she had ever seen in her entire life. The school was absolutely huge, with dozens of floors and thousands of windows all lined up perfectly. The white brick looked beautiful, and it complimented the dark blue tiled roof beautifully. The building was perfectly symmetrical and stretched the length of what seemed like half a mile. Even from afar, Jazzy could see the school was without flaw.

A splash drew Jazzy's attention behind her, where she saw a never-ending blue sea. Jazzy couldn't believe how much water she saw. As she saw ships sailing through the water, she wondered how they didn't get lost in the blue abyss. Stone docks lined the coastline, and people were climbing onto them from the sea. But on further inspection, Jazzy didn't see regular people pulling themselves onto the dock. One minute she saw a tail and fins, and the next there would be a pair of legs!

Jazzy tapped on Elsif's shoulder. "Are those-"

"Mermaids," Elsif said offhandedly, while she looked in a different direction.

"Whoa," Jazzy breathed, as she stared at the mermaids. One girl with long brown hair was swimming near the shoreline, and pulled herself onto the nearest dock. Her long dark green, shimmering tail stretched up her whole body to just below her collar bone, only her arms, neck, and head looked human. But half a second later, the green tail transformed into blue pants with feet at the bottom, and a yellow blouse appeared over her abdomen and shoulders. She stood up casually and headed towards the school. A normal looking girl was in the place where a mermaid just was. "Elsif? Elsif, how does-"

Jazzy turned to see Elsif, staring off at another student. A girl with dark hair was walking past them and towards the front doors of Merlin. As the girl passed them, Elsif gave her a small smile and a wave. The girl kept walking and didn't notice Elsif, which made Elsif's hand drop immediately followed by her smile.

"Elsif?" Jazzy asked again.

"What?" Elsif turned toward Jazzy. "Did you say something about mermaids? You probably don't see many of those in Mellberg."

"Not at all," Jazzy said. "Who did you wave to?"

"Um," Elsif looked back towards the girl who was on her way to the front doors. "Just an old friend. She didn't see me." Elsif then gestured towards the long brown haired girl that Jazzy had previously been admiring. "Did you see Misty transform? It's pretty cool to see in person."

"You know her?" Jazzy asked in wide-eyed wonder.

"Kind of," Elsif shrugged. "Misty is dating my cousin Monty."

"You have more cousins?" She asked in astonishment. "More than just the ones you live with?"

"Yeah I have-" Elsif began counting on her fingers. "Seven."

Jazzy shook her head in disbelief. "This is the most exciting day of my life."

Elsif patted Jazzy on the shoulder with a forced laugh. "Let's go check in."

As the girls walked towards the front doors, Jazzy got a closer look at the magnificence of the school. The front lawn was a perfect shade of green with not a single blade of grass out of place. The path and stairs leading up to the front doors were flawless white brick. They led right up to double glass doors that were framed and decorated with gold. But the extravagance did not stop at the doors.

If the outside was impressive, then the inside was unimaginable. The ceilings were about a mile high and in the distance Jazzy could see several staircases, corridors, and hallways branching off from the foyer. Jazzy couldn't decide what was more impressive, the giant fountain in the middle of the room or the golden chandelier above their heads. Every direction Jazzy looked she saw the most pristine architecture of her life, all covered in gold motif.

"This way," Elsif motioned for Jazzy to follow her as she made her way across the room.

Elsif walked up to a table with a middle-aged man with a neat handlebar mustache. She began talking with him and arranging everything for Jazzy. Elsif set up Jazzy's room assignment, arranged her class schedule, and filled out all her paperwork. Jazzy's mom never had the opportunity to drop her off on the first day of school, but she imagined it would be similar to that moment.

"Jazzy, what's your last name?"

"I don't have one," Jazzy stated.

Elsif glanced at Jazzy with a surprised expression, then back at the man behind the table. "Mr. Lukin, should I make up a last name for her if she doesn't have one?"

"Sure," Mr. Lukin shrugged, not appearing too concerned. "You should use Thomas. That's my middle name, and I always thought it was a rather good one."

"Jasmine Thomas?" Elsif asked Jazzy. "Does that sound good?"

"Sure," Jazzy agreed.

"Okay," Elsif said, then handed Jazzy a few items. "Here's your class schedule, Merlin ID, and chamber room assignment."

Jazzy gratefully took the items. She looked at the Merlin ID and noted the numbers in the corner, like Ms. Princey said there would be.

After Elsif finished checking Jazzy in, they headed to the ladies' dormitories located in the east wing. Elsif led them to a chamber on the third floor that had a view of the Dextram Sea. When they finally reached the door, Elsif's hand hesitated on the doorknob.

"Remember," Elsif began. "My cousins can be a little *much* sometimes. They enjoy being loud and obnoxious and not following social cues."

"Okay," Jazzy said with ignorant optimism.

They are going to eat her alive, Elsif thought as she turned the handle.

For a split second, Elsif saw a glimmer of hope. Her three cousins were sitting nicely in the common area of the dorm, looking like completely normal individuals who contributed to society. But alas, it only lasted for a single split second. With one foot in the door, a bucket filled with water and orange glitter fell on Elsif's head.

The cousins laughed as Elsif wiped her eyes and tried to control her breathing. "Jazzy, meet my cousins," Elsif muttered.

"Hi," Jazzy said as she attempted to muffle her laughter.

"Jazzy's a new student," Elsif explained. "She's going to be staying in room A, and I'm going to be in room C with Ruth."

"Yes!" The girl, who Jazzy assumed was Ruth, exclaimed in excitement. She wrapped Elsif in a big hug, then turned to Jazzy and wrapped her in a hug as well. "Hi I'm Ruth! Sorry, I just got wet glitter on you," she said while releasing Jazzy from her grasp. She was short with hazel eyes, and dark blonde hair. She wore a cute pink sundress with white lace.

"I love glitter," Jazzy responded.

Elsif attempted to wipe off her shirt. "Who put the bucket above the door?"

"Do you have to ask?" The girl sitting in the closest chair responded. She had long brown hair tied back into a ponytail and dark brown eyes. She was wearing cargo pants and a white flowy shirt. "I'm Milly," she said to Jazzy. "Nice to meet you. Do you like sailing?"

"I don't know," Jazzy said, keeping her smile in place despite her confusion.

"Rose," Elsif grumbled towards the last girl who sat on the couch with a mischievous grin. "I told you no pranks directed at me if I was going to live here this year."

"The glitter water wasn't directed toward *you*," Rose clarified. "It was directed toward *Milly*."

"*Milly*," Elsif copied Rose's tone. "Was already inside the room."

"That's not my problem!" Rose defended herself. Rose was a tall, lanky girl with long, messy auburn hair with blue eyes that matched Elsif's. She wore overalls that were covered in rips, burns, and mystery colors. "You should consider it a welcome gift."

"What a great reception," Elsif muttered.

Rose walked over and shared a cheeky smirk with Jazzy. "Would you like a mushroom?" She dangled a piece of fungi in front of Jazzy's face, but it was quickly snatched away by Elsif.

"Stop it Rose," Elsif chided. "You're not allowed to scare off any more roommates."

"I'm trying to set a new record," Rose remarked with a dramatic twirl.

"Our last roommate left in three days," Ruth stated.

Elsif shot a look at Ruth, before adding, "But that was a year ago, Rose is much more mature now."

"Yes, I am so much more mature now," Rose agreed with a sly smile. "How about a muffin?"

"No!" Elsif shouted, clearly exasperated.

Ruth leaned over to Jazzy. "You don't want to eat anything that Rose gives you."

"Or anything that comes from Mirabilis for that matter," Milly added. "My skin had purple dots on it for three weeks when she tricked me into some of her berries."

"You're from Mirabilis?" Jazzy asked Rose.

"Born and raised," Rose announced proudly. "Well except for a day and a half when I was seven and decided to run away from home and start a new life in Viverra."

Elsif rolled her eyes. "Aren't you seven now?"

"No," Rose boasted. "I'm thirteen! A grown young woman I assure you."

Milly eyed Elsif. "Did you really not know how old she was?"

"I knew she was thirteen," Elsif stated. "Obviously."

"Okay," Milly challenged. "How old is Ruth?"

Elsif shrugged. "Also thirteen?"

"Fifteen!" Ruth protested.

"Yeah," said Milly. "I'm the other one who is thirteen."

"So close," Elsif joked. "Well in my mind you guys are still five years old."

"I'm sixteen," Jazzy added, trying to join in the conversation. "And I'm from Koronia."

"Koronia!" Rose exclaimed. "I've never met someone from there! I didn't know you were allowed to leave! Are you allowed to be here right now? Are they watching you? Blink twice if you need help!"

Ruth pulled Rose out of Jazzy's face. "You can go ahead and ignore her. That's what we all do. I'm also from Regium, the Bellator district to be exact."

"I'm from Navisia," Milly added.

"You all don't live in the same place?" Jazzy asked in a sad tone. "Don't you miss each other?"

Milly shook her head. "Nope."

Ruth hugged Milly. "I do!"

"I miss pulling pranks on them," Rose noted. "Especially Elsif."

Elsif rolled her eyes. "We see each other plenty during the six months at Merlin, and when our families go to the Stellae region. That's where our family is originally from. Our grandparents are still there along with some other family, so we visit a lot."

"How much family do you all have?" Jazzy asked, amazed. She couldn't keep track.

"Too much," Rose joked.

"Our grandparents had six children," Milly began. "My mother is the oldest of the siblings and married a pirate from Navisia. They lived in Stellae for a while and had my older brother David, but thirteen years later when I came along they decided to raise me in Navisia. David goes to Merlin too, but this is his last year of advanced schooling."

"My mother was the second sibling," Elsif continued. "And moved to Gelida after she went to Merlin, where my father is from. Our Uncle Oliver is next and he and our Aunt Monica had three boys, Monty, Michael, and Max who all go to Merlin, but are from Stellae. Then Ruth's dad, Uncle Benjamin, was next and married and moved to Bellator."

"And they had a perfect daughter," Ruth commented.

"Then who's next?" Milly asked. "Uncle Louis or Uncle Earnest?"

"Uncle Louis," Ruth replied. "He died before any of us were born."

Elsif interrupted, "I was born."

"Why are you so old?" Rose accused with a side eye.

Milly shook her head. "Anyway, the youngest was Uncle Earnest who met Aunt Rainbow at Merlin and moved to her home region of Mirabilis, where they raised Rose."

"Wow." Jazzy was overwhelmed by all the information.

"You can meet them later if you want," Ruth offered.

"Yeah later. Let's go unpack all our stuff," Elsif said then looked at Jazzy. "Welcome to the family."

Jazzy went into the first room to the left. She was neighbors with Milly and Rose who had the second room to the left. Ruth and Elsif were across the living room, and next to the bathrooms.

Jazzy set down her two bags, and began to unpack her few belongings. Once she put her clothes, toiletries, and her little trinket box on the bed, she walked back into the living room to explore the chambers.

There was an oval coffee table in the middle of the room, with two couches and four chairs around it. Next to Jazzy's room was a little kitchen and a closet, and across from her was the bathroom. Walking into the living room, she saw a glass door that opened to a balcony. She stepped outside and felt a cool breeze. The sun was setting on the Dextram Sea while students continued to stream into the school.

"Let's go to dinner!" Jazzy heard Milly call from inside. She rushed back inside to join the girls, excited about her first meal with her new friends.

*****

Delicious smells wafted towards the girls as they walked through the large ornately carved archway, and into the spacious dining room. On either side of the long room, two fireplaces blazed, cheerfully inviting the students to relax and enjoy a good meal.

"That's my brother David over there," Milly told Jazzy. "He's the one standing on the table having a sword duel."

"And the one he's dueling is our cousin Monty," Elsif commented. "Who do you think is going to win?"

Milly and Ruth voted for David, while Elsif and Rose voted Monty. Jazzy wondered how they didn't impale each other, and grew nervous that it would happen any moment. After several minutes of lunges, blocks, twists, and a few flips, they abruptly stopped to start eating dinner.

"I think it was a draw," Milly commented, as the boys started talking to two other guys. "Those two are Michael and Max."

Rose stood up and began frantically waving to the four boys. They saw the signal after a moment and walked over to the girl's table. Jazzy was introduced to each of them and grew even more amazed at the close family connection. After a few minutes, they went to different tables, and the girls continued their meals.

"In our family, there are two gangs," Rose explained. "The girls against the boys. We must be superior to them in every way."

The girls talked about the different contests they had won over the years, and strategies they must implement for future competitions. After staying in the dining chambers for hours laughing, talking, and eating way too much sugar plum stew, the girls decided to head back to the dormitories for the night.

As they walked down the hall, Elsif stopped suddenly. "Hey, let's step into this corridor for a second."

Jazzy was confused but followed the other girls into an adjacent hallway. The other girls leaned against the wall and began chatting softly. Confusion engulfed Jazzy until she glanced back into the main hallway.

A group of five students passed their corridor. There were two girls who were identical with brown hair, pale skin, and two different eye colors, one amber and one dark brown. A guy with spiky red hair followed them, saying something that made both girls snarl at him. Bringing up the rear was a tall guy with jet black hair, vivid green eyes, and a permanent glare. Beside him the last girl had dark hair and a complexion that seemed almost green. Upon further inspection, her hair also had a green tinge when it caught the light.

As the greenish girl passed, she glanced over and caught Jazzy's eye. Her eyes were green as well and held Jazzy's gaze for a split second before she moved on. Jazzy had never seen anyone that looked like her before.

After the group disappeared down the hall, the girls continued walking as if nothing happened.

"Oh my gosh," Rose teased after a minute, grabbing Elsif's arm. "They almost killed us!"

"Who were they?" Jazzy asked with curiosity.

"That's Melissa's infamous gang," Ruth stated. "Paisley and Piper were the twins. Bernard had the red hair, and Juniper was the tall guy. They're from Versario, so people tend to avoid them. Scared babies like Elsif."

"They enjoy murdering people," Rose said with a smile.

"They don't murder people," Elsif voiced. "They just might possibly be related to murderers."

"That's so mean," Ruth replied.

Elsif scrunched her nose. "I mean historically all the regions of Fantasma sent their criminals to the region of Versario for like five hundred years, and the practice was only banned seventy-six years ago. And there's rumors that governments still send their unwanted to that region illegally. So they might be perfectly nice people, but they could also be *loiterers*."

"We don't even know them," Milly complained. "Who cares about their region's history? They're people like us."

"Of course they are," Elsif agreed. "And they deserve respect and a great education, but I'll be keeping my distance because I'm scared of them."

"Because they're from Versario?" Jazzy questioned.

"No," Elsif stated. "Because Bernard bit me when we were eight, and any friends of his are enemies of mine."

The girls laughed and talked about the nefarious activities that Melissa and her friends might have done as they arrived at their chambers and got ready for bed. They went to bed with great anticipation for the first day of classes.

Chapter 3: Raiding the Weaponry

Elsif was going to kill her cousins. It was five in the morning on the first day of classes, and all the girls thought it was an amazing idea to have a full-blown conversation right next to Elsif's bed. Practically smothering herself with a pillow, Elsif could still hear the sounds of laughter and the comparison of schedules.

"I'm really looking forward to my advanced sailing class," Milly commented. "My regular sailing class is going to be boring in comparison."

"You're taking two?" Ruth questioned.

"It's better than being in another literature or magical science class," Milly replied. "But flying class will be cool too."

"I can't wait to fly!" Rose exclaimed. "I'm going to fly all the way home when I decide to drop out."

"I'm in flying too," Jazzy said happily. "During the last hour?"

"Yeah," Milly confirmed. "It's a good last class to have. The field is right outside the dining chambers, so we can be the first ones to dinner."

"I'm most excited for my advanced Animalium culture class, I can't wait for the unit on-" Ruth was cut off by a pillow hitting her head. "Elsif, do you mind? We're trying to have a conversation."

"And I'm trying to not strangle you all," Elsif muttered from underneath her covers.

"Did you get into the history of Magicis?" Ruth asked. "That's all you talked about in July."

"No," Elsif took the covers off her head. "My schedule was filled up. They made me take a stupid magic class about inanimate objects. Magic is a waste of time when I could be learning about the politics of Magicis in the Ancient Age."

"Says the person who has magic," Ruth complained. "I would do anything to have powers."

"Me too," Milly agreed. "You'd have such an advantage in a battle."

"Not me," said Rose. "I'm perfect the way I am. I can become an evil dictator with or without magic."

"You have magic?" Jazzy asked in awe.

"I don't have much. I can only do this." Elsif held out her hand and a little snow flurry started to dance across her palm.

"Wow," Jazzy said, absolutely dazzled by the snowflakes.

"It comes in handy when your drink is lukewarm," Rose added.

"Yeah," Ruth agreed with sarcasm. "She's amazing, but we should get ready for school. We only have two hours."

"Two hours to sleep," Elsif covered her head again. "Everyone please get out."

*****

The first day of school was an average day for all the girls except Jazzy. After several minutes in each of her classes, Jazzy was completely lost and confused. It was a little tough, but fortunately, her last class was much more enjoyable because she had Milly and Rose.

The first session of flying class was spent trying to get off the ground for at least five seconds. The girls scooped up a shimmery substance that was half gas and half liquid from a bowl and poured it over themselves. The substance was called *vish* and was supposed to help an individual fly if they concentrated.

Rose and Jazzy took turns jumping off a tall rock with the rest of the students, while Milly stood to the side and prepared her mind. While she waited, she noticed something interesting happening across the field.

Juniper and Melissa appeared to be having a heated argument over a long bag, which appeared to be a beige-ish color. Melissa tried to hand Juniper the bag, but he shoved it back at her. Milly couldn't hear what they were saying, but she could tell they were both angry. They continued their disagreement for several minutes before Melissa stormed off with the bag. Juniper shook his head and walked off in the other direction.

"Milly!" Rose yelled, floating upside down over Milly's head with her arm extended. "High-upside-down five!"

Milly rolled her eyes, high fived Rose, and promptly forgot about the interaction she had witnessed. She ran over to the vish bucket so she could join Rose in the sky. Jazzy couldn't figure out the lesson on the first day, but she was happy to watch from the ground.

Once class was over, the three girls walked inside and met Ruth and Elsif for dinner. As the girls chatted about their first day of school, Elsif shoveled food in her face faster than Ruth could describe the dreamy boy in her Magic of Everyday Life class. After three and a half minutes Elsif stood up to leave without saying a single word.

"Elsif, where are you going?" Ruth questioned. "I need your opinion on whether this man is my future husband or not."

"I need to talk to Professor Henson about my August break paper for Advanced Humilis and Struth History," she said as she sprinted out of the dining chambers.

"I didn't understand a single word of that," Rose muttered.

"Me either," Milly agreed. "But to answer your question Ruth, no he's not."

Elsif made her way to the second level of the lecture wing. When she arrived at Professor Henson's office, he was meeting with another student so she waited in the hallway. Elsif was already uneasy about talking to her professor, but wanted to completely bail on the endeavor when another student joined her in the hallway.

"Hi Tinsley," Elsif spoke to her old friend. Actually she was never *her* friend; she was Libi's friend.

Tinsley smiled politely. "Hey, how are you?"

"Good," Elsif replied. "You?"

"Good," Tinsley said. "Are you going to trivia night on Friday?"

"No, I'm busy." *I wasn't invited.* "Looks like it's my turn."

A disheveled young boy walked out of the office with a look of defeat in his eyes. "Good luck," he mumbled to Elsif as she walked past him.

Elsif took a deep breath and tried to get in the right headspace as she entered the classroom. Seeing Tinsley threw her mind for a loop and her thoughts were scrambling to remember why she was seeing Professor Henson.

"Elsif, good to see you again," Professor Henson said while waving her in. "How are you doing?"

"Good," Elsif replied. "But I had a question about the paper that you graded today." She pulled the paper from her bag and placed it in front of him. "I received a 73% on my paper about the separation of Humilis and Struth in the year 3949 and I'm not sure if that was the grade that I was supposed to receive."

"That grade's accurate," Professor Henson assured.

"Well," Elsif continued quickly. "Could you explain your reasons behind the grade? Because I spent the entire August break on this paper and think it's one of the best papers I've ever written. I even dragged my parents to Humilis for a holiday in the region and interviewed two dozen people on their opinions of the war and separation. Everything in the paper was accurate with first person accounts and covered the topic fully and extensively. I'm not sure where you are taking points off."

The Professor took a deep breath before responding to Elsif. "The problem with your paper was that the opinions you wrote do not align with the Academy's views."

"I didn't write an opinion paper," Elsif attempted to explain without sounding disrespectful. "I wrote an informational paper. I reported on all sides in an unbiased manner."

"The assignment was to write on the separation of Humilis and Struth that the Academy teaches," He rebutted. "These ideas are what they teach in Humilis, not here. You, especially, should learn from this mistake if you plan on pursuing a teaching position at this school."

Becoming a professor at Merlin Academy had been Elsif's dream since she was five. She finalized her whole life plan at the age of seven, and there was no other option in all of Fantasma for Elsif. She would graduate from Merlin Academy this year, attend one year of advanced classes for teaching, get her teacher's license, and finally attend Merlin for her last three years to receive her advanced history degree. After graduation she would be a teacher's assistant at Merlin for five years, then become a full time professor when she was twenty-eight. She would leave her legacy as Merlin's youngest professor in history.

"I wasn't saying that I disagree with Merlin's views," Elsif remarked. "I didn't give any of my opinions. I stated what the people in Humilis told me about the separation. It would be dishonest of me to only include the positive views of Magicis and their government during that time, because some people had negative views. I wrote all the views that I found."

"How does that make this school look?" Professor Henson questioned. "When you apply for the advanced program the administration will review your papers and question your loyalties if you continue writing papers like this. Take this grade as a teaching moment and remember to focus on the views of the Academy in the future."

"How, *in all of Fantasma*, was I supposed to know about this?" Elsif demanded, her frustration growing. "You gave me the parameters of the paper and I wrote the best paper that you've probably ever read. If you don't think that this paper is at least an A- then you're crazy. This is ridiculous!"

"The only thing ridiculous is this behavior," Professor Henson announced. "Your paper was graded properly and fairly. You are now dismissed."

"Fairly!" Elsif exclaimed, forgetting where she was, who she was, and what she was doing. All she cared about at that moment was her hard work not being recognized. "If this is how you evaluate great work then I'll just quit!" Elsif grabbed the paper from the table and tore it in half. She proceeded to throw the paper in the trash and stomp out of the room. The whole scene was bad, but Elsif had the potential to recover if she hadn't done her next actions.

A globe sat next to the door and Elsif had always been bothered by the fact that Humilis was missing from Fantasma. The globe was made before Humilis seceded from Struth, but Elsif thought in a Humilis and Struth class, then Humilis should obviously be on the globe!

Elsif pushed the globe onto the ground where it shattered into pieces. "Your globe is geographically incorrect!" Elsif yelled while she slammed the door behind her.

Elsif took one step before she froze in place, paralyzed by the realization of her actions. Elsif had never done anything remotely like that before. She was always the teacher's pet with perfect grades and a star sticker on every assignment. Bad behavior was not tolerated at Merlin. Elsif had no doubt that she would be expelled by morning.

Every single one of Elsif's aunts, uncles, and cousins had gone to Merlin, and she was going to be the first one to be expelled. Well, not the *first* one, Uncle Louis was thrown out too. But he ended up being shunned from the family, and to this day no one can bring up his name at family gatherings.

That would be Elsif's fate. Abandoned by her family, a disgrace to her lineage, and to never be a history teacher. That was the worst fate that Elsif could imagine.

"Elsif?"

"What?" Elsif snapped out of her thoughts.

Tinsley stared at Elsif. "You're blocking the doorway."

"Oh, sorry," Elsif muttered as Tinsley walked past her.

Elsif watched Tinsley close the door behind her and thought that maybe leaving Merlin wouldn't be the worst thing in the world. She would never have to see her old friends again.

Fuming with anger, shock, confusion, and a few other emotions Elsif couldn't place, she decided to go for a walk in the gardens behind the school. The walk quickly turned into a staggering run before she found a quiet corner to have a meltdown. She began to cry as an unwelcome guest came over to her.

"Hi Gertrude," Elsif forced herself to say while wiping her tears.

"SQUAWK!" Gertrude replied with a lopsided tongue.

Gertrude was a goose. She was a student at Merlin Academy who was enrolled as a Loquanim, a magical animal from Mirabilis. Although she was a bit different from the other Loquanims at the school. Typical Loquanims were in animal bodies but acted a lot like regular humans since they could talk, wore clothes, and had jobs. Gertrude was different because she wore a pink bonnet on her head and a blue ribbon bow around her neck, but nothing else. She also didn't exactly know how to speak. She either only knew how to squawk or really liked to say the word squawk. No one was quite sure.

"You know Gertrude," Elsif stated. "I hate politics. Politics, politics, politics! I didn't know that's all this school cared about."

"SQUAWK," Gertrude agreed, or at least she thought it sounded like a squawk of agreement.

"Thanks Gertrude," Elsif said and patted her on her feathery back. "That means a lot. If Monty and Misty ever break up, I'll make sure to put in a good word for you."

"Squawk," Gertrude peeped with a wiggle of enthusiasm. It was also a known fact that Gertrude had been in love with her cousin Monty for the last five years.

Curfew was quickly approaching so both Elsif and Gertrude went to their own chambers. Taking small, slow steps, Elsif took her time getting back to her room. Before walking in the door, Elsif pushed down her emotions, and crossed the threshold of her chambers.

"Hi Elsif," Jazzy greeted from the living room where she sat with Ruth, Milly, and Rose. "How was the meeting with your professor?"

"Good," Elsif lied. "I'm tired so I'm heading to bed."

"Last to rise," Milly commented to Jazzy. "First to go to bed. That's our Elsif."

Elsif rolled her eyes. "I like my sleep, sue me."

"Loser!" Rose exclaimed with a big thumbs down.

Ruth nodded in agreement. "She's really lame sometimes. Too lame to play board games with us apparently."

"Fine," Elsif conceded and joined the girls for a couple rounds of magic dice and angry elves. Since it was her last night at school, it would probably be a good idea to spend time with her cousins.

Laughter quickly filled the room as the girls tried to defeat several angry elves. As Jazzy rolled her dice to see if she would fight the elves with fire or a candy cane scythe, a door slammed in the hallway followed by several footsteps. The girls were surprised since the Academy had a very strict curfew rule of no students out of their chambers after ten.

"It's at least 11:30," Milly commented.

Jazzy looked at the clock on the wall. "It's almost midnight."

"Who was that then?" Ruth asked standing up to check the door.

Elsif stood up quickly. "I'll look." She hoped it wasn't the administration waiting to escort her away.

Opening the door, Elsif peeked her head out. Almost immediately, Elsif shut the door and her mouth fell wide open.

"Who was it?" Milly snapped.

Whispering loudly, Elsif replied, "It's Melissa!"

"Well she's not concerned about fighting stereotypes," Ruth mumbled.

Rose jumped up and ran to the door. "We should go after her."

"It's past curfew," Milly reminded Rose.

"And we were about to start goblin chess," Ruth added.

"Who cares where she's going?" Milly stated.

Rose groaned. "You guys are so boring! Where's your sense of adventure?"

"The rules are the rules," Milly stated.

Ruth began to set up the board. "Who's playing me first? Jazzy?"

"Sure," Jazzy smiled, joining Ruth at the table.

Elsif's automatic response was to ban anyone from leaving the room, but then she began to think. She may not be at the school much longer. If she was caught out after curfew then what was the worst thing that could happen? Expel her twice? She already had one foot out the door, might as well make the best of her last night. She had never done anything remotely rebellious in her whole life, and this might be her only chance.

"I'm in," Elsif stated.

Everyone turned and stared at Elsif in confusion. Ruth was the first to speak up. "Who are you and what did you do with our cousin?"

"Maybe I feel like doing something exciting," Elsif declared, her mood rising sharply. "Maybe I want to break a school rule to see why another student is breaking a school rule!"

"Exactly!" Rose agreed with joy. "This is our chance to no longer be boring losers. If we get caught we'll just blame Melissa and say she mind controlled us."

"You know," Elsif added. "Melissa could be planning some super top secret mission to destroy the school and we could be the ones to find out and alert the authorities."

"Yes!" Rose jumped around. "Or we could join her? We'll decide in the moment," she said with a sly wave of her hand.

"I'm not going," Ruth muttered, returning to her chess game.

"I don't know if I want to go," Jazzy remarked. "I'd rather play goblin chess."

"Fine," Rose stated, then turned to Milly. "Mildred, think about how heroic you could be."

"Not my name," Milly noted.

"Shh," Rose latched on to Milly. "Think about Melissa, a potential villain, running around the school with no one to stop her. We must rise to the occasion, Milicent!"

Milly was torn inside as she toggled with her two major values, following the rules and protecting society. After a minute of debate in her head, she had decided. "Let's go."

The three girls ran out of their chambers and down the hallway where Elsif saw Melissa. After a few minutes of running around aimlessly, Milly spotted a green shadow turn down a hallway on the west side of the school.

"Rose, you have to be quiet," Elsif urged Rose as they followed from a distance.

"I am," Rose argued a little too loudly.

Milly, who was leading, spun around. "Shut up."

"That's rude," Elsif chided as she hit Milly's arm. "You shouldn't say that."

"She swore at me Elsif," Rose claimed, her hand on her heart.

Milly had to restrain herself from strangling the two. "Just be quiet." Turning back around, Milly found that Melissa was gone.

"She must have gone down either the hallway that leads to the boys' wing, the hallway that leads to the teachers' wing, or this room," Elsif concluded as she checked what the room was labeled. "The Weaponry."

"Going to the teachers' wing would be stupid," Milly stated. "But we're more likely to be caught if we go to the boys' wing."

"So that just leaves," Rose said, her voice brimming with excitement. "The Weaponry!"

"Oh no," Milly muttered.

Bursting into the room, Rose found herself in paradise. The large room contained hundreds of shelves with hanging weapons, dozens of stands with dangerous looking objects, and long tables with thousands of different blades. Elsif and Milly had to summon all their strength and willpower to stop Rose from creating pure chaos. Unfortunately, Melissa was nowhere to be found.

"She's not here," Elsif stated. "Should we try the boys' wing?"

"She could be anywhere by now," Milly assumed. "We'd never be able to find her without being caught at this point."

Elsif frowned. "Then we should probably head back."

"Are you joking?" Rose demanded, two different weapons in each of her hands. "We can't leave when this is the best thing that has ever happened to me! Imagine all the mayhem I could cause, the battles I could win, the wars I could wage, the fear I could strike!"

"We definitely need to get her out of here," Milly agreed.

"Never!" Rose yelled while running around, picking up everything she could reach, and evading her cousin's grasps. Rose was quick but Milly was finally able to grab her when she suddenly stopped. "I think Melissa *has* been here."

Rose had stopped in front of a large and decorative stand with a glass covering, but was completely empty. Milly let go of Rose to look at the plaque on the stand, and Elsif joined her.

Malum's Staff

This staff was first created by Malum in the 3190s. Malum was the most powerful Mimpius before their extinction, and she put all of her power into the staff. In 3199 Malum used this staff to assassinate the Elven King and in turn began the Elven Wars and the Bloodshed Age. In the year 3210 Malum was defeated and killed which ended the first Elven War. Merlin Academy claimed the staff and it has been on display ever since. Whoever wields the staff is said to wield the power of Malum. The staff is the second most powerful object recorded in history, after the Warlock's Hat.

"This isn't good," Elsif concluded.

"She has it. Melissa has Malum's staff," Milly said in disbelief.

"We need to tell a teacher or something," Elsif stated. "We need to go to the President of Merlin."

"We'll get expelled," Rose insisted. "We can't tell anyone!"

"Don't worry," Elsif assured, deciding mentally that she would go to the President in the morning and take the fall for everyone. But instead said out loud, "We can write an anonymous letter."

"Wait, there's something else missing," Rose said. "Look, oh nevermind, she didn't take it."

"How do you know?" Milly asked and walked over to the empty stand.

Warlock's Hat

The Warlock Hat was first recorded in 3158 in a journal belonging to Ren Siid. It possesses power beyond any other magical object that has been known to exist, combining the power from all magical people groups. There have been only two individuals that have been known to control the Hat. The first was Xen Siid, the famous Warlock and creator of the Hat, who ended the Elven Wars. The second is Quay Muse, apprentice to Xen Siid, who was able to use the Warlock's Hat, but not to its fullest abilities. The Warlock's Hat was last seen in Viverra on the eve of Quay Muse's passing in 3213. As far as anyone knows, the Hat vanished.

"At least she doesn't have that," Elsif spoke.

Milly backed away from the stand. "We should head back to the room and figure out what to do next."

"Hold on a minute," Rose said when Elsif and Milly moved toward the door. "I'm not leaving until I get some good weapons."

"Rose this seriously isn't the time for your craziness," Milly rebuked.

"I'm not talking about stealing weapons for fun," Rose said with a serious tone. "We should take some weapons for protection. What if Melissa uses the Staff tomorrow to turn us all to frogs? We need to protect ourselves."

Once again Elsif's first reaction was to stop Rose, but in the back of her mind, she thought Rose had a point. Elsif didn't think stealing weapons was the answer, but being prepared for potential danger given the circumstances seemed well within the realm of reason. Borrowing a few weapons for a few days probably wasn't a big deal, and they could return them once Melissa was caught. Besides, if they were caught then Elsif could always take the blame.

"That's actually very smart of you Rose," Elsif noted. "Go ahead and grab a couple things."

"We can't take weapons!" Milly claimed.

"Out of all people, you should know self defense is important," Elsif stated. "You're from Navisia, weapons are part of your culture. Besides, it will only be for a couple days, until the Staff is found."

"We'll be in huge trouble," Milly argued.

"They didn't notice that a deadly Staff was taken," Rose insisted. "They aren't going to miss a couple of measly knives. Or this machine gun."

Elsif confiscated the gun. "Something smaller Rose."

Milly crossed her arms and shook her head as Elsif and Rose rummaged through the room.

"I've picked out my weapon," Rose said, holding two long whips made of chains with blades on the ends.

"No," Milly groaned.

"I'll allow it," Elsif teased. "They were in the corner Milly, no one cares about them. They're dull so it's fine." A dagger on the table caught Elsif's eye. "Look at the jewels on the handle. They look like they are from the Magic Age, maybe from Monstrum? I think I found my weapon."

"I refuse to be a part of this," Milly demanded.

Elsif motioned Milly toward one of the walls. "Look at these swords from Navisia."

Milly loved weapons so it was a great temptation to borrow one for a few days. Her parents always made her keep her swords and knives at home, so she could focus on her studies at Merlin. A sword named *Tuccley* caught her eye along with a magic knife contraption. She had never seen a sword so pristine and she had never heard of a knife machine with built in magic. The knife contraption could be strapped to a forearm and it would produce unlimited knives. Eventually she caved and took both, but promised herself she would return them as soon as she practiced with them a few times.

Rose also grabbed a stun blaster for Jazzy and a bow for Ruth so they didn't feel left out in their thievery.

After collecting their loot, the girls quietly snuck back to their chambers. They were very eager to tell Ruth and Jazzy about their crazy adventure, but there was one problem. Ruth and Jazzy were not in the room.

Chapter 4: OooOOoooOoh Juniper

"Check," Ruth declared as Jazzy cautiously made her next move. Ruth glanced at the door, like she had been doing every other minute since the girls left. She wondered if they were having fun, and if she should have gone instead of playing goblin chess.

Jazzy moved her goblin king so it was out of Ruth's reach. She was also thinking about the girls and hoped that they weren't in any trouble.

"Checkmate," Ruth stated. "I killed your goblin queen."

"Good game," Jazzy said. "How do you think they're doing?"

"They're probably alright," Ruth replied with uncertainty. "I'm sure they'll be back any minute."

Jazzy shifted nervously in her seat. "You don't think they've been caught?"

"They're fine," Ruth repeated, right before faint noises came from the hallway. "That must be them," Ruth said, jumping to her feet. Jazzy followed her as Ruth peeked into the hallway. Who she found was in fact not Elsif, Rose, Milly, or even Melissa, but none other than Juniper Miller.

"I think you might be lost," Ruth told Juniper. Previously, Ruth was feeling bad about missing out, but suddenly a good feeling came over her.

Juniper was standing in front of Melissa's chambers, two doors down. When Ruth spoke, Juniper looked around startled for a split second, but relaxed once he saw Ruth.

"I was just looking for my friend," he replied in a low monotone voice.

"Melissa?" Ruth questioned with a smile, deciding she was going to have some fun. "She left her chambers half an hour ago. But it's odd when you think about it, since it's past curfew. Isn't that odd Jazzy?" Ruth looked at Jazzy, but Jazzy shuffled behind her.

"Yeah," Juniper agreed apathetically. "Odd."

"But then again you're out past curfew too," Ruth noted. "What a coincidence that is, or maybe it isn't. I guess we'll find out since my cousins are following her, as we speak."

"I don't know anything about what Melissa is doing," Juniper said plainly.

Ruth scoffed dramatically. "Then why are you trying to see her?"

"That's not your business," Juniper stated.

"It actually is my business because you two are breaking school rules," Ruth replied. "And I, as a law-abiding citizen, should really report you, since I'm a firsthand witness to you both being out past curfew. It's only my civic duty as a student of Merlin Academy."

Juniper rolled his eyes and leaned on Melissa's door. "If you report me, fine. I'll just report your cousins. Word to the wise, when you threaten someone, don't give them information they can use against you."

"I wasn't trying to threaten you," Ruth quickly rebutted. "I was just-"

"Yeah you weren't trying," Juniper agreed. "You were failing. Why don't you head back inside your chambers, go to bed, and forget all this happened."

"Tell us what Melissa is doing and you have a deal," Ruth offered, summoning all her boldness and hoping Juniper didn't see right through her.

"Yeah, of course I'll tell you," Juniper said with a hint of sarcasm. "Then you'll go running off to the President's office. Sounds like a great plan."

"Why would I do that?" Ruth pondered out loud. "You have valuable information about my cousins, don't you?"

"Then why do you want to know?"

"I don't know," Ruth shrugged suspiciously. "I guess I'm just curious."

"You know curiosity killed the cat," Juniper warned.

"Well, *I'm* not a cat."

"Well, *I'm* still not going to tell you," Juniper stated.

As Ruth opened her mouth to retort, a light turned on at the end of the hallway, and the monitor's voice was heard from a distance.

"Fine," Ruth declared, stepping back into her chambers with Jazzy. "Then you can be caught by the monitor."

"Wait," Juniper said with gritted teeth.

Ruth popped her head back out with a grin. "Yes."

"Let me hide in your room, and-" Juniper paused, debating his options. He'd rather be anywhere else in Fantasma, but it didn't look like he had a choice. "I'll tell you anything you want, if you let me in."

"Anything?" Ruth asked.

"Anything."

Ruth pulled Juniper in the room by his sleeve, and quickly shut the door just in the nick of time, because footsteps were heard seconds later.

"The lights are on," Jazzy said with a panicked tone. "Do you think the monitor is going to check in here?"

"Don't worry," Ruth assured, grabbing Juniper's arm and throwing him in her room. "Hide in here and don't make a sound."

"You better have a good alibi of why your cousins are missing and an even better reason for why you have a guy in your room," Juniper told Ruth as she flung the door closed in his face.

"Would you just trust me," Ruth said with exasperation through the door. Turning to Jazzy she pointed to the other side of the room. "Shut both the bedroom doors." Jazzy obeyed when a knock was heard on the chamber door. "Act natural," Ruth instructed right before she answered the door.

Taking a deep breath, Ruth opened the front door slowly and calmly. "Hi Sabrina, can I help you?"

"Hey, I hope I didn't wake you," Sabrina greeted. The monitor for the third floor of the girls' wing was Sabrina, a twenty two year old advanced student from Magicis. She was known for being a tremendous stickler when it came to the rules, but luckily for Ruth she had always made a good impression with her.

"No," Ruth assured. "Jazzy and I were just playing goblin chess."

"Oh good," Sabrina replied. "I'm so sorry for coming around so late, but I heard some voices in the hallway and it's protocol for me to check all the rooms. I have to make sure no one is breaking curfew."

"Well we're all here," Ruth said with a big smile.

"Amazing," Sabrina sighed with relief. "Have a goodnight." She waved goodbye and left to knock on another chamber. Ruth closed the door with a superior attitude.

Juniper walked into the living room, his face completely perplexed. "Why didn't she check to see if the rest of you were here? Did you bribe her? Hold a knife to her throat?"

"Nope, nothing like that," Ruth responded with a toss of her hair. "You can get away with a lot when you're considered a good student."

Juniper snorted. "My room is searched every other week."

"It's one of the perks of following the rules," Ruth told Juniper. "So now you can sit down and tell us everything you know about Melissa leaving in the middle of the night."

"Slow down, first I need your names," Juniper established.

Ruth crossed her arms. "Maybe we want to remain anonymous."

"I already know you're Ruth Walker. You've been a student here for years," Juniper stated while Ruth pouted. Juniper then turned to Jazzy. "Who are you?"

"Jazzy," she mumbled meekly. "I'm new."

"Okay," Juniper said. "Now I need a reason why I can trust you two. Some type of collateral for the information."

"Collateral?" Ruth questioned. "That wasn't the deal. You don't have a choice unless you want me to go get Sabrina."

Juniper opened his mouth to argue, but briskly closed it. From his expression it was obvious he was fighting a battle of inner turmoil and conflict in his head. After a minute he finally said, "Fine, whatever. Let's go."

Ruth and Jazzy shared a look of confusion while Juniper walked over to the door. "Where are you going?" Ruth asked.

"To show you what Melissa's doing," Juniper said matter of factly.

"The deal was for you to tell us," Ruth argued. "Not to take us somewhere. It's past curfew!"

"And we don't know you," Jazzy added timidly.

Juniper rolled his eyes again which was beginning to annoy Ruth, but was also starting to allure her. "It's easier if I just show you."

Ruth crossed her arms. "We're not going to blindly follow you out of our chambers!"

"Would you just trust me?" Juniper said, reciting Ruth's words from before.

Ruth looked from Juniper, then at Jazzy. Even though Jazzy shook her head with worry, and her own head was flashing warning alarms, Ruth decided to trust her gut. "Fine, we'll go."

Jazzy grabbed Ruth's arm. "Don't you think this might be a bad idea?"

"It's all going to be fine," Ruth assured, linking arms with Jazzy. Both girls walked out of their chambers, and followed Juniper. "Where are we going?" Ruth whispered to Juniper as he led them through the hallways.

"Stop talking or we'll get caught," Juniper snapped in a low tone. "You'll see for yourselves soon enough."

Juniper led them out of the girls' wing, through the south side of the school, and out the back doors into the gardens. The girls shivered as they wandered through every section of the gardens at Merlin. First they entered the picnic area with lots of tables under shady trees. Then they made their way through the grassy field where classes took place. They walked through the animal enclosure area, then the fruit orchards, and veggie gardens. Then they strolled by the waterfalls and followed one of the streams to the butterfly grove and flower patches. By the time they had entered the extensive maze at the back of the gardens, the girls had lost all hope that Juniper knew where he was going.

"Are we lost?" Jazzy stuttered through her chattering teeth.

"Or are you just as confused as us?" Ruth said in an accusing manner. "*Or* maybe he's trying to lose us so we freeze to death?"

"It's September," Juniper muttered. "Calm down."

"You obviously don't know where you're going!" Ruth exclaimed. "We've been wandering for what? An hour?"

"It's so cold," Jazzy fussed.

"I know it's out here," Juniper assured. "I haven't been to the place myself, but we're close. I know it."

"A place?" Ruth questioned the first bit of information that Juniper finally decided to share. "What's the place? Maybe I've seen it before. I come to the gardens all the time with my cousins. It's Rose's favorite spot to wreak havoc."

"I don't know what the place looks like," snapped Juniper.

Ruth stopped in her tracks. "You don't know what we're looking for?"

"I don't know exactly," Juniper said vaguely, stopping to face Ruth. "I have an idea of what I'm looking for. I'll know it when I see it."

"*An idea*?" Ruth questioned, shaking her head. She grabbed Jazzy's arm and decided enough was enough. "What a waste of time! I should have listened to you, Jazzy!" Ruth said over her shoulder as they walked away.

"Wait a minute," Juniper said, while stomping after them. "I didn't invite you to come out here with me in the first place. You're the one that insisted on knowing what Melissa was doing. You butted into this whole ordeal, and now you're quitting right before I find it?"

"You're never going to find it," Ruth retorted, not letting go of Jazzy, and not breaking her stride. "I'm cutting my losses before we're all caught."

"So you're giving up?" Juniper asked.

Ruth whirled around to face Juniper. "No, I'm not. I'm finally coming to my senses. Why do you even care if we leave? I thought you wanted to be left alone this entire time."

"I don't care if you leave," Juniper argued. "I just thought you might want to witness this."

"What's *this*?" Ruth urged.

Juniper hesitated to answer, but when he finally opened his mouth he was cut off by a bright light and a voice from above. "What are you kids doing down there?"

Before Ruth could think, she felt herself being dragged into the wall of the maze. Juniper had grabbed her and Jazzy and pulled them into the tall, thick brush that was used to line the walls of the maze. Sticks and branches protruded into their personal space as they tried to find a position that didn't hurt.

"We can't go through the walls you idiot," Ruth whispered at Juniper through a mouth full of leaves. "The magic prohibits anyone from passing through to avoid cheating."

"We're not going *through it*," Juniper hissed back. "We're hiding *in it*. He's flying above us, so if we're out of his view he'll think that we ran. Don't go too far into the bush."

"Good plan except the part where the bush throws us out and we land ten feet away with broken arms," Ruth retorted. "It's happened to Rose three times."

"You're making up this Rose person." Juniper grumbled as he tried to stop a branch from poking his side.

"Guys," Jazzy whispered. "He's coming towards us."

Silence washed over them as they tried their hardest not to move, as the bright light from above came closer and closer. The light shone right at the spot they were hiding, but went by quickly. To the girl's dismay, Juniper was right, and the guard began to shine his light in another direction, probably assuming they ran.

"Come on," Juniper said, making his way out of the bush. "We'll take the long way back so he doesn't catch us." The girls didn't argue, and followed Juniper through the gardens and back to the school. He was very careful to make sure they weren't followed, and everyone was confident that they were off the hook once they got to the back doors of Merlin.

"That's why you can't wander around for eight hours because you have *an idea* of a location," Ruth said to Juniper as they stepped inside.

"We didn't get caught," argued Juniper. "But now Merlin is going to have double the guards out at night so we'll have to wait until the next school month to look again. We can meet here at the back doors on the first Friday in November, at midnight."

"Who says we'll show up?" Ruth retorted.

Juniper gave a look of disbelief. "You'll show up."

"Maybe," Ruth muttered. "But why do we have to wait all the way until November? That's almost two months."

"You'll have to," Juniper stated. "And don't go around telling people about this."

"Do we look stupid? Actually, don't answer that," Ruth added as Juniper opened his mouth. "Should we be worried about Melissa?"

"No," Juniper said without further explanation. "We should all get back to our chambers before we get caught again."

"I thought you said we didn't get caught," Ruth teased.

"Funny," Juniper said in a dry tone. He turned in the direction of the boys' wing and headed back to his chambers.

"Bye!" Ruth called after him, but Juniper didn't respond or turn around. "Rude," she mumbled under her breath, then turned to Jazzy with a smile. "Wasn't that fun?"

Jazzy shook her head. "Not really."

Ruth shrugged with a smile that refused to leave her lips. "I had fun."

The two girls walked back to their chambers carefully and cautiously. When they got back, they walked in to find a very concerned Elsif and Milly. Rose, on the other hand, was cool as a cucumber, playing with her new weapons.

Another hour had passed as all the girls told their stories, interrupting each other to tell details, and rebuking each other for making bad decisions.

After all the stories were told Ruth asked in disbelief, "You let Rose in where?"

Elsif frowned and said, "And you went with who?"

"Letting Rose have a dangerous weapon is far worse than going with Juniper," Ruth defended.

"No way!" Elsif exclaimed. "You went with *the* Juniper Miller. The potentially evil and villainous Juniper! He could have *murdered* you!"

"Rose is going to *murder* us all!" Ruth yelled.

"Okay, fair point," Elsif grumbled. "But you still should have been more cautious."

"And why would you take weapons?" Ruth questioned. "And why would my weapon be a bow with no arrows? It's useless!"

Rose replied with distaste, "You don't have arrows?"

"Why would I have arrows?"

"You're from Bellator," Rose said with an obvious tone.

Ruth crossed her arms. "My district has a couple war museums and you think I carry around arrows?"

"Didn't you go to archery camp every other month when you were a kid?" Elsif added.

Ruth grimaced "That still doesn't mean, you shouldn't have gotten me a cooler weapon!"

"Guys, we need to focus," Milly advised, trying to steer the conversation to a more important topic. "We need to figure out what to do about the missing Staff. What's our next step?"

"Tell the President of Merlin," Elsif stated. "We'll write an anonymous letter and I'll drop it off at his office tomorrow." Elsif's words did not exactly match up with her own plans. She knew that the next day she would be personally delivering the letter and telling the President she alone went into the weaponry and followed Melissa.

"I'm not sure we should do that," Milly stated. "I still think we should go directly to him and accept the consequences of our actions. The administration needs to know this is serious."

"You'll get in so much trouble," Ruth retorted. "You could say that you accidentally went into the weaponry."

"Accidentally?" Milly questioned. "He's not going to believe we accidentally went in there."

"Yeah," Rose agreed. "How does one accidentally wander into a weaponry?"

"I don't think anyone would doubt that *you* accidentally wandered into a weaponry," Elsif stated.

"How did you guys get inside?" Jazzy asked.

"It was unlocked," Milly answered. "Melissa must have left it open after she stole the staff."

"So she stole it tonight?" Ruth concluded.

"No," Milly replied with certainty. "I saw her show Juniper the staff in a bag during flying class today."

Everyone looked at Milly, and Elsif voiced what the others were thinking. "You're just saying this now?"

"I just remembered it," Milly argued. "It didn't seem like a very significant moment at the time. But that means Melissa stole it sometime prior to tonight. So she has snuck out before, and she wasn't going to the weaponry when we followed her tonight. There's a lot to unpack but we need to start with who we can trust. Melissa, Juniper, and their whole gang aren't looking good at the moment."

"I agree," Elsif nodded. "All of them are suspicious."

"Juniper is trustworthy," Ruth contended. "Melissa was the one doing the evil plotting and he was trying to show us. Right Jazzy?"

"I suppose," Jazzy agreed half heartedly. "He did keep us from being caught. But I didn't like going out after curfew with him."

Elsif turned to Ruth with a serious expression. "He was leading you guys around and trying to distract you so you didn't catch Melissa. And he only protected you guys so that you didn't rat him out when you were caught."

"You weren't there," Ruth claimed. "You don't know anything about Juniper."

Elsif sighed. "Let's just agree to be careful of both of them."

Ruth frowned and didn't agree.

"Okay, so next steps," Milly stated again. "We are going to write an anonymous letter to give to the President tomorrow morning. Can we at least settle on that?" All the girls agreed. "Should we be worried that he won't read it in time?"

"Juniper made it sound like we didn't have to worry about Melissa for a while," Ruth said, embellishing Juniper's one word statement.

"Okay," Milly nodded. "Let's write the letter now so it's ready for the morning."

"I'll take it," Elsif volunteered quickly. "I'll take it before classes."

"Be careful," Jazzy worried.

Elsif nodded. "I'll be super inconspicuous."

Rose laughed, and said while twirling her new chain whips, "Nerd." Rose often teased Elsif for using big words.

The girls drafted the letter to the president of the Academy. They described how Melissa left her chambers and how she probably (or most definitely) had Malum's staff. They left out everything about them being away from their chambers and them stealing weapons. They also left out Juniper, per Ruth's request. After they had finished the letter, there was only a couple of hours before sunrise. The girls went to bed, but none of them slept.

Chapter 5: A Threat Of No Major Significance

The girls woke to knocking. Ruth shot out of bed and answered the door. Deja vu washed over Ruth as she faced Sabrina again.

"Hi Sabrina."

"Good morning," Sabrina said. "Sorry to bother you for a second time, but I have to do another mandatory room check."

"Really?" Ruth said, raising her voice. "You have to do another room check?"

"Yeah," Sabrina confirmed. "I'll be quick, don't worry. I know you all will have to get ready for classes soon."

"No worry here," Ruth said, continuing to talk in an unnaturally loud voice. "Come on in, and check our room."

"Thanks," Sabrina said, walking in. "Some things have gone missing from the Academy so every monitor is checking their floor."

"Interesting," Ruth mumbled, hoping that someone had removed the contraband from the living room table. She turned around as Sabrina entered the room, and to her relief, saw a weaponless table.

Milly walked out from her bedroom after overhearing the conversation. "Hi Sabrina," Milly said with a forceful tone and stiff limbs. "How odd it is that you're here."

Ruth threw a panicked side glance at Milly behind Sabrina's back.

"I'll be quick," Sabrina assured, taking a look at the room. She lingered for a few seconds, then like the previous night, she promptly left without actually checking anything.

Ruth and Milly let out huge sighs of relief once the door was shut.

"That was a close one," Milly said, wiping the nervous sweat from her forehead.

"You didn't help," Ruth accused Milly. "*How odd is it that you're here?* Could you be more suspicious?"

"You were literally yelling and repeating everything that Sabrina said," Milly argued. "You were way more suspicious than me."

Elsif walked into the room, "You two were both suspicious, but it's fine. Sabrina didn't catch on, and we aren't likely suspects anyway."

Jazzy peeked out of her room. "Are you sure we aren't suspects?"

"We're not," Elsif assured.

"Since they are checking everyone's chambers," Jazzy said, coming out of her room. "Maybe we don't have to give the President our letter."

"We should still give him the letter," Milly countered. "We don't know how closely they checked Melissa's stuff."

"They definitely checked her room closely," Ruth stated, remembering Juniper's comment from last night. She suspected Melissa also received similar treatment of getting her chambers searched often. "But we should still give him the letter just in case."

"Let me get dressed and I'll take it," Elsif said, mentally preparing herself to be thrown out of school. "Where are the weapons anyway? They were on the table when I went to bed."

Rose cartwheeled into the room. "Is someone wondering where the weapons are?"

"Rose, it's too early," Ruth muttered.

"I actually don't mind the dramatics," Elsif mentioned. "Helps me wake up."

"I hid the weapons," Rose declared, standing on the table. "Aren't you proud of me for being a forward thinker."

"Where are they?" Milly asked.

"I'm not saying unless you solve my riddle."

"We don't have time for this," Ruth griped.

"Come on," Milly grumbled.

Rose ignored them both. "They are in the deepest, darkest corner of this dorm."

Elsif interjected, "They're under your bed."

"Where an oddly large number of bunnies like to swarm," Rose continued in a sing-song voice. "Far from Milly, further from Ruth, Jazzy, and Elsif too. They are the farthest away from everyone else's view."

Elsif walked to Rose's room. "They are definitely under your bed."

"Laying with the one matching sock, I'm seldom seen," Rose sang on. "Who am I, in this place, where I always stay unseen?"

"Found them!" Elsif exclaimed, and strolled back into the living room with two arms full of weapons.

"Why can't you just tell us things?" Milly questioned.

"What's the fun in that?" Rose responded. "I spent all night coming up with that riddle!"

Once the weapons were back on the table, Ruth said, "We need a better place to hide these."

Rose spoke first, "I have a plan." She danced and twirled out of the chambers before the girls could ask further questions.

"Let's hide it under our bunk for now," Elsif said to Ruth.

"Smart," Ruth agreed, taking the weapons.

Elsif dressed quickly, grabbed the letter, and left to throw away her future. She walked straight to the President's office and braced herself for expulsion. Elsif finally arrived and knocked on the President's door, labeled: *President of Merlin Academy: Mr. Edgar Coleman.*

As Elsif waited for the door to open, her heart pounded uncontrollably inside her chest. Each second that passed was an agony to wait. She was moments away from being expelled from the best school in Fantasma, a drop-out, a shame to her family, and a disgrace to society. *Why is this taking so long?*

Turning to the secretary, Elsif asked, "Excuse me, excuse me." The secretary finally looked up from her papers, and realized Elsif was standing in front of her. "Is Mr. Coleman here?"

"No," she responded apathetically. "He's very busy along with the rest of the administration. You'll have to come back after the school day, though I doubt he'll have time for you then either."

"Oh," Elsif said, not knowing if she should go to her class. She wasn't technically expelled yet, so her teachers were probably still expecting her. Elsif decided to slip the letter under the President's door, and come back to explain everything once she was officially expelled.

Elsif was nervous when she arrived at her first class. She waited for her teacher to throw her out in a dramatic fashion. But surprisingly they did not. Nor did the next teacher, or the one after that. No one said anything about Elsif's behavior from the previous day. Even during her fourth class with Professor Henson, he didn't yell at her to leave his class the second she entered the room. It was odd, to say the least.

After class, Elsif walked up to Professor Henson's desk reluctantly. He looked up from his book with a slight smile. "Are you here to destroy any of my other inaccurate historical documents?"

"Am I expelled?" Elsif asked nervously.

"Of course not," Professor Henson remarked. "You are not the first student to have a nervous breakdown in my office. I was meaning to replace that globe anyway. You are one of my most promising students Elsif and I look forward to having you as my colleague one day."

"Thank you."

Elsif left the Professor's class completely and utterly perplexed. She should have been relieved to not be expelled, but Elsif wasn't. She felt worse than ever, but she couldn't come up with a reasonable explanation as to why. While she walked to her next class, Elsif was so lost in her thoughts that she forgot to avoid a certain group of people.

"Hey, where you headed?"

Elsif looked up to see Bernard, Piper, and Paisley standing in front of her. There was no one else in the hallway, so the question had to be for Elsif.

"Where are you going?" Bernard repeated.

"Literature in Regium?"

Paisley snickered. "Sounds fun. What was your name again?"

"Elsif."

"Elsie?" Piper asked.

"Elsif," she repeated in a clear tone.

"Oh," Piper mocked. "El-*sif*. Did Gelida run out of names? They had to come up with random words to call their kids?"

The three laughed at Piper's joke as Elsif stood uncomfortably.

"How's your day been Frosty?" Bernard asked. "Did anything interesting happen? Talked to anyone new? Deliver any letters?"

Elsif tried to reply but couldn't. Every word in existence escaped her mind. She could feel her face grow red and her hands began to shake. She willed herself to say something, or anything. She didn't know if she was more nervous with them talking to her or that they knew about the letter. *Come on Elsif, just say something! They're staring and judging you and you look like an idiot!*

"What's wrong Frosty?" Piper demanded. "Did you forget how to talk?"

Elsif shrugged. "I just really don't know why you guys are talking to me."

"Keep it like that," Paisley warned.

They walked away from her, leaving Elsif alone in the hallway. As they left, Elsif heard them discussing something about happy stones, but Elsif was so alarmed that she didn't understand their words.

Was I just bullied? Elsif wondered as she walked to her next class. *I don't know if I've ever been bullied before. I could use this in a future essay about the struggles of adolescence. Besides that little benefit, I'm so confused about what just happened. They have never acknowledged my existence in the past. I'm not used to people acknowledging me. What did they say about a letter?*

Arriving at class, Elsif tried her best to push the encounter out of her mind, but was unsuccessful.

*****

Milly sprinted to Ruth and Elsif's table at dinner right after her flying class. Jazzy and Rose jogged behind her, and eventually joined the table.

"Was the letter delivered?" Milly asked, breathing heavy.

"Yes," Elsif answered.

Milly sat down relieved. "Good. So it all went smoothly?"

"Yeah," Elsif said. "Except I think I might have been threatened by Melissa's friends. I'm not really sure."

"Oh no," Jazzy said. "Are you alright? What happened?"

Elsif thought for a moment. "They said I had a stupid name."

"You *do* have a stupid name," Rose agreed, half listening to the conversation, half trying to fling cheese balls at Michael's head a couple tables over.

"They also said to forget everything I know," Elsif defended. "It sounded like a threat."

"Forget what?" Milly questioned.

Elsif threw her arms in the air. "I don't know! Maybe something to do with the letter? I think they mentioned that. All I know is I am going to write a fantastic article about the whole encounter."

"Why are you writing an article about the Staff being missing?!" Ruth shouted loudly. A split second after the declaration, Rose dove over the table to cover Ruth's mouth. Realizing her mistake, Ruth looked around to see if anyone heard her.

"What's wrong with you," Rose spat through clenched teeth. "Do you want us all to be *killed*?"

"Who would kill us?" Milly asked with a dismissive tone.

"Bernard already bit Elsif once," Rose stated. "Who says he's not going to come back and finish the job?"

Ruth tried to regather the meeting. "We just need to lay low right now, and when we get back from October break Juniper will tell us everything."

"Juniper, Juniper, Juniper," Elsif muttered.

"I'll agree to that plan," Milly remarked. "Let's just focus on passing our classes for now."

*****

The first month of school came and went in a flash. Classes were challenging, sleep was lost, and time was well spent in laughter. The girls enjoyed living together and there was no more sneaking out at night. Elsif slowly went back to her normal self, worrying about doing extra credit and what the best topic for her next paper would be. Jazzy learned something new about magic everyday, and was continually amazed. Ruth did as well in her classes as she could but spent most of her time trying to find Juniper in hallways and the Dining Chamber. Milly focused on her sailing classes and joined the crew of a Merlin ship. Rose blew up a total of fourteen objects in the month of September, and painted all the flowers purple in the gardens.

The last day of September classes was spent packing and making carriage arrangements. The girls were returning to their home regions for the October break, and were waiting for their carriages in the dining chambers.

Overhead an announcement noted that the carriage for the Koronia district was ready. Jazzy grabbed her things. "I'll see you all in November." She waved and left through the front doors.

"Have fun in Mellberg!" Elsif called to her.

Rose banged her head impatiently on the table. "Who's carriage is next?"

"Mine is coming in five minutes," Milly responded. "Your's will be shortly after mine."

"That's too long!" Rose groaned.

"You're lucky," Ruth mumbled. "I have to stay for almost another hour. I missed the first carriage to Bellator."

"Ah poor Ruthie," Rose mocked. "One more hour that you can't see your cute neighbor."

"Yes," Ruth agreed. "It *is* terrible."

Elsif raised her eyebrow. "I thought you were in love with the assistant librarian?"

"That was three months ago," Ruth said with an obvious tone. "A new guy moved in across the street from my house in August."

"Danny?" Elsif questioned. "I can never keep them all straight."

"Yeah." Ruth nodded in confirmation. "You guys would also be complaining about going home late, if you had seen him."

"I doubt that," Milly spoke. "Rose and I should head out to the front. See you later."

"Bye," Ruth and Elsif said in unison.

Rose bowed. "Salutations." She then stood up and yelled to the other side of the dining chambers, "GERTRUDE! THE CARRIAGE IS HERE!"

Gertrude the goose squawked in return then led a group of other dressed animals through the front doors. Rose bounded over to them and began planning their journey home to Mirabilis. Milly walked behind the group and felt relieved she wasn't going to be stuck in a carriage with the boisterous group. She was going to be in a civilized carriage full of pirates who were planning their looting escapades for the break.

Once Milly and Rose were gone, Elsif immediately began listing all the assignments she was going to be working on during October break. She was interrupted around assignment seventeen by an unexpected visitor.

"Did you have any trouble during the chamber searches?" Juniper asked, after sliding in next to Ruth.

"Of course not," Ruth proclaimed with pride. "Sabrina didn't even take four steps into our chamber."

"That's ridiculous," Juniper muttered. "They searched my room twenty times this month."

"Did they find anything?" Ruth wondered with concern.

"Of course not," Juniper echoed. "I'm not stupid. Bernard had a couple of stolen magical rocks from his class, but he only got a detention for it."

"How about Melissa's chamber's?" Ruth asked. "We gave a letter to the president."

"I heard," Juniper commented. "They searched her room the most out of anyone. She was fuming over it. But they didn't find anything. She hid it well."

"That's what we were looking for in the garden then?" Ruth spoke. "The place where she hid the staff?"

Juniper shrugged. "Kind of, you'll see when we get back."

"Sounds like a plan," replied Ruth.

While Juniper and Ruth talked, Elsif sat across from them, completely baffled. She was confused as to why Juniper was talking to them, but even more puzzled over why Ruth was talking back. They were talking so casually, like they were friends.

Elsif couldn't help but blurt out, "Why are you sitting with us?"

Juniper looked over at Elsif in an unfriendly manner. "I'm going over the plan to make sure you guys don't mess it up."

"We know the plan," Elsif stated. "And we're not doing the plan."

"Yes, we are," corrected Ruth, with a dismissive tone.

Elsif stared at Ruth. "No, we aren't going back in the gardens in the middle of the night." She then turned to Juniper. "You can leave now."

"Fine," Juniper said as if the disagreement wasn't worth his time.

Once Juniper walked away, Ruth hissed at Elsif, "You are the absolute worst."

"What was that?" Elsif spat at Ruth, ignoring her comment.

"What do you mean?" Ruth retorted. "And stop rolling your eyes at me! He was confirming plans with us and you totally embarrassed me!"

"Yeah he was updating us, but what was that look you were giving?"

"What look?" Ruth demanded.

"The gazing look, *this* look." Elsif gave a very exaggerated gazing, loving look.

"That was not my face!"

"It was *so* your face," insisted Elsif. "You can't see your face, but I can see your face, and trust me that was the look."

"Liar," Ruth stated. "And why would you tell him we aren't doing the plan? We never agreed not to do it."

"We never agreed that we were doing it either," Elsif countered. "We did agree that we can't trust him or Melissa. Since we can't trust him, we really shouldn't be wandering around at midnight with him. Nothing good happens after midnight!"

"You may not want to go but I'm going."

Elsif snorted. "Over my dead body."

"I'm done talking about this," Ruth said while crossing her arms. "You're ridiculous."

"I'm ridiculous?" Elsif said in astonishment. "I'm not the one crushing on Juniper."

"I am not," Ruth declared, then reconsidered. "Okay, maybe just a little."

Elsif looked Ruth in the eyes and said in a very serious tone, "Ruth, you better stop right now."

"What do you want me to do, deny my feelings?"

"We can't trust him," Elsif stated, then sighed knowing stopping one of Ruth's crushes was impossible. "Just- be careful. Please."

Ruth brightened up. "Does that mean you approve? Even a little bit?"

"No," Elsif quickly corrected. "I don't trust him and I think he's wrong for you. Also, he's too old."

"He's not," Ruth insisted. "He turned seventeen right before school started, so he's one year and three quarters older than me."

"How do you know all of that?" Elsif said in disgust. "I prefer your neighbor."

"I don't," Ruth smirked. "Now we have to find you a guy. Then we could go on a double date."

"First of all, no. I don't have time to date if I'm going to be Merlin's youngest professor," Elsif stated. "Second, I will never double date with you as long as I live because you are literally the lamest person I have ever known."

The call for Elsif's carriage came, so Elsif was forced to pick up her things and leave. As she boarded her carriage, Elsif hoped that Ruth wouldn't make any bad decisions with her remaining time at Merlin. Elsif was beginning to think Ruth missed her carriage on purpose so she had time alone to try to talk to a certain someone...

Chapter 6: The Beige Bag

Milly was the last to arrive at the chambers in November. She had taken the late carriage from Navisia because she had been so busy plotting about what to do about the Staff. Milly's best solution was to ambush Melissa in the middle of her least favorite class and interrogate her until she told them the location of the Staff.

"Honestly," Rose said, laying across the couch. "I forgot about the Staff."

"I didn't have time to think about it," Elsif said, reading a book on the floor because Rose kicked her off the couch. "I spent all month researching the Loquanim and human peace alliance of 3211."

"No one cares," Rose said, poking Elsif with her foot.

"I did nothing," Ruth sighed. "Besides think about our meeting with Juniper on Friday."

"I thought about the Staff a little," Jazzy admitted. "I spent most of my time working in the bakery, practicing my painting, and I also turned down a proposal."

If Milly had been drinking water, she would have spit it out. "Wait, hold up. What happened?"

"The baker's son Kent," Jazzy explained casually. "He proposed and I said no."

Ruth clutched her chest. "You said no!"

Elsif hit Ruth's leg. "She's sixteen, of course she did."

"Yeah," Milly agreed. "You're so young. Why would he propose?"

"Hold up a minute," Rose interrupted. "Was he proposing marriage or an illegal animal smuggling agreement?"

"Marriage," Jazzy stated plainly. "It's common for girls in Koronia to get married between fifteen and eighteen."

"That's crazy," Ruth muttered. "In an unrelated note, Jazzy, could I move in with you?"

Milly rolled her eyes. "We need to get serious. Who's going to meet Juniper on Friday?"

"No one," Elsif said.

Ruth countered, "I think that I should be the only one to go."

"Why, in all of Fantasma, would we send you alone?" Elsif demanded.

"*Because*," Ruth exaggerated the word. "He knows me and he invited me. The only other person that should go is Jazzy, but Jazzy doesn't want to go."

Jazzy shook her head in agreement. "I would rather not."

"And you don't have to," Ruth assured. "So I'll go alone."

"No," Elsif declared. "You're not."

"Yeah," Rose agreed. "I'll go and mess him up. I've been practicing my punches on Milly."

"That's true," Milly stated. "She's getting really strong."

"No," Elsif crossed her arms. "I don't want any of us to go, but if Ruth insists on going then we all need to go. Safety in numbers."

"Fine," Ruth mumbled. "Don't embarrass me."

Elsif and Ruth began to argue but were interrupted by a note sliding under the chamber door. Milly bounded across the room and swung open the door. There was no one in the hallway. Disappointed, Milly grabbed the note and trudged back into the room.

"They must have ducked into a nearby chamber," Milly said while opening the note.

"What does it say?" Rose questioned, jumping up and trying to steal the note from Milly. "What does it say!"

Milly pushed Rose aside and read the note aloud, "Juniper has the Staff."

*****

The girls quietly walked through the Merlin hallways a few minutes before midnight on the first Friday of November. Juniper was waiting at the entrance of the gardens with a look of annoyance as the gang walked up.

"Oh good," he muttered. "You brought the whole circus."

"Oh good, you still have that charming personality," Ruth mocked.

Elsif leaned over to Rose. "If she gets any more embarrassing, please put an end to it. Or me, whatever you have to do."

"Do I have permission to stuff her in a duffel bag?" Rose questioned.

Elsif shrugged, but Milly responded with a stern, "No."

Jazzy began to look around. "Where's the bag?"

"Hey!" Juniper barked, which got the girls' attention. "We don't have all night. Are we going or what?"

"Actually," Ruth mentioned. "We were hoping to have a little chat first?"

The only way Elsif agreed for the girls to go out after curfew was if they confronted Juniper about the note. She still didn't think it was a good idea, but Elsif was secretly intrigued by the thickening plot.

"No," Juniper stated and began to walk toward the gardens.

"We know *you* have the staff!" Rose shouted.

Juniper turned around, with a crease in his brow. "You're not serious."

"We don't think that," Ruth corrected. "Well, some of them might, but not me."

"Why would you come if you think I have the Staff?" Juniper demanded. "Or are you all idiots?"

"Ruth is," Rose and Elsif mumbled at the same time, then proceeded to high five.

"We're here so you can prove that we can trust you," Ruth explained.

"I don't need to prove anything," Juniper snapped.

"Awesome," Elsif responded, then turned to usher the girls back to Merlin. "Let's go back to bed then." Ruth refused to move.

"Just show us the thing in the garden," Ruth pleaded. "Or explain what's going on with Melissa. Just tell us something to prove your innocence."

"I can't," Juniper admitted to Ruth. "I don't know what's going on."

Ruth blinked, perplexed. "What do you mean?"

Juniper's jaw tightened as he debated his next words. "I don't know what's going on," Juniper repeated. "A couple days before classes started in September, Melissa told a couple of us that she was going to steal Malum's Staff because she saw something in the gardens that gave her 'perspective' or whatever that means. Then on the first day of class, she showed me the Staff and she said everything was going to be different. I didn't know what that meant. I didn't even think she was going to steal it in the first place. Melissa is always talk, but never any action, and I only half remember what she said about the gardens but I know it's important. I tried to get her to return the Staff, but it ended in a fight, and now my group isn't too happy with me. I'm the only one with any sense, Melissa has some crazy plan, and my only hope is finding the *thing* in the garden and using it as leverage."

"That was perfect!" Ruth exclaimed. She turned around to the other girls with excitement. "I told you guys I wasn't aiding a potential villain."

The girls exchanged glances of uncertainty. Elsif spoke up first, "Or he could be saying gibberish to make us pity him so we don't rat him out."

"I don't need anyone's pity," Juniper barked. "And we all need to stop talking before we're caught."

Ruth turned back. "You still haven't explained why you're tolerating us by letting us get involved."

"What do you want me to say?" Juniper said with an irritable, sarcastic tone. "That I don't want to do this alone?"

"Yes, that would be lovely," Ruth confirmed. "So we're all in agreement to trust Juniper, right?"

"We still don't have proof that he doesn't have the Staff," Milly countered.

"What do you all want from me?" Juniper groaned, his patience growing thin. "Do you want to check my room?" He said with an air of sarcasm.

"That's a great idea," Ruth perked up. "Let's go!"

Despite Juniper's protests, the girls walked straight to the boys' wing and demanded to search his room. Reluctantly, Juniper opened his chambers and allowed the investigation. Walking in, the girls saw the typical guy chamber, which was decorated with dirty clothes and half eaten food.

"Ew," Rose sniffed around. "I'm going to throw up."

"Welcome to living with Bernard," Juniper remarked, leaning against the doorway, hating every single second of his life.

"What?" Bernard said, who emerged from one of the rooms as if he was summoned. He didn't look concerned about five random girls being in his chambers in the middle of the night. "Hey Frosty."

"I'm going to throw up too," Elsif mumbled to Rose.

"Can you leave?" Juniper snapped at Bernard.

He was met with a distasteful scorn, but he left the chambers without a fight. It was evident that the roommates weren't on great terms.

Jazzy stared at the door after Bernard left. "Does everyone ignore the curfew?"

"Only cool people," Rose bragged.

"Let's start searching," Milly suggested.

The girls split up and searched different rooms. Elsif and Milly were quite determined to search every corner, while the others were a little distracted. Rose found a puzzle, Jazzy decided to clean, and Ruth stopped to talk to Juniper every three minutes.

Half an hour later, the girls hadn't found anything too suspicious. Rose was unsure about a glass jar of marbles she found, *but* she couldn't produce any proof based on her suspicions so she had to let that hunch go. The search was about to conclude when Elsif tripped on a broken floorboard and crashed to the ground.

Rose laughed. "Embarrassing."

Elsif ignored the comment and stood up. "You should really tell maintenance to come and fix that."

"I'll get *right* on that," Juniper stated. "Are we done here?"

There was a mutter of agreement while Milly walked over to the broken floorboard. "I think it's loose." She began to pull on the board, and without much effort the large plank became completely dislodged into Milly's hands. Putting the piece of wood aside, Milly looked into the hole. She saw something sitting at the bottom, and reached her arm inside. The space was about a foot deep, five inches wide, and a couple feet long. Milly caught hold of some fabric and brought it into the light. It was a long beige bag.

"This is the bag the staff was in," Milly reported, looking frantically at her cousins. "I'm positive."

Accusing eyes landed on Juniper. His expression was neutral as everyone examined him, forcefully neutral. "I didn't know that compartment existed," he demanded sternly. "That bag isn't mine, it's Melissa's."

Ruth walked over and took the bag in her hands. "Milly, are you absolutely certain this is the bag you saw during flying class?" Milly nodded without hesitation. Ruth turned to Juniper. "Why is this in your room?"

"*I don't know*," Juniper stressed every word. "Melissa must have put it there."

Elsif interjected, "Melissa wouldn't have been able to access your room without your permission. There's magic to restrict access to other chambers."

"I don't have the staff," Juniper insisted. "Why would I let you guys in here if I did?"

"You didn't think we would find your secret little hideout," Rose answered.

Juniper rubbed his brow. "I don't know how it got in here, but *I* didn't put it there. Even if I have the bag, that doesn't mean I have the Staff."

"Maybe we should go," Jazzy suggested in a soft spoken voice.

"Yeah," Elsif agreed. "Let's go."

"Fine by me," Ruth said, throwing her hands up in the air and walking out of the room first. Her emotions ran high and she regretted her actions. She scolded herself for being naive and stupid over a guy she didn't know. She hated that Elsif was right all along, she was always right. *Stupid, stupid, stupid.*

"Ruth, wait," Juniper ran after her. "I swear I had no idea about the bag."

"I don't care about the bag," Ruth said, wheeling around to face Juniper. "It's the fact that it was hidden. You could have just told me that you had the bag and I would have trusted you."

"How could I have told you about the bag if I didn't know about the bag?" He argued.

"Just leave me alone!" Ruth exclaimed. "I obviously can't trust you, Juniper!" She ran down the hallway and Juniper watched her go.

"Wow," Elsif commented to Rose as they walked back to their chambers. "That was really dramatic."

"*It's not about the bag*," Rose mocked Ruth. "*You lied to me! I'll never trust you again!*"

Milly frowned. "I give that impression a six out of ten."

"What?" Rose questioned defensively. "That was my best Ruth impression I've ever done!"

"The wording wasn't accurate," Milly replied.

Rose waved her off. "I was taking creative liberties. A simpleton like yourself could never understand. Jazzy loved it."

"I feel really bad for Ruth," Jazzy said in response.

"Don't worry," Elsif muttered. "I'm sure Ruth will move on to another boy next week."

*****

Days went by and the girls silently agreed to not bring up the beige bag incident to spare Ruth's feelings. They assumed she would be over the whole affair in a few days, but Juniper's betrayal was harder on Ruth than they originally thought.

"Remember that time we were all helping Juniper catch Melissa with Malum's Staff but we found out *he* actually had the Staff," Rose said on a random Thursday evening in the chambers.

The girls were not amused.

Ruth gave Rose a deathly glare. "Permission to hit Rose." The council were in agreement of the motion so the offender received a swift smack from the suffering party.

"Probably would be best to never bring it up again," Elsif suggested.

Jazzy nodded. "Probably best."

"Fine," Rose announced. "We can just wait around until we're killed by the Staff."

"We're not going to be killed by the Staff," Milly chided Rose.

"Merlin Academy won't let anything happen to us," Elsif said with certainty.

"But," Jazzy spoke with uncertainty. "If Malum's Staff is the second most powerful object in history, and Merlin doesn't have the *most* powerful object, then could they defend us?"

Silence filled the room as the weight of the realization left no room for options. It was more than a fun fact, it meant life and death.

Rose slouched in her chair. "I was just joking," she said in a solemn tone that she rarely used.

"I thought the Hat didn't even exist," Ruth said, confused.

"It exists," Milly explained. "It's just been missing for hundreds of years."

"Then maybe someone from Merlin will find the Hat before Melissa uses the Staff," Ruth suggested with hope. She may have not trusted Juniper anymore, but she still found comfort in his words that it seemed like they had time before Melissa acted.

"Are they even looking?" Milly asked with doubt in her voice.

"There haven't been any major searches for awhile," Elsif rattled on. "There was a big trend about a hundred and thirty years ago for the Warlock's Hat but it died out after fifty years or so. All the major historians moved on to try and find this magic book called Enkantiis and that has been the trending archeological find since."

Rose sighed. "Why are you such a nerd?"

"I don't know." Elsif returned the sigh.

"So no one at Merlin is looking for it?" Ruth clarified.

"Basically no," Elsif replied. "If they were, then they would have to publish their research and findings. They could potentially be 'asking' some smaller historians to look into it and they wouldn't technically need to publish their work since they aren't an established institution. But if Merlin was officially looking for the Hat, then they would have to record it, and Merlin is only investigating Enkantiis right now."

"We'll just have to be ready to protect ourselves," Milly interjected. "We'll need to keep the weapons and we should actively keep an eye out for Melissa."

"Too bad we couldn't just find the Hat," Jazzy said with melancholy.

"Jazzy, you're a genius," Elsif said, rising to her feet. "We can find the Hat!"

Rose laughed. "Someone needs a reality check."

"I'm serious!" Elsif said, her whole face lighting up. "We have more access to professional research and resources than anyone else in Fantasma. If you think about it, we are in the perfect position to find the Hat. Tons of research has been done for us but no one else is trying to find it at the moment. We actually have a chance to find it, a rather small chance, but a chance nonetheless!"

Jazzy looked unsure. "But we're teenagers."

"Teenagers at the most elite academy in all of Fantasma," Elsif countered. "We already have a leg up on the competition."

"Elsif," Rose spoke. "Are you suggesting a good old fashioned, impossibly difficult, treasure hunt that could endanger and change our lives forever?"

"Maybe not that last part," Elsif responded. "But yes, yes I am."

Rose stood and raised an invisible glass. "I'm in."

"What are you doing?" Milly inquired.

"DON'T JUST SIT THERE!" Rose screamed. "CHEERS ME BEFORE MY ARM GETS TIRED!"

Milly was hesitant. "I don't know. The odds aren't in our favor."

Elsif raised her invisible glass "When have the odds ever been in favor of saving the world? Heroes don't look at the odds."

Milly knew Elsif was only saying those words to convince her, but they were the *exact* right words for her. She stood up and raised her invisible glass.

Elsif turned to Ruth. "You don't want to miss out on all this fun do you?"

"Obviously not." Ruth rose from her seat and raised her invisible glass.

"Jazzy," Elsif finally said. "This idea was inspired by you. We can't do it without you."

Smiling, Jazzy stood up and joined her imaginary glass with the others. They cheered to the treasure hunt, and an imaginary vow bonded them all to the new adventure.

Elsif was excited for her future once again, which had been dwindling the last few months. She knew the treasure hunt for the Hat could seriously elevate her in the historian world, but secretly that wasn't the true reason she suggested the idea. Even if she would never admit it to herself, Elsif loved the thrill of all the dramatics that the Hat and Staff had brought to her life. It was dangerous and exciting, which were feelings Elsif had never fully experienced before. She wanted to feel them a little bit more before she had to give them all up for a responsible adult life. One more little taste and Elsif would be able to get it out of her system forever, and return to her normal, dependable life.

Chapter 7: Struth Is A Weird Region

"**W**hat's better than setting the entire library on fire?" Rose asked.

"Many things," Milly stated.

Rose and Milly were in the library reading about the Warlock's Hat. The girls all agreed to spend the rest of November researching and trying to find any clues to help lead them on their quest. It was, unfortunately, Rose and Milly's turn to spend their lunch hour researching in the library. So far the gang had only found general information and history about the Hat, and nothing concrete to help them on their treasure hunt. Milly was reading multiple books at once, comparing her notes from each one, and taking the search very seriously. Rose was planning twelve different ways to set fire to the room.

"Can we leave now?" Rose begged. "All these books just talk about the boring history of the Hat. Elsif already knows about the entire history of everything so we really don't need to read about it too."

Milly picked up another book without looking at Rose. "We still have fifteen minutes."

Rose grabbed Milly's book and threw it behind her. "What could we possibly discover in fifteen minutes?"

Milly opened up another book. "You know Numterram was discovered in fifteen minutes."

Rose eyed Milly suspiciously. "That's not true."

"Probably not," Milly flipped through a few pages, while Rose went around and collected the biggest books she could find. She stacked them up next to each other and made a book family. Their names included Branson, Beatrice, Bobby, Bobert, Blake, Betty, and Jeff. Milly ignored Rose as usual.

"We can head to class now."

"FINALLY!" Rose stood up and knocked down her book family. "Good luck fending for yourselves, you stupid little orphans."

"You're going to make a fantastic mother," Milly muttered sarcastically as the girls headed to their History of Struth class.

"Oh Milly no," Rose assured. "I will be the amazing, funny, charismatic, mysterious Aunt that your kids will love more than you and you will resent me for it."

"Okay," Milly accepted her fate without a second thought.

Once the girls arrived at their classroom, Rose realized her grave mistake. This class was just as boring as reading books in the library. Trying to pass the time, Rose crumpled up small pieces of paper and threw them at Milly's head when the professor wasn't looking.

Milly tried to pay attention but Struth was so boring that she kept drifting to other activities like doodling or glaring at Rose. Finally Milly shook her head and was determined to pay attention.

"There is a misconception in most regions," Professor Henson said in a voice that was monotone and slow. "That Struth is academically behind the rest of Fantasma and our citizens aren't particularly bright. But that-" He paused so he could take a deep breath in. "Is not the case. Not the case at all. We have done great things just like the rest of Fantasma..." Milly summoned all her strength to not bang her head against the table out of desperation to escape her boredom.

She hadn't known that her own language could be so hard to understand. Milly was pretty sure that Professor Henson wasn't speaking Elfish or Glordin, because the words all made sense but somehow they didn't make sense in the order he was saying them. She kept hearing Struth and achievements but she couldn't repeat the overall message of his lesson even if a wand was loaded up with a curse and pointed at her head.

Rose had given into the temptation and was currently hitting her head against her desk as Professor Henson continued to speak. Rose also didn't like to hear Professor Henson, but she couldn't stand looking at him even more. He looked like a weirdo! In his defense, most people from Struth did in her opinion. He had beady little eyes and wrinkles that looked like whiskers. He bore a non-human essence to him, and Rose found that quality very distrusting.

"The Struth region," the Professor said, in between unnecessary pauses. "Also has great restaurants with great food, really great food. A restaurant in my hometown was awarded..."

Milly silently wished she could leave and arrive at her Advanced Sailing class early. Rose was daydreaming about eating orange marmalade out of a jar that was twice her size.

"But besides food," Professor Henson drawled. "We have many other great accomplishments. Our museums for instance. My personal favorite is the Warlock's Hat Museum, a really great museum. You should all visit sometime. You'll be thoroughly impressed."

The girls' heads shot up and they both finally learned something worthwhile in the class. They turned to each other with the same knowing smirk.

"Looks like we have plans for December break," Milly whispered.

"Teaching a bat to eat a cat?"

Milly shook her head with disappointment. "Why do I talk to you?"

After class Milly went to talk to the professor about the Warlock Hat Museum, but she had to wait awhile because half the class had questions on the lecture. Milly and Rose weren't the only ones that couldn't focus on a single word he said. While she waited, out of the corner of her eye, Milly saw Juniper walk into the room for the next class. He looked in her direction and for a moment she thought that he was glaring at her, but she quickly realized he wasn't looking at her but rather the girl behind her. Piper was in line behind her to also talk to Professor Henson and she exchanged an unfriendly glance with Juniper as he walked to his seat.

Milly had never talked to anyone in that particular group before, but there was a mystery around them, and Milly was not immune to curiosity. She was on a mission to not only find the Hat but find out the secrets of the Versario students.

"Are you guys not friends anymore?" Milly asked, trying to sound casual.

Piper looked over at Milly with a mixture of surprise and disgust. "What?"

"Sorry," Milly replied, attempting to sound. "I just thought you guys were in the same friend group, but it doesn't look like that now."

"That's not your business," Piper snapped.

"It's not," Milly agreed, and turned forward. *That did not go well.*

The interaction created an uneasy feeling in Milly's stomach as she began to talk to Professor Henson. She looked over at Juniper several times to judge if he could overhear her or not. She wasn't sure, so she lowered her voice. Professor Henson did not pick up on Milly's cues because he practically shouted when he talked about the Warlock's Museum. Apparently it was his favorite subject because he went on and on without pausing, like in his lectures. He was probably thankful that one student had been interested in something he said, and didn't want to miss the opportunity to elaborate.

Milly eventually interrupted his rambling and thanked him for his time, but explained that she unfortunately had to get to her next class. She promptly left without looking at Juniper on her way out so as to not draw his attention.

*****

"Where's Ruth?" Rose demanded.

At the end of the school day Rose, Milly, and Jazzy (who was practically dragged) ran straight to the library after their last class. They immediately found Elsif which was no surprise because she practically lived in the library during the school months.

"Am I not enough for you?" Elsif demanded while reading her book.

Rose smacked the book out of Elsif's hand. "No." Accustomed to the behavior, Elsif picked up her book, unaffected and continued to read.

"Is she coming?" Milly asked impatiently.

"Why are you all so obsessed with Ruth?" Elsif demanded. "I've met her, she's not that great."

"We have something important to talk about," Milly explained, her voice brimming with anticipation.

"We had to run here," Jazzy explained, sitting down next to Elsif. "I don't know why."

Rose twirled with agitation. "You'll learn why when that stupidly late girl gets here!"

"Does she know that we are meeting in the library?" Milly asked.

"We've been meeting everyday," Jazzy said. "I would think she would assume."

"Ruth's an idiot!" Rose claimed loudly. "We can't *assume* she knows anything."

"Don't call her an idiot," Elsif chided Rose. "It's rude."

"Your face is rude," Rose retorted back.

"Should I go find Ruth?" Milly interrupted, fidgeting in her seat.

Elsif began to read her book again as she answered Milly. "You're going to search all of Merlin?"

"We have to talk about Struth!" Milly wailed with impatience.

Elsif chuckled slightly at Milly's passionate statement. "No one has to talk about Struth *that* badly."

"We do when they have the largest Warlock's Hat Museum in Fantasma," Milly stated.

Elsif eyed Milly. "They have museums in Struth?"

"I was surprised too!" Rose exclaimed. "I thought Struth was nothing but an open field where boring people sprouted out of the ground. That or it was made up entirely and it was the most boring joke of the century."

"Mr. Henson told us about the museum," Milly said. "How did you not know? You're obsessed with everything in history."

"Well," Elsif said, her cheeks growing a slight shade of pink. "I might have a little trouble paying attention in his classes. He's just so boring. But I should probably start now because- nevermind."

Rose reached out and cupped Elsif's face and leaned awkwardly close. "I can't believe it. You actually are human." Elsif, in response, shoved Rose's face away. In retaliation, Rose grabbed Elsif's book again and flung it across the room.

"Can't I just finish the chapter?" Elsif moaned.

"Focus Elsif!" Milly snapped in her face. "Struth could be our answer for all of this."

"I really doubt Struth has anything interesting to say that we can't learn here," Elsif retorted. "The only thing interesting about Struth is that Humilis used to be a part of their region."

Rose blinked slowly. "Elsif, they're in the same region."

"No they aren't," Elsif began, as Milly and Rose groaned. Everyone knew Elsif took every opportunity to lecture useless information that she had compiled in her classes whenever someone said an incorrect historical fact.

"In 3949, the district of Humilis, which previously was in the region of Struth, was uncomfortable with the influence that the four Magicis ambassadors were having on the Chancellor of Struth. Struth and Magicis had always had a close alliance since they were both originally human regions and stood together during the Elven Wars to keep the human race alive. But the ten towns of Humilis argued that it was over 600 years ago and they should try to be an independent region. Struth and Humilis kept disagreeing on Magicis' role in their government so they both agreed that Humilis should secede and begin their own government and they could decide for themselves what role Magicis would play in their govern-"

Elsif was cut off by a harsh '*shh*' from the librarian who was walking by. "This is a library full of intellectual Merlin students," the librarian chided Elsif. "Not a tavern full of hooligans."

"I'm sorry Mrs. Gessner," Elsif said sheepishly.

"You should know better Ms. Menzie," Mrs. Gessner spoke harshly, which Elsif was not used to hearing. "You're about to graduate and you're acting as if this is your first year at the Academy. I don't want to hear you raise your voice again in my library."

"Yes ma'am," Elsif nodded.

Mrs. Gessner walked away and all four girls were a little unsure if they were allowed to continue speaking to each other or not. Rose only lasted twenty-seven seconds before she whispered, "Third best moment of my life."

"Was I really that loud?" Elsif questioned in a whisper.

"No," Jazzy assured, patting Elsif on the shoulder. "Maybe Mrs. Gessner is having a bad day."

"You weren't any louder than the rest of us," Milly added.

Rose had begun to crumble up little pieces of paper and flick them at Mrs. Gessner when her back was turned from them. "Honestly, any noise you make is too loud."

"Stop it," Elsif snapped at Rose once she saw where she was aiming her tiny paper cannonballs.

"I'm defending your honor," Rose barked back. Elsif's reflexes reached out to grab the paper, but on second consideration, she decided to leave Rose alone. Instead, she went to pick up her book and coincidently moved a library cart so Rose had better aim at Mrs. Gessner.

"Where's Struth and Humilis?" Jazzy asked Milly.

"Between Navisia and Vulputate," Milly explained.

"Okay," Jazzy nodded. "Where's Navisia and Vulputate?"

"You don't know where Navisia is?" Milly asked in confusion. "They're pretty vital to the economy of all the regions on the North Sea. We trade with Regium a lot. I think we might trade with Koronia specifically, but I'm not sure."

"They don't teach a lot about the other regions in Mellberg."

"Can you name all fifteen regions?" Rose questioned with wide eyes. Jazzy shook her head in response. "That's okay," Rose replied. "I can't either."

"You can borrow one of my maps, Jazzy," Milly said, pulling out a large folded map from her bag.

Elsif frowned. "Why do you randomly have maps of Fantasma?"

"Your hobby is learning about dead people," Milly stated. "Don't judge me."

"But I've been learning so much more about Fantasma," Jazzy added. "I learned about Andorae yesterday. I never knew about the Vaniians, but after class the teacher introduced me to one. They're green skin is so beautiful, it's like the color of emeralds."

"Fantasma used to be full of different people groups," Elsif added. "There used to be Elves, Fairies, Dwarves, Sostomi, Goblins, and Mimpius. They all had different magical abilities and lived in different areas of Fantasma."

"Where are they now?" Jazzy asked with excitement.

"Dead," Rose said dryly.

Jazzy's mood dropped. "Oh."

"Well, they tried to kill all the humans," Elsif quickly explained. "So during the Elven Wars we fought them and their people ended up dying out."

"Why did they want to hurt humans?" Jazzy asked sadly.

"They wanted to enslave us," Milly said.

"The Elves did," Elsif corrected her. "But when humans fought the Elves and they started losing, they recruited the Fairies, Dwarves, and Sostomi. But the Mermaids and Loquanims joined our side and we ended up winning. The Vaniians remained impartial during the wars, and the Mimpius died out on their own because the Elves had killed most of them before the Elven Wars. But it's lucky for us that the Elves took care of the Mimpius because they were more evil than the Elves. More powerful too, but there were a lot less of them than the Elves."

Rose coughed loudly. "*Nerd.*"

As Jazzy received an extensive history lesson from Elsif, Ruth finally showed up.

"Hey," Ruth said.

"Hey? Hey!" Rose demanded, slamming her hands on the table. "You were a whole fifteen minutes late and all we get is a *hey*? What did you expect us to do while we were waiting for you? Discover Numterram?"

"What?" Ruth said with a scrunched face.

"Nothing," Milly muttered. "Unlike Rose, I *actually* have important news."

Milly filled Ruth in on the discoveries they made during their class with Mr. Henson. Ruth was also surprised to discover there was anything worthwhile in Struth.

"Now we have to decide what we do with this new information," Milly stated. "What are everyone's thoughts?"

Rose stood up. "I am bored." After her proclamation Rose walked away to collect some chairs, so she could make herself a fort.

"We need to go to the museum," Ruth stated. "It's the obvious next step to our quest."

"When did we start calling it a quest?" Elsif questioned. "I wasn't given the memo on the name update."

"I like the sound of a quest," Jazzy beamed. "It sounds exciting."

"We can come up with the name later," Milly said, reeling everyone back to the original conversation. "So we are in agreement? We should go to the Warlock's Museum in Struth." Everyone nodded, including Rose who was lining up several chairs. "Now our only problem is we can't travel to Struth on our own. You need to have an adult to stay at an Inn, and we don't know anyone in Struth that we can stay with."

"We can ask Professor Henson if he has a weird nephew we can bunk with," Rose suggested, then proceeded to tackle Elsif out of her chair.

"Rose, get off-" Elsif sputtered as she fell to the floor, and Rose stole her chair.

Rose dragged Elsif's chair next to the rest of her chairs and said, "I needed a sixth chair."

"Hey," Ruth said. "We do happen to have an older, mature cousin who is going to become a legal adult on November 29th."

"Oh yeah," Elsif said, standing up from the floor. "I guess I can keep all you from dying in a ditch. Except for Rose, I would let Rose die in a ditch."

"Not if I kill you first, you old maid," Rose grumbled, while laying on all six of her chairs.

"This is a good plan," Milly stated. "We should go at the beginning of December break, before we head to Stellae. We'll leave from Merlin, go to Struth, stay a week, then head to Stellae."

"Sounds good," Elsif said, then turned to Jazzy. "You should come to Stellae with us. Our extended family always stays at my grandparent's house during December because our family has like six birthdays in two weeks."

"I'd love to," Jazzy replied. "As long as it's alright with the rest of your family?"

"Of course," Elsif said. "Our grandparents love it when we bring friends."

Rose smirked. "They'll love to find out that Elsif *finally* made a friend."

"You'll love Stellae!" Ruth told Jazzy. "There's so many amazing shops, pretty views, and our grandparents have flying carriages."

"Flying carriages?" Jazzy asked.

Elsif nodded. "We can show you all over Stellae. It'll be so much fun, but just a heads up, our family is crazy."

Jazzy laughed. "I don't mind that."

"Think of twenty Roses and Ruths everywhere."

*****

The girls were walking back from dinner, talking about their plans for December break when Rose jumped in front of the group and made a declaration, "I have to show you all something right now or Fantasma may end!"

"Okay," Elsif said, rolling her eyes. "Make it quick, I have a paper to write."

"Follow me!" Rose said and ran down the hallway with a heel click here and there. The girls followed at a normal pace. Along the way the girls had a weird encounter with Melissa. As they passed her in the hallway she waved and smiled at them. Jazzy waved back but the other girls stared at her without moving their arms.

"That was weird," Milly commented.

"Why is she acknowledging our existence?" Elsif questioned.

"Who knows and who cares what Melissa is up to," Ruth added with a hostile tone.

"She looked nice," Jazzy suggested.

"Nice and evil," Rose agreed, who had run back because the girls were walking too slow.

Ruth crossed her arms. "We should go back to hiding every time we see that group."

Rose began to push the girls. "Keep moving ladies, we are almost to our destination." She led the gang to the first floor of the girls' wing and stopped in front of a closet door. "Tada!"

"Woah, a door!" Ruth said with sarcastic amazement, as Milly opened the closet.

"It's filled with cleaning supplies," Milly reported, stepping inside. "Is this a not so subtle way to ask us to clean the chambers?"

"Yes," Rose answered. "But also no. Remember when I said I would find a perfect place to hide our weapons?"

"No," Elsif stated.

"Not really," Ruth agreed.

Milly shook her head. "Nope."

"Vaguely," Jazzy added.

"Well I did and I have." Rose said proudly. "You all may follow me to the perfect place for our precious weapons."

Rose walked into the closet and began pushing a tall shelf on the back wall. The shelf looked big and had tons of different items on it, so the girls doubted Rose would be able to move it, but the shelf slid easily. Or Rose had super strength. One or the other.

The empty floor space revealed a trapdoor with a little metal handle sticking out. Rose grabbed the handle and opened the trapdoor to reveal a black hole big enough for someone to fall down. The girls gathered around the hole and couldn't see the bottom. Without any explanation, Rose jumped into the hole and disappeared.

Silence followed Rose's disappearance down the hole.

"After you," Ruth gestured to Elsif after a moment.

"I'm not following Rose into a dark hole in the ground. Did you not hear her earlier when she was threatening me?"

"I'll go next," Milly volunteered. She got down and put her legs into the hole, and tried to judge the distance to the bottom when her foot hit an object. "Oh, there's a ladder," Milly said happily.

"That's only for the wimps," Rose called up from the dark abyss.

Ignoring the taunt, Milly climbed down the ladder, and the other three girls followed her. The hole was not very deep, only a little less than six feet. Once all the girls had climbed down, Rose finally turned on a light. They found themselves in a small, empty room with a dainty chandelier hanging from the ceiling, a table with their weapons on it, and a bolted door on the south wall.

"Nice job Rose," Ruth said, impressed.

"Thank you," Rose said with a low bow. "I thought we could use this place for secret meetings, harboring our illegals, and torturing sessions."

"Good idea," Milly said, ignoring Rose's last comment. "We don't want people overhearing us if we are talking about delicate things." Milly remembered her conversation with Professor Henson and how Juniper could have been in earshot.

"How did you find this?" Elsif asked.

"Oh you know," Rose shrugged. "I just checked every room to see if there was a hidden passageway or space somewhere. I moved a lot of shelves, paintings, and desks until I found a secret room suitable enough for us."

Milly looked at Rose in shock. "Were there other secret rooms?"

"Duh," Rose said harshly. "What kind of magical school doesn't have secret rooms? I picked this one because it was close to our chambers, it had a spooky door, and this chandelier sets the mood."

"Does this place have a name?" Jazzy asked.

"I've been calling it my dungeon," Rose said casually. "But I'm open to other amazing, cool, and intimidating names."

"The bunker," Ruth suggested.

"The meeting room," Milly countered.

"Down the rabbit hole," Elsif added.

Rose rolled her eyes. "Too obvious, too boring, and too I don't even know what that means. This place will henceforth be named Rose's dungeon."

Milly interrupted Rose's announcement, "Don't you think people will get suspicious if we keep talking about meeting in *Rose's dungeon*?"

"Milly, Milly, Milly," Rose said in a condescending tone. "No one will ever question *me* having a dungeon."

The girls continued to argue about the name of the room as they left and went back to their chambers. Eventually the arguing turned into exciting chatter about their plans for December break.

Chapter 8: Rose Swears She Didn't Do It

On the last day of November the girls took a carriage from Merlin Academy to Struth. The carriage ride was about nine hours to New Greenville, where the Warlock's Hat museum was located. The girls told their parents that they needed to travel to Struth for an extracurricular school project, and since Elsif was eighteen and could buy a room at an Inn, they had no objections.

"Are we there yet?" Rose exclaimed.

Milly sighed. "For the millionth time, no."

Rose closed her mouth for a couple minutes before asking again, "Are we there now?"

"We have two to three more hours," Ruth said, looking out the window. "We're about to cross the bridge into Struth."

Jazzy's eyes grew wide. "We're already in Struth?"

"Vulputate lets the carriages travel really fast," Elsif said. "I think they allow the fastest travel for carriages out of all the other regions."

"Carriages go up to 175 mph on the Adsit roadway," Milly said. "That was the main road we were on when we were passing through Vulputate."

"How fast is that?" Jazzy asked.

"Fast," Ruth replied, still looking outside. "You use horse carriages in Koronia and horses can only trot up to twelve mph. So we're going fast."

"Are we still going that fast?" Jazzy remarked with amazement. "It doesn't feel like we're moving quickly."

"Struth has a max speed of sixty," Milly replied indifferently. "It's so slow. I hate having to travel through Struth. Navisia doesn't have limits on how fast you can go in carriages. Usually the carriages won't go beyond 150, but sometimes they can be persuaded on certain roads."

"Wow," Jazzy mumbled.

"The magic in the carriages make the ride completely smooth," Elsif explained to Jazzy. "So we can't feel how fast we're going, at any speed."

"So interesting," Rose interrupted with sarcasm. "Are we there yet?"

"Rose," Elsif stated. "This is why nobody likes you."

Pouting in her seat, Rose yelled in response, "Why don't you love me Elsif!"

"Don't worry Rose," Jazzy said with a smile. "I'll always love you."

Two hours later the girls arrived in New Greenville. The town was supposedly the second-largest town in Struth, but none of the girls were impressed by what they saw as the carriage passed through town. All except for Jazzy, who was impressed by everything she saw outside of Mellberg.

The carriage pulled in front of the Hickory Well Inn, and the girls got out. As they strolled into the Inn, Jazzy turned to Elsif. "Where is the carriage going?"

Elsif turned her head to see the carriage rolling away independently. "I'm not sure. It probably has someone else to pick up."

"Will it know when to pick us up when we leave for Stellae?" Jazzy asked.

"Yeah," Elsif replied. "I already gave the date and time back at Merlin, but if we change it then we can send a letter to the school."

"So Merlin owns all the magic carriages?" Jazzy asked.

"Of course," Elsif said. "Magicis controls all the carriages in Fantasma."

"Do you have to pay to use them?" Jazzy continued to ask.

"Um," Elsif paused. "No, the carriages are public transportation. Anyone can use them."

"There aren't any in Koronia though," Jazzy commented.

Elsif searched for an answer. "Oh, that must be because the government of Koronia doesn't allow magic."

Jazzy nodded, "That makes sense."

At the front desk, Elsif checked the girls into their room. She had mailed a letter to reserve a suite that had six beds so there was plenty of room for all of them, and Elsif wouldn't have to share a bed with any of her cousins.

"Alright, I will need to see an ID to confirm the room," the woman behind the desk said as she filled out paperwork.

Elsif rummaged through her bag and pulled out her wallet. "Will my student ID suffice?"

"If it has your name and ID number it will be fine," she said, while taking Elsif's ID. "Oh, you're a Merlin student." She looked at Elsif with a big welcoming smile. "How impressive. We love to see well-accomplished Merlin students here in Struth."

"Thank you," Elsif said while unsuccessfully smothering her prideful smile. Elsif wasn't the proud type, but she did enjoy the reaction from strangers when they found out she was a Merlin student. That's usually why she used her Merlin ID instead of her Gelida ID.

"What brings you to town?" The woman asked.

"The Warlock's Museum," Elsif answered. "We have an extracurricular project at Merlin for the Hat."

"Oh our museum is quite impressive," the woman replied. "Lots of books."

Elsif nodded. "That's what we're here for."

"Alright then," she returned to her paperwork. "That will be $2,100 for the suite for ten nights."

"Sounds good, here's a Pecuun bill and let me see if one of my cousins has a gold coin," Elsif said, turning to the other girls.

"My only currency is rocks," Rose said, holding out her hands to reveal several small stones.

"I only have Denii bills," Ruth stated. "Coins are too heavy."

Milly reached into her wallet. "I have one."

"Thanks," Elsif said, taking the gold coin from Milly and giving it to the front desk woman.

"Okay," the woman replied counting the money. "Your change is going to be $8,000." She handed Elsif back eight Denii bills.

Jazzy watched the interaction in shock. She had never seen paper money before, she didn't know it existed. Her village had only ever used coins. Copper and silver were the main coins and once in a while someone would use gold, but that was a rare occasion.

Jazzy whispered to Ruth, as Elsif finished signing the paperwork for the suite. "That's a lot of money."

"Not really," Ruth said offhandedly. "Our grandparents give us five Denii bills for every month we complete at Merlin."

"Are they rich?" The words popped out of Jazzy's mouth before she realized the question was rude.

Ruth didn't seem to be offended. "No, just well off. You should see some of the really rich homes in Magicis or Stellae. They're as big as Merlin."

Once Elsif was done checking in, the girls dropped off their bags at the room, and headed to the Museum. Elsif chose the inn that was only four blocks away so the girls could easily walk.

The Warlock's Hat Museum may have been the only impressive thing in all of Struth. Most of the region was filled with average looking homes and a few businesses scattered around, but the museum was a large modern structure. The girls found out the cause of the grand architecture from the large plaque outside the entrance.

Donated by:

The President of Merlin Academy,

Robert Chapicky, 3949

"That was the year Humilis seceded," Elsif commented to herself because no one else cared about history. "Interesting."

As the girls walked in they were immediately greeted by a thirty foot tall Hat statue. The Hat was tall, with a small brim, and came to a point at the top.

"We know what it looks like now," Rose said as she twirled into the museum.

"One step closer," Milly pointed out. "Let's go."

The girls went to the history corridor, and spent the first day strategizing. They talked about which sections to go through, what historians they needed to focus on, and divided all the work between them. Elsif, Ruth, and Milly ended up doing most of the research because Rose found the games for children and forced Jazzy to play with her.

After a few solid hours of research, the girls went back to the inn for a good night's rest. They were up early the next morning for another full day of work. The same routine continued for the girls day after day as they read book after book. Even though they made a valiant effort, nothing groundbreaking was found. After several days it began to look like the trip to Struth had been a mistake. But day six took a different turn.

"I'm not eating another burger," Ruth stated.

"Then starve," Rose declared.

"It's right next door," Elsif countered. "And it's Rose's turn to grab lunch. Do you really want her walking across town? Think of the civilians, Ruth."

"The taco place is only two blocks," Jazzy suggested.

"I'm not a big fan of tacos," Milly chimed in.

"The chicken place?" Ruth asked.

Elsif shook her head. "That's four blocks. How many people will die in those four blocks?"

"I'm leaving." Rose stood up. "I'm getting something edible and I will force it down all of your throats if I have to!" Rose bounced out of the library and the girls continued their research, hoping Rose would obey the laws of Struth.

Elsif was reading a book about the Hat in the Bloodshed Age while trying to determine its whereabouts from 3250-3310. Ruth scanned an article written recently about Xen Siid. Milly looked at a map of Fantasma and was tracing where they knew the Hat had been throughout history. Jazzy was debating what book she should read next. She never truly knew what she was supposed to look for and felt bad for not contributing more.

The authors the girls found at the museum were the same ones that they had been reading at Merlin for the last month. They had become very accustomed to seeing the names Walten Elian, Leslie Perkins, Wayne Allwine, Chris Diamantopoulos, and Britt Iwan.

Jazzy picked up another book by Walten Elian titled, *The Warlock's Hat and Common Misconceptions*, and began flipping through the pages. Immediately something odd caught Jazzy's eye. There were handwritten notes in the margins.

She realized the book was full of added annotations in the margins with words like WRONG or definitely incorrect or how dumb was this author??? And on the last page of the book there was a loose note that read:

Idiots List

Andorae Region/ Saladana Tavern 11/14

Vulputate Region/ New Shield 12/1

Numterram Region/ Darling Dashing 12/28

Struth Region/ Warlock's Museum 12/8

Currus Region/ Bender's Auto Repair Club 1/15

Silvia District/ Audley's Tavern & Pub 2/3

Mirabilis Region/ Cheshire Cat 3/19

Viverra Region/ Kolvig Kernels 4/11

"I think I may have found something-" Jazzy was cut off by a loud siren. The girls looked around in confusion, but there was a quick answer to their questions. Smoke began seeping in all around them. Within seconds, the room grew dark, thick, and hot.

"Fire!" Ruth exclaimed, grabbing all the stuff on the table and jamming it into her bag.

"Leave everything, we have to go," Milly said, standing up, and entering a cloud of smoke. She was overtaken by a coughing fit and forced to hunch down.

Elsif grabbed Milly. "Get lower to the ground. And cover your mouth!"

"Where's the exit?" Jazzy asked, her voice shaking.

The girls frantically looked around the room, but the darkness confused them and they didn't know which direction led to the nearest exit. While they debated their options, a flaming shelf came crashing down next to them. Screams filled the air as the girls scattered away from the burning shelf that nearly missed them.

"Door," Milly choked amid coughs.

Elsif saw the faint door through the smoke, that the shelf had been blocking before it fell. Ruth grabbed the bags, Elsif grabbed Milly, and Jazzy took the book that was in her hand as they all ran out of the building.

The door led outside where the air was fresh, clean, and not life threatening. The girls took a couple steps away from the building before Milly and Jazzy collapsed to the ground. Milly was coughing her lungs up and Jazzy trembled from head to foot.

"We need to get farther away," Elsif said, grabbing Milly again. "The building could explode.""What?" Jazzy said, looking up at Elsif with fear in her eyes.

"Buildings don't explode from fires," Ruth retorted, while helping Jazzy to her feet.

Elsif's mouth opened to respond, but the words snagged on her lips when she saw someone who looked familiar, exit through the door behind the girls. The guy ran in the opposite direction from where the girls stood, but even though smoke filled the air, it was hard to miss the red hair. .

"Elsif!" Ruth yelled at her, which brought her attention back to the present. "Why would the building explode?!"

"I don't know," Elsif snapped as she came back to the moment. "That's what they do in books!" She ignored what she saw, grabbed Milly, and began dragging her towards the street where groups of people were congregating.

As they walked further from the building, the air grew cooler and relief washed over the girls. Once the girls joined the crowd, the library was almost completely engulfed by the flames.

Firefighters began showering water on the building, but the fire wasn't slowing. The air was full of smoke but the girls were far enough that Milly's cough was beginning to subside.

"You alright?" Elsif asked.

"Yeah," Milly said between deep breaths. They were sitting on a bench, with a perfect view of the Museum's demise. "But I think an ember caught my arm when the bookcase fell."

Elsif examined Milly's arm and noticed a small hole had been singed in her shirt. Rolling up Milly's sleeve, Elsif found a small red burn on Milly's upper arm. The burn was a deep shade of red but didn't appear too serious.

Elsif put her hand gently on the burn and attempted to cool the sore. Milly slightly winced at Elsif's touch, but appreciated the slight coolness that Elsif was able to produce.

As Elsif concentrated on producing all the frost she could muster, a firefighter walked up to the girls. "Is everyone in your group accounted for?"

"Yeah we have everyone-" Ruth began but Jazzy cut her off.

"We don't have Rose."

"But she wasn't in the museum," Elsif assured, or at least she hoped that Rose was not inside when the fire started. "She was grabbing us food. She's around here somewhere."

"If you don't find her soon, make sure you report her missing," the firefighter stated before moving to the next group.

Ruth stood. "I'll go find her."

As Ruth walked away, Elsif looked around for Rose, but someone else once again caught her attention. The same familiar red hair popped up in the crowd in the distance. Elsif let go of Milly and walked a few steps towards the recognizable stranger. Her eyes must be playing tricks on her.

"I'm going to look for Rose too," Elsif blurted and took off into the crowd.

Her eyes were locked on a sliver of the stranger's hair, as she weaved through the crowd. As Elsif grew closer, the guy stopped for a moment and started to turn around to look back. Smoke and onlookers still blocked her view, but she thought she recognized the face, and he seemed to recognize Elsif as well, because a moment later he bolted away.

There was no reason to chase him, but Elsif did. If this was who Elsif thought it was, then usually she would ignore him or hide, but something came over her and she ran after him.

She broke through the thick of the crowd and had a clear shot towards him. He ducked behind a building, and as Elsif rounded the corner in pursuit, she ran straight into a woman and crashed to the ground.

"Oh my, are you alright?" The woman asked, still standing.

Elsif's head had been knocked in two ways. One from the ground and the other from her foolish actions. Why was she chasing a semi-stranger for no good reason? Elsif should have been tending to her cousins after a traumatic incident, not running after a mysterious red headed guy.

"Are you alright?" The woman repeated, helping Elsif to her feet.

"I'm fine," Elsif said sharply, turning away from the woman.

"Are you hurt?" She continued to ask. "Are you looking for someone?"

Elsif ignored her and tried to shake the moment of insanity from her mind. She hustled back to her cousins, and forced herself to ignore the suspicion that was consuming her.

Ruth had found Rose and all the girls were sitting safely on the bench where Elsif had left them. Milly was no longer coughing, Jazzy had her usual smile back, Ruth was eating soup, and Rose was trying to do a handstand.

Once Elsif walked up to the group, Rose sprung to her feet with a proud smirk. "I got soup!" She announced to Elsif with a grand gesture to the bowl that Ruth was holding.

"*One* bowl of soup," Milly added.

"It's a big bowl," Rose defended. "We can share!"

"There's no soup places around here," Milly told Elsif. "We don't know what's in it."

Rose kicked Milly's foot. "Stop it! Just eat!"

Elsif ignored the current conversation and turned to Rose. "I'm going to ask you something and you're going to be honest."

Rose's expression grew somber. "There is definitely no turtle in that soup. And I definitely didn't mock it before stuffing it in my soup."

"Rose," Elsif continued. "Did you start the fire?"

Rose gasped. "How dare you, good sir! You have insulted my honor! We duel at dawn!"

Elsif took a deep breath. "I need you to promise me you didn't have anything to do with this fire because if you did then our family owes millions to Struth because you destroyed their most popular- and probably the only good- tourist attraction."

"Actually," Rose began. "We are ladies so we cannot duel. We will both send one of our elder male cousins. I choose Michael."

"I'll take Monty," Elsif stated. "But I need you to promise me that you had nothing to do with the fire."

"Even by accident," Ruth added between sips of soup.

"You do talk about setting things on fire a lot," Milly interjected.

"No one would blame you," Jazzy said assuredly.

"Wrong," Elsif told Rose. "I would blame you."

Rose groaned dramatically. "No! Even though it was a super impressive fire and I would love to take credit, alas I cannot. Twas not thy!"

The girls decided to walk back to the inn and rest from their interesting afternoon. Elsif thought Milly should be checked out at a hospital but Milly refused. Milly knew she was fine and she was never one to go running to the hospital after every scrape or burn she obtained.

That night the girls debated whether or not to leave for Stellae or stay in town for the next three days, like they had originally intended. As the girls were discussing their next course of action, Jazzy looked down at the book that she was still holding.

"Hey," Jazzy said, interrupting Ruth and Milly's argument. "I think I may have accidentally stolen this book from the museum. It's sort of interesting though. Someone wrote notes correcting the author."

Elsif took the book and began flipping through the pages, while the other girls looked over her shoulder. The note in the back of the book had fallen out, and Ruth scooped it up off the floor.

"Who does this guy think he is?" Elsif criticized. "I think that Walten Elian knows what he's talking about. He's one of the best historians to ever live."

"I think he's making some good points," Milly countered.

Elsif scoffed. "Like what?"

"He says that the Hat was crafted by the Elves," Milly explained. "And that would make sense since you said that the Elves had control over the most variety of magic, and were even trying to learn other people's magical abilities. And that's what the Hat was, it contained magic from all the people groups."

Elsif shook her head. "No, it's ridiculous. Everyone knows the Hat was created by Xen Siid and he was human. Wait-" Elsif's eye caught a section that piqued her interest. "Dwarven collateral?"

"That's my favorite type of collateral," Rose mentioned.

"What's that?" Jazzy asked Elsif.

"No one's been able to figure out where the Hat was during the Bloodshed Age between 3250-3310," Elsif explained. "It disappeared from Merlin Academy in 3250 and reappeared in the Merlin gardens in 3310. The mystery guy has a little note that says 'Dwarven collateral' with a question mark. That's an interesting theory, I wonder why he thinks that."

"Is he right?" Jazzy asked.

"Well," Elsif muttered. "After the Elven wars, the Dwarves were feuding with the other magical people groups and dying out, so I could see them stealing the Hat from the humans to try and sway us to help them. Maybe that's what he means by collateral? But then again-"

"Hey," Ruth interrupted. "Isn't *that* today's date?"

Struth Region/ Warlock's Museum 12/8

"And that was our location," Milly added.

"That's crazy," Rose said. "It must be a list of places he wants to start fires."

"Which section did you find the book in?" Milly asked Jazzy.

"I think it was on one of the tables," Jazzy said.

"Hm," Elsif thought aloud. "Maybe they're appointments? And that would mean he was at the museum today, where he left behind his book?"

"Appointments to start fires," Rose added.

"He seems knowledgeable about the Hat," Jazzy noted.

Elsif frowned. "I wouldn't go that far, but I'm interested in the Dwarvian collateral theory."

"It's new and different information," Milly countered. "A new lead from all the stuff we've been reading. Too bad we missed him."

"Yeah," Elsif agreed, then changed back to the original topic. "We should just leave for Stellae now. We can't do any more research here and Struth is too boring to find something else to entertain ourselves."

"I didn't know this was a dictatorship," Rose grumbled.

Everyone agreed, some more reluctant than others, and the girls packed up their things. Elsif went to the front desk and arranged for a carriage to come. Fifteen minutes later, the girls were rolling away from town. They passed the remains of the Museum on their way to Struth. The building was completely burned down and black rubble was all that remained.

"Do you think it was arson?" Milly said as the carriage pulled away.

"Of course it was," Rose said.

"Why?" Elsif asked. "Because you did it?"

Rose punched Elsif before replying. "I didn't! I was getting soup!"

"Do you think anyone was hurt?" Jazzy asked with a concerned expression.

"No," Ruth assured. "We would have heard about it."

Jazzy shook her head. "Why would anybody want to burn down a harmless museum?"

"I don't know," Elsif muttered to herself, while watching the museum disappear in the distance. The suspicion from earlier that day gnawed at her again, and she feared that she had to say it aloud or she might go crazy. "Did any of you see someone come out of the museum right after us?"

"I was too busy coughing to death," Milly remarked.

"I was busy getting soup and *not* starting fires," Rose declared.

Ruth and Jazzy both shook their heads in response to Elsif's question.

"It's weird but," Elsif hesitated. "I swear I saw Bernard leaving the museum. It couldn't have been him right?" Saying the words out loud for the first time made Elsif feel extremely foolish. She knew it wasn't him; there was no reason for it to be him. Elsif must have chased some random guy and he was probably telling all his friends about some crazy psycho girl.

"Maybe," Ruth started with a cheeky grin. "He's hopelessly in love with you and is stalking your every move?"

"That's a terrifying thought," Elsif commented.

Ruth's smile grew. "It's romantic."

"Could he have been the one that started the fire?" Milly said unprompted.

Elsif stared at Milly in horror as her stupid little thoughts were realized through another's mouth. She'd suspected that Bernard was the culprit behind the fire since she caught a glimpse of red hair, but she didn't want to admit it to herself. Elsif didn't want to admit that her worries could be a possibility. The whole situation was too dramatic, it couldn't be true.

"Why would Bernard want to burn down the museum if he was in love with Elsif?" Jazzy questioned. "That doesn't make sense."

"Bernard doesn't love Elsif," Rose corrected harshly. "No one could, it's impossible."

"Guys I'm serious," Milly insisted. "It all makes sense. "I was talking about the museum to Mr. Henson after class-" Milly was cut off by Rose.

"MR. HENSON DID THIS! I KNEW HE WAS ALWAYS ONE OF MY MORE SUSPICIOUS TEACHERS!"

"Not Mr. Henson," Milly continued, placing a hand over Rose's mouth. "I was talking to Mr. Henson about the museum and mentioned going in the beginning of December, and Juniper walked into the class. He could have overheard everything and sent Bernard to stop us."

"No," Ruth said without skipping a beat.

"Come on Ruth," Milly opposed. "You have to admit, it adds up."

"No," Ruth said, anger growing in her tone. "We said we weren't going to talk about him!"

"He may have almost killed us," Milly argued. "We have to talk about him!"

"No! He didn't do this!" Ruth yelled, and began banging on the wall. "Stop the carriage!" The carriage obeyed and came to a quick stop. Ruth burst through the door and ran off into an empty field.

"Ruth wins most dramatic of the week," Rose snickered.

Elsif sighed and tried not to roll her eyes. "I'll go talk to her."

Following Ruth into the field, Elsif walked through the tall wildflowers and weeds.

"Go away," Ruth told Elsif.

"Ruth," Elsif said, her patience running out. "Can we talk-"

"It wasn't him!" Ruth insisted, facing Elsif with a pleading expression. "Elsif, it can't be him!"

"It could be him," Elsif stated plainly. "Or it could have been some deadbeat smoker in the bathroom. I honestly don't know what to think at this point. But why are you so upset at the *idea* of Juniper being the bad guy?"

"He's not," Ruth demanded. "No matter what has happened, deep down I need to believe that this is Melissa and not Juniper."

"Ruth," Elsif said calmly. "I understand that you have a crush, but seriously, don't let it take over your life and cloud your judgment. Can't you get over him and pick some other stupid boy?"

"I will never get over him," Ruth declared. "I'm in love with him."

Elsif pinched her brow. "You barely know him. You've spent a total of thirty minutes together."

"It was love at first sight."

"Of course it was," Elsif muttered.

"I know you don't believe in it," Ruth spoke. "But I know what I felt when I first saw him."

"You just think he's cute," Elsif argued. "Cute guys come and go, but that doesn't mean it's love. It's temporary."

"The way I feel is not temporary!"

Elsif sighed. "You're like twelve, calm down.."

Ruth kicked the ground. "Juniper isn't evil."

"Fine," Elsif conceded, her patience completely drained. "Fine, Juniper isn't evil and he's the love of your life. You'll both end up happily ever after. Can we get in the carriage and go to Stellae now?"

Meanwhile, Milly, Rose, and Jazzy watched Ruth and Elsif from afar, attempting to see what they were talking about.

"Rose," Milly whispered. "Can you still read lips?"

"Yep," Rose stated. "They are either talking about how Ruth is in love with Juniper or about catching moonfish in June."

"I think it might be the first one," Jazzy stated.

"I don't know," Rose countered. "Ruth likes her moonfish."

Chapter 9: Family Makes The Heart Ache

During the fifteen-hour carriage ride, the girls couldn't help but bring up the note a million different times.

"We should meet him," Milly insisted. "We're at a dead end, it's our only hope."

"What if *he* was the one responsible for the fire?" Ruth suggested, trying to find anyone else to blame.

"What if someone- *not me*-," Rose theorized. "Started the fire to kill him before he was able to spread his knowledge about the Hat."

"Even more reason for us to find him," Milly stated.

Elsif looked at the note. "We wouldn't be able to go to Currus in January. We have school."

"What about February?" Jazzy suggested.

"We can't," Milly answered sadly. "The Winter Games at Merlin are during February break. We can't miss those."

"Oh yeah," Ruth agreed. "I don't want to miss those either."

"I don't mind missing," Jazzy mentioned.

"It's your first one," Ruth protested. "You can't miss it."

"Yeah," Rose agreed. "I always dominate. You have to see my awesomeness in person."

Elsif looked out the window. "We're here. We can figure out what to do about it later."

Secretly Elsif thought that going to Silvia would be the perfect opportunity to miss the Winter Games. In the past she had always competed with her friends and it was always the highlight of the year. But for obvious reasons, Elsif wouldn't be competing with them this year. She didn't need another reminder that Libi and her weren't friends anymore, so Elsif thought skipping the Games all together would be the easiest solution.

As the carriage pulled into the driveway Jazzy stared at the house in awe. She had already been mesmerized by the tallest buildings she'd ever seen, but the girls' grandparent's house was even more awe-inspiring.

The house was encapsulated in its own world. The city around the house was filled with huge buildings and busy streets, but the house was surrounded by trees and bushes that blocked out the bustling metropolis.

As the carriage approached, Jazzy could see that the house was inside what seemed to be a large glass bubble. There was also a narrow but deep stream that ran through the yard and around the house. The house itself was unique looking with lots of large windows and rounded architecture. The nature surrounding the house looked like it was melding with the house in a few areas. The trees grew from outside to inside to back outside, and there were several waterfalls coming from the house and falling into the stream. There were also a couple bridges that connected the upper levels of the house, and lots of balconies. There were many different aspects of the house but somehow it all came together in a natural way.

At first glance, it seemed impossible to get to the house without swimming, but as the carriage approached, a bridge appeared that led the carriage to the front entrance. Once they were over the bridge, a glass door shut behind them, closing the bubble. Jazzy was amazed that she could no longer hear the city life. The only sounds surrounding Jazzy was the running water, rustling leaves, and the faint voices from the house.

The girls left the carriage, and Jazzy followed them into the house. Once again, Jazzy's jaw was on the floor. She was currently standing on a glass floor that had a perfect view of the rushing water that contained a wide variety of fish and other small creatures. There were also more trees and foliage inside that created unique decorations for the house.

But the technology went completely beyond what Jazzy's mind could have imagined and she struggled to take it all in. There were hundreds of buttons and blinking lights on a panel on the wall one moment, but then they were gone the next. Most of the technology was invisible to the human eye until someone pointed it out.

Jazzy only had a moment to be overwhelmed by the technology because she was soon swarmed by a large number of people. Parents, aunts, uncles, grandparents, and cousins all surrounded the girls as they walked in and attacked them with hugs and questions. Jazzy stood alone in the crowd watching everyone chaotically communicate with love and laughter.

Apprehension crept across Jazzy's face as her pure delight changed into an unknown dread. She watched the happy reunion with a pit in her stomach that Jazzy had never experienced before. As everyone embraced around her, Jazzy had a sudden realization that she was lacking something. She didn't have what her friends had. She felt lonely, which didn't make sense because Jazzy was surrounded by people.

Jazzy watched Elsif with her parents and overheard a few words of their conversation.

"She didn't even say hi to me," Elsif confessed to her mom and gladly accepted her encouraging hug. "Of course I got a perfect score," she boasted to her dad a moment later with a huge grin. "Struth was so boring, I never want to go there again," she told them both as she glanced over and saw Jazzy. "Oh! This is Jazzy!"

A forced smile spread across Jazzy's face as she met Elsif's parents and the rest of the family. The forced smile soon became genuine as Jazzy's odd feelings melted away and she became herself once more.

"I don't think I'll ever remember everyone's names," Jazzy said with a laugh as she and the girls walked up the stairs to the room they would be staying in.

"It's not that complicated," Rose told Jazzy. "Everyone in the house is my personal servant. So don't bother remembering their names, just call them Rose's peasants."

"We'll help you when you forget," Milly said.

The girls' room was the highest room in the house and had a view of the city above the trees. The room was filled with six loft beds that were built into the wall and overlooked huge windows.

Jazzy went to bed with a smile on her face, but once the lights were out and she was alone with her thoughts, her expression dropped. Something was missing from Jazzy's life and she had realized it for the first time.

*****

"I'm mixing the salad," Elsif said. "You've got a problem with that?"

"Yeah, I do! Because," Rose barked at Elsif while trying to rip the bowl from her hands. "I WAS GOING TO MIX THE SALAD!"

Elsif pulled the bowl away from Rose's reach. "That sounds like a *you* problem."

As Rose chased Elsif, the other girls set the table for dinner. The Walker family owned a thirty-foot long dining table and had dinner together every evening they could. Even with Ruth, Milly, and Jazzy helping, the set up took awhile.

Eventually Rose caught up to Elsif, and they compromised on the salad by agreeing to mix it together. It did not go well, but at least they weren't fighting. They filled the bowl with every single ingredient they could find until it was overfilling. Elsif didn't want to dirty another bowl so they had to deal with the consequences of their actions. It was nearly impossible to mix their ginormous salad with utensils, so Rose had the bright idea to toss the salad in the air. Elsif encouraged Rose to throw the salad higher and higher until there was more salad on the floor than in the bowl.

In the middle of the chaos, their cousin Monty walked in. "What are you two doing?"

"You know," Elsif replied. "Mixing salad."

"That's not mixing," he commented. "It looks more like a food fight."

"Look," Rose said, gesturing to the bowl. "It's mixed!"

"Oh yeah," Monty agreed with sarcasm. "That one carrot and two pieces of lettuce look real mixed, but you forgot about all the salad on the floor."

"Wow," Elsif muttered. "Everyone's a backseat salad-mixer these days."

"How do you mess up salad?" Monty argued.

"It's because," Milly answered from the other room. "They share a brain."

"You've never even eaten a salad before," Rose sniped at Monty. "How would you know what it's supposed to look like or how much of it should or should not be on the ground?"

"He ate a salad once," David said as he walked through the kitchen. "I made him eat one when he was six, after he broke my toy dragon."

"I still get flashbacks," Monty shuddered.

Rose held the bowl in Monty's face. "Fear for your life!"

After throwing away most of the salad, the leftovers were placed on the table along with the rest of the food. Luckily, no one complained about the lack of salad at dinner.

*****

The next day the girls took Jazzy to some of the shops downtown. Walking around sounded fun until Jazzy realized that they would not be walking at all.

"Are you sure it's going to fly?" Jazzy asked for the seventh time. "With all of us in it?"

They were standing on the roof of the grandparents house, in front of the flying carriage that they were about to take out. It was a small carriage with three rows.

"Get in and find out," Rose said, pulling a lever that created an opening in the glass bubble above them.

Milly climbed into the carriage first and took the left front seat, which had a steering wheel in front of it and several buttons. "It's super safe Jazzy," Milly called out. "I'm a very safe driver, I promise."

Rose bounded into the spaceship and sat next to Milly. "And I'm a very dangerous copilot."

"She's not the copilot," Elsif assured Jazzy, climbing in next and sitting behind Rose. "Flying carriages only have one driver."

"Driver?" Jazzy asked. "I thought it was magic?"

"Flying carriages work differently than regular carriages," Ruth explained, while taking a seat next to Elsif. "Since there aren't roads, we need to help steer. And altitude gets tricky so we control that too. Get in!"

Jazzy hesitantly climbed inside and took a seat in the back row. The carriage was similar to the ones at Merlin, but Jazzy had the feeling it was going to be a very different experience.

The other girls grabbed a strap next to their seats and pulled it across their laps, and Jazzy copied their actions. But once the belt clicked into place, Jazzy felt trapped and panic began to rise in herself.

Milly pushed several buttons and cranked a lever, until the carriage rose from the ground. Jazzy watched the house grow smaller as the carriage flew into the air.

As the carriage soared, Jazzy's stomach turned and thought she was going to throw up. It was unnerving to look out the window and not see the ground. But once Jazzy saw the skyline and twinkling lights in the distance, her stomach forgot about all her worries. It was breathtakingly beautiful.

They spent the whole day exploring Stellae and showing Jazzy the sights and shops. Whenever they went into a building, Milly would park the carriage on a balcony that was so high up that the girls couldn't see the ground. The view made Jazzy nauseous, so she learned to not look down.

The shops were filled with technology, gadgets, and items Jazzy knew she would never understand, but she was content to just look.

The girls picked up a few things for themselves here and there and shared some interesting snacks with Jazzy. Her favorite was a purple liquid that tasted like boysenberry pie. Most of the food was a little strange for Jazzy but she appreciated the experience.

After a long day of activities, the sun began to set, and the girls were ready to head home. They boarded the carriage and began to fly to their grandparents' house.

"It's getting cloudy," Milly commented.

"Is that bad?" Jazzy asked nervously from the back.

"No," Ruth assured. "It just means we can't see the pretty views."

Jazzy looked into the distance. Even through the fog and clouds, she could see the lights of the city.

"We have a navigation system," Elsif explained. "So even if we couldn't see anything outside, the system would still be able to guide us home."

"Too bad I destroyed the navigation system," Rose stated.

"It's right here," Milly gestured to an area with flashing lights.

"I replaced it with a fake navigation system," Rose announced. "Watch, I'll prove it." Before anyone could stop her, Rose lunged forward and grabbed the lever that controlled the altitude. She pulled back as far as she could and pressed the button that flung the ship into full speed.

The carriage flew upward at a rapid pace, as Milly tried to shove Rose off the controls. But her attempt was futile because momentum held her back against her seat.

Red lights flashed and a woman's voice repeated the words, "Your craft is beyond the legal altitude, please fly down."

"Rose, stop it!" Elsif yelled helplessly from her seat.

"You're gonna get us into trouble!" Ruth demanded. "Pull down!"

Rose ignored the girls as she clung to the lever. "Best day ever!"

Eventually the carriage had flown so high that gravity had lessened and Milly was able to reach the lever. She grabbed it from Rose and pulled it level so the craft was flying at a normal angle again. Milly turned off the voice and alarm, so the girls were able to take a breath of relief.

Elsif grabbed Rose. "Get in the backseat."

"You're boring," Rose grumbled as she was shoved in the back next to Jazzy, who was trembling. Elsif took the seat next to Milly so Rose wouldn't try to sneak back up.

"I can't believe you Rose," Milly fumed. "I'm the captain, you can't just take over!"

"This isn't a ship," Rose complained with her arms crossed, slouching in her seat.

"We're over the legal altitude level!" Milly yelled at her. "We're breaking the law!"

"Law, shmaw," Rose mumbled.

"You could have killed us," Ruth grumbled.

"That was the hope," Rose snickered. "And flying higher than the limit isn't even dangerous."

"It's illegal!" Milly countered angrily.

Elsif turned to Milly. "Can you take us back down?"

"Yeah," Milly replied, pushing a few buttons.

"What's that?" Jazzy asked. After enduring a small heart attack, Jazzy had been distracted by the views while the girls yelled at Rose. They were so high that their carriage was above the clouds. It was hard to see Fantasma below but Jazzy could see peaks through the clouds and she realized she could see the outlines of both the East and West coasts of Fantasma. . It was exactly like the maps that Jazzy had seen at Merlin and it was a breathtaking sight. But right after taking in the most magnificent view Jazzy would ever see in her life, she saw something that she didn't understand.

The girls looked west, where Jazzy pointed. In the distance, past the coastline, they saw some green land with speckled lights that eventually disappeared on the horizon. But the image they saw didn't make sense. The land they saw in the distance was not a part of Fantasma.

"What is that piece of land over there?" Jazzy repeated, waiting for an answer. The girls stared with confused expressions.

"That has to be," Elsif hesitated. "Animalium, I guess."

"We can see the edge of Animalium right there," Ruth countered, pointing at the southeast corner of Fantasma.

"What else could it be?" Elsif stated. "Fantasma's a globe. There's nothing else west of the KidaKash Ocean than Animalium, Viverra, and Currus."

"Maybe it's a mirage," Milly added. "You can see some pretty weird things in the distance sometimes."

"A mirage in the sky?" Rose questioned. "A more probable situation is we're all hallucinating right now and are actually in comas in a large monster's belly."

Jazzy looked at the girls with a confused expression. "So you all don't know what that is?" Jazzy wasn't used to the others not having all the answers.

Milly grabbed the lever and began their descent. "We have to get back down to a legal altitude."

"I think it's a mirage," Elsif stated.

"No, it's not," Ruth countered as the mysterious land disappeared from view.

"I don't think so either," Milly replied. "But I'll figure it out. At a legal altitude."

"How?" Jazzy asked.

"I'm going to sail across the KidaKash Ocean," Milly declared. "As soon as I become a captain of my own ship."

"That was a quick decision," Elsif said. "What happened to the mirage theory?"

"Rose convinced me, there's no mirages in the sky." Milly replied. "Plus I've always wanted to discover something, and this is my perfect opportunity. But of course it will be my second discovery after we find the Hat."

The girls continued to travel downward through the clouds, until red blaring lights began to fly behind them. A large patrol carriage had caught them above the legal altitude level.

"We can outrun them!" Rose shouted. "They'll never take us alive!"

"No," Elsif chided. "Milly you need to slow down and let them pass so we can follow them down to the ground."

"I know, I know," Milly replied, while maneuvering the carriage. The patrol carriage pulled in front of them and led them down to the ground level. They parked on an empty street on the outskirts of town where it was less busy.

"We must flee for our lives!" Rose yelled.

"Calm down," Elsif chided Rose. "We're only going to get a fine, not a death certificate."

"Is a fine bad?" Jazzy asked.

"It's not a big deal," Milly replied.

"As long as it doesn't go on our permanent records," Elsif muttered.

"Either way Grandma Theadora will kill us," Ruth muttered.

Once both carriages had landed, a man stepped out of the patrol carriage. He was wearing a clean, pressed uniform with a blaster on his left side. He wore a solemn expression as he approached the girls.

Ruth opened the carriage door, and the man climbed inside. He walked to the front and stood between Milly and Elsif.

"Identification card," He said in a sharp voice to Milly.

"Yes sir," Milly said, reaching into her pocket.

"You were flying at 14,835 feet and the legal height is 10,000 feet. Is there a reason that you were flying above the legal limit?"

"It was an accident sir," Milly said as she handed him her ID card.

"We got lost," Ruth added.

"We were on our way back down," Elsif assured.

The guard took the ID card without looking at it and began to scold the girls. "I was talking to the flyer of the craft, if that is not you then remain silent. Who was flying the craft?"

"I was sir," Milly stated.

The guard looked from Milly to Elsif. "You weren't the one flying?"

Elsif frantically shook her head. "No."

"So I'm supposed to believe you let someone half your age fly the carriage instead of you two swapping seats so you wouldn't get in trouble?"

"I'm the more responsible flyer," Milly explained.

"I'm responsible," Elsif defended herself. "But the buttons overwhelm me."

"I should remind you all that lying to a guard of the Stellae government can be punishable to life in prison," he said sternly. He then turned to Elsif. "This is your last chance. Were you in any way impaired which kept you from being able to fly the carriage properly?"

"Of course not," Elsif replied nervously.

The guard frowned. "The laws of Stellae are very strict when it comes to the flying altitude level and we don't take these things lightly-" He abruptly stopped talking when he finally looked at Milly's ID card. "Oh, you're a Merlin student?" He asked in a much friendlier tone.

"Yeah," Milly said, surprised by the change in his voice. "We all are."

"That's awesome," he commented with a smile. "I graduated there in 3981 and then graduated advanced classes in 3985. It's a great school." The girls nodded in agreement. "Well, I'll leave you guys off with a warning," he continued and handed back Milly's ID. "Make sure you're paying attention when you're close to the legal altitude line next time. A good tip I tell my kids is to make sure you're never too far from the highest building around you since the limit is only a half mile over the tallest building in Stellae. Also make sure you don't fly out of Stellae. Flying carriages aren't legal in any other regions so you'll get in real big trouble for that. Have a good rest of your day!"

He gave the girls a wave and left. He got back into his patrol carriage and flew away.

"That was a close one," Milly said.

"I don't know what I'm more offended by," Elsif muttered. "The fact that he thought I was twice Milly's age or that he thought I would be an irresponsible flyer."

"Elsif, he doesn't know you," Ruth stated. "Who cares?"

"If he knew you then I'm sure he would think very highly of you," Jazzy added.

"I'm surprised he didn't arrest you for being a huge nerd," Rose told Elsif.

"Whatever," Elsif replied. "Let's just go home before more crazy stuff happens."

*****

One afternoon all the cousins played board games in the living room of their grandparents house. During the final round of a particularly intense game of Dwarves, Caves, and Hidden Jewels, Milly and David were up against each other and their round would determine whether the girls or guys won.

"I'm done!" David declared, slapping down his last card. He raised his arms triumphantly. "I'm done!"

Milly threw her cards across the room, and stormed out. "You cheated!" She yelled from the next room.

"It's not my fault that you're a loser," he yelled back.

Elsif shook her head. "I'll never understand this side of the family." Her and Max were reading in the corner after they got out early in the game.

"Let's play again," Michael suggested. "I want to try a new strategy."

"Yes!" Rose twirled to the table.

"Max and I are passing," Elsif announced.

Ruth, Monty, and Jazzy both agreed to play again. Right before the cards were shuffled and passed out, Milly came running back to the table.

"You're going down," Milly warned David.

David rolled his eyes. "In your dreams."

Milly and David didn't see each other often because of their age difference and since they lead very different lives. But when they did get together, the sibling rivalry was intense.

"You can't lay down a Dwarf King when I have a Destroyer on the table," Milly accused David.

"We aren't playing blocking rules," David retorted. "It makes the game too long."

"We didn't say that before we started playing," Milly argued.

"This family only plays with our made up rules," Monty stated. "It's an unspoken rule."

"Unspoken rules are not contractually binding," Michael pointed out.

David refused to pick his card up. "House rules trump game rules."

"Fine," Milly muttered. She would later blame that one move on the reason the girls lost once again.

"Rigged," Ruth announced. "When you write your memoir after finding the hidden land in the KidaKash Ocean, make sure to include this moment of defeat. It will humanize you to your millions of fans."

"Oh," David said with interest. "Mills, are you going to look for Menkensma?"

The girls looked at David with confused expressions. Even Elsif put her book down to pay attention to the conversation. "What's Menkensma?" Milly asked.

"The secret island where the KidaKash, Moania, Trionton, and Nemoa Oceans meet," David explained. "Where pirates sail and never return. But that's if they can get there in the first place. Magic currents steer all ships away, and only the best sailors can get through, but they'll pay the ultimate price. To never be seen again."

"I didn't know you liked old pirate tales so much," Monty said with a laugh. "One of these days you're going to have to trade in your flying carriage for a ship."

"So this Menkensma place is real?" Milly asked.

"It's only a theory," Michael clarified. "Nothing has been officially discovered."

"I'm going to discover it," Milly said plainly. "I'm going to be the first to sail there and back."

"Not if I beat you to it," David said.

"You'll get a head start on it," Ruth commented. "Milly's already busy searching for something else with us."

"What is it?" Michael asked. "Maybe we could help."

"We're looking for the-"

"Nothing," Elsif interrupted Ruth. "It's just some extracurricular thing."

"Don't leave us in suspense," Monty teased.

"It's nothing," Elsif repeated, going back to her book. "It's a stupid school thing."

Once the cousins returned to the game, Ruth leaned over to Elsif. "Why don't you want to tell them?" Ruth whispered.

"They'll make fun of us," Elsif muttered.

"Who cares," Ruth whispered sharply. "They won't be laughing when we find it."

Elsif's first reaction was to tell Ruth to stop being stupid and that they would never find the Hat. But she stopped herself, and shook the intrusive thought away. "Please don't say anything until we find some real leads."

"Fine," Ruth mumbled as she went back to the game.

As Monty shuffled the deck of cards to get ready for round three Milly turned to David. "Are you actually going to look for Menkensma one day?"

"Are you?" He asked.

Milly nodded. "Yes."

"Then I am too," he replied. "I might as well find something else to beat you at since these games are too easy."

Milly extended her hand to David. "May the best sibling win."

They shook and the race began.

*****

On December 30th, the girls traveled back to Merlin Academy, and shared a carriage with their other cousins. There was never a dull moment in the fifteen hour ride because it was filled with games, trivia, charades, and a guessing game of 'What was Rose thinking?' Before the ride, Elsif made the other girls promise to not bring up the Hat, which was harder for some than others.

After a long day they finally arrived at Merlin Academy. January had approached far too quickly and the girls were back in classes before they knew it. Other than papers and tests, nothing extraordinary happened. No fires, no sneaking out, and no overheard plots to destroy Fantasma. The only semi-odd thing that happened was Milly ran into an eight legged cat, but other than that, the month was normal.

Jazzy, Ruth, Milly, and Rose looked forward to the Winter Games the following month, and Elsif planned to visit Silvia, which she finally agreed to. Little did the girls know what grand adventures were waiting for them in the month of February.

Chapter 10: Why Are They Shooting At Us?!

Elsif found a knife in her bag, which would normally be alarming, but since she lived with Milly and Rose, it was not. The knife was the one that Elsif had *borrowed* from the weaponry. There was a small note attached to the knife.

Dearest Elsif,

If it pleases thee, it would be enjoyable for my entertainment if thee could stay alive long enough for

thy to torture thou at the maze race. So I oblige you to stab anyone who may want to hinder a fire neareth you.

Sincerely your favorite cousin,

Rose

(P.S. You probably won't need it but Struth was weird so it's better to be safe than sorry. Remember slash, don't stab.)

Your actual favorite cousin,

Milly

Elsif left Merlin the morning of the second day of February, and took a seven hour carriage ride to Silvia. She was staying at Audley's Tavern & Pub, the next location for the secret historian, according to the 'Idiot's List.' She purposely arrived three days earlier than the Lists' date so that she would have plenty of time to scope out her surroundings, and get some homework done.

She arrived at the tavern around dinner, so Elsif checked in and ordered food up to her room. Elsif had anticipated being completely wracked with nerves since she was traveling alone for the first time, but she found herself almost giddy. She knew Regium was the safest region in Fantasma and she had overexaggerated the Struth/Bernard situation in her head, so her logical side had nothing to worry about. Instead her imaginative side soared out of control as she imagined meeting the mysterious and wise old stranger.

The food on Elsif's plate grew cold as she fantasized about learning new things about history that no one else knew, becoming the stranger's prodigy, and being the most famous historian in Fantasma by the age of nineteen. After imagining herself shaking the hand of Merlin's President several times, Elsif pushed those thoughts away and chided herself for being foolish.

She knew none of those things would happen, and they were not worth her time thinking about. Homework was a much more productive thing to focus on, but since Elsif couldn't concentrate she decided to go to bed and prepare for the meeting she hoped would happen.

*****

Elsif forced herself to wake up before the sun so she could be the first one to enter the tavern. It was torture to wake up that early, but Elsif knew she needed to fully commit to finding the stranger, and that meant being at the tavern all day for the next several days.

Elsif liked to be overprepared and she knew others didn't hold time schedules as sacred as she did, so she thought showing up a few days before and after would be the best plan.

Grabbing her bag, Elsif remembered the knife, and debated where it should go. If it was in her bag, then she might not be able to reach it if there was trouble. But the knife was also too big to hide in a pocket. The only thing Elsif knew was that she shouldn't be brandishing a weapon for all to see so she had to find some way to hide it.

After a few minutes of problem solving, Elsif found a clever solution. She took one of the few dresses she owned, and slit a hole in the pocket. She then slipped on the dress and a pair of pants underneath. The knife was then tucked in her left pants pocket, hidden by the dress, but easily accessible through the ripped pocket.

It was the perfect plan and Elsif mentally patted herself on the back for thinking of it. Unfortunately, Elsif had allowed herself to get so caught up in her pride that she had to run down to the tavern to be the first to enter the establishment.

She sighed with relief when she saw no one else in the pub, and found a perfect spot at the end of the bar so she could observe the whole room. Elsif pulled out her homework and worked while she assumed the role of secret spy.

Who are you mystery guy? Elsif lost herself in thought as people began to trickle into the pub. *How about I call you Jerry. Yeah, that's a good name. Jerry, you're probably a little on the older side, wise with age. You've got a bit of a sharp tongue because you like to call people idiots. Personally I think that's a bit rude, but I guess you could be using worse language. You also think you know where the Warlock's Hat was during the Bloodshed Ages so you are probably either extremely clever or an idiot yourself- sorry I shouldn't call you an idiot, my bad. But I guess that's all I know about you Jerry; that's all I got.*

Elsif examined each person that came into the pub but no one seemed like a potential match to the character of Jerry that Elsif had created inside her head. Eventually, Elsif began working on her homework again because there was nothing else to do. She tried not to become discouraged and reminded herself that it was only the 3rd and Jerry would most likely not come until the 5th.

Halfway through the day Elsif began to contemplate whether or not to talk to a very old gentleman who was eating oatmeal. He seemed *too* old to be Jerry or to be of any use to Elsif, but there was a strange manner to his oatmeal eating ways that set alarm bells inside Elsif. But when she leaned back in her chair to stand up, she abandoned the idea and went back to her homework.

Even though the whole reason Elsif traveled to Silvia was to find Jerry, she was still hesitant to talk to strangers. It was ridiculous, but Elsif grew flustered every time she thought about approaching someone at the tavern. Her body was glued to her seat and couldn't will herself to stand up.

"Is this seat taken?"

"What?" Elsif tore her eyes away from the old man and saw that a young guy was inquiring about the seat next to her. She glanced at the chair next to her, then at the two dozen empty chairs around the bar, and wondered what this guy's problem was. "No?" She said with a questionable undertone.

"Thanks," he said, taking a seat and ordering a meal.

With subtle annoyance, Elsif moved her papers closer to herself and hoped her new neighbor wouldn't give her weird looks when she analyzed people as they walked in.

Wait, Elsif suddenly thought. *Could this guy be Jerry? No, that wouldn't work, he's way too young. He can't be more than a couple years older than me. But on the other hand Jerry could be a young guy. Maybe he's some super wise and cranky young guy? But most likely he's a middle aged guy- SHOOT! What if he isn't a guy? It could be a woman! Dang it Elsif, stop being sexist! I never even considered Jerry being a girl. Did the notes in the book say anything about being a certain gender? Maybe I should get the book out of my bag? Then maybe Jerry (Or Jenny?) would see the book and come up to me and talk to me! But darn it, this guy is sitting on the side that my bag is on! I'd have to say excuse me and I hate talking to people! Well I shouldn't say hate, hate is a strong word, and I don't know this guy personally. But why in all of Fantasma would he sit right next to me? Maybe I could move my chair and then grab my bag-*

Elsif's thoughts froze and her jaw dropped as she glimpsed long brown hair and fair skin through a window, across the town square. The figure was only visible for a single second before it disappeared into a bakery.

That can't be Piper, Elsif desperately thought while her heart pounded loudly. *Or Paisley- it can't be either of them! I'm seeing things, I'm going crazy, I need to check, to make sure-*

A sound of glass shattering rang in Elsif's ear as she saw something whizz past her head. She saw an arrow stuck in the wall in front of her, between her and her neighbor's heads. Elsif turned around to see a masked man outside loading up another arrow through a broken window.

Before the assailant could reload his bow, Elsif grabbed her bag and frantically climbed over the counter and hid under the bar. Her mind raced as images of Piper, fire, Paisley, arrows, and Bernard swirled around but Elsif couldn't make sense of anything.

"How did they find me?" Elsif mumbled aloud as she covered her face and tried to make sense of the reality around her.

"Are they shooting at you?" A surprised voice asked beside her.

Elsif looked up from her hands and saw the boy that had previously been sitting beside her. He must have jumped over the bar to escape the attacker as well. But Elsif realized he was looking at her with a confused expression, which rapidly changed her perspective on the situation.

"Are they shooting at you?" She asked in disbelief.

He opened his mouth but hesitated before quickly saying, "No! No, they're definitely shooting at you. So we need to get *you* out of here." The stranger grabbed Elsif's arm and dragged her to her feet. Before Elsif could say a word, they were running through the pub's kitchen, a few hallways, and stopped at a locked backdoor.

"Shoot," the guy grumbled, shaking the door handle. "Who locks doors from the inside?"

"Maybe it's locked on both sides," Elsif suggested for no good particular reason.

The stranger gave Elsif a sideways glance before letting out a slight laugh. "That makes me feel better. You don't know how to pick locks do you?"

"I know how to freeze them," Elsif joked because her brain was clearly not working due to the shock.

"That'll work," The guy said and backed away from the door.

"Oh, okay," Elsif said with uncertainty. She reached for the knob, but knew there was no way she'd be able to conjure up enough magic to even make the door knob cool to the touch. She bluffed for a few seconds and made her hand as cold as she could muster. "It's frozen," Elsif said with false confidence.

"Back up." He motioned Elsif away from the door. "I'm going to kick it down."

Elsif listened, but inwardly cringed because she knew the door wasn't going anywhere. Secretly she hoped the armed attacker would catch up to them and end Elsif before the guy discovered she was a fraud.

He swung his leg and kicked the door, but the lock didn't budge and he fell to the ground from the force. Elsif felt terrible for the poor guy but also had to cough to cover up a laugh that was rising in her throat.

"There's probably another door," Elsif suggested, as the guy stood up.

"That was a warm up," he assured Elsif as he rubbed his knee. "Here's the real one." To Elsif's surprise, his second attempt was successful. He kicked the handle so it went through the door and disconnected. They were able to swing the door open while the lock fell to the floor.

Elsif didn't have time to be impressed because the stranger grabbed her arm again and set off running into the forest. Looking behind her, Elsif saw a glimpse of a few sheriffs but didn't see the attacker.

The two continued running in the forest until they couldn't see the town any more, and they were surrounded by dense trees. Elsif wasn't sure how much time passed but since she could no longer breathe, she came to the conclusion that they had put an adequate distance between them and the tavern.

Elsif stopped running and sat down, her legs giving out as soon as she touched the ground. After gasping for breath, Elsif looked around and saw that the stranger was laying down a couple feet away from her.

"That was fun," the stranger said with a tired smile.

"That's one way to describe it," Elsif stuttered through heavy breaths. Her mind was finally calming down and she was able to think rationally again. Which was amazing because she was able to fully grasp the situation she was in. Elsif was alone in the middle of a forest with a completely random man.

On one hand there were no attackers trying to shoot her. But on the other hand, Elsif didn't know if this guy was a murderer. Maybe he helped her out of the goodness of his heart, or maybe he wanted to get her alone so he could cut her to pieces. Elsif didn't know.

"What's your name?" Elsif asked, hoping that it was a non-murderous name.

"Um," he said while looking up at the cloudy sky. "Grey," he replied, looking back at Elsif.

"Is that your actual name?" Elsif asked with skepticism.

"Nope," he replied casually.

I'm so getting murdered today, Elsif thought to herself.

"And your name?" He asked.

Elsif laughed. "I can't tell you my name if you don't tell me yours."

"Make one up," he countered with a smile.

"Alright," Elsif said, sorting through all the names she knew in her head. "How about Gertrude?"

"Okay Gertrude," Grey said. "Why was that guy shooting at you?"

Elsif shook her head. "I'm pretty sure he was shooting at you."

"Fine," Grey relented. "Let's say there's a seventy-five percent chance he was shooting at me. I want to know the twenty-five percent reason he was shooting at you."

"It's a dumb reason," Elsif insisted. She knew there was no way that was Paisley or Piper. It was just a random girl with similar hair and skin tone. Neither of those girls were in Silvia, neither of them were stalking Elsif, and neither of them would have hired a hitman for Elsif. Bernard hadn't been in Struth and that fire didn't have anything to do with Elsif.

"I don't know what I was thinking," Elsif said. "No need to worry about it."

"Actually I'm very concerned about it," Grey admitted. "I might lose some sleep."

Elsif tried to hide her chuckle, but was glad Grey wasn't going to press her on the issue. She was already embarrassed about the lock, she didn't need this random guy to judge her about her paranoid thoughts too. "Why were they shooting at you?"

"That's not fair," Grey countered in a lighthearted tone.

Elsif stood up and shook her head. "It doesn't matter. I'm going to head back to the tavern."

"Wait," Grey frantically scrambled up and blocked Elsif's path. "You're in grave danger, you can't go back."

"We've established the hitman wasn't after me," Elsif said, continuing to walk. "I'll be fine and I have things to do."

"But you were seen with me," Grey warned while walking beside Elsif. "And *if* that guy was shooting at me, then he'll think you're with me. My family is kind of a big deal so he might think you're associated with us."

Elsif couldn't help but roll her eyes. "The last time someone described themselves as a *big deal* was when I was twelve and my cousin told me she just did her first cartwheel."

"I'm just looking out for your wellbeing," Grey stated.

"So you're not a thief or a criminal?" Elsif asked. "Or possibly a murderer?"

"I am actually a murderer," Grey joked. "Thanks for asking, not many people do. It's nice to be acknowledged."

Elsif found herself trying not to laugh again. "I *really* need to go back to the tavern."

"You can't," Grey begged. "We're accomplices now, we need to go into hiding."

"I'm not your accomplice," Elsif stated. "And I don't really want to be around a potential murderer."

"I was kidding," Grey assured with a smile. When Elsif didn't break her stride, Grey grew more serious. "I seriously was joking. I have never murdered anybody, ever. The worst thing I've ever done was punch my brother in the face, but trust me, he deserved it." The town began to appear in the distance, and Grey stopped walking. "It's too dangerous to go any farther."

"Bye Grey," Elsif said and walked on.

"Fine," Grey called to Elsif as she walked farther away. "Go then. Get killed. See if I care. It won't be on my conscience!"

Elsif knew there was no danger waiting for her back at the tavern, but as usual, Elsif's overthinking mind started to create doubts. There was a very small chance that the psycho was sent to kill Elsif, but there had been too many coincidences for Elsif to have peace of mind. She really didn't want to go back to the tavern alone, so she slowly turned back to Grey.

A smug grin spread across his face. "Let's go."

As they walked back Elsif's hand brushed against her left pocket, and she was reminded of the protection that she had forgotten about.

"Just so you know," Elsif said casually. "I have a knife." She was almost completely certain Grey wasn't a murderer because he already had ample opportunity to kill Elsif, but to be on the safe side, she thought this warning would definitely keep her alive.

"You're telling me now?" Grey demanded in a joking manner. "That information would have been useful back when we were under attack."

Elsif shrugged. "Better late than never."

"Well take it out," Grey insisted. "You may have to defend both of us, you know."

Elsif reached into her ripped pocket and pulled the knife out. "It's either a fairy dagger from the 1900s or a Dwarven knife from the Magic Age. I haven't figured it out yet," Elsif said, proudly brandishing her knife.

"You call that tiny little blade a knife?" Grey retorted. "How are you going to defeat the bad guys with that? It's not even sharp."

"It's an important relic," Elsif defended the dagger, while holding it close to her heart. "This has survived thousands of years of history."

"I had no idea," Grey said in fake awe. "I'll never disrespect the sad little knife again."

Forcing herself not to smile, Elsif and Grey arrived back at the edge of town. They didn't see any crazy people with bows, but noticed a couple sheriff's talking with the tavern owner. Grey went over to talk to the sheriff and owner to assess the situation. After a short conversation, he walked back to where Elsif was waiting in the tree line.

"I guess we're off the hook," Grey noted. "He was arrested."

"Did they say which one of us he was after?" Elsif asked with sarcasm.

"Neither of us," Grey said earnestly. "He had a vendetta against the tavern owner and wanted to scare away his patrons."

"Really?" Elsif said, not knowing if she could trust Grey's words. But she decided to cautiously believe him because this outcome meant she was safe.

"Yeah," Grey confirmed. "He must have been a real idiot to get caught so easily."

Siren bells pounded in Elsif's head as a familiar word hit her ears. Her eyes widened as she looked at Grey. "Why did you come to the tavern today?"

Grey thought for a moment. "Their chili is pretty good."

"There was no other reason? None at all?" Elsif asked desperately. Grey shook his head, but Elsif was determined to not give up. She grabbed the book out of her bag in one last futile attempt. "Is this yours?"

His eyes narrowed. "Why do you have my book?"

"Oh my gosh." Elsif's entire world exploded. "I can't believe it's actually you. I never thought that I would actually find you. Oh man, this is amazing." Elsif bubbled over with excitement as she tried to figure out what to ask first.

Grey took the book from Elsif's hands and began flipping through the pages. "Where'd you find the book?"

"You left it at the Warlock's Hat Museum in Struth," she happily answered.

"Of course," Grey mumbled. "My favorite museum."

"Why do you think the Warlock's Hat was with the Dwarves in the Bloodshed Age?" Elsif began to rattle off questions. "Do you really think it was collateral? Also could you explain your note about the peace treaty of Aduna? I've studied history at Merlin for a decade and have never heard of that. And why did you say that Xen Siid was an elf? There's thousands of records saying he was a human from Navisia."

"First," Grey shut the book. "I have to tell you something *really* important."

"What?" Elsif said in anticipation.

"This isn't my book."

Elsif's face dropped. "What?"

Grey laughed. "I was joking."

Elsif snatched the book. "Are you kidding me?"

"You set me up," Grey defended. "I couldn't help myself."

Even though deep down, Elsif thought it was funny, she was in no mood to be teased. She was now the one that felt like an idiot after rambling about Dwarves and the Hat to this stranger, who probably thought she was crazy.

Laughing, Grey asked, "Now I need to know what's so important about this book."

"Nothing," Elsif said, stuffing the book in her bag. She was determined to walk away and never see him again, but her frustration boiled over and she wasn't able to contain herself.

"And I wasn't looking for the owner of the book, this book belongs to the Warlock's Hat Museum in Struth! I'm looking for the guy that vandalized the book because I'm stupid and think that if I find the Warlock's Hat, I'll become a famous historian and maybe save the world! I also think this random friend group from my school might be stalking me but that's completely unrelated, or maybe it's not. I don't really know!"

To Elsif's surprise, Grey didn't call her a nerd and walk away, but instead asked, "You think he's here?"

"Yes," Elsif professed. "There was a note in the book that had this tavern's name and the date February 5th on it."

"It's the third," Grey clarified.

"I know," Elsif said with annoyance, more at herself than Grey. "I thought I should come early in case he arrived early or got his dates wrong. Actually that's not true, I came early because I didn't want to be at Merlin Academy during the stupid Winter Games." Elsif knew she was rambling, but she had stopped caring sometime between being attacked by arrows and that moment. "I'm starting to think Jerry doesn't exist and I came here for nothing."

"His name's Jerry?" Grey asked.

"No, that's the name I gave him," Elsif replied. "I should go home. I've had too much excitement for one day."

"I don't think you've had *enough* excitement for one day," Grey opposed, grabbing Elsif's hand and pulling her towards the tavern. "We are going to find Jerry if it's the last thing we do."

They walked into the tavern and spent the whole day talking to random people and trying to find Jerry. Grey was committed to the mission and took the lead. Elsif was usually the silent partner that observed Grey's conversation and took mental notes to determine if the candidate could potentially be Jerry.

By the end of the day there were no Jerry sightings but Grey was determined to try a new strategy the next day. Each day the two met at the tavern and tried new techniques to find Jerry. One day the two spoke in strange accents, took up fake names (or faker names than they were using before), and talked loudly about the Warlock's Hat, hoping Jerry would come up to them and correct them.

Another day they decided to walk up to strangers, introduce themselves with random names, then ask the stranger if they had read any good books about the Warlock's Hat lately. When the stranger inevitably said no, they would walk outside, change into a different hat or jacket and walk back in and do the same ordeal over and over again.

One day they even pretended to be law enforcement and went around interrogating the guests of the tavern and asked where they were on all the dates of the idiots list.

Grey had started calling himself Duke, and Elsif preferred that name so she began using it regularly. Elsif also used fake names and went through all of her cousins' names plus a few extras like Ellie and Kara.

Time passed quickly and Elsif had stayed at the Tavern for over a week past the 5th. She told herself it was to ensure that she did not miss Jerry, and she was doing a thorough job in the Warlock's Hat search. But after a while Elsif had to admit to herself that she wasn't staying to find Jerry, she wanted to be around Duke for a little while longer.

Eventually sense came back to Elsif and she knew that she had to head back to Merlin. She promised her cousins that she would watch them compete in a few games and Elsif had gotten no homework done. She needed to say goodbye and return back to reality.

"Well Duke," Elsif said, sitting in the pub as she waited for her carriage to come. "I think this is the end of the line."

"We did all that we could, love," Duke said with his horrible fake accent from earlier that week.

"Yes, darling we did." Elsif said copying Duke's tone. "Jerry shall forever remain a mystery."

"Don't talk like that, love, Jerry shall be found," he insisted. "Someday."

Elsif switched to her normal voice when she saw her carriage pull up. "Well, I guess this is goodbye."

"For now," Duke replied, helping Elsif with her bags. "We still haven't found Jerry."

As they walked outside to the carriage Elsif had to admit her thoughts out loud. "I've given up on Jerry. Maybe the Hat is supposed to remain a mystery."

"Don't worry," Duke assured. "I'm not giving up on Jerry. He's out there somewhere and I'll find him for you."

Elsif chuckled. "If that happens then write to me at Merlin Academy, chamber 3718."

"Got it," Duke said, loading her luggage in the carriage. "Well see you soon Gertrude, or Ruth, or Kara, or whoever you are."

"Elsif Menzie."

"Well goodbye Elsif Menzie," Duke said, which Elsif enjoyed hearing.

"And your name?" Elsif asked.

Duke shrugged in response. "See you around, love." He walked away before Elsif could protest and demand his name.

She climbed into her carriage and thought maybe not knowing Duke's real name was for the best. Elsif would never see him again, and didn't need the distraction from her studies. But it didn't stop her heart from hurting when he waved as Elsif's carriage pulled away.

Chapter 11: The Amazing Maze Race

"**T**he list is up!" Milly exclaimed.

The biannual Merlin Academy Games were the highlights of Milly's year, and she always tried to be the first to sign up for the events each season. All the girls (except Elsif who was in Silvia), came up behind her to see which events they had this year.

Winter Games Events

Archery   February 3rd

Sword Dueling   February 5th

Magic Dueling   February 7th

Ship-Racing   February 10th

Interpretive Dance   February 12th

Dress-Making   February 13th

Sled Racing   February 15th

Hand-to-Hand Combat   February 18th

Independent Flying   February 20th

Cannon Shooting   February 23rd

Maze Race   February 25th

"These are good events," Milly announced, grabbing a pen to sign up. "Way better than last year."

"They change?" Jazzy asked, perusing the list.

"Yup," Milly replied, as she signed her name for a third time. "They switch up most of the events, but usually keep the biggest event the same. For the Winter Games, they always have the maze race as the last event, and for the Summer Games it's the carpet race. They're crowd favorites."

"I win them both every year," Rose boasted.

"She doesn't," Milly corrected.

"Darn it," Ruth grumbled. "They don't have pole climbing this year. They better be in the Summer Games."

"They have dress-making?" Jazzy questioned. "I thought these were going to be athletic games."

Rose responded first, "They always add one non-athletic event in the games, you know, for the dweebs."

"It's so the games are well-rounded and show the skills of all Merlin students," Milly countered.

"Well, I think dress-making is the perfect event for me," Jazzy stated.

"You also have to do the maze race," Milly insisted. "It's arguably the best event that Merlin has ever hosted."

Jazzy agreed to sign up for the maze race and dress-making. Ruth signed up for archery, sword dueling, and the maze race. Rose signed up for interpretive dance, hand-to-hand combat, independent flying, and the maze race. Milly signed up for archery, sword dueling, magic dueling, ship racing, hand-to-hand combat, cannon shooting, and the maze race.

"Should we sign Elsif up for the maze race?" Milly asked the other girls.

Ruth nodded. "Yes, she needs to be forced into having a little school spirit."

As Milly signed Elsif's name, Rose laughed maliciously. "She's going to hate us. I love it."

*****

On February 3rd, the school was filled with people from all over Fantasma who came to watch the Winter Games. The first event was starting and Ruth and Milly were among the hundreds of students who were participating in the archery event. Jazzy and Rose found a place to sit in the crowded bleachers that were set up on the edges of the field in the gardens.

The archery event was one of the few that Ruth was semi-decent at. This was because Bellator was known for its archery camps, and it was practically mandatory for children growing up in that district to attend. Milly was also fairly good at archery, but that was because Milly was good at most things that had to do with athleticism and weapons.

After a couple hours of competition Ruth placed 36th and Milly placed 41st out of 600 participants. Milly was not too happy about Ruth beating her and she may or may not have broken a bow over her knee when the scores were announced. Ruth wore her smug winning smile for approximately two days before Milly excelled in the next event.

Sword dueling was an impressive spectacle to watch as Milly took down several competitors who were twice her size and weight. But eventually, her luck ran out as she faced a boy from Vulputate who was too strong for her. She placed 21st out of 200 in sword dueling, which to anyone else would be impressive, but if Milly wasn't first then she wasn't satisfied.

The next event was magic dueling, where Milly and Rose performed terribly. In their defense, magic wands were not their forte. Milly placed 113th and Rose placed 89th out of 150. Except for Rose's scorched eyebrow, there were no injuries.

Milly started to take the competition seriously during the ship racing event. She had convinced some of the advanced students from Navisia to let her join their crew for the games. She started as assistant helmsman and by the end of the event she was second mate. Their team scored 2nd overall.

Interpretive dancing was an interesting event for Rose since she was disqualified within the first fifteen minutes. In the judges' defense, nothing was supposed to explode during the dance so Rose couldn't dispute the decision.

Jazzy immensely enjoyed the dressmaking event, and scored first out of twenty five contestants. Which made sense since Jazzy had been making her own clothes or tailoring hand-me-downs for as long as she could remember. Her dress was simple but well made, especially compared to the others who's stitching could barely stay together. Jazzy's dress was made from a dark plum-colored cotton and had a simple empire waist. The dress also had short sleeves and went past Jazzy's knees. It looked like something Jazzy would wear on any regular day but the judges were quite impressed by her handiwork and that brought great joy and pride to Jazzy.

The next event was hand-to-hand combat, and Rose and Milly both participated. Rose, once again, was quickly eliminated because hand-to-hand combat was obviously not clear enough for her. She apparently had misunderstood and brought several hand grenades. Milly placed seven places higher than the year before, and got 31st out of 300.

Cannon shooting was always a favorite of Milly's and she was able to place 9th out of 350 participants. She may have walked away with two bruised arms, but Milly was more than willing to pay the price of a few injuries if she was able to get in the top ten.

Finally the most anticipated event of the season arrived, but Elsif was nowhere to be seen. At the end of the first week, Elsif sent a letter to the girls explaining that Jerry had not been spotted so she was going to stay an extra couple days. Then the day before the maze race, Elsif sent another letter saying she was stuck at the edge of Magicis because of a snow storm, but she would try her best to get to the school the next day. But the morning of the maze race came and she had still not arrived.

"We need to go." Milly urged the girls out of their chambers. "I heard almost everyone signed up this year so we need to get there early to get a good spot at the line."

The girls walked out the back of the school and joined the dense crowd at the edge of the maze. Milly had worn her running shoes, black pants, a breathable shirt, jacket, and tied her hair extra tight in her low ponytail. Ruth, who usually opted for dresses, wore some old clothing and a coat so her nice clothes wouldn't get dirty when she went through the maze. Jazzy wore a shawl and the dress she made in the competition because she liked having something new to wear and she was planning to leisurely walk through the maze anyway. Rose wore four hats.

"Good morning students!" The President's voice boomed over the crowd as everyone got into position to start. "Now racers, on your marks, get set, go!"

Everyone in the crowd began to pile into the giant maze. Rose ran toward the front of the pack and disappeared. Milly ran and took the first left, while Jazzy wandered to the right. Ruth walked in with the end of the crowd and walked straight until she came to a dead end. When she turned around, she screamed.

"Why are you yelling?" Juniper asked a bit too harshly.

"You scared me," Ruth demanded, trying to defend herself. "Obviously."

"When you get over your fright," Juniper stated, turning away. "Follow me."

He began walking away, and Ruth knew she shouldn't take the bait. She *couldn't* take the bait. He had lied and betrayed her. Elsif would be livid. It would be such a dumb decision. She had to forget about him. She was not in love with him and she would not follow him. Despite telling herself all this, Ruth couldn't help herself.

"Follow you where?" Ruth asked as she ran after Juniper.

"To wherever Melissa is headed," Juniper said, like it was the most obvious thing in the world.

Ruth matched Juniper's pace and waited for him to elaborate on why they were following Melissa. No explanation came, and Juniper clearly was not going to talk first. Ruth couldn't contain herself any longer and blurted out, "What are we doing? Why should I go with you? Why should I trust you? What am I even doing?"

Juniper didn't respond and didn't look at Ruth.

"Elsif is going to kill me," Ruth continued. "If she ever finds out, then I am literally going to die."

"She *isn't* here," Juniper corrected. "So she won't find out."

"How do you know she's not here?" Ruth asked with suspicion.

"I haven't seen her glower at me from across any rooms lately," Juniper stated. "So she must have left for February break."

Ruth chuckled to herself. "Do you actually catch her glaring at you?"

"Are you doubting her hatred for me?" Juniper asked in a tone that suggested he was bordering on a joke.

"I don't think she's doing it on purpose," Ruth teased. "I'm sure she's doing it subconsciously."

"She's subconsciously planning my death," Juniper retorted.

"You can't blame her," Ruth stated. "She thinks that you have Malum's Staff."

"You *don't* think I have the Staff?" Juniper asked in a steady voice. He always talked in a way that revealed no emotion, no way of interpreting any hidden meaning. Ruth hated it.

"I never said that," Ruth said plainly.

"You said *she* thinks," Juniper repeated. "You didn't say *we* think."

Ruth grew flustered as she snapped back at Juniper, "Don't put words in my mouth."

"I didn't," Juniper replied. "They were your words."

Tongue-tied and without a good comeback, Ruth decided to change the subject. "We should pick up the pace if we're going to find Melissa."

"Fine," Juniper agreed, leading the way through the maze. "The one thing you can rely on Melissa to do is to not trust anyone. She won't like all these students scouring through the maze. She'll be checking to make sure her thing is still safe."

"And if we find the thing in the garden," Ruth began to ask. "Then that will prove her guilt for stealing the Staff?"

"We'll find out," Juniper said cryptically.

A half hour passed before they finally found Melissa. They saw her from a distance and began following her through the twists and turns of the maze. It didn't take long for the pair to realize that Melissa was turning in random patterns. She either was participating rather poorly in the race, or purposely walking in a haphazard way to throw someone off.

Ruth was about to suggest that Melissa might know they were following her, when suddenly she disappeared. Juniper ran to catch up to her but was stopped by a dead end. Melissa was gone, but there was no place where she could have gone without passing Juniper and Ruth.

Juniper began tearing away at the bushes all around him. "She must have gone through the walls."

"That's impossible," Ruth stated matter of factly. "Remember? The magic prevents it. Even if she was hiding in the bushes like we did in September, we'd be able to see her from here."

"Would you stop talking?" Juniper complained as he struggled through the bushes. "We would find her a lot quicker if you would help me."

Placing her hands on her hips, Ruth glared at him. "Why would I help you with a completely useless task?"

"If she didn't go through the walls, and if she wouldn't be able to hide from us," Juniper turned to Ruth with an annoyed expression. "Then how did she disappear?"

"I know it wasn't from the going through the walls," Ruth said, matching his annoyance. "It's impossible."

"It's very possible," he retorted.

Ruth scoffed. "I'm walking away now."

Juniper stopped fighting the wall, and ran after Ruth as she tried to return to the race. "I was almost through," Juniper stated.

Ruth rolled her eyes. "Sure you were."

"I was," Juniper muttered through gritted teeth.

"No," Ruth spat back. "You weren't."

"At least I was doing something to find Melissa," Juniper snapped. "All you did was stand there and criticize me."

"I wasn't going to waste my time," Ruth stated. "And I was trying to stop you from wasting yours."

"Well, now we completely lost her," Juniper grumbled.

A female voice came up behind Juniper and Ruth, and asked, "Who did you lose?"

Ruth and Juniper whirled around to find Melissa. "Who are you looking for?" She restated, with a wicked smile. "I could help you."

"Oh," Ruth said, looking at Juniper then back at Melissa. "We were looking for-"

"Ruth's cousin, Milly," Juniper finished Ruth's sentence.

"You were looking for Milly?" Melissa questioned with an even wider smile.

"Yep," Ruth mumbled. "Apparently we were."

"I just saw her," Melissa said earnestly, reaching out to touch Ruth's shoulder in a way that was probably intended to be comforting but instead every muscle in Ruth's body tensed. "I'll show you. Come with me."

"No thanks," Juniper snapped.

"We're fine," Ruth agreed.

"Please let me help you," Melissa said with her unsettling smile. "You'll find her much faster with my help. She went this way, follow me."

Melissa linked arms with Ruth and ushered her through the maze. Even though Ruth attempted to protest, she was now trapped in the snake's coils. Juniper followed behind the girls with a solemn expression.

After walking aimlessly for twenty minutes, Melissa turned to Ruth with her flashy smile. "I wonder where your cousin could have gotten to. I was sure she wasn't far."

"Yeah," Ruth mumbled, trying to find a way to get away from the clutches of her sworn enemy. "I wonder."

Eventually, Melissa just so happened to lead them straight out of the maze and to the end of the race. "Oh look at that," Melissa commented innocently. "We're out."

Juniper shot Ruth a skeptical look. "Yeah, look at that."

At that point, around half the students had finished the race and Melissa, Ruth, and Juniper placed 924th, 925th, and 926th.

Melissa sighed. "We still haven't found Milly, have we? Should we go back in?"

"They won't let us go back in once we finish," Ruth stated.

"Oh, right! Well, that's a shame," Melissa said with fake pity. "Why did you need to find her anyways? Was it an emergency?"

"Um, well I, uh," Ruth struggled for words. "I wanted to check up on her, because, well, she has a phobia of mazes." Ruth regretted the lame excuse as soon as it left her lips, but she had to commit at that point. "Yeah, one time when she was in a maze, when she was around eight, she, uh, got lost and it was dark and she was alone for days and almost died, and was scared and hungry and lonely. Also she lost her dog, did I forget to mention she had a dog? She was discovered like forty-something hours later by some friendly hikers. But before that she ran into some not-so-friendly hikers who tried to eat her. It was a very traumatic experience so every year when we do the maze race, I try to check up on her."

Melissa nodded along sympathetically. "That sounds terrible."

"Wow," Juniper said in a monotone voice. "Too bad we didn't find her."

"Why does she compete in the race?" Melissa asked.

"Uh," Ruth stuttered. "It's because she- there she is!" Just in the knick of time, Milly emerged from the maze. Ruth began to walk away from Melissa. "I should go check on her."

"Yeah," Juniper agreed. "We should go make sure she's okay."

"Why would you go with her?" Melissa questioned Juniper, judgment brimming her tone. "You're not friends with them."

Before Juniper could respond, Ruth interrupted, "You're right, he's not." She ran toward Milly before she was tempted to see Juniper's reaction.

Once Ruth reached Milly, she immediately embraced her and whispered in her ear, "Please keep hugging me and don't ask why."

"I'm concerned," Milly said with stiff arms.

"Would it be an inconvenience for you to cry a little?" Ruth asked.

"I'm not doing that," Milly stated. "Let go of me."

"Fine," Ruth released Milly, and tried to stop her head from swerving in Juniper's direction.

"How did you do?" Milly asked, stretching her muscles from the race.

"I don't know, good," Ruth muttered. "How did you do?"

"Well at first I was intimidated by..." Milly began to rant about the whole event and described her journey in excruciating detail. Ruth tried to listen at first, but her mind and eyes wandered across the garden. Ruth hated that her eyes were drawn to Juniper.

Juniper and Melissa were talking closely, a little too close in Ruth's opinion. They were speaking in low voices so Ruth couldn't hear a thing. Melissa still had her fake smile plastered across her face. Juniper remained expressionless with a slight expression of annoyance, as his face usually did. At one point Melissa said something that made Juniper's face change into the smallest smile for a half second. Ruth's jaw dropped.

Why did he smile, Ruth thought desperately. *Melissa made him smile. What could they possibly be talking about that made Juniper smile?*

Ruth thought she might cry or scream when suddenly Juniper and Melissa both looked in her direction. She quickly turned her attention back to Milly who was still going on and on about the stupid maze race.

"And I went to the same dead end three times!" Milly exclaimed. "I couldn't believe how dumb I was. I'm definitely better at navigating on water, that's for sure."

"Hey Milly," Melissa walked up to Ruth and Milly. "You are so brave." She gave Milly a hug, then flashed a smile at Ruth as she sauntered away.

"Was that Melissa?" Milly questioned. "Why did she hug me? Why is everyone hugging me?"

"You're a huggable person," Ruth commented as she saw Juniper walk over to them.

His expression was back to normal. "That was a waste of time."

"What were you and Melissa talking about?" Ruth blurted. She hoped that it came off casual, but she knew herself too well to be delusional.

"Nothing."

Milly turned to Ruth. "Aren't we mad at him?"

Ruth shot a sideways glance at Juniper. "Yes, we are."

Juniper rolled his eyes. "I thought we were over this."

Milly felt awkward so she slowly backed away. "I'm going to find Jazzy and Rose. Hopefully they won't hug me."

Juniper waited until Milly walked away before asking, "Why are you mad at me this time?"

"I never stopped being mad in the first place!" Ruth stated, her short temper bubbling to the surface. "You might have the Staff, you lied to me about it, you smiled at something Melissa said, and she's a jerk so that makes you a jerk for smiling at whatever she said!"

"What?"

"Leave me alone!" Ruth yelled and stormed off before her embarrassment kicked in.

Ruth went straight to the front of the school and stood by the carriage arrival and drop off area. She sat down and refused to stand back up until Elsif had arrived back at Merlin. It took several hours, but eventually her carriage rolled up.

"Hi," Elsif said, spotting Ruth. "Why are you sitting in the dark?"

"I just had the most embarrassing moment of my entire life," Ruth stated plainly.

"You embarrass yourself everyday. I'm sure it wasn't that bad," Elsif assured. "Did everyone survive when I was away?"

"Everyone except Rose."

"Oh good, everyone I care about is still alive. How were the games? How did you do in the maze?"

"Fine," Ruth said, standing up and preparing her story. "You'll never guess what happened." As Elsif and Ruth walked back to their chambers, Ruth began her long story about Juniper, Melissa, and his stupid smile. She didn't leave a single detail out. Elsif listened intently and booed every time Ruth mentioned Juniper.

Once Ruth finished Elsif assured her that she made the right decision in the end. "Juniper's playing games with you."

Ruth nodded and agreed outwardly with Elsif, but deeply she regretted her words. "Did anything eventful happen in Silvia?"

"No," Elsif said flatly. "Nothing eventful."

After a few minutes the girls arrived at the chambers and were reunited with Jazzy, Milly, and Rose. Elsif gave Milly a big hug for an uncomfortable amount of time.

"Why is everyone awkwardly hugging me!"

The girls laughed at Milly's confusion and took turns hugging her. After that, the girls asked Elsif a million questions about her trip. Elsif reported that it was unsuccessful and boring. While she described her visit, she conveniently left out Duke. She didn't really know why, she hadn't planned on keeping him out of the story, but she did. Maybe someday she would tell them the whole story, but not today. Elsif sort of enjoyed keeping a little of the adventure to herself.

Chapter 12: Can We Throw Rotten Tomatoes At Him??

"Rose," Milly said while sitting in their chambers on a boring March afternoon. "What did you get for number ten? I got Currus."

"Striped hippopotamus."

"I don't think we're doing the same assignment."

"I'm writing my hit list," Rose mentioned casually.

Jazzy walked in with a heavy sigh. "That was a tough week. I have so much homework."

"But now it's Saturday," Rose declared. "We have the day off tomorrow and can fulfill as many shenanigans as we desire."

"I'll have to do homework the whole day," Jazzy replied.

"Me too," Milly added

"My homework will have to wait," Rose stated. "I have plans."

Ruth walked into the chambers in time to hear Rose's statement. "What plans? I have a ton of work this weekend, so I'm not available for any plans."

"They're private plans," Rose clarified.

Milly muttered under her breath, "Remind me to tell Elsif to stay away from you."

As Rose opened her mouth to give a charming comeback, a *clink* was heard from the balcony window. The girls turned toward the noise, but didn't see anything outside. The clink repeated again, and again. By the fourth *clink*, the girls realized the noise was coming from a pebble that was being tossed at the window from the ground.

"Not it!" Ruth screamed.

Milly glanced at Ruth with confusion. "What?"

"I don't want to look first," Ruth stated calmly.

Jazzy slouched down in her chair. "I would rather not look either."

"I'm busy," said Rose while she intently worked on 'homework.'

Milly reluctantly stood up. "I guess I'm looking."

She walked over to the balcony and peered into the dark. Milly couldn't see anything so she slid the door open and stuck her head outside. She looked down and saw a shadowy silhouette of a man.

"It's a guy," Milly said, closing the door behind her. "Throwing rocks from the ground."

Ruth perked up. "A cute guy?"

"I don't know," Milly stammered. "It's dark."

"Is he young?" Ruth continued in an eager manner. "Is he a teenager?"

"I don't know."

"Go back and check!"

Milly groaned but obeyed Ruth's urgent request. She went back to the balcony and tried to catch a better look at the stranger. Ruth, Rose, and Jazzy all stumbled out after Milly to see for themselves. Once each girl was satisfied by their investigation, they went back inside.

Once the door closed behind them, Ruth declared, "I call dibs!"

"Ew no," Rose replied. "He's weird looking. We should throw something back at him."

"No Rose, don't hurt him!" Ruth begged. "He might be the love of my life. My future husband!"

"He is *not* cute," Rose demanded. "Get some standards!"

"I think he's good looking," Jazzy commented.

Milly shook her head. "But why is he throwing rocks at our room?"

"Because he's the love of my life," Ruth insisted.

Milly exhaled sharply while massaging her brow. "He is not the love of your life, Ruth."

Elsif walked in during Milly's last statement. "Who's not the love of Ruth's life?"

"The really cute guy who's throwing rocks at our window," Ruth stated.

Elsif laughed. "I call dibs."

"No," Ruth shot back. "I called him. He's mine!"

"That's not fair," Elsif retorted. "I wasn't here so we obviously need to draw straws or something for this imaginary guy."

"Fine," Ruth began to barter. "If he is younger than eighteen, then he's mine, and if he's older, then he's yours."

"Deal," Elsif agreed, shaking Ruth's hand.

"Lame," Rose interjected. "We need to throw something back at him. Like rotten tomatoes! Do we have any of those?"

"Do you want to see him?" Jazzy asked. "We're deciding if he's handsome or not."

Elsif paused. "Is there actually a dude outside our window?"

"On the ground," Milly explained. "He keeps throwing rocks at our glass door."

Elsif nodded slowly, while she emptied her backpack. She had just returned from the library after writing a twenty-five page paper about Elf cruelty in the first century. "Why?" She finally asked. Another *clink* was heard from the door.

The girls shrugged in response.

"Is someone going to ask him?" Elsif inquired. "Or are we going to live with this slightly inconvenient noise for the rest of our lives? Or we could get security."

"No," Ruth begged, falling to her knees. "Cute guys don't belong in jail!"

"I already went out," Milly said. "It's someone else's turn."

Jazzy attempted to hide under her blanket, while Rose ran to the fridge to find anything rotten. Ruth refused to face the love of her life because she was too frightened of his rejection, but also because she was comfy on the floor.

Elsif conceded and went to the balcony to shoo the guy away. But she was greeted by an unexpected, but definitely not unwanted, stranger. After quickly closing the door, Elsif walked to the edge of the balcony.

"What are you doing here, Grey?" Elsif asked, leaning over the rail and keeping her voice low.

"I thought you were calling me Duke?" He asked, looking up at Elsif from the ground.

Elsif repeated the question, "What are you doing here, *Duke*?"

"I know Jerry's real name."

"What!" Elsif shouted, then immediately covered her mouth. She looked behind her to see the girl's faces pressed against the glass. Turning back towards Duke, Elsif continued to talk in a soft voice, "How, in all of Fantasma, did you find Jerry?"

"I didn't find Jerry," Duke clarified. "I just know his name."

"But how?" Elsif questioned, completely amazed but trying to keep her body language neutral so her cousins wouldn't know what was going on.

Duke shrugged, but had a smug smile plastered across his face. "I have my ways."

"So who's the infamous Jerry?"

"I can't yell out his name," Duke stated in a mockingly obvious tone. "Have you ever done a secret mission, love?" He asked, while switching to his fake accent from Silvia. "Climb down and I'll tell you."

"I'm on the third floor," Elsif argued. "I don't fancy dying today, darling."

"Fine, I'll climb up," he said and reached for the trellis on the side of the building.

"No!" Elsif blurted. She grasped for all the common sense she had left, and scrambled for a response. "It's past curfew, and my monitor will kill us if she finds you."

"I'm not scared of your monitor," Duke assured. "I'll be stealthy, practically invisible."

"It's not a good idea," Elsif said curtly.

Duke surrendered and backed away from the wall. "Fine, let's meet tomorrow. I'll be by the waterfalls in the garden at ten tomorrow morning. See you then."

He disappeared into the night before Elsif could conjure up a reply. She stood alone on the balcony for a moment, dazed by the unexpected conversation. Eventually she walked back inside before she drowned in her thoughts. The second Elsif opened the door, a million questions flooded her.

"Why was he throwing rocks?" Milly questioned.

"How old was he?" Asked Ruth.

"What did he say?" Jazzy inquired.

"Where did he go?" Rose demanded, arms full of produce.

Elsif waved off the girls. "He had the wrong balcony."

Ruth pouted as she flopped into a chair. "So he wasn't here to declare his love for one of us?" Elsif shook her head. Ruth frowned and asked, "How old was he?"

"Older than eighteen," Elsif answered quickly.

Ruth hit the arm of her chair. "Darn it!"

Milly interjected, "He's lucky we didn't call security on him."

"Hopefully he finds the right balcony," Jazzy commented.

Rose sighed dramatically. "What am I going to do with all these stinking tomatoes?"

*****

The next day Elsif left for the gardens as soon as she woke. She was so excited about meeting Duke that she didn't acknowledge her cousins on her way out. Which in turn caused some confusion within the girls, since Elsif never left her bed before noon on Sundays.

In the garden, Elsif saw that Duke had beat her to the waterfall even though she was early. "I never thought I'd see you again," Elsif admitted as she walked up.

"I told you I'd see you soon," Duke countered. "How could you forget so quickly?"

"I didn't forget," Elsif mumbled, then changed the subject before her embarrassment set in. "What's the name?"

Duke reached into his pocket and pulled out a little slip of paper.

"Joseph Ellison," Elsif read. "Who is he?"

Duke replied plainly, "No idea."

"You must have *some* idea," Elsif insisted. "You got the name."

"An anonymous third party got the name," Duke stated. "It came with no description but complete assurance that this is his real name."

"An anonymous source?" Elsif questioned showing her lack of confidence. "How do we know your source is honest? He could have written the first name that came to mind."

"I trust him," Duke assured. "So you'll have to trust me."

"And what if I don't?" Elsif asked.

"Ouch," Duke said as he touched his heart.

Elsif rolled her eyes. "I'm not trying to be difficult. But I'm not one to trust random people's words. I need sources or proof. And this whole Hat, Jerry, Staff situation has already been too dangerous for my liking. So I'm not going to risk my or my cousin's safety over an anonymous source."

"Don't tell me you're worried about the risk *now*?"

Elsif frowned, not understanding Duke's comment. "Of course I'm worried about the risk. Who wouldn't be?"

"You traveled to Silvia by yourself," Duke stated with emphasis. "You were going to meet Jerry alone. You even fraternized with a guy who was being shot at, then aided and abetted his escape."

Elsif tried to keep her frown plastered on her face even though Duke was far too charismatic to be frowned at for long. "Fair point, but I'm not as irresponsible as you're making me out to be."

"I'm not saying you are," Duke said, raising his hands in defense. His tone suggested he was under attack, but his smile revealed the joke behind it. "But in Silvia you were ready for any experience that came your way. You have to admit it was more fun that way."

"Silvia was different," Elsif continued sternly. "It was just me. But my cousins are going to want to meet Jerry in April when he's in Viverra, and I don't want them to be nearly burned alive again."

Duke shook his head, not buying Elsif's excuse. "You can't live your whole life worried about risks. Or you won't have any worthwhile memories on your deathbed."

"I'm not planning on dying any time soon," Elsif retorted, while inwardly debating. She didn't want the search to be done yet, and Viverra was the natural next step. "Maybe a trip to Viverra next month wouldn't be the end of the world," Elsif conceded.

"Amazing," Duke beamed. "Jerry better exceed all my expectations when I meet him or I will be sorely disappointed."

Elsif's mouth dropped at Duke's statement. "Are you coming to Viverra with us?"

"Of course," Duke said. "I *have* to meet the infamous Jerry."

"Good," Elsif mumbled, looking down at her restless hands so Duke wouldn't see her grin.

"What are you doing today?"

Homework. Papers. Studying for a million tests.

"Nothing," Elsif said. Usually her day off would be spent sleeping and studying, but in that moment Elsif desperately wanted to escape the mundane routine.

"Same here," Duke replied.

"Do you want a tour of Merlin?" Elsif offered, crossing her arms to hide her shaking hands.

"Sure, might as well."

*****

"Why are the windows so symmetrical?" Duke questioned as the pair walked along the path that ran parallel to the Dextram Sea. "The building has no personality."

"It's only the most impressive building in all of Fantasma," Elsif replied with a tease. "But I'll let the administration know you think it needs more character."

Several dozen students enjoyed the warm March day on the front lawn of Merlin. Elsif was telling Duke about how her cousin Monty tried to push her in the lake last year, when Elsif's least favorite person made an appearance.

"And then he dangled me over the water-" Elsif stopped when Juniper approached. "Hi?" She said in an unwelcoming tone.

"Where's your shadow?" Juniper asked bluntly.

"She's not around."

"Letting her have the day off?" He asked Elsif, while shooting a glare at Duke. "You're not a student."

"I'm not," Duke confirmed, extending his hand. "I'm Fox."

Elsif chuckled at the new name, but quickly covered her mouth.

Juniper didn't accept the handshake. "Visitors aren't allowed when school's in session. Except for balls and the games."

Duke lowered his hand. "Good thing I'm not *in* Merlin then."

"You're on school grounds," Juniper stated in an accusatory tone.

Duke grew amused at Juniper's attack, while Juniper grew increasingly annoyed. "I'm on the sidewalk. I could be passing through to the next town."

"Then you should keep walking."

"I'm taking my time, taking in the views."

"It's the same sea as the next town."

"Who are you? The lawn monitor?" Duke asked, completely flabbergasted. "Or maybe you're the President of Merlin? Here to make sure the unintelligent stay off the property."

"I'm an *actual* student," Juniper spoke harshly. "And I'm trying to keep the student body safe."

Elsif accidentally allowed a laugh to escape her. The interaction between the boys was both comical but also baffling to her. But the laugh was costly because it turned Juniper's attention to her.

"You've been a student for years," Juniper said in a hostile manner. "You should know better."

Elsif's face dropped. "No one cares about visitor rules."

"It's my fault-" Duke interjected, but Elsif continued.

"Ruth's not here so you can leave," Elsif remarked. "And she doesn't want to talk to you anyway."

Juniper didn't respond immediately, which concerned Elsif. She squirmed slightly as Juniper debated his next words. "I need to speak to you over there." Before Elsif could question Juniper, he walked several feet away.

Elsif looked between Juniper and Duke. She then turned to Duke with a remorseful expression. "Give me three seconds, and I'll be back."

She figured complying with Juniper would be the fastest way to get rid of him.

"You're not seriously going along with this, are you?" Duke asked with shock.

"Just three seconds," Elsif explained desperately. "I promise that I hardly know him. He's just weirdly obsessed with my cousin. I'll be right back. Three seconds!"

Duke protested, while Elsif walked over to Juniper. The sooner Elsif talked to Juniper, the sooner she could get back to Duke. "What do you want?"

Before Juniper answered he walked around Elsif, so Elsif was forced to turn her back to Duke. She found it weird, but Elsif only wanted to get out of the conversation as fast as possible

"What do you want?" Elsif demanded, her voice nearing a shout. "I don't understand your infatuation with Ru-" Elsif's words got stuck in her throat as she saw an unwelcome sight over Juniper's shoulder. Bernard was standing thirty yards away from them, looking in their direction. When they made eye contact, he quickly looked away.

Elsif's eyes moved to her shoes, as she took in the situation. How long had Bernard been watching her? Was he watching her? Or was she crazy? Paranoid? Did Juniper want her to see Bernard? It would explain the awkward shuffle from before. Why would Juniper want her to see Bernard?

Juniper broke the silence, "You need to explain to Ruth that I need to talk to her."

It's a trade, Elsif realized. Juniper was trading the information about Bernard for Ruth.

The last thing, in all of Fantasma, that Elsif wanted was for Juniper and Ruth to talk. But if the situation confirmed that Elsif wasn't delusional and Bernard was stalking her, then Juniper was doing her a huge favor. And Elsif hated not returning favors.

"I'll mention it," Elsif muttered.

"Do it today."

Elsif held her hands together so they wouldn't flail around in frustration. "I'm not making any promises that she'll actually talk to you, but I'll relay your message."

"Good," he said and walked away.

Elsif frowned as she imagined the joy Ruth would feel later. Elsif would have to figure out the perfect way to tell Ruth while also discouraging her from speaking to Juniper. She was lost in thought when Duke snuck up behind her.

Elsif jumped once she saw Duke was beside her. "Sorry," she muttered, her face growing warm.

"What did he want?" Duke asked, his smile disappearing for the first time that day.

"He wouldn't leave until I agreed to tell Ruth that he needed to talk to her," Elsif explained. "I really can't stand him."

"I could tell," Duke said, his grin returning. "What's his deal with Ruth?"

"I don't know," Elsif said, then began her tirade. "But ever since they snuck out to find something of Melissa's- none of us even know what the thing is- Ruth has been convinced she's in love with him and he's been dragging her around through mazes and stuff. And he might have the Staff or Melissa might have it. I don't know anymore."

"Is Ruth the cousin who likes to sail?" Duke asked.

"No," Elsif shook her head. "That's Milly. Ruth is the one that likes animals, wears dresses, and is obsessed with finding a husband before she turns seventeen."

"And you don't approve of Juniper being the groom?" Duke teased.

"I'd lock her up in my other cousin's dungeon before that ever happened," Elsif stated. "Honestly I don't think I would approve of any guy dating any of my cousins. *Ever*. Ruth's completely harmless neighbor Danny looked in her direction once and I tried to convince my Aunt and Uncle to move."

"Your cousin has a dungeon?" Duke asked with a laugh. "That's cool."

"It's not going to be cool when I end up shackled and upside down in it," Elsif joked.

"How often are there balls here?" Duke asked. "Since that's the only time Juniper will let me on Merlin property."

"You're also allowed during the Summer Games in June," Elsif countered.

"Will *you* be at the games?" Duke asked. "Because you skipped the Winter Games to go to Silvia. So if I wanted to be at Merlin at the same time as you, then I think the ball is the only guarantee."

Elsif's heart skipped a beat. "We have the Felix Finis Ball once a year on July 31st to celebrate the end of the academic year."

"I might have to swing by," Duke commented casually.

The whole world turned upside down as Elsif realized she might have a date to the Felix Finis Ball. There was no way that Elsif 'Nerd of the Year' Menzie could have a date to the ball. Excitement was quickly replaced by fear as Elsif's mind flashed a million horrible scenarios that could happen at the ball.

"Fox is a stupid name," Elsif blurted, desperate to change the subject.

"I panicked," Duke admitted light-heartedly. "Your laughing didn't help."

"Sorry about that," Elsif said with a chuckle, as she once again saw Bernard in the distance. "What should we do next?" Elsif asked, looking around to see if they could get out of Bernard's eyeline.

"Do you have a favorite place?"

"Well," Elsif said with uncertainty. "My favorite place is the library, but Juniper might attack you if you go inside."

"I'll take my chances," Duke said, grabbing Elsif's hand. "Lead the way."

Butterflies erupted in Elsif's stomach, as she walked hand-in-hand with a boy. It must have been a weird fever dream, because there was no way Elsif was living in her reality.

Even though it may have only been an illusion, Elsif took Duke to her favorite spot in the library. They walked to the back corner with several comfy chairs and a great view of the gardens. They were also surrounded by Elsif's favorite subjects, or as Rose called them, the most boring subjects.

"I read this one last week," Elsif said as she pulled a book off a shelf. "It's about how the humans started Merlin Academy in 1096 and how they were in constant conflict with the Elves who were trying to enslave them. The basis of the book is that those times were basically a pre- pre- pre- prerequisite of the Elven wars."

"Spoiler," Duke teased, as he took the book from Elsif. He plopped a chair and began flipping through the pages.

"It was published 600 years ago," Elsif stated. "I think the time clock on the spoiler rule ran out."

"Actually the spoiler rule is 800 years," Duke replied. "You're 200 years too early."

"Oh I thought the cut off was 599 years, my mistake-" Elsif was cut off by Rose, who appeared out of nowhere and decided that out of all the chairs in the library, she had to sit in Elsif's lap. "Rose get off of me!" Elsif pushed Rose off of her, only for Rose to crawl right back.

"How violent you are today, my dear," Rose mocked, as she clung back to Elsif. In all the excitement, Rose didn't notice the guest. "Who are you?" She asked when she finally saw the boy sitting across from Elsif.

"Jax," Duke replied, entertained by the antics.

"You're new?" Rose questioned as she started her investigation.

"Yup," Duke answered. "Elsif is showing me around."

"Really?" Rose turned to Elsif with astonishment. "I didn't know you knew how to talk to the male species. Or anyone outside our family."

"Ms. Princey asked me to give him a tour," Elsif stated. Rose laughed in Elsif's face, which was uncomfortably close since Rose was still in her lap.

"Why you?" She demanded. "You're the third most awkward person I know. Were there no socially active people available to welcome the new student. Is that why Ms. Princey had to resort to you?"

Elsif frowned. "Go away."

Rose stood up and disappeared behind a bookshelf but not before she yelled over her shoulder, "I'm going to get to the bottom of this!"

"I'm so sorry," Elsif said, her face growing warm again. "She's my cousin."

"She seemed- stimulating," Duke said, hesitating to find the right word to describe Rose.

"Yeah," Elsif nodded. "Rose is definitely *stimulating.*"

Elsif tried to steer the conversation away from Rose and onto any other subjects, but unfortunately another cousin showed up.

"Elsif! Rose said you had a boy back here," Ruth's voice was heard before she was seen. When she appeared from behind the bookshelf, Ruth gasped. "There *is* a boy back here."

"He's a new student and you're scaring him," Elsif scolded Ruth. "Go away."

Ruth shook her head as she left. "Out of all the places to show him, and you chose the library?" She disappeared, but Elsif wasn't able to take two breaths before another cousin appeared.

"What do you want Milly?" Elsif asked, exasperated.

"Nothing," Milly admitted. "Rose said she'd pay me three silver coins if I walked back here."

"I'll give you a Pecuun bill to leave and keep Rose and Ruth away," Elsif offered.

"You need to manage your money better."

Elsif's patience was growing thin when Duke extended a hand to Milly. "I'm Kay. I'm a new student." Milly shook his hand. "I'm Milly, Elsif's cousin. Do you like sailing? My ship is in dire need of an engineer's assistant. I don't need an answer right away but you should think about it."

"Okay Milly," Elsif interrupted. "Bye."

After Milly left, Elsif was over the moon thankful that there were no other interruptions. She made a mental note to give Jazzy a big hug for not being as weak willed and embarrassing as her cousins.

"I'm *so* sorry," Elsif stressed. "I wish I could say they aren't always like that, but I'd be lying." Duke had been his charming self throughout all the chaos and Elsif was thoroughly impressed.

"I'm sure Jerry is going to love meeting them," Duke said.

"Yeah," Elsif agreed, realizing if Duke planned to come to Viverra, then he would have to interact with her cousins again. Panic flooded Elsif's senses as she imagined more embarrassing incidents happening. But the panic subsided a moment later as Elsif thought about how well Duke handled them. Maybe next month wouldn't be terrible if they were all together.

"Hey," Elsif began. "Since my cousins are going to Viverra and you're planning to go too, would you want to be formally introduced to them now? Just so it's less chaotic in Viverra and we can focus on Jerry."

"Um," Duke began in a hesitant tone. "Maybe not. I wouldn't want to end up hated like that Juniper guy."

"That's a whole different situation," Elsif assured eagerly. "I promise they won't hate you."

"Better not risk it though," Duke said.

Elsif nodded, but knew this was Duke's polite way of rejecting the invitation. "Yeah, definitely," Elsif mumbled. She quickly grabbed another book off the shelf and began rattling off facts.

After several hours, the sun was beginning to set, and Elsif had a pile of homework waiting for her. She loved spending the day with Duke, but she was still a student who needed to prioritize work.

"I need to head back," Elsif eventually said. "I have a paper on the Magicis Peace Alliance of 3503 due tomorrow. It's supposed to be twelve pages and I wrote eighteen, so I've got to shorten it."

"You can't just put a big X through the last six pages and turn it in?" Duke asked.

Elsif smiled sadly. "Unfortunately no. Can I walk you to the carriages?"

"I'm not taking a carriage," Duke explained. "I'm walking."

Elsif looked at Duke with a quizzical expression, "Walk? The nearest town is at least an hour's walk."

Duke shrugged. "I like walking."

"Did you walk from Silvia?" Elsif asked comically.

"I did, actually," Duke said. "Walked and borrowed a couple horses."

"Do you have a vendetta against carriages or something?"

"No," Duke replied. "I just prefer not to ride in them."

"Okay," Elsif replied, not completely understanding what that meant. She had never heard of anyone not riding in carriages. Seemed like an odd preference to her. But Elsif soon forgot about those thoughts when Duke leaned over and planted a kiss on Elsif's cheek.

"See you in Viverra," he said and left Elsif sitting in her little corner of the library.

Elsif sat completely frozen, her thoughts empty. She sat there for a while, not thinking. Just sitting frozen in the chair. After a while, Elsif snapped back to her old self. She chided herself for acting foolish over a boy, and left to go back to the chambers.

*****

"Are you crazy?" Milly asked Rose. "His name was Kay."

"Maybe I am?" Rose stated, crossing her arms. "What does that have to do with his name being Jax."

"He looked more like a Jax," Ruth interjected.

Milly wanted to bang her head on the coffee table in their chambers.

"It doesn't matter what he looked like," Milly argued. "His name *is* Kay."

"He said Jax!" Rose yelled at Milly.

On the edge of losing her sanity, Milly snapped at Rose. "You need to clean out your ears."

"I don't think it was nice to embarrass Elsif," Jazzy said with a hint of guilt.

"You didn't do anything," Ruth told Jazzy. "You're in the clear."

As Milly and Rose argued, and Ruth assured Jazzy of her innocence, Elsif entered the chambers. The entrance caused an eruption in the living room.

"Elsif, his name is Jax right?" Milly asked.

"The foreigner's name was Kay!" Rose declared, standing on her chair.

"I'm so sorry Elsif," Jazzy pleaded. "I didn't think it was funny."

"Is he single?" Ruth jumped in Elsif's face. "Not for me of course. Not my type. But he's perfect for you! You finally won't be single, lonely, and pathetic."

Elsif swatted the attacks away. "His first name is Jax and middle name is Kay. He goes by both. Jazzy, it wasn't a big deal, and I'm used to it by now. And I don't know and don't care."

"That makes sense," Milly replied, easing back into her seat.

Rose eyed Milly, not giving up her height advantage. "Sounds suspicious if you ask me."

"I didn't," Milly retorted.

Ruth sat in the other chair. "You should really find out if he has a girlfriend. I become more concerned each day that you're going to become a crazy cat lady."

"I'm allergic to cats," Elsif stated.

"Oh Elsif!" Ruth exclaimed. "You're doomed!"

Elsif ignored Ruth and sat on the couch so she could sort out her homework. Before she dove into editing, Elsif decided to bring up the subject of Jerry.

"Do you guys want to go to Viverra next month?" Elsif asked. "It's the last item on the Idiot's List."

"I'm down," Milly responded.

"I'll go," Ruth added.

"I'd love to come," Jazzy smiled.

"I hope we get into a fight!" Rose bounced in her chair.

Jazzy frowned. "We're not going to fight anyone, right?"

"No," Elsif assured.

*****

As Elsif tucked herself into bed after a long day, she remembered a commitment from earlier.

"Ruth?" Elsif called to the bed above her.

"You're awake?" Ruth questioned.

"I forgot to mention," Elsif hesitated. "Juniper walked up to me today and said that he needs to talk to you. Goodnight!" Elsif rolled onto her back and closed her eyes.

Ruth was never good at boundaries which was evident by her jumping on top of Elsif. "What did he say to you? What was his tone? Did he look good? Why does he need to talk to me!"

"I don't know," Elsif said, giving into the conversation and sitting up. "He was very persistent though."

"Persistent?" Ruth said with wide eyes. "That's good- I mean bad. Very bad. I don't want to talk to him."

"Good," Elsif agreed. "Goodnight."

"But!" Ruth grabbed Elsif before she could lay back down. "Tell me this. Was there desperation in his eyes?"

Elsif considered slapping Ruth, but was too tired. "I don't know. I didn't notice his eyes."

"How could you not notice his eyes?" Ruth pleaded. "Those beautiful green eyes. I dream about those eyes!"

"If you want my advice," Elsif stated plainly. "You shouldn't talk to him. Ever." Ruth rolled her eyes but Elsif continued. "I'm trying to protect you. He's going to use you and hurt you."

"I promise that I'll be careful around him," Ruth answered sincerely. "But I can't promise to stay away."

Elsif groaned, "Fine, whatever, goodnight." She laid her head back down and covered her face with her blankets before Ruth could protest. Eventually Elsif felt a weight lift from her bed and heard Ruth back in her bed.

For several minutes, rhythmic breathing was the only noise in the room, until Ruth cut the silence. "I know you think I'm crazy, but I love him."

Elsif swallowed her groan, and forced herself to fall asleep.

Chapter 13: Eating Popcorn And Not Getting Married

The girls were traveling to Viverra, a region that none of them had been to before. Elsif had made arrangements for them to stay at the Kolvig Inn, which was down the road from Kolvig Kernels, the best popcorn joint in town. Viverra was known for their fields of flowers, vegetation, and small farms. Right away they noticed that everything seemed to move at a slow pace and the locals were friendly, overly friendly.

"They're planning something," Rose claimed while she eyed the check-in lady over her shoulder as the girls walked to their room.

"She was sweet," Jazzy said, who was already in love with Viverra. It felt more like home than any other region she had visited.

Rose blew out hot air. "They're *definitely* planning something."

The girls arrived in town the day before Joseph Ellison was supposed to appear, so the girls had a little free time to kill.

"What should we do?" Ruth asked after the girls had settled in and boredom started to take over.

"Build a bomb," Rose responded.

"Not today," Ruth answered. "I don't want to get my dress dirty."

"We could play cards," Milly suggested. "We haven't played Fairy Rush in awhile."

Rose groaned so everyone in the region could hear her. "We play those stupid games every day! It's boring! We don't ever do anything fun! Elsif, make them do something fun with me!"

Elsif, who had learned how to tune Rose out, was busy writing in her journal. She hadn't realized Rose was talking to her until a shoe flew at her face. "Stop," she chided Rose, while chucking the shoe back at her. "If you're bored, you can journal with me."

"No one likes journaling but you," Milly stated, then grabbed the shoe from Rose. "You need to stop taking my shoes."

"It's fun," Elsif encouraged, resuming her writing.

"Lame!" Rose drawled.

"I'd rather play a game," Ruth added.

"Maybe we could do it another time," Jazzy suggested.

Even though her idea was rejected, Elsif continued to write. Journaling had become a common habit for Elsif in the last couple years. Whether she needed to list out all her favorite Magic Age topics for a future paper, or try to convince herself she wasn't going crazy because she kept seeing certain people everywhere.

"We should talk about the mission," Milly vocalized.

Ruth let out an exasperated breath. "That's all we talk about! Do we have lives anymore without the Hat?"

Milly frowned at Ruth. "What do *you* want to talk about? *Boys*?"

Ruth cheekily beamed in return. "Now that's a wonderful idea Maylee."

"No," Milly grumbled. "And stop calling me the wrong name."

"Do we know any boys?" Jazzy wondered aloud. "I suppose we know Juniper, but we're not allowed to talk about him, right?"

"Right," Elsif muttered, nose deep in her journal.

"Elsif, stop being boring and join us!" Ruth chided.

With a heavy exhale, Elsif took her time tying up her journal and reluctantly joined the conversation. Elsif had a habit of taking the leather ties on the ends of her journal and knotting them in a very intricate way so that she knew if someone (Rose) had untied her journal and read her private thoughts.

"Obviously," Rose interjected. "We should be talking about how we're going to take over Numterram. It's the smallest region so it should be simple."

"I think-" Milly began to recommend another grand idea but Elsif stopped listening because she heard a 'clink' against the window. She shot out of her chair and peered outside to see a familiar face.

"What happened?" Jazzy asked Elsif when she saw her at the window.

"Nothing," Elsif lied through her teeth, as she rushed to the door. "I'm going to get coffee or something, so I'll see you guys later."

Elsif was out the door before anyone could reply. The conversation continued as normal until Milly had a strange realization. "Elsif doesn't like coffee."

"Maybe she wants to try it," Jazzy commented.

"Who cares?" Rose complained. "Let's do something fun."

"Back to the drawing board," Ruth muttered.

*****

"You should really stop throwing stuff at my window," Elsif said, meeting Duke in front of the Inn. "It's getting a little old."

Duke's mouth curved into a smile. "How else am I supposed to get your attention, love?"

"I don't know," Elsif teased, as her fingers fidgeted around her journal that in her hurry she forgot to put down."Maybe knocking?"

"Where's your sense of excitement?"

The pair walked to a nearby field filled with wildflowers that were beginning to bloom in the fresh April air. The sun was on the verge of setting so the sky's colors changed into hues of pink and orange. There was a warm breeze lingering in the atmosphere which felt amazing against the skin after a long winter. In the distance, the snow covered mountains of Animalium could be viewed through the clear sky. It was the perfect moment.

"It's weird to think that we're here because we're trying to track down the Warlock's Hat," Elsif said out of the blue. "It's ridiculous when I say it out loud. We traveled across Fantasma for something that's practically a fairytale. I think I've been living too far out of reality recently."

"Don't say that," Duke said in a tone that was a tad more serious than Elsif expected.

"I'm just saying that maybe after this I need to take a break from adventure," Elsif replied. "Return to some normalcy."

"I wouldn't say traveling to a few different regions is a real adventure," Duke said in the same tone that Elsif was growing to dislike.

"I know it's not," Elsif hastily replied even though the words stung.

"You could experience a real one," Duke suggested, taking Elsif's hand. "Have a life that matters. Go on adventures everyday."

Elsif's heart didn't go into spastic shock like the last time Duke held her hand. Instead she stood in hollow confusion. "What are you talking about?"

"Leave Merlin," Duke proposed, his normal smile returning. "You don't want to live that boring and stuffy life that all Merlin graduates go on to live. Nobody from that school has ever done anything worthwhile."

Elsif slowly withdrew her hand from Duke's reach, as her heart dropped. "I do plenty of worthwhile things with my life."

"Do you?" Duke questioned as if he was mocking Elsif. "You could if you left Merlin. Imagine traveling all over Fantasma and learning about its history firsthand instead of reading it in your books. You'll never regret your life choices again."

Elsif found herself shaking her head and her defenses rising. "Who says I regret my life choices?"

"Why would you be here if you didn't?" Duke asked. "You're looking for Jerry and the Hat to try to fill a void that Merlin will never be able to fill. Merlin raises people who only care about themselves and do whatever they need to to protect their perfect bubble. Being here proves that you don't want to live that privileged, fragile life. You want to see the world and do something that makes life worth living."

Something snapped inside Elsif as color flooded her cheeks and her muscles tensed. "Is that what you do?" Elsif retorted bitterly. "Travel to every region, do whatever you want, with no responsibilities?"

"Your life has been chosen for you since the day you were born," Duke reasoned. "Don't you want to choose what you want to do for yourself? To have freedom for the first time in your life!"

"I have *chosen* every step of my life," Elsif snapped. "I *chose* to be top of my class, I'm *choosing* to go to advanced schooling, I'm *choosing* to be a professor, and I'm *choosing* to become a great historian. That sounds like *choosing* to me."

"You've chosen everything Merlin has wanted you to choose," Duke argued in frustration. "The only thing that you've ever done that wasn't Merlin-approved was sneak out of your chambers and travel around to look for the Hat. You can't tell me those things haven't been a million times better than whatever Merlin homework you've been assigned." Elsif wanted to counter but her mouth was lacking an answer. For a moment she was struck dumb and her mind was overloaded.

Duke continued in a softer and kinder tone. "You may never find the Hat, but this whole adventure hasn't been pointless. It brought us together and it showed you what you really want in life."

"You don't think I can find the Hat?" Elsif asked in disbelief.

"Forget about the Hat," Duke begged. "Forget about Merlin, forget about your family, and come with me."

Elsif's head snapped up. "What?"

"Come with me," Duke repeated, his face serious and his voice earnest. "We'll travel and have our own adventures. We'll figure out what *we* want for our lives, and not be confined by what others think our lives are supposed to be."

"I can't-" Elsif stuttered, not able to complete a sentence. "I have- there's school. I'm going to graduate. My cousins- I have a plan!" Elsif paced, trampling many of the flowers around her. When her mind finally collected her thoughts she turned to face Duke. "I don't even know your name."

"Marry me and I'll tell you whatever you want to know."

Disbelief, shock, then laughter overtook Elsif. "Now I know you're crazy! Is this all some big joke to you? Are you possessed? What is wrong with you!"

"I'm not going to run away with you and *not* marry you," Duke said matter of factly.

Elsif shook her head and took a step back from Duke. "No. No!" She screamed. "I'm eighteen! I'm in school! I have a plan! I'm going to be a professor! I don't know your name!"

"You're really hung up on the name," Duke attempted a joke, as he tried to close the gap between them.

"I don't know how old you are!" Elsif continued to back away. "I don't know anything about you! Your favorite color! If you want kids! Where you're from-"

Elsif stopped in her tracks. "You're from Koronia. Only a person from Koronia would think this proposal is okay."

An uncomfortable expression flashed over Duke before he quickly hid it with a half smile. "Yeah, I'm from Koronia. But that doesn't matter, none of that matters! Elsif, I'm in love with you and I want to spend the rest of my life with you!"

"I don't love you," Elsif said without a second thought. All of her confusion left as she was consumed with anger. "How arrogant are you to think I would abandon everything I have worked for just to be with you? I have a life, a family, and a school that I *do* love and I will never leave."

Duke's expression slowly matched Elsif's enraged face. "I'm not arrogant," he demanded. "I'm just not *scared* to admit what I want. I'm not scared to say how I feel, and I'm not scared to pursue the life that others have deemed unfit for me. I'm not scared of being who I am despite what others may think of me."

Shame was not a feeling that Elsif was expecting to feel when she began the conversation, yet it slammed into her. Elsif had been driven by fear her whole life and now a guy she hardly knew had discovered her dirty little secret.

She was scared of never being successful, so she pushed herself at school. She was scared of her family not accepting her, so she wanted to attend advanced classes. She was scared of not doing anything worthwhile, so she planned to become a great professor. She was scared she wouldn't like her future life, so she threw herself into a treasure hunt so she would have a distraction. She was scared of a lot of things. She was scared of almost everything.

As Elsif pushed away the shame, a new thought emerged. She hated Duke. Hated him for shedding light on her unconscious feelings that she had buried deep.

"I'm not scared of rejecting a man I don't love," Elsif ruthlessly said, not caring about her harsh tone. "I loathe you Duke, or whoever you are. You're a jerk, you're arrogant, and you're too stupid to ever have any real responsibility in your life. I have never met such a foolish idiot and I hope I never have the displeasure of meeting you again."

She turned to leave, but Duke followed her. "Elsif, wait!" He begged, trailing her. "I didn't mean to hurt-"

"Leave me alone!" Elsif yelled and threw the only thing she had in her hands at him. She stormed off and this time Duke didn't follow her. He let her go.

The sun finished setting as Duke watched Elsif leave. She disappeared in the darkness, leaving the swaying flowers in her wake. Duke stood alone in the field, his shoulders slouched, while holding tight onto Elsif's journal.

*****

The girls woke early the next morning so they could be at Kolvig Kernels when it opened, ensuring they wouldn't miss Joseph Ellison.

Milly woke first and appointed herself the responsibility of time management over everyone else. As the girls roused, Milly made sure to keep everyone on a strict schedule. Milly went to wake up Elsif because it was her turn to use the bathroom, but found an empty bed instead.

"Elsif?" Milly called loudly.

"What?" Milly heard a voice behind her. Elsif was sitting on the ground by the window, peering out, fully dressed and ready for the day.

"You're not sleeping," Milly said with confusion.

"I'm not," Elsif confirmed, continuing to look out the window.

Milly shrugged off Elsif's odd behavior and moved Jazzy to the next bathroom slot. After half an hour, all the girls were ready and on their way to meet Jerry. They walked into the restaurant a few minutes after opening and began their exciting day of interrogations and eating popcorn.

Elsif ordered caramel popcorn for herself and plopped down at a table in the corner. Jazzy made polite small talk with an odd-looking woman with a bird on her shoulder. Ruth was eating garlic pepper popcorn and wandering through the restaurant. Milly greeted each person as they walked in and asked if their name was Joseph Ellison. Rose sat at a table with every flavor of popcorn that Kolvig Kernels offered and shoveled it in her face.

Most of the day passed with no Jerry sightings, but at two o'clock everything changed. An older gentleman passed over the threshold of the restaurant and life as the girls knew, would never be the same.

"Are you Joseph Ellison?" Milly questioned the man, like she had questioned all the popcorn patrons.

The older man had white sparse hair, and was hunched over a cane. He had wrinkly grey eyes that were scowling down at Milly. "You're not Sterling Hollow."

"I'm not, sir-" Milly stated, as Jerry walked beyond her and sat down at a table. Milly signaled for the other girls to approach slowly. Unfortunately, Rose rushed to the table first.

Slamming her hands down on the table, Rose yelled, "Tell us what you know Jerry!"

Ruth grabbed Rose and dragged her backwards. "I am so sorry. She's from Mirabilis."

The old man grunted with understanding. But he did not look happy to have five teenage girls hovering over him.

Milly sat down across from Jerry and led the conversation. "Sorry to disturb you, sir, but we were hoping to talk with you for a moment."

"No," the man snapped with a croak.

Ruth and Jazzy shared a concerned look while Milly continued. "We have something important to discuss with you."

"Not interested," he muttered.

Milly glanced behind her with uncertainty but continued, "You *are* Joseph Ellison, right?"

The old man looked up with a glare. "Who's asking?"

"We are," Milly clarified.

"And who's *we*?" The man demanded condescendingly.

Milly gestured to the girls one by one. "That's Jazzy, and these are my cousins Rose, Elsif, and Ruth. I'm Milly."

The man continued to glare. "And how do you know my name?"

"My cousin Elsif found it inscribed in a note from this book we found," Milly explained.

Elsif darted her eyes away as Milly explained her lie to Jerry. Milly didn't know it was a lie, she would be furious if she knew. Milly hated lying. But Elsif had an easier time bending the truth when it saved herself. She was going to admit the truth one day, that's how Elsif justified the lie, but now she knew she'd never have the courage.

"The book was about the Warlock's Hat," Milly continued. "That's why we're here. We were hoping to ask you about the Hat."

"You and all the other idiots."

Elsif rolled her eyes. "So you obviously wrote the idiot's list."

Joseph resumed glaring at the girls, without a response.

"Mr. Ellison," Jazzy piped up in a timid voice. "We're interested in finding the Warlock's Hat and were hoping you could help."

"You're wasting your time," barked Joseph. "And more importantly, *my* time. I came here to eat popcorn and meet with an old colleague. Nothing more, nothing less."

"It's taken us months to find you," Ruth spoke. "You have to talk to us!"

He crossed his arms and grumbled to himself. "Everyone wants to know about that blasted Hat, but no one wants to hear the truth."

"We'll listen," Milly insisted, leaning forward.

"Where have I heard that before?" Joseph said through gritted teeth. "Each month, I meet with people who insist they'll listen to me but when I tell them the truth, they just babble about this and that, and those idiots don't know left from right or up from down. Even my own grandson, Adam, won't listen to reason and insists the Hat is out there somewhere-"

Milly interrupted, "So the Hat is still missing?"

"No!" Joseph snapped. "I'm saying it's gone. Disappeared. Destroyed. I don't know, but it's not out there."

Milly leaned forward. "How can you be sure? Maybe it's just lost? The Hat would really help us right now."

"Yeah, yeah," Joseph shook his head with a scoff. "The Hat would *help* a lot of people. The Hat is better off gone, trust me. It's too powerful. It corrupts people and it will only be used for foul things."

"We won't misuse it," Milly stated firmly. "We want to defeat a potential evil threat, and when we're done with it then we'll hand it over to Merlin Academy. They're more trustworthy than anyone."

"Merlin Academy is the last place I want the Hat," Joseph spat in disgust. "Darn school, darn region! Don't waste your lives searching for the Hat like I've wasted mine. Forget about it."

"You don't know anything about Merlin Academy!" Elsif unexpectedly shouted at Jerry. The girls whirled around to see Elsif red with anger. "You probably don't know a thing about the Hat. You're a bitter old man who likes to make up things like the Hat being with the Dwarves during the Bloodshed age because you're bored and have nothing better to do with your life."

"Elsif calm down-" Ruth began but Elsif kept talking.

"This whole idea was stupid," Elsif stated, shaking her head. "This was so stupid. Of course he doesn't know anything and of course we'll never find the Hat. This is so stupid! I could be writing a paper right now or be reading about the Magic Age! Why are we even here!?"

Jerry shot Elsif a scathing look. "You shouldn't bother reading those fictional books Merlin Academy writes. You're just reading their brainwashed propaganda."

"History isn't propaganda-" Elsif snapped, but was interrupted by Rose shoving her drink in Elsif's face.

"My drink is warm," Rose said casually, as if she wasn't in the middle of a fight between fire and ice.

Elsif pushed the drink out of her face and shot an accusatory finger at Jerry. "You're a lunatic if you think the most prestigious school in all of Fantasma wouldn't have accurate historical records."

"Elsif, my drink!"

Jerry groaned with frustration. "You probably think the Elves were the villains and killed off all the magic people groups and themselves in the Elven Wars."

"Yeah, I do," Elsif said while dodging Rose's drink. "That's basically a perfect summation of the Elven Wars. Obviously- Rose, stop it- there are years of more details but yeah, the Elves were jerks."

"Elsif!" Rose screamed, and Elsif finally gave up and stuck her whole hand in Rose's drink. After ten seconds, Elsif withdrew her hand and faced Jerry once more. "Ah, perfect," Rose said in contentment after a sip.

"Who are you, that you know more than Merlin?" Elsif demanded.

A comical smile slowly grew over Jerry's face. "You have ice magic?"

Elsif's expression changed from anger to confusion. "Yes."

"Life is truly ironic."

The peculiar comment drove Elsif to the edge of her patience. She stormed out of the restaurant and didn't look back. Ruth and Jazzy ran after Elsif, but Milly and Rose stayed behind to continue the conversation.

"Sir," Milly began. "There has to be more to the story than the Hat just being gone. Whatever you have to say, *we'll* listen."

"I don't talk to idiots," Joseph stated flatly.

Rose brought her fist down onto the table. "Yeah *we* might be idiots, but we're *stubborn* idiots! And we'll track you down every other month and we will annoy you to no end until you tell us everything you know. Long live Fantasma!"

Joseph and Rose entered an epic staring contest but eventually Jerry conceded. His expression softened as he said, "Whoever sent you girls should know better than involving a bunch of children in this business."

"No one sent us," said Milly earnestly. She then explained how the girls came across a book by Walten Elian and found his notations in the margins alongside his idiots list. She described how they wanted to meet him because he had a different take on the Hat than every other historian.

"It's a darn shame about the museum," Joseph muttered with a solemn expression. "It was a good museum. Misguided and a puppet to Magicis, but at least they still cared about the integrity of the Hat. Anyways, you haven't explained how you knew my name."

"You wrote it in the book," Milly explained. "My cousin Elsif found it written very small in a corner in the middle of the book."

"I most certainly did not," Jerry grumbled. "But that's beside the point. You girls don't want anything to do with the Hat. I can promise you it will lead to nothing but unwanted consequences. I appreciate your inquisitiveness but I can't in good conscience tell you what I know."

Even though Milly was disappointed with the outcome, she nodded in understanding. "Thank you for your time. If you change your mind and want to share your knowledge about the Hat then you can write us a letter at Merlin, chamber 3718. Thank you again and sorry for bothering you."

Rose didn't want to leave, but Milly grabbed her arm and forced her to leave the poor man alone. As the pair left the restaurant they saw another patron walk past them and up to Jerry. Milly concluded that he was Sterling Hollow, the old colleague Jerry was meeting. Milly selfishly hoped that Joseph wouldn't tell Sterling anything about the Hat either.

Milly and Rose walked back to the inn to find an interesting scene playing out. Elsif was frantically packing her things, Ruth was yelling at her, and Jazzy was sitting on a bed with a long face.

"What's going on?" Milly questioned.

"Besides Elsif going insane!" Ruth exclaimed. "She's also going back to Merlin right now!"

"We're not leaving for another week," Milly told Elsif. "We were going to explore Viverra."

Elsif didn't stop as she answered Milly. "I need to go back to Merlin. I've wasted too much time."

"It's break Elsif!" Ruth pleaded. "There's nothing to do there!"

"David, Monty, and Michael stay during breaks," Elsif shot back. "If you're an advanced student then you need to take the breaks to study! I can't waste my time searching for stupid relics that will never be found!"

"Searching for the Hat isn't a waste of time," Milly argued.

"Yeah," Rose agreed. "The only waste of time here is your face."

Elsif violently threw her clothes into her bag. "It *was* a waste of time! It was stupid! We were never going to find the Hat! It's been missing for 700 years! How could I be so stupid! I hate the Hat! And I hate Duke!"

"Who's Duke?" Ruth questioned.

Elsif froze, as she filled with dread. The secret was out, and Elsif might as well come clean.

"He proposed to me last night," Elsif mumbled, zipping up her bag. Silence overtook the room before an explosion of questions.

"Was he cute?" Ruth asked.

"Why is everyone getting proposed to?" Milly wondered out loud.

"How did you meet him?" Jazzy inquired.

"Where is he?" Rose shouted. "I've been wanting to break someone's nose!"

"Did you say yes?" Milly asked with dread.

"No ring," noted Ruth. "She said no."

"He could be cheap," Rose countered.

"Tell us about him," Jazzy insisted.

Elsif raised her hands to stop the flood of questions. "I don't want to talk about it right now. All I want to do is go back to Merlin."

"Okay," Jazzy said. "Maybe if you feel up to it, then you can tell us about it on the ride back."

"You guys don't need to come," Elsif assured. "You should all stay in Viverra."

Ruth scoffed, "You said you were proposed to and you think we're going to leave you alone?"

Milly started packing her things. "I wouldn't mind getting some extra sailing time in."

Rose grinned. "I've always wanted to see what kind of damage I could do when Merlin was completely empty."

Elsif sighed with exhaustion but also relief. She was relieved that she wouldn't be sitting in the carriage alone with only Duke's words repeating in her head.

*****

Elsif tried to avoid the topic as long as possible, but patience was not a strong suit of the cousins. After twenty-three minutes, Elsif was forced to tell the whole story. Elsif chose to be brutally honest about the whole encounter, from the beginning to the harsh end. It was embarrassing and hard to relive, but afterwards Elsif finally felt relieved.

"You *should* have said yes!" Ruth exclaimed once Elsif finished the story.

"No!" Milly yelled at Ruth. "She really *shouldn't* have!"

"I think it's a *little* romantic," Jazzy mentioned. "He wanted to run away with you."

"He's ugly," Rose said with disgust. "It's not romantic to run away with an ugly guy."

Elsif laughed at herself. "I can't believe it happened."

"What if he was your soulmate?" Ruth speculated. "You had the opportunity to travel Fantasma with your soulmate!"

"He wasn't my soulmate," Elsif said sternly. "Soulmates don't exist."

Ruth's jaw dropped. "How are we related?"

Elsif rolled her eyes. "I want to forget about everything."

"I can hit you over the head," Rose offered.

"Thank you Rose," Elsif replied. "I appreciate it."

The girls laughed and joked the rest of the carriage ride back to Merlin, distracting Elsif from her crazy last few days.

Chapter 14: Stalking Should Not Be A Common Habit

The girls were rarely at Merlin during breaks when there were no games, so they took full advantage of the circumstance. Elsif practically took over the library. She spread her papers, books, and belongings over every table she could find. Milly spent her days at the docks, sailing with every ship that Merlin owned. Jazzy practiced her sewing in empty classrooms that overlooked the gardens. Ruth split her time between her favorite spots in the garden. The two areas that got the most attention were her favorite fountain and the animal enclosure. Rose did nefarious things that should never be talked about.

On one boring evening, Ruth was sent to the dining chambers to retrieve dinner for all the girls. As she was returning with a large tray of food, she ran into Juniper. Literally. Ruth rounded a corner and almost slammed into him.

"What are you doing here?" Accused Ruth while steadying her tray.

Juniper looked down at her with a frown, then stole a roll. He took a bite out of it before Ruth could protest.

"That's Milly's!" Ruth complained. "You owe her a roll!"

"Yeah, I'll get right on that," Juniper muttered. "Your warden didn't give you my message."

Ruth shrugged and darted her eyes away. "I got it."

"You were planning to ignore me then," Juniper said with his usual tone of annoyance. "Real nice."

"I wasn't ignoring you," Ruth corrected. "I was contemplating what to do with the information that Elsif shared with me."

Juniper took another bite of the roll. "You needed a month to contemplate?"

Ruth wasn't sure how to answer so she changed the subject back to her original question. "Why aren't you home? It's April break."

Juniper scoffed at the question. "You obviously never stay during breaks."

Ruth rolled her eyes. "I have a food delivery, so if you don't mind I'll be leaving." She began to walk slowly away, but paused to give Juniper the chance to stop her. When he made no attempt, she whipped around and marched back. "What did you want to tell me?" Ruth demanded.

"Too late," Juniper grumbled, not moving from where he was propped against the wall.

Ruth would have crossed her arms if she didn't have a tray in her hands. "Well I didn't even want to know," Ruth insisted. "I never cared about what you had to say to me and that's why I never asked in the first pla- Melissa just went around that corner."

"What?" Juniper asked, taken aback, while Ruth sprinted past him. "Ruth, wait-" Juniper caught up to Ruth and grabbed her by the arm.

"Hey, watch the food," Ruth snapped, while yanking her arm out of reach from Juniper. "And she's getting away, we have to go!"

Grinding his teeth, Juniper stated in a serious voice, "We shouldn't follow her."

"Why not?" Ruth urged. "It's the perfect coincidence and we can't let that opportunity slip us by!" Anticipation coursed through Ruth's veins and a smile crept onto her mouth as she trailed Melissa and had Juniper at her side once again.

"It's not a coincidence," Juniper said sharply, which made Ruth stop in her tracks.

"What are you talking about?"

Juniper appeared conflicted for a fleeting moment. "Nothing," he blurted, then went in the direction Melissa went.

"So we *are* following her?" Ruth asked, rushing after Juniper to keep up with his long strides.

"If that's what *you* want to do," Juniper stated.

Ruth wanted to throw her arms up in frustration but unfortunately, she still had the tray. "You don't want to follow her? All of a sudden you don't care what Melissa's doing? And what do you mean it's not a coincidence?"

Juniper sighed, obviously annoyed. "Why do you always have so many questions? Just be quiet so we can follow her."

"I do not *always* have questions," Ruth grumbled. "*You're* just *always* so cryptic!"

Juniper ignored the comment as they followed Melissa. Ruth considered Juniper's silence as a win. So she wore a smug expression as they walked.

A few minutes later, the pair saw Melissa walk into a closet in the teachers' wing. She was in there for about three minutes before she strolled out casually.

"That must be where she's hiding the staff," Ruth said with quiet excitement. She ran to the closet and gestured to the door with her head since her hands were still full. "Open it! Open it! Open it!"

"If the Staff is in here, then Melissa is the dumbest thief in Fantasma," Juniper grumbled, as he opened the door.

The closet appeared to be a regular janitor's closet, but Ruth learned from Rose that closets at Merlin could actually be hidden passageways. Juniper and Ruth stepped over the doorstep, but before they could look around, the door slammed behind them.

*****

"Where is our food?" Rose groaned, lying in the middle of the floor in the girls chamber.

"Should someone check on Ruth?" Milly suggested. "She might need help. We asked her to bring a lot of food back."

"Yeah," Elsif agreed while engrossed in a book. "You should go help her."

"Rude," Milly replied

Jazzy put down her sewing. "I could go."

"Fine. I'll go," Elsif said, placing a bookmark in her book. "I've been meaning to swing by the library anyway."

Milly stood up as well. "I'll come too. I want to make sure Ruth grabbed plenty of rolls."

As the pair walked to the dining chambers, Milly thought it was the perfect time to convince Elsif that they needed to continue the treasure hunt for the Hat.

"Hey," Milly said with a forced casual tone. "I was thinking about the Hat the other day and what if-"

"I'm going to stop at the library," Elsif interrupted. "I'll meet you at the dining chambers." Elsif turned around and left before any chatter of the Hat could ensue.

The library was completely vacant as Elsif entered her favorite space. She wandered the shelves and enjoyed the complete freedom of being alone. Next year she would be in advanced classes and she would be learning even more about all the amazing books Merlin had to offer .

She needed to find a book about the mass exitus of the Loquanims from Magicis to Mirabilis and she was hoping her favorite author, Kathleen Beaumon, had written about the topic. Luckily enough, Beaumon had written a number of books on the subject, along with all of Elsif's favorite authors. Walten Elian had written at least a dozen, Ev Gabora had several, Lee Thomp wrote a handful, along with all of Elsif's preferred authors. As Elsif scanned the shelves, she realized she couldn't find a book that *wasn't* written by one of her favorite authors.

Elsif began wandering shelf after shelf searching for an author that wasn't among the couple dozen she knew of, but she couldn't find a single one. Book after book was written by Allwine, Iwan, Diamantopoulos, Perkins, Elian, Gabora, Thomp, Beaumon, Numen, Jule, Kidd, Russ Jones, Soner, Rodlor, Chell, and Fidler.

Even in the sections Elsif never read, like zoology or the magical science section, the authors were the same. Finally Elsif found two new authors, Lyn Venble and Ralph Ritt, in the medicine in magic section. But besides those two new additions, Elsif didn't see any other names. Elsif counted nineteen authors that filled the entire Merlin library.

Elsif wandered aimlessly around the library, not quite sure how to process the new information. On one hand, Merlin wanted the best books written by the best authors. But on the other hand, it felt a little irresponsible not to house a bigger variety. Almost like Merlin was cheating their students out of more ideas-

A pair of mismatched eyes were peering at Elsif through a shelf. When Elsif made eye contact, her thoughts stopped and her mouth gasped. She stumbled backwards into a chair, and fell to the ground. Even though her heart pounded, Elsif sprung to her feet and raced to the other side of the bookshelf, but found no one. There was a sound of scurrying footsteps several shelves away, so Elsif hurried after them. She only caught a glimpse of brown hair escaping through the front door of the library.

There were only two people in the whole Academy that had two different colored eyes, and Elsif didn't like the prospect of either spying on her. She debated following the stalker, when she heard another noise behind her. Elsif grew too nervous and ended up running out of the library to the dining chambers.

She found Milly standing outside of the dining chambers, eating a roll. Elsif stopped running once she saw Milly and staggered slowly up to her, completely out of breath. Once she reached Milly, Elsif leaned over, put her hands on her knees, and took several deep breaths.

"Why were you running?" Milly asked, unimpressed with Elsif's lack of athletic ability.

"Exercise," Elsif said between gasps. "Where's Ruth?"

"She's not here," Milly reported, finishing her roll. "We must have missed her when she was on her way back to the chambers."

Elsif grumbled to herself, "Are you kidding me?"

"Hurry up," Milly said, gesturing to Elsif to follow her. "You took forever and I'm hungry."

"Let me catch my breath, Mallery," Elsif mumbled as she reluctantly followed Milly.

"Not my name," Milly stated to Elsif.

As the girls hiked back to their chambers (Elsif basically hobbling) a forbidden topic was brought up once again.

"I heard there are some pretty large libraries in Vulputate," Milly commented to Elsif. "I'm sure they would have some more information about the Hat. What if we go-"

"Hey!" Elsif exclaimed out of blue, while checking over her shoulder. "Let's talk about this in Rose's dungeon."

Milly shot an inquisitive look at Elsif. "Why?"

"Because," Elsif began stumbling over her words. "We said- uh- that we were going to talk about sensitive subjects down there. But then we didn't. So we should do that now. Right now. If we don't then it's just a waste of space where Rose does dubious activities, and we don't want that."

Milly didn't understand why Elsif kept looking around while they walked, but she was willing to go *anywhere* if Elsif would talk about the Hat. So Milly agreed to wait until they were at Rose's dungeon to further discuss the Hat.

"So Vulputate?" Milly questioned Elsif as soon as her foot stepped off the ladder. "What are your thoughts?"

Even though Elsif was glad to be out of sight of any hostile eyes, she slightly regretted agreeing to Milly's tirade. But she put on a brave face and listened to Milly as she went on forever and ever. It felt like three hours had passed by the time Milly had finished her spiel, but it was probably closer to ten minutes.

"So," Milly said with anticipation. "What do you think?"

"You have fun with all that," Elsif told Milly. "I'm going to be focusing on my classes."

Milly frowned as passion filled her veins. "Come on Elsif! You're our leader! You can't abandon the mission!"

Elsif rolled her eyes. "I don't want to be the leader of anything. You can be the leader now if it'll make you happy."

"Are you serious?" Milly asked earnestly.

"Sure," Elsif teased, and took off her imaginary crown and placed it on Milly's head. "Congratulations, you are the new leader for finding the Hat."

Milly smiled with pride as Elsif climbed back up the ladder and out of Rose's dungeon. They made their way back to their chambers, but when they finally arrived, Ruth was nowhere to be found. The news of Ruth being missing was particularly troubling because the girls were very very hungry.

*****

"It's not going to open." Ruth sat crossed legged on the floor with the tray in her lap, and ate her dinner as she watched Juniper try shoving different things through the lock of the closet door. "Rose locks Elsif in closets all the time by jamming a chair under the doorknob. It's impossible to dislodge the chair from the inside."

Through the peephole of the lock it was apparent that 'someone' had shoved a chair under the handle of the closet so that Juniper and Ruth could not escape. Juniper had been trying relentlessly for the last half hour to stick several long slender items into the peephole to attempt to remove the chair, but all his attempts were unsuccessful.

"At least I'm doing *something*," Juniper grunted, as he jammed a screwdriver into the lock. "You gave up and started eating."

"It's dinner time," Ruth defended. "And I'm hungry. Besides, someone will find us eventually."

Juniper put down the screwdriver for a moment and looked at Ruth. "You're making it even more *obvious* that you don't stay during breaks. No one is around to make sure we're in our chambers or aren't dying somewhere in a closet."

Ruth smiled smugly in response. "My cousins will have noticed I'm missing by now and they'll be looking for their food, and maybe even me."

Juniper shook his head and returned to jamming the screwdriver in the peephole. "Lucky you," he mumbled under his breath.

"You should eat something," Ruth told Juniper.

"I'm busy," Juniper grumbled while looking for another tool. He walked around Ruth in the tight space, and almost tripped over her while he reached for a file on the top shelf. "Can you get out of the way?"

"This closet is three feet wide," Ruth complained. "Where would I go?"

"Fine," Juniper muttered, sticking his next tool in the peephole.

Several moments of silence passed and Ruth didn't enjoy a single second. She was in a unique situation and Ruth knew she had to take advantage of it. This was the perfect time to get answers to her very important questions.

"How many girls have you kissed?" Ruth asked casually.

Juniper's tool froze mid-shove, as he slowly turned towards Ruth. "What?"

Ruth shrugged. "I'm just making conversation."

"Well stop it," Juniper snapped, returning to the door.

"Fine," Ruth mumbled, then added. "Why did you say it wasn't a coincidence? And why are you here for April break? Also what were you going to say to me last month?"

Juniper sighed loudly. "What will it take for you to stop talking?"

Ruth thought for a moment. "Answer one question and I'll be completely silent until we are rescued."

"What is it?" Juniper groaned, while putting down the tool. He waited for the question, still facing the door.

Heart pounding, Ruth knew there was only one question that she truly needed the answer to. "What's your deal with Melissa? Is she your ex or something?"

Something resembling a laugh escaped Juniper's mouth as he shot Ruth a surprised look. "You're kidding right?"

"Uh," Ruth stuttered, feeling self conscious under Juniper's undivided attention. "I don't know. She made you smile at the maze."

"What are you talking about?"

Ruth closed her mouth and regretted her words immediately. But she had already started digging her grave, so she might as well lie in it. "At the maze once I walked away. You and Melissa were talking and you smiled at something she said."

"She *said*," Juniper replied with annoyance. "She'd love to show me exactly what I was looking for in the maze as long as I did her a favor. It was so ridiculous that I laughed at her."

"Oh," Ruth breathed, embarrassment rushing through her. "It just looked like you guys were friendly."

"Do you really think so little of me?" Juniper asked, his tone lighter than it had ever been before.

"No," Ruth said a little too quickly as her heart fluttered. "I mean," she added, as she broke eye contact. "I hardly know you, and I want to know if I'm doing all this just to get back at your ex."

"Melissa is the worst," Juniper insisted. "I've never liked her."

"Why did you hang out with her then?" Ruth questioned, looking back up at Juniper who was still holding her gaze.

Juniper shrugged. "She's from Versario."

"That makes no sense," Ruth stated. "I don't hang out with other people from Bellator."

"It's different," Juniper mumbled, his muscles tensing. Ruth opened her mouth to ask what he meant, but her words dried up when Juniper sat down next to her unexpectedly. He took half a sandwich off of Ruth's tray and began eating.

"At least we won't starve to death," Ruth said with a smile, while grabbing the other half of the sandwich.

They ate in silence for several minutes. Ruth didn't mind being stuck in the small closet, eating next to Juniper. She smiled to herself as she realized that this whole situation was very similar to a date. Sitting together, talking, and eating alone are all the ingredients for a perfect date. In her mind, Ruth was counting it, and claiming she was the first of her cousins to go on an official date. Elsif and Jazzy may have been proposed to, but technically neither of them had been on a date.

"Why are you here during April break?" Juniper asked after some time.

Ruth perked up at Juniper's question. "We were in Viverra to find someone who knows about the Warlock's Hat, but then Elsif was proposed to and it freaked her out so she wanted to come back and study to get her mind off it all. We all decided to come with her."

"Fun," Juniper said with dry sarcasm.

"And why are *you* here for April break?" Ruth said with interest.

Juniper was quiet for a few seconds. Ruth lowered her head and focused on her sandwich, assuming Juniper would never give up his mysteries. But her head snapped up when he finally answered. "Because I'm not allowed to go home."

"What?"

"I'm not allowed to go home," Juniper repeated flatly. "No one from Versario is. Once you accept a position at Merlin then you can't go back. Ever."

Ruth listened intently and absorbed every word that Juniper said. Once he was finished, she didn't have any words to respond but she tried anyway. "That stinks, especially in the winter time. I'd do anything to get away from the cold," Ruth said in a joking tone.

"It's the worst part of Merlin," Juniper agreed.

"Do you miss home?" Ruth asked.

"No," Juniper stated but did not elaborate.

"But you're still allowed to leave Merlin, right?"

"It's complicated," Juniper said. "We're 'encouraged' not to, but the others do. I've never left because I didn't want to give them any reason to kick me out."

Ruth's mouth fell open. "You've *never* left Merlin."

"Not since I was nine."

"Wow," Ruth breathed.

Juniper shifted uncomfortably for a moment then changed the subject. "And no, I don't think it's a coincidence Melissa appeared behind us. She's been acting like a ghost, practically haunting me lately. Everywhere I go, she's lurking around. She probably thinks I know more than I do."

"What do you know?"

Juniper paused. "Not as much as I want."

Though she thought the phrase was odd, Ruth let it go. "You know," she added. "You've answered almost all my questions except one. You haven't told me what you wanted to tell me last month."

"And you're never going to find out," Juniper countered.

"That's what you think," Ruth said with a tease. "You don't understand how crafty I can be."

Juniper's mouth curved up in a smile and Ruth thought a heart attack would erupt in her chest at any moment. Juniper- the secretive and stoic Juniper- had smiled at something *Ruth* had said. She knew her life would never be the same.

Hours passed as Juniper and Ruth sat side by side in the closet, waiting to be rescued. Ruth rattled on for most of the time they were trapped, with Juniper adding short responses. After the pair had eaten all the food, they placed the tray on one of the shelves next to the cleaning supplies.

The plethora of food had Ruth growing sleepy. She closed her eyes and tried to lean her head back but the shelving was extremely uncomfortable. Bracing her neck, Ruth tried to sleep while sitting upright but she knew that she would never fall asleep that way. Suddenly, a devious idea came into her mind. If her head *happened* to fall on Juniper's shoulder while she was *asleep* then that wouldn't be *her* fault. If she could get him to answer almost all her questions *and* smile, then maybe Ruth actually had a chance with him.

Ruth executed her plan slowly and deliberately. Her head tilted slightly to the right and then her body followed the motion of her head until she landed on Juniper. Every muscle in her body froze as she waited for Juniper to shove her off. But he didn't.

If death befell Ruth in that very moment then she wouldn't have even cared. Her life was complete. Her life was perfect. Nothing in life would ever compare to the moment when Ruth matched her breathing precisely to Juniper's. If this wasn't love, then Ruth didn't think love was possible. She would never be able to move on from the feeling that was overflowing inside of her.

At some point Ruth fell asleep, deep and sound. She knew she had fallen fast asleep because she was awoken abruptly to the door opening and Juniper jumping to his feet. Once Ruth realized what was happening, she also shot up to her feet.

As the closet door finally opened, Ruth and Juniper laid eyes on their rescuer, Michael.

"Michael!" Ruth exclaimed as she gave Michael a big hug. "You've saved us."

"Yeah," Michael said while prying Ruth off of him. "Elsif said you never brought them dinner."

"I didn't," Ruth confirmed with enthusiasm as a result of finally being free. "Juniper and I got trapped in the closet by Melissa."

Michael looked at Ruth with a puzzled expression. "I don't know either of those people."

"Well this is Juniper," Ruth said. "And Melissa is-"

Michael interrupted, "I don't really care. I need to get to bed, it's almost midnight."

"Okay," Ruth said, waving to Michael as he left. "Goodnight."

"Your cousins took a little longer than expected," Juniper said sarcastically.

"Yeah," said Ruth. "I thought that Elsif would have scoured the whole school in under thirty minutes- Wait!" A bad thought crept into Ruth's mind and she had to set it right immediately. "I've got to go," she told Juniper. "See you later!"

"Bye," Juniper said as Ruth ran after Michael.

After catching up to Michael, Ruth began to plead. "Michael, please don't tell Elsif about Juniper. She will freak out for no reason, and I will have to hear about how I'm going to ruin the rest of my life. Please, please promise me you won't tell Elsif!"

"Okay," Michael mumbled carelessly.

Ruth sighed with relief. "Thank you Michael, you're a lifesaver."

Light as a feather, Ruth floated back to her chambers with a smile. She ran into Milly on her way back to the girls' wing, and Milly flagged down the rest of the cousins to stop the search for Ruth.

When Ruth told the girls she was trapped in a closet (while not mentioning the mysterious tall man that was with her) they all assumed Rose had something to do with it. Rose- who couldn't deny or affirm the claims- said that Ruth deserved it whether or not she had done the action.

After complaints of going hungry at dinner, and Ruth accusing Melissa of heinous crimes, all the girls went to bed. The rest of April passed and the girls enjoyed their restful break without any more stalking situations or trappings in closets.

Chapter 15: Stupid Conch Shell

Milly walked around Merlin Academy on the last day of April with a storm cloud of defeat over her head. It appeared that no one was interested in searching for the Hat anymore. Elsif wanted to focus on her studies, Ruth said she had other things to do, Jazzy would search *if* everyone else wanted to, and Rose had moved onto another impossible task because the Hat wasn't dangerous enough.

Milly was walking back to her chambers from the library, where she continued to research the Hat. She had invited Elsif to go with her, but Elsif said she was taking a break from the library. There was no elaboration, and Milly didn't care enough to ask.

Back in the chambers, Milly found most of the girls in the living room, but Rose was missing, which was always a cause for concern. But Milly's panic only lasted half a second when a large crashing sound came from her bedroom.

"You guys have to watch her when I'm not around," Milly complained as she went to assess the damage.

"Oh sorry Milly," Jazzy said as she took some muffins out of the oven. The girls never used the oven in the past, so it was a pleasant surprise when Jazzy moved in and they were able to enjoy baked goods regularly.

"I'm in the middle of a research paper on Elven enrollment at Merlin in 3002," Elsif stated, writing at the coffee table.

Ruth was playing the card game, Hermit Spells, on her own while she sang a lullaby about love under her breath.

Milly groaned as she opened the door to see Rose in the middle of a completely rearranged room.

"Looks nice, right?" Rose asked with pride.

"Yeah," Milly said sarcastically. "I love how you stacked our desks on top of each other, so the top one is unusable."

Rose waved off Milly's concern. "It's still usable, you just have to be creative. And now we have more room!"

"Room to do what?" Milly asked.

"To practice our weapon skills!" Rose exclaimed.

"You haven't-" Milly's thought trailed off as she looked to her left and saw Rose's chain whips dangling from a hole in the wall. "*You're* explaining that to the custodial staff."

"The hole isn't even that big!"

Milly saw her dagger contraption sitting on Rose's bed. She snatched it up and strapped it to her right forearm under her shirt. "Don't touch my weapons again," she warned.

*****

May classes started out well and dandy. Normal things were taught and average days were had by all. It seemed like the girls were going to have an uneventful month without any crazy adventures- but little did they know, May was going to be the most preposterous month for one of them.

After the third day of classes, Ruth stomped into the dining chambers and made an announcement. "Life is almost over."

"Is it?" Milly asked dryly.

"May is already here," Ruth stated as she joined the girls in the living room. "That means we have this month, next month with the Summer Games, finals in July, the Felix Finis Ball, and then the end of the school year. Jazzy's first year! Elsif's last year!"

"That's how time works," Milly confirmed.

Rose scowled in her seat. "Time isn't real. It's a lie. It was invented to sell clocks."

"I'd have to agree with that," Elsif replied.

Jazzy smiled fondly while thinking about the last eight months. "It's been a lovely year."

"But it's almost over," Ruth insisted. "And then Elsif will leave us forever!"

Elsif frowned. "I'm still taking classes here and living here. My bed will still be under yours every night."

Ruth sighed solemnly. "It'll be different."

"How?" Elsif questioned. "I'll be in advanced classes but you won't notice a difference. It's not like we ever took classes together in the regular program."

"But we had the potential to," Ruth argued. "And that was comforting."

"Elsif?" Jazzy asked. "When did you decide you wanted to become a history professor?"

"When I was around six or seven," Elsif answered.

"Wow," Jazzy replied. "And you've always wanted that? You've never second guessed?"

"No," Elsif replied quickly without clarifying if she was answering the first or second question.

"I wish I had your decisiveness," Jazzy said. "I'll be graduating next year and I have no idea what I want to do. I always thought I would take the first job that was offered to me in Mellberg. Maybe in the bakery or in the dress shop."

"You'll figure it out when you take advanced classes," Elsif assured.

"I'm going to Captain my own ship," Milly interjected. "Live on the open water and travel the Dextram Sea. There's no better life."

Ruth scoffed, "Maybe except for marrying the love of your life and having two perfect children."

Rose rolled her eyes. "I want to do whatever the opposite of *that* is."

"So," Milly responded. "You want to be a homewrecker and kill people?"

Rose beamed from ear to ear. "Exactly."

"But," Ruth continued, ignoring the side conversation. "Until that happens I'm planning to be an Animalis Curantis."

"Nerd," Elsif muttered.

Ruth gave Elsif a swift punch in her arm. "Shut up."

"Watch your language," Elsif warned as she shoved Ruth.

It was one of those moments when the cousins were reminded that Elsif was not only their friend or cousin, but also their second mother. They were all waiting for the day that Elsif would stop bossing them around, but that day was not coming soon.

An unexpected knock interrupted the conversation. Jazzy answered the door to find Sabrina. "Hi," she greeted. "Sorry for interrupting but I was asked to bring Milly down to the docks."

Milly shot out of her seat and left with Sabrina without a second thought. She never needed an explanation to go to the docks.

"That sounded suspiciously like an execution," said Rose.

Elsif shrugged. "I guess we'll find out later."

"Anyone else a little offended we weren't invited?" Ruth commented. "Even if it *was* an execution, I would have liked to watch."

*****

"I don't know how to tame a kraken!" Milly exclaimed.

"Well we don't need you to tame it, exactly, " Misty explained. "We just need help getting the kraken to stop terrorizing us."

"I'm sure it's not *that* hard," Sabrina assured. "I'll leave you guys to it." She then conveniently walked away right before a giant tentacle splashed everyone within thirty feet of the docks.

Milly regretted not asking Sabrina any questions before coming down to the docks, because now she was in the middle of a death trap. She was now expected to vanquish a hundred-foot monster with no knowledge or prior experience.

"What do you want me to do about it?" Milly questioned.

"You're from Navisia," Misty said as if that explained everything. After Milly continued to look confused, Misty continued. "You're from Navisia and people from Navisia know how to deal with krakens."

"Fifty years ago!" Milly replied pessimistically. Every sailor in Navisia knew the havoc that a kraken brought to the sea. They were giant sea creatures who knew no mercy and had very few rivals. There was a famous pirate tale that said the only way to deal with a kraken was to either tame or kill it, but both were impossible tasks.

According to her family history, Milly's grandfather on her father's side had tamed a kraken. But he had passed several years ago and Milly didn't know anyone else who had even seen a kraken in person. Krakens were, fortunately, rare creatures to come across because they hated humans. Most lived in the Nemoa Ocean near Versario and Monstrum. Sometimes a baby kraken would wander north and get stuck in some currents that trapped it into the Old Yama River, and into the Dextram Sea.

"Yeah," Misty agreed with optimism. "So we're asking all the students from Navisia to help out. You'll be excused from classes until we get the situation under control."

Milly looked around at the empty docks. "Where's everyone else?"

"Um," Misty hesitated. "We're still working on the crew."

"Can I be captain?" Milly asked without hesitation.

Misty thought for a second. "How old are you?"

"Fourteen."

"How about first mate?" Misty offered.

Milly forced herself not to leap for joy. "Deal. Have you, or the other mermaids, tried talking to it?"

"Yes. He's exceptionally rude and none of the mermaids will go back in the water until he's gone."

Misty excused herself and left to find more people for the crew. Milly went down to the ship, so she could prepare for the coming days (or weeks) of sailing. She chose the largest ship that Merlin owned, and hoped it would be strong enough.

Once aboard the ship, Milly began tying loose rope and checking for any rips in the sails. As Milly walked around the ship and prepared for the next day's exertion, the boat began to rock back and forth. Since there had been such little movement from the waves that night, Milly knew she had *company*.

She dashed off the ship and onto the stone dock in hopes that the kraken would have a harder time capsizing something that wasn't floating. On the ground, Milly had a better view of the monstrosity that was lurking beneath the ripples of the water.

"Hey there," Milly spoke softly, walking towards the edge of the deck. "My grandfather told me about you." The ripples began to grow and Milly could make out a faint monster shape deep under the water. Milly crouched down and peered over the dock.

The shape became more distinct as it rose closer to the surface. A large tentacle with a thousand blue scales of different hues was only a dozen feet below Milly. It slowly rose toward the surface and Milly could see the details of the beautiful beast. She was so close to the famous myth that every pirate heard in their childhood. So close to the strong, infamous, and mysterious brute that only the greatest could tame.

"He told me that you weren't that scary of a creature," Milly said as she reached her left arm into the water. "Just misunderstood."

Her hand reached deep into the water and the tentacle rose towards Milly. Stretching her fingers, Milly grazed the giant tentacle and felt the hard scales of the kraken. It was the greatest moment of her life. Well, it was great for three seconds before the tentacle wrapped around Milly's wrist and abruptly pulled her under the water.

Milly was ten feet under when her brain finally registered she was about to die. The tentacle was grasped tightly around her wrist and pulled her down fast. Milly's autopilot turned on and her right arm shot a dagger into her hand, from her contraption

Adrenaline rushed through Milly's body as she slashed the tentacle that held her captive. Blood filled the water and the pressure on Milly's wrist disappeared. Without hesitation, Milly swam as fast as she could to the surface.

Milly gulped the air in big gasps as she grabbed the dock. It took the last of Milly's energy to pull herself out of the water and to safety. As she laid on the dock Milly said between ragged breaths, "Now this is personal."

*****

"That kraken is going to kill me!" Milly exclaimed, soaking wet, as she walked to her room and slammed the door. Ruth, Rose, and Jazzy, who were still awake, exchanged confused glances.

Elsif popped her head out of her room. "What was Milly yelling about?"

"A coven is going to bill her," Rose replied.

"Okay," Elsif said, and went back to bed.

A week went by with no progress on the kraken situation. Misty and the other mermaids had convinced *just* enough people for a functional crew, and they spent every day from sun up to sun down, attempting to control the kraken.

After the first day, the crew unanimously agreed that it would be easier to kill the kraken, but the President sent them a memo that said Merlin was a pro-preservation school. So they had two options: escort the kraken out into the middle of the Dextram Sea or tame the beast.

By day five the crew had sunk two ships, lost a dozen volunteers (as in quit, not died), and Milly had thought about transferring twenty eight times. By the end of the week Milly was filled with hopelessness, dread, and rage. The only bright side of the whole escapade was that the previous student captain dropped out after the second capsizing. Milly was now the leader of the ship that was fighting a losing battle.

After a particularly hard day Milly walked into the chambers completely exhausted and defeated. She slumped down on the couch and began contemplating her life choices.

"How's it going, Mills?" Elsif asked even though she already knew the answer.

"Terrible," Milly complained. "It's a kraken! A KRAKEN! This is a job for professionals! Why are they asking a fourteen year old student! It's because I'm the only one stupid enough to stay on the crew!" After she was tired of yelling, she added in a normal tone, "I would have given up by now too, but the President said that he was going to cancel the Summer Games if the kraken wasn't taken care of. I love the Summer Games!"

"I know you do," Elsif sympathized.

"It could be worse," Ruth interjected. "At least it's not a dragon. Those things destroy everything in their paths."

Milly gritted her teeth as she responded to Ruth, "How about you fight the kraken then?"

"I'll fight it," Rose volunteered. "Let me at 'em!"

Jazzy shook her head with concern. "That sounds dangerous."

"Danger is my middle name," Rose bragged.

Ruth rolled her eyes. "It's Kali."

"Same thing!" Rose insisted.

Milly sighed. "I'm too young to be dealing with this kind of stress. I'm only fourteen."

"I thought you were thirteen?" Elsif questioned.

"My birthday was in September."

"Oh," Elsif said with surprise. "That was a while ago. Happy birthday."

"Thanks," Milly said. "You can give me a tamed kraken for my gift."

Elsif wrinkled her nose. "That's a tad out of my price range."

"I'm doomed," Milly declared. "I am a dishonor to my grandfather."

"Just copy whatever your grandfather did," Ruth stated

"I would," Milly said with sarcasm. "Except for the fact that he had a full crew, had been a captain for over two decades, he had the strongest nets in all of Fantasma, and the stupid conch shell- wait!" Milly jumped to her feet and ran out of the chambers.

She sprinted across the Academy until she arrived at the mail room. Milly asked for a pen and paper so she could write a quick letter to her parents.

Dear Mom and Dad,

I need to tame a kraken so I need Grandpa Han's conch shell. ASAP! I think I saw it last in the attic. Please send it immediately! I am desperate!

Love, thanks,

Milly

Milly sealed her letter and gave it to the mailroom attendant to send immediately. She waited impatiently in the hallway as she waited for her parents to respond. After a few minutes the attendant handed Milly a letter, without a conch shell.

Hi My Darling Mil,

Is this for a school project? Merlin has really advanced their lessons since your father and I went there. It will probably take a while to find the shell but we'll start looking. Besides the kraken assignment, are you enjoying your classes? When will you be home next? I want to make sure we aren't sailing somewhere. I'm assuming you aren't coming home next month because of the Summer Games, at least I hope not because we're sailing to Numterrum then. Anyway, I'll send the conch shell sometime this week.

Love you,

Mom

Milly grabbed more paper and replied.

MOM!

I NEED IT NOW! BEFORE SUNRISE! THIS IS LIFE OR DEATH! THEY WILL CANCEL THE SUMMER GAMES IF I DON'T TAME THIS KRAKEN! SEARCH LIKE YOUR LIFE DEPENDS ON IT BECAUSE MINE DOES!

Love, thanks,

Milly

She brought the letter to the attendant and waited for a response again. This time, nothing came. "We can bring the mail to your room," The attendant told Milly.

Milly crossed her arms. "Fine."

*****

The next morning, Milly woke before the sun, and got ready for another day of kraken wrangling. She crossed her fingers as she approached the front door, hoping to find the magic conch shell. To Milly's overwhelming relief the conch shell had arrived with a note.

Good luck on your school assignment sweetie! -Love, Mom and Dad

Scooping up the item that was going to save her life, Milly bounded for the docks. For the first time since the escapade began, Milly felt hope.

Milly boarded the ship with the few remaining crew members, and they set sail for another day. After half an hour of preparing the ship, Milly began exploring the sea, searching for the kraken. It didn't take long to find him, because they were found first.

The boat shook ominously back and forth for a moment before tentacles rose from the water and wrapped around the vessel. The ship started to *crack* as the tentacles tightened their grip and the crew ran around in complete chaos. It looked like the third capsized ship was about to happen under Milly's control.

Several sailors drew their swords and attacked the tentacles but they could not penetrate the kraken's hard scales. Their swords bounced off the krakens armor or bent under their force. This was the hundredth time that the sailors had tried to fight off the kraken from their ship and the outcome was always the same. The attack was an inconvenience to the kraken at best.

As Milly gripped the steering wheel and tried to stay afloat, she knew it was the time to bring out the conch. "Professor!" She yelled across the ship. Since the monster hunt was technically a school sanctioned activity, the crew needed a teacher to oversee the escapade. "Professor!"

Professor Thompson turned toward Milly. "What!" He yelled frantically. Professor Thompson was from Navisia but he was from the inland, so he wasn't exactly familiar with sailing. Everyone wondered why he was assigned to chaperone instead of one of the sailing teachers, but Milly knew that the sailing teachers knew better.

"I have this conch shell from my grandfather!" Milly yelled to him. "It can help tame the kraken! Can I use it?"

"What does it do?" The professor called back.

"Uh," Milly paused. She wasn't actually sure what the conch shell had to do with taming the kraken. Her grandfather would always add it into his stories here and there, but she couldn't recall what the conch's purpose was. She suddenly feared that the conch shell may have been nothing more than a prop in her grandfather's stories to make the story feel real since he could show the item to Milly as he told the tale.

Milly finally decided to say, "You'll see when I use it!"

Professor Thompson raised one arm and gestured for Milly to do whatever she wanted, then quickly grabbed a nearby pole as another *crack* echoed through the ship.

Milly asked a sailor who was running past her to take the wheel, and she ran to the edge of the ship. She reached into her satchel and pulled out the conch shell. Milly gripped the sides of the conch and raised it to her lips. She blew steady and strong but no noise came out. Trying again and again, Milly didn't understand why nothing was happening. In her grandfather's tales he would always blow the conch shell then the kraken would be tamed.

Lowering the conch shell, Milly realized the conch was an old wives' tale. She went to take back the wheel when she saw all the sailors had stopped running around the ship. The tentacles had sunk back to the water.

"It worked!" Milly said in disbelief. The conch shell must have been only audible to the kraken himself! Milly began jumping in celebration but was knocked off her feet when the boat was once again seized by tentacles and lifted into the air. The tentacle dropped the boat about fifteen feet in the air, and the boat crashed back into the water and capsized. Sailors began falling into the water as parts of the ship broke and sank.

Milly swiftly raised the conch shell to her lips again and blew, but this time she didn't stop until the kraken had swam far away. The ship continued to sink but the lifeboats were still intact so the crew made their way back to shore safely.

"Well, at least it's kind of tame now," Milly said on the docks.

"Why didn't you do that to begin with?" A sailor named Kell asked.

Milly laughed but didn't respond as she hugged her conch shell. In the distance, she could see the kraken splashing around.

Over the next couple days Milly returned to the docks, attempting to communicate with the kraken through the conch shell. The kraken grew less aggressive over time, and stopped all attacks on ships, people, and mermaids.

Milly didn't fully understand how the conch shell worked but continued figuring out the relationship between it and the kraken every day.

On the last day of May, Milly visited the kraken again. She blew the conch and he arrived at the edge of the docks. A small portion of his head rose out of the water, and Milly could see one of his giant eyes looking up at her.

"Are we good now?" Milly asked. "It's been fun but the Summer Games are coming up and I'll need to return to classes in July."

The kraken blinked slowly and stared at Milly.

"I'll be around though," Milly assured. "I'm here almost every day. But I can't be here *all day* every day anymore." The water rippled violently for a second. "I'll come as often as I can."

She knelt down at the edge of the docks like she had done at the beginning of the month. Again she reached her hand into the water, and gently brushed against the kraken's scales.

"You're quite beautiful," Milly complimented as she admired the different shades of blue. A tentacle rose from the water and splashed Milly playfully.

*****

"I did it!" Milly exclaimed, bursting into the chambers. "I tamed the kraken!"

Rose tilted her head. "What's a kraken?"

"The thing I've been taming."

Rose frowned. "That gives me no context."

"The monster you wanted to fight."

"I want to fight a lot of things, Mila."

Milly rolled her eyes while Ruth commented, "I told you that it wasn't going to be that bad."

Milly walked into her room and shut her mouth.

"Hey," Elsif called to Milly in her room. "Do we have a pet kraken now?"

"Kind of," Milly shrugged as she crawled into bed. "I guess."

"Well," Jazzy commented. "If he's your pet then you need to give him a name."

Milly shut her eyes and began to fall asleep. "I don't care. You guys can name him. But make it something fit for a kraken."

"How about," Ruth suggested. "Elwin!"

"Sounds great," Milly mumbled as she rested for the first time in a month. "Goodnight, and please don't talk to me until the Summer Games."

Chapter 16: The Good Old Days

On June 1st, a huge crowd gathered to see the list for the Summer Games. The girls, mostly Milly, fought through the crowd to finally see the anticipated events for the season.

Summer Games Events

Archery   June 2nd

Sword Dueling   June 5th

Magic Dueling   June 7th

Ship Racing   June 10th

Classical ballet   June 13th

Baking   June 15th

Mirabilis Croquet   June 17th

Wyvern Riding   June 19th

Horse Racing   June 22nd

Synchronized Flying   June 24th

Carpet Race   June 28th

"Yes!" Milly pumped the air in anticipation. "There's some good events this year," she said as she began signing up.

Ruth crossed her arms in disappointment. "They still don't have pole climbing."

"They only have pole climbing every three years," A voice commented from behind the girls. Turning around, they saw Juniper lurking behind them.

Elsif leaned over and whispered to Rose. "This guy *seriously* needs to get a life."

"Totally," Rose whispered back and then said loudly. "Elsif thinks you need to get a life."

Ruth turned to Juniper and tried to hide her smile. "There aren't specific schedules for events. The Games Committee decides them at random."

"Then why has pole climbing been held every three years for the last thirty seven years?" Juniper asked.

"A girl can hope," Ruth grumbled.

Milly leaned over to Jazzy. "Where do we stand on the Juniper issue? I can't keep track."

"Um," Jazzy mumbled, trying to remember. "I thought we didn't like him, but I could be wrong."

"We don't," Elsif told the girls bluntly.

"Good to know," Juniper said with heavy sarcasm, and left.

Once Juniper was out of ear shot, Ruth snapped at Elsif, "You don't have to be so mean."

"Excuse me if I don't like jerks," Elsif said. "Especially evil jerks."

"Whatever," Ruth muttered. "Let's not go down this rabbit hole again."

Rose perked up. "What about a rabbit hole?" Rabbit holes were Rose's third favorite type of hole.

After Milly was done signing up, the rest of the girls took turns signing up for various events. Milly signed up for everything except ballet, baking, and croquet. Ruth signed up for archery, horse racing, and the carpet race. Rose signed up for sword dueling, classical ballet, mirabilis croquet, synchronized flying, and the carpet race. Jazzy signed up for baking and the carpet race. Elsif was forced to sign up for the carpet race by Rose and Milly. The first attempt at forging Elsif's name was on wyvern riding, but Ruth and Jazzy outvoted that decision.

"We have someone participating in every event this year," Milly said. "And all of us are doing the Carpet Race!"

"I can't remember the last time Elsif participated in an event," Ruth commented.

Rose laughed. "I can. Three years ago in the Winter Games. She tried Magic Dueling and ended up with a black eye."

"You fought really dirty Rose," Elsif defended.

"It's ironic that you did the worst in Magic Dueling when you're the only one of us who has magic," Milly observed.

"I would have done better if Rose didn't tackle me."

Rose immediately tackled Elsif. "You have to be prepared for anything!"

*****

The Summer Games were even more popular than the Winter Games. People from all over Fantasma came to watch, hundreds of students participated, and the girls became very competitive. On June 19th, Elsif, Jazzy, Ruth, and Rose stood in one of the Merlin's towers to watch Milly compete in the wyvern riding event.

"If no one gets eaten by a wyvern, then I'm suing," Rose stated.

The girls saw Milly in the distance, waiting with the other contestants at the edge of the gardens, for the Vaniians to bring out the wyverns. As they waited, the referees explained the flying course. They would be around fifty feet in the air, start in the gardens, fly out to the Dextram Sea, and then back to the finish line in the gardens.

Wyvern riding was a rare event at Merlin for many reasons. First of all, wyverns were not the most safe or reliable animals. They were somewhere between a small dragon and a large snake, and had the worst qualities of both animals. Another reason for the rarity of the event was that wyverns were only found in Andorae and usually only Vaniians rode them. The Vaniians had a special magical connection with the wyverns that allowed them to ride them peacefully. They normally didn't like to share their animals or anything for that matter with other regions but once in a while Magicis would convince them. The final reason this event didn't come around more often was the last time the school hosted this event, a student ended up in a coma for thirty-three months.

Only five students were participating this year.

Finally the five Vaniians walked up with five wyverns. The Vaniians were tall, with the shortest six feet and the tallest over seven feet, and they had a dark green complexion. There were only a couple dozen Vaniian students at Merlin and only one professor so it wasn't common to see them walking around Merlin, but they were a more common sight than wyverns. The wyverns had long necks, wiry wings, sharp jagged teeth that didn't fit in their mouths, and rough dark green skin.

Milly and the other contestants climbed onto the wyverns and settled into the saddles, while the Vaniians continued to hold onto the creatures. The girls watched Milly tighten her grip on the reins and prepare herself for the race.

"Riders, on your mark," The President of Merlin announced. "Get set." Milly held her breath as she focused on the wyvern's breathing. "Fly!"

The Vaniians let go of the wyverns and complete chaos ensued. All five wyverns shot into the air and began screeching and jerking uncontrollably. Each wyvern completely ignored the designated race course and flew in different directions. Two flew over the water where they bucked off their riders. One wyvern circled over the crowd, while another flew straight up. Milly's wyvern headed to the tower that neighbored where the girls stood.

Milly's wyvern landed on the roof next to the tower and perched for a few minutes. It appeared Milly's wyvern was calming down but suddenly two more wyverns flew over. Both wyverns attacked Milly's wyvern, one with a rider and one without. They snapped their teeth and dived into each other. Milly and the other rider clung for their lives, and it looked like Milly's wyvern was the most aggressive.

"Is no one going to do anything?" Elsif demanded, looking around frantically.

"What could anyone do?" Jazzy asked.

"We attend a magic school!" Elsif shouted. "I'm sure *someone* can do *something*! What did the school think was going to happen when they had students riding these things?"

"Milly needs to jump off and onto the roof," Ruth said with urgency in her voice.

Rose gestured to the Wyvern fight. "She's a little busy!"

"Look," Jazzy pointed at the ground. "Some professors are trying to do something."

Jazzy was right. Several professors were taking out wands and potions and one of them had a rock. But no matter what they said or what they pointed at the wyverns, nothing happened.

"They're idiots!" Ruth yelled in frustration. "Everyone knows that wyverns can only be controlled by Vaniian magic. And Vaniians have to be touching them to control them!"

"No one knows that!" Rose yelled back at Ruth. "Why do *you* know that?"

"Because!" Ruth shouted. "I like animals!"

"Guys!" Elsif snapped. "Milly is about to die! Be quiet!"

Fear washed over Jazzy's face. "You think she's going to die?"

"No," Ruth assured Jazzy. "She'll-" Ruth's words failed to come out when she saw something alarming on the tower nearest Milly. Someone was carrying a large gun and it was pointed straight at Milly. And that someone was Juniper.

"Juniper is going to shoot Milly!" Ruth exclaimed and ran off toward the other tower.

"Of course it's *him*," Elsif groaned as she followed Ruth.

"Oh no," Jazzy muttered as she also ran

"That's a nice gun," Rose said as she joined the others. "Do you think he'll let me borrow it sometime?"

Ruth was the first to arrive at the top of the next tower. She found Juniper halfway out a window with a giant blaster that was aimed towards the warring wyverns. Bernard was standing next to him with his arms crossed and an irritated expression, as if the whole scene was an inconvenience to him.

"Juniper stop!" Ruth screamed. "You're going to hit Milly!"

Juniper only glanced over his shoulder for a second before he returned to his hunt. "I know what I'm doing Ruth," he said as he fired another shot.

Ruth continued to argue with Juniper, when he finally shot one of the wyverns. It was the wyvern that was attacking Milly, who still had a rider. Ruth braced herself to see a deadly crash, but to her surprise, the wyvern grew weak and instead flew to the ground. Once he reached the ground, the wyvern collapsed, and the rider was safe. The blaster was a stunner.

"Good shot," Ruth said sheepishly.

"Thanks for the vote of confidence," Juniper muttered, as he took aim again. Several clicks sounded from the gun, which meant Juniper was out of ammo. "Bernard," he tossed the blaster forcefully towards Bernard. "Reload it. Quickly."

Catching the gun, Bernard rolled his eyes and took out a magazine clip from his back pocket. "I'm adding another twenty to your bill."

"Fine," Juniper spat back. "Whatever. Hurry up!"

The other girls finally arrived at the tower and joined the mayhem. "Why did you stop shooting?" Elsif asked frantically, as she watched Milly barely hanging onto her wyvern.

"Calm down Frosty," Bernard muttered. "We're working on it."

"*I'm* working on it," Juniper corrected with a snap. "*You* need to move faster!"

Sighing, Bernard handed the gun back to Juniper. "This is the last time I'm letting you borrow my stunner."

"Merlin's stunner," Juniper grumbled as he returned to shooting at the two remaining wyverns.

"Oh gosh!" Jazzy exclaimed, covering her face. "Milly almost fell!"

"Hit the wyverns!" Elsif urged.

"What do you think I'm trying to do?" Juniper demanded in annoyance.

Elsif crossed her arms. "Do as much damage to Merlin as possible."

"Let him focus!" Ruth yelled at Elsif.

Raising her hands in surrender, Elsif conceded, and remained quiet. After several more shots, Juniper finally hit Milly's wyvern. Sighs of relief were breathed a moment too soon when the girls saw that instead of Milly's wyvern flying to the ground, he fell onto the roof and rolled several times. Milly was violently knocked off and sprawled onto the rooftop. Her wyvern recovered an ounce of strength and flew to the ground, leaving Milly behind. For a moment, it appeared Milly was going to be fine, but that was before the last wyvern laid eyes on her.

Milly saw the final wyvern dive towards her a half second after everyone in the crowd saw. She had just enough time to shove herself under an awning that was sticking out of the roof. Luckily, the wyvern's head was too big to reach Milly, but its long jagged teeth were inches away from her.

Juniper shoved the blaster into Ruth's hands. "Aim for the wyvern." Before Ruth could ask any questions, Juniper jumped out of the window and onto the rooftop.

"Shoot the blaster!" Elsif screamed.

"I'm trying!" Ruth said as she attempted to raise the blaster, but it was too heavy to aim. With Elsif's help holding up the blaster, Ruth pulled the trigger in the direction of the wyvern.

Juniper continued to climb across the roof towards Milly, as Ruth and Elsif fired off shots that served as a distraction. The wyvern would fly away for a few moments when a shot came near him, but would quickly fly back to terrorize Milly each time.

Once Juniper had reached Milly, he waited behind a roof vent until the wyvern flew away. He quickly rushed to the awning and helped Milly out from under her shelter. Milly put an arm around Juniper's shoulder, and he dragged her back to the tower.

It was a close call but they made it back to the window in the nick of time. Juniper hoisted Milly in first, and Jazzy helped her inside. Ruth and Elsif continued to shoot towards the wyvern, while Juniper climbed inside. Rose slammed the window shut right before the wyvern slammed into the glass.

The wyvern fell backwards onto the roof, and was dazed for a moment. Juniper grabbed the stunner, opened the window again, and had a clear shot. The wyvern was hit with one blast, and flew weakly to the ground.

Juniper dropped the gun and wiped the perspiration from his brow.

"Can I have my stunner back now?" Bernard asked. "And the seventy you owe me."

Rolling his eyes, Juniper handed Bernard the gun and pulled out four silver coins from his pocket. "I owe you thirty."

Bernard snatched the money and hissed, "Are you kidding? You're never going to pay me back."

"Here!" Ruth quickly reached into pocket.

"No," Juniper snapped. "You don't owe him anything."

"His stunner helped save my cousin. So I'll happily pay the man." Ruth pulled out a dennii bill and handed it to Bernard. "Keep the change."

"Actually," Rose interjected. "The extra is so that I can borrow the gun whenever I want."

Bernard took the money, ignored Rose, and walked away.

Juniper shook his head. "The gun isn't even his. If he hadn't stolen it from the weaponry then Merlin would have been able to take down the wyverns without our help."

"Well you're preaching to the choir," Ruth said, putting a hand on her hip. "Because we've all stolen weapons."

"So while all of *you* are enjoying your new toys, *I'm* the one that the professors keep accusing of stealing."

"I guess you have one of those faces," Ruth teased.

Elsif rolled her eyes at Ruth and helped Milly up. "We need to get you to the nurse's chambers."

"I'll help you," Jazzy said while steadying Milly's other side.

Milly winced while the girls propped her up. "Thanks Juniper," she said as the girls took her away.

Juniper nodded in return.

As the girls walked away Rose made an announcement. "We need a rematch. I couldn't tell who won."

*****

Milly was carefully examined and bandaged by the nurses at Merlin while the girls stayed for moral support. She ended up having two cracked ribs, dozens of bruises, and a broken nose. The head nurse assured the girls that despite the numerous injuries, she was positive that Milly would make a full and quick recovery.

"The ribs should be healed in five weeks, the nose in two, and the bruises will fade within a week," the nurse told Elsif while Milly forced herself to drink the disgusting medicine. "She'll need to have plenty of rest for two weeks, take it easy for the following three weeks, then she should be back to normal. But only if she takes the peony elixir twice a day."

"Thank you," Elsif told the nurse as she left to tend to other patients. Turning to Milly, she asked, "Are you sure you don't want your parents to come down?"

"No," Milly insisted. "It's not that bad and they're in Numterram. I don't want them to leave and come all the way here for nothing."

"Okay," Elsif said hesitantly.

"Good thing Juniper was there," Ruth mentioned with a wide smile.

Elsif rolled her eyes. "Yeah, yeah, thanks for bringing it up every five minutes."

"I'm just saying," Ruth argued. "He saved Milly's life."

"I could have saved Milly," Rose boasted to everyone. "It wasn't that impressive."

"Then why didn't you?" Elsif asked.

Rose thought for a few seconds. "I didn't want to break up a perfectly good wyvern fight."

"We are very thankful for Juniper," Jazzy agreed with Ruth. "He was very brave."

"I suppose," Elsif grumbled.

"I TOLD YOU!" Ruth began to chant in a sing-song voice. "I TOLD YOU!"

Elsif covered Ruth's mouth with her hand to stop the annoying noise. "Milly is already suffering enough without your annoying voice."

Ruth smacked Elsif's hand away. "You're the worst."

"Does anyone have playing cards?" Milly interrupted. "I need to win something to lift my spirits."

"Let's play Goblins vs Gryphons!" Rose exclaimed.

Jazzy agreed, "I'll play too."

"I have cards you guys can use," Ruth said. "But I have to go."

"I need to get my homework done," Elsif said. "But I'll finish today so we can play for the rest of break."

Ruth and Elsif walked out of the nurse's chambers together, but split in different directions once they went down the corridor.

"Ruth?" Elsif questioned. "Where are you going?"

"The bathroom," Ruth replied innocently.

Elsif gestured in the direction she was walking. "There's a bathroom in our chambers."

"I don't like that bathroom."

"Okay," Elsif said suspiciously. "Bye then." Elsif continued to walk in the direction of her chambers for a minute, then turned around and stealthily followed Ruth.

Except she wasn't sly because Ruth saw her almost at once. They held eye contact for a moment before Ruth ran in a dead sprint away from Elsif. Left with no other choice, Elsif chased after her.

The girls ran through almost the entire school and outside. Elsif usually wasn't the sprinting type but she was filled with adrenaline, determined to keep her younger cousin out of trouble. Eventually, Ruth outran Elsif near the docks. Elsif looked around desperately, and saw Ruth disappear behind some bushes on the east side of the school.

She quickly realized Ruth was headed to the east side of the gardens. Ruth often talked about how it was the most romantic area of the gardens, and Elsif had a feeling she was going to meet a certain someone there.

Even though she was exhausted, covered in sweat, and breathing hard, Elsif walked in the direction where Ruth disappeared. As she walked on a path that went around Merlin, Elsif decided to take a peak inside the window of her chamber, in case Ruth went back there.

Elsif walked off the perfect white brick path, and trudged through the flawlessly lined foliage of trees and bushes. Her steps left muddy marks in the nice landscape, which made Elsif feel bad, but taking care of Ruth was more important.

When Elsif arrived outside of her chambers, she realized there was a small flaw to her plan. Since they lived on the third floor, Elsif could hardly see inside from the ground.

Looking around, Elsif thought that if she climbed a tree, she may have a better vantage point. Climbing trees wasn't Elsif's favorite activity, but she didn't trek through the mud for nothing. The trees at Merlin were manicured often so the lowest branch was a few inches above Elsif's head. The other problem that Elsif faced was that she had zero upper body strength, because the heaviest thing she lifted on a regular basis was her 'Comprehensive History of the Ancient Age.'

Elsif pulled herself up with all of her strength, but it wasn't enough because her grip slipped and she ended up falling back into the mud. Elsif sat defeated at the base of the tree. Her pants were covered in mud, her shirt was lined with sweat, and her hair was the frizziest it's ever been.

At that moment, Elsif had reached a new low, but unfortunately things were only going to get worse. The man who had proposed to her a few months earlier, just happened to be walking towards her.

Horror coursed through every vein in Elsif's body as she spotted him through the tree line. Elsif had never wanted to see Duke again in her life, but especially not when she was filthy, sweaty, and frizzy!

Moving quickly, Elsif crawled under a nearby bush so Duke wouldn't see her. He walked right past the bush and headed in the direction of her chamber. Dread washed over Elsif as she saw him through the leaves of the bush and saw how clean he looked. After crawling under the bush, she was now covered from head to toe in mud. She had no choice but to live under the bush for the rest of her life, or until Duke left.

But Elsif looked up with terror as she realized Duke wasn't planning on leaving the area, but instead climbed the trellis that led up to her chambers.

What is he doing? Elsif inwardly panicked. Did he want to talk to her? Was he going to trash her chambers in the name of revenge? Was he going to propose to one of her other cousins?

But a worse thought crossed into Elsif's mind. If Duke was caught climbing the walls and said he was trying to visit her, then Elsif could get in trouble. She had already been on the brink of expulsion once, and did not want to risk that happening again.

Duke was already a third of the way up the trellis and even though Elsif would rather die, leaving Merlin would be worse. Against her better judgment and every logical thought in her head, Elsif crawled out from under the bush.

"What are you doing!" Elsif demanded.

Duke froze mid climb and looked behind him. "Hi."

"Hi," Elsif said irritatedly. "Can you get down before you're caught and *I* get in trouble."

"Yeah," Duke said while quickly descending the trellis. "Sorry."

Once Duke was on the ground, Elsif's inward dictionary short circuited. She had nothing to say to him. She didn't want to say anything to him. She couldn't say anything to him. Because as soon as she started talking to him, then she would start thinking about him, and then soon enough Elsif would be in a deep dark hole with all of her feelings and she would never escape.

Elsif kept her mouth shut and forced herself to not let any emotion show on her face.

"How are you doing?" He eventually asked with a half hearted smile.

"Good," Elsif replied coolly.

"I didn't mean to run into you," Duke said apologetically. "I was just returning your journal." He pulled Elsif's diary out of his jacket pocket. "I was going to leave it on your balcony."

Elsif's jaw and heart dropped. She had completely forgotten that she had thrown her diary at Duke in her fit of rage. She hadn't known it was missing. Her innermost thoughts, her private confessions, everything that she didn't dare think was in that book. She would have been mortified if any of her cousins had read it, but the thought of Duke reading her thoughts made Elsif want to tear her clothes and wail in agony.

Elsif stood in shock as Duke extended the journal, and her shame-filled hands took it. Elsif couldn't imagine what Duke must think of her now.

But Elsif urged herself to not care what Duke thought of her. She couldn't care! Her thoughts must not be consumed by the opinions of a stupid random boy. She didn't care that she was covered in dirt, she didn't care what Duke thought of her, and she didn't care what he read in her diary-

Elsif's inner monologue stopped when she saw the tie on her journal. Her complicated knots and binding were exactly the same as when she last saw it. Her security binding was not undone or re-tied. No one had opened her diary. Duke didn't read her journal...

Elsif couldn't believe it. She was in shock in a completely different way. Who has access to someone else's private thoughts and doesn't read them? Elsif had read Ruth's, Rose's, and even peeked at Jazzy's diaries. She was yet to find Milly's, but not for lack of trying. She wanted to know what other people thought about. She had never done it vindictively or shared the information. Elsif just wanted to know others better.

Everything changed for Elsif at that moment, even if she wouldn't know that for years to come.

"Thank you," Elsif said in a softer tone. "How have you been?"

"Good," Duke said. "How are the Summer Games going?"

"Good," Elsif said, then doubled back. "Actually not *that* good. Milly almost died a few days ago, but besides that good."

"What?" Duke asked.

"Well there was a wyvern race that got out of control, magic apparently doesn't work on them, and Bernard stole the blaster from the weaponry," Elsif explained. "And then *technically* Juniper saved her, but it was more of a group effort."

"I bet you did most of the saving," Duke assured, his standard smile appearing.

"I wish," Elsif said, a smile creeping onto her face as well. "But unfortunately Juniper did everything. Ruth's overwhelmingly happy and annoying at the same time. I'm actually trying to find her now, so she doesn't go crawling back to him."

"Did you think that Ruth and Juniper were under the bushes?" Duke asked, trying to hide his laugh. He said it in his charming way that Elsif realized she had missed dearly.

"They could've been," Elsif replied. "Got to check everywhere."

"Naturally," Duke agreed. "Well, I don't want to keep you from finding them."

"Yeah," Elsif said, a little surprised at the disappointment in her tone. "I guess I should go to the gardens-"

"Could I ask you for a favor first?" Duke interrupted.

Elsif slowly nodded her head. She wasn't completely sure she wanted to do something for Duke, but on the other hand, she wasn't quite ready to walk away from him forever. "Sure."

"I wanted to-" Duke paused, then reached into his other pocket and grabbed an envelope. He gave it to Elsif. "I was going to leave this with your journal."

Elsif took the envelope and turned it over in her hands, feeling paper and a small lump. "What's inside?" Elsif finally asked.

He rubbed the back of his neck and looked away from Elsif. "Can you wait to open it until after I leave?"

"Sure," Elsif agreed. Duke began to fidget with his hands since they were now empty. Elsif had the feeling that he was on the edge of saying something else. "Was that the *only* favor?"

"Yes," Duke said then quickly added. "Actually, no. I wanted to ask you something as well."

Elsif couldn't believe it, but it seemed like Duke was actually nervous. In all their time together, Elsif had always been the one wracked with nerves, while Duke was always relaxed and easy-going. She enjoyed seeing the tables turn. "Yes?" Elsif prompted.

"Once in a while," Duke said in a serious tone. "Could you think about me? Not all the time, or anything crazy like that, but- I just can't stand the thought that in a few years you might forget about me."

Elsif didn't know if she could agree. She had been trying to forget about Duke, and she knew it would be painful to remember him for the rest of her life. But inwardly Elsif knew that he would never be able to fully escape her mind.

"I won't forget you, Duke."

"Will," he corrected. "My full name is William, but I prefer Will."

Her heart melted and pulse raced as Elsif repeated her words. "I won't forget you, Will."

He smiled when Elsif said his name. "Only once in a while," he repeated. "Maybe when you meet the guy that finally convinces you to marry him, then you can tell him the hilarious story of an idiot named Will, who tried to convince you to marry him."

"I don't know if that will happen," Elsif admitted. "I don't think any other guy will have the guts to propose to me on the second meeting, and it's the third meeting when people usually start running from me."

"It *was* the third meeting," Will corrected. "And I know some lucky guy will finally convince you, and you'll have a lovely life."

Elsif didn't have a response.

"I should go," Will said. "It was nice to see you, love." He turned and took a few, slow steps.

Dread suddenly filled Elsif. She didn't want him to walk away. She didn't want him to leave her. She didn't want to go back to a stupid life. She didn't want to read a book, write a paper, or even boss around her cousins. Elsif wanted Will to stay.

Conflict raged in Elsif. There were so many different emotions swirling inside her head, and Elsif didn't know what to do. Will was someone she barely knew, but also knew completely at the same time. Elsif didn't even know if there was room for him in her concrete future.

So many different thoughts crossed Elsif's mind, but once she looked down at her journal Elsif had no doubt about her decision.

"Will!" She yelled desperately. He turned around and faced Elsif, several yards away from her. "Do you want to go to the Felix Finis Ball with me?"

Will smiled. "I'd love to."

Elsif breathed a sigh of relief. "It's on July 31st at seven."

"I'll be there," Will confirmed confidently.

"Good," Elsif said breathlessly. "Bye!" She ran away before her overthinking brain could take over. Elsif ran all the way to her chambers, burst through the door, and fell onto the couch. Her heart pumped loudly, as she tried to calm down.

Elsif had never had a date to the Felix Finis Ball, but now she was going with a boy that she was absolutely enamoured with.

After half an hour, the door opened and Elsif was joined by Ruth.

"How's it going?" Ruth asked nervously.

Elsif smiled to herself from the couch. "Good."

"Before you scold me," Ruth warned. "I wish to request amnesty because of Milly's near death experience."

Elsif would have argued if she wasn't so absurdly happy. "Sure, whatever, sounds good."

Ruth eyed Elsif, as she walked into her bedroom. "Okay then. You know you're getting dirt all over the couch."

Elsif didn't care.

*****

The rest of the Summer Games went well with minor incidents. All the girls, except Milly who was extremely upset, participated in the Carpet Race. The teams were Ruth/Jazzy and Elsif/Rose. Elsif and Rose went through several rough patches during the race but finished in one piece, although they did finish dead last. Ruth and Jazzy got in the top fifty out of five hundred teams so that was rather impressive.

The girls spent the rest of July hanging out in the nurse's chambers and trying to find activities for Milly to do while sitting. There was no chatter of boys, or Hats, or Staffs. It was a restful time, as the girls hung out and prepared for the last month of the school year. One of the last moments for all the girls to hang out before Elsif graduated.

Years later the girls would look back on those weeks and wish for them again. They were happy, healthy, and together. They joked, laughed, and spent hours hanging out in the nurse's chambers without a care in the world. Yes, it was truly the good old days.

Chapter 17: New Beginnings Can't Erase A Painful Past

Eleven days went by and Elsif had still not opened Will's letter. She enjoyed holding it in her hands and feeling the small object inside. She liked to imagine and wonder what was inside. Her cousins, who noticed the letter and strange behavior, begged Elsif to open it.

"What if it's ten million little pieces of sand glued together?" Rose suggested.

"What if it's a treasure map?" Milly proposed.

"It's obviously a love letter," Ruth stated.

"It could be solidified milk," Rose went on.

"A key maybe," Milly added. "A key to something important. Like a treasure chest."

"His favorite rock!" Rose exclaimed.

"Whatever it is," Jazzy told Elsif. "I'm sure it will be wonderful."

Elsif rolled her eyes at the ridiculous guesses that she had become accustomed to, and refused to open it until she was good and ready.

"You *know* what it's most likely to be, right?" Ruth asked Elsif.

"A letter?" Elsif asked with sarcasm.

Ruth gave Elsif a telling look. "A ring."

"It's not," Elsif replied flatly.

"He's going to propose, *again*?" Rose questioned. "What is this guy's problem? Does he come from a land with no girls?"

"Stop it," Elsif insisted. She didn't want any negative thoughts thrown at her, so her fairytale imaginations wouldn't end.

"Open it then!" Ruth begged. "I failed a test today and I need good news."

"An engagement is not good news," Milly retorted.

"I'm not engaged!" Elsif yelled.

Jazzy patted Elsif's arm. "I'm sure you aren't."

Elsif sighed. "I suppose I *should* open it soon."

The girls crowded around Elsif and leaned over her in anticipation. With hesitant hands, Elsif slowly tore open the envelope, to find two items inside. A necklace with a locket that had a crystal snowflake on it, and a handwritten note.

"It's beautiful," Elsif said breathlessly as she held the necklace.

"Looks expensive," Ruth said, invading Elsif's personal space to get a better view.

"Looks old," Milly commented as she eyed some discoloration.

"Looks stolen," Rose muttered.

"It looks thoughtful," Jazzy assured.

Elsif clasped the necklace around her neck and admired the beautiful locket. She found the small lip on the side and tried to open it, but it wouldn't budge. "I can't get it open," Elsif said while struggling.

Ruth reached for the locket. "Let me try."

Milly grabbed the locket from Ruth. "I'm stronger."

"But my nails are longer," Ruth argued, trying to steal it back from Milly.

"Guys!" Elsif exclaimed while trying not to be strangled, from the yanking of the chain around her neck.

Milly and Ruth released the locket so Elsif was able to breathe normally, but it only lasted a moment. Rose seized the necklace as soon as the opportunity arose. She pulled at the locket with all her strength.

"You're going to break it," Elsif scolded while snatching the necklace back.

"What does the note say?" Jazzy asked.

Elsif took the note from the envelope and read it silently to herself.

Dear Elsif, I wish you the best in your future endeavors. I hope you remember me once in a while because I'll be thinking of you often. -With love, Will

"Nothing." Elsif smiled as she tucked it into her pocket.

"Boo!" Rose jeered.

"It's a proposal isn't it?" Ruth questioned.

"No," Elsif said with a smirk as she stood up. "Goodnight."

Elsif walked to her room and went to bed as the girls begged her to come back.

*****

Ruth kept a watchful eye as she walked through the gardens. Classes had just ended for the day and Ruth had dinner plans with her cousins in half an hour. So she had a very limited 'sneaking off' window.

Once she was at the entrance of the maze, Ruth casually walked, while smoothing down her clothes, and made sure her hair still had a subtle curl that she had perfected that morning. Her plan was executed flawlessly when she just so happened to bump into Juniper.

"Oh hey," Ruth said offhandedly. "What are you doing here?"

"You know what I'm doing here."

"You're literally here every day looking for Melissa's thing. It's getting pathetic," she teased. "Don't you have any hobbies?"

"Yeah," Juniper said with dry sarcasm. "I'm only in the maze when I'm in between saving people from wyverns."

Ruth laughed as she walked with Juniper through the maze. "We still don't know if Melissa's thing is in the maze area of the gardens. We should try checking other areas. We could start in the east section. There's this one fountain-"

"We saw Melissa disappear in the maze," Juniper interrupted.

"Fine," Ruth huffed. "Do you have a vendetta against fun or something?"

"I don't have time for fun," Juniper argued. "There's a more pressing matter that needs my attention."

"Yeah, yeah," Ruth muttered. "But I'm sure that the fate of Fantasma can wait if you want to take a break once in a while."

Juniper shot a glance at Ruth. "What would that be?"

"Maybe," Ruth smiled. "Off the top of my head, we could go to the east side of the gardens or maybe the Felix Finis Ball?"

"What?" Juniper demanded, caught off guard.

"I'm just giving you options," Ruth defended herself. "*I'll* be going to the ball and *I'll* be having a super fun time."

"I don't do balls," Juniper muttered.

Ruth frowned, but refused to give up. "Okay. While you're alone in the maze, I'll be having the time of my life. Eating, socializing, and dancing with a ton of cute guys. I'm going to have a great night."

Juniper's face clouded over, then relented slightly. "I guess I could stop by."

"Good for you. I *might* see you there," Ruth said enthusiastically. "I'll be having fun with *whomever* asks me to go." Ruth had zero other prospects, but Juniper didn't need to know that minor detail.

Juniper glared, while Ruth grinned back. "You want us to go together?" He asked in his usual emotionless tone that was always mixed with a hint of annoyance. But Ruth was not deterred.

"No," Ruth corrected. "I want *you* to ask *me* to go to the ball with you. And we'll see how I respond."

"Seriously?"

Ruth smiled as she tilted her head.

After a moment of debate Juniper said, "Fine."

"Fine, what?"

"Fine, let's go."

"Go where?"

"The ball," Juniper grumbled, his annoyance growing

"Oh yes, I'm going to the ball," Ruth answered, enjoying herself. "With Elsif at this point unless someone wants to *ask* me."

Juniper gritted his teeth. "Do you want to go to the ball with me?"

"Yes, that would be wonderful," Ruth beamed. "I'll see you at the end of the staircase, at seven."

She bounded back to the school so she could meet her cousins for dinner and so that Juniper didn't have time to change his mind.

*****

It was the last week of classes for the year and Elsif was on her way to the admissions office to sign up for the advanced program. Her plans for the future were full steam ahead, and nothing would stop her from becoming a history professor at Merlin. *Right?*

Elsif shook her head free of the doubts that she had no time for. She may have had a rough year and teetered slightly from her perfectly planned future, but that was all in the past. She was staying at Merlin because that's what she wanted.

The lack of diverse authors at Merlin didn't really bother her. Being scolded for writing other points of views wasn't that big of a deal. Elsif trusted Merlin, and that's all she needed.

"Can I help you?" The impatient voice of Ms. Princey asked from behind her desk.

"Oh yes," Elsif said, snapping back to reality. "I'd like to sign up for advanced classes for teaching. The one year program."

Ms. Princey grabbed a form from a shelf and slid it across the desk. "I'll need your full name, ID number, date, and signature."

Elsif filled out the form quickly so her thoughts wouldn't paralyze her. "Done," she said and slid the paper back to Ms. Princey.

"Approved," Ms. Princey said without looking at the paper, and stamped her seal on the top.

"Thanks," Elsif said, then turned to leave the office, but jumped when she saw the person behind her.

"Hi Frosty," Bernard said mockingly. "Signing up for advanced classes? Sounds fun, I think I'll sign up myself."

"*You're* doing advanced classes?" Elsif questioned. She had never seen Bernard awake during a class in her life.

Bernard shrugged. "Guess so."

Elsif frowned and left the admissions office. But once she was on the other side of the door, she lingered for a moment.

"Whatever is easiest," Elsif heard Bernard say.

"That would be," Ms. Princey paused. "Psychology."

"Perfect," Bernard said.

"I'll need your full name, ID number, date, and signature," Ms. Princey repeated. There was a minute of silence before Elsif heard the word, "Approved."

Elsif left the admissions office full of apprehension as she anticipated another year of being stalked.

*****

It was July 30th and the girls had completed their finals. They celebrated by eating all the best food in the dining chambers while talking about the Felix Finis Ball.

"There's no way that you're going," Elsif commented. "You have to be at least fifteen."

"I turned *sixteen*," Ruth replied. "In January."

"I thought your birthday was in July," Elsif mumbled.

Milly shook her head in disappointment. "When's my birthday?"

Elsif batted her eyelashes at Milly. "I don't think you've shared that with me, Molly."

"Not my name," Milly said. "And how could you not know my birthday? You were there when I was born."

"Gross," Elsif muttered. "I was *not* there. Maybe right outside the door, but I definitely didn't witness your birth."

"What's my birthday?" Rose asked while bouncing in her seat. "I'll give you a hint- I'm a gazillion years old."

"I'm a busy person," Elsif defended herself. "It's hard to remember everything."

"It's not everything!" Milly argued. "We remind you of our birthdays and ages every other week!"

"Well it's obviously not working," Elsif stated. "How about you all wear name tags but instead of your names it's your age and birthday."

"Don't worry Elsif," Jazzy said. "I can help remind you."

"No Jazzy!" Rose exclaimed. "Don't enable her bad behavior."

Ruth brought back the conversation to her original topic. "Guys, I need to know if I should wear my hair up or down!"

"I think I'm going to wear my hair up," Jazzy said. "I always wear my hair down and since this is my first ball I want it to be special."

"If you go up then maybe I should go down," Ruth commented.

"You're like nine," Elsif said exasperated. "You can't go!"

"We literally talked at the ball last year?" Ruth announced. "Don't you remember?"

Elsif didn't remember much about last year's Felix Finis Ball. Her defense mechanisms blocked most of that night. The night that Elsif found out that she and Libi were no longer friends.

She sat alone for most of the evening, wondering where Libi and the others were. Elsif had found herself alone for most of that day. The other girls in her chambers weren't around when she started getting ready for the ball. Then, they arrived separately and disappeared into the crowd shortly into the evening.

Elsif also wasn't sitting next to Libi, which was odd. When their friend group was together, Libi and Elsif were always right next to each other. Inseparable. But when Elsif sat down in the seat next to Libi, a few minutes later Libi moved to the other side of the table. It wasn't a big deal to Elsif, but it was strange. But then several minutes later, the girls began disappearing from the table, until Elsif was alone.

"Hey," a girl named Loretta came up behind Elsif. "You're not with the others on the balcony." It wasn't quite a question but more of a statement to let Elsif know she was missing out.

Elsif had never been good friends with Loretta. Partly because Loretta usually didn't pay attention to Elsif, but the other reason was that Elsif often found Loretta's comments rude or back handed.

"I'm not," Elsif observed with an attempt at a chipper voice. It was difficult to keep a smile on her face in the presence of Loretta, but Elsif tried her best.

Loretta laughed at seemingly nothing, but then bore a serious expression. "I hope there's no hard feelings between us."

Elsif shook her head. "Why would there be?"

"Well because," Loretta said with an obvious tone. "Libi is rooming with me next year."

Any semblance of a smile dropped from Elsif's face. "What?"

"Libi's moving into my room in September," Loretta clarified. "And of course Claudia, Paula, Brookie, and Brynn are also moving to the other rooms in my chambers. But you already knew that, right?"

Elsif's lower lip trembled as she tried to respond in a level voice. "I didn't."

"Oh no," Loretta said with a frown. "I'm sorry. I bet Libi was waiting for the perfect time to tell you."

"Yeah," Elsif mumbled, as her whole world collapsed. All five girls in her chambers, who she had been living with for years, were moving out, and none of them had the decency to tell her.

"But you know," Loretta said with a shrug. "It's nothing personal. These things happen."

"Yeah," Elsif repeated, feeling completely hollow.

"Were you going to the midnight play in the neighboring town after the ball?" Loretta asked.

"I, uh," Elsif hesitated. "Didn't know about it."

"Well I think tickets are sold out," Loretta said with fake disappointment. "So maybe you can join next year. I promise there's hardly anyone going. Just Libi, Jenn, Tinsley, Brynn, Magdalyn, Claudia, Paula, Jessa, Brookie, Britt, and me."

Everyone but me? Elsif thought but instead said, "Sounds fun."

"Yeah," Loretta said, then stood up. "See you later."

She walked away and Elsif watched as she joined Libi and the other girls, who had just walked in from the balcony. The group began laughing about something, and they forgot about Elsif completely.

Elsif got up and walked towards the exit while wiping away her tears. She was so distracted that she didn't see Ruth. "Hey!" Ruth exclaimed. "Look at my dress," she said with a twirl.

"Cute," Elsif said and kept walking.

Ruth followed Elsif. "You hardly looked!"

"Hey," Elsif stopped in her tracks. "I'm moving into your chambers next year."

Ruth's mouth fell wide open. "Really? That's awesome! We're going to have so much fun every night. We can play magic dice and angry elves every night-"

Elsif didn't hear the rest of Ruth's spiel because she left the ball and went to her chambers. She walked into her bedroom and packed all her things. Elsif had lived in that room for ten years, and now she was leaving. Within five minutes the world she had known, had ended.

Thirty minutes into packing, the front door opened and Libi walked into the room. Elsif glanced at her and waited for Libi to talk first. No explanation came, so Elsif tried to save some of her dignity.

"I'm moving into my cousin's chambers next year," Elsif said. At least she could pretend that it was her decision.

Libi didn't look over at Elsif. "Nice." After a few minutes, she left.

That was the last conversation Elsif and Libi had. After ten years of friendship, it was over on a random Saturday night, for no apparent reason.

Elsif had taken all her stuff to her cousin's chambers that night and cleared out her old room. She sorted out her new living arrangements at the housing office before leaving for home.

She went to the carriage drop-off area, and Elsif's bad luck continued, because she ran into her old friends as they waited for a carriage to the next town over.

They were still wearing fancy dresses with hair and makeup, while Elsif wore baggy pants, an old shirt, and tear-stained makeup.

Again, Libi didn't look in Elsif's direction. It didn't take long for their carriage to arrive, and they all shoveled in with screams of laughter and joy. Elsif saw them roll away while she was left alone.

"Elsif," Ruth interrupted Elsif's thoughts, bringing her back to the present. "Don't you remember?"

"Uh," Elsif hesitated. "No, I don't remember."

Chapter 18: Fab Fancy Favorable Felix Finis Ball

Milly and Rose were eating lunch on the day of the Felix Finis Ball. The other three girls were getting ready in the chambers, while the two girls were excluded from all the fun.

"What should we do tonight?" Milly asked.

"We could either blow something up in our room," Rose suggested. "Or sneak into the ball and blow something up there."

Milly continued to eat her food like she was having a normal conversation. "We can't sneak into the party. We'll get in trouble."

"So," Rose said with hope in her heart. "Blowing stuff up is still on the table?"

Milly sighed. "I need to start hanging out with normal people."

Elsif, Ruth, and Jazzy came to join the pair for a quick lunch before returning to their pampering. Elsif was wearing makeup, Ruth had curlers in, and Jazzy had her hair pinned up.

"Milly and I are going to ignite some explosives at the ball in protest of not being able to go," Rose announced. "So beware."

"Aren't you still recovering Milly?" Elsif questioned. "You should take it easy tonight."

Milly shot Elsif a questioning glance. "Rose said she was going to blow up the school and you're worried about my healing process?"

"That was like a month ago," Rose said while rolling her eyes. "She's completely fine. Stop acting like a baby Mertle."

Milly ignored the aggravating comment from Rose. "The nurse said I'm fine as long as I don't do anything too strenuous."

"Well you guys can explode whatever you want," Ruth stated. "As long as you stay far away from the ball. I finally have a date and you two aren't going to ruin that for me."

Elsif turned towards Ruth in horror. "What?"

Ruth widened her eyes to give a false appearance of innocence. "You have a date, so why shouldn't I?"

"Please tell me that it's your cute neighbor," Elsif begged.

"Is it Juniper?" Jazzy asked. Ruth smirked but didn't reply.

Elsif massaged her brow as she felt a tension headache creeping in. "Are you trying to give me a heart attack?"

"We trust him now!" Ruth demanded.

Elsif scoffed. "When, in all of Fantasma, did we start trusting him?"

Ruth crossed her arms. "Well *I* trust him."

"Obviously," Milly muttered.

Ruth gaped. "He saved your life Milly! You of all people should trust him!"

"Calm down," Milly said, overwhelmed by Ruth's volume. "I never said I didn't."

Perking up, Ruth beamed. "So you do?"

"Maybe," Milly remarked. "I'm still weighing the pros and cons."

"I think I might be starting to trust him," Jazzy said then turned to Elsif apologetically. "Sorry, but he was very brave when he rescued Milly."

"Fine," Elsif stated. "But I'd rather we just didn't talk about him."

Rose interjected energetically, "Then let's talk about how it's age discrimination for Milly and I to not be let in the ball!"

"Hey we all had to wait our turns," Ruth snapped. "So you two can wait one more year!"

*****

The Felix Finis Ball was the most famous ball in all of Fantasma. The ballroom at Merlin was only used once a year so that it would remain in pristine condition. All Merlin students who were fifteen and older were invited and outsiders were only allowed if they were the date of one of the students.

The ballroom had high vaulted ceilings with millions of twinkling lights scattered around and a giant chandelier that hung in the center. There were dozens of columns lining each wall, and large decorative windows on the north wall with beautiful curtains. The entrance to the ballroom had a large staircase made of white tree branches that encased different gems, and each person would be announced at the top before they entered the ball. The other side of the ballroom overlooked the gardens, and there was a large balcony that had a staircase that led to the gardens.

The decorations were different every year but they were always exquisite. Hundreds of tables would line the walls and a unique centerpiece would be placed at each one. Ice sculptures, statues, banners, greenery, and flower arrangements would also be scattered throughout the room. In the middle of the ball there was a large dance floor with a prominent fountain placed at the center that changed with the theme of each ball. Around a hundred musical instruments would play for the dance, and around half of them would be accompanied by a person while the others were played by magic.

The girls arrived at the ball and made their way down the staircase one by one, as their names were called.

"Elsif Menzie." Elsif walked down the steps in a traditional light blue ball gown with hints of sparkles in the ruffles. Will met her outside the doors to the ballroom so they could enter together, but he did not give his name to be announced.

"Ruth Walker." Ruth glided down the steps in her soft pink, mermaid style, sleeveless gown that had layers of lace and flowers that traveled down her skirt. She met Juniper at the bottom of the staircase, and they walked into the crowd together.

"Jazzy Thomas." Jazzy stepped forward as her name was called and traveled down the staircase with her simple plum, empire waist dress that she made herself.

The girls had made a deal prior to coming, that the three of them would stick together for the whole night. It was quickly broken.

Ruth met Juniper at the bottom of the staircase, and they quickly disappeared together. Elsif, who did not approve of Ruth's fast getaway, went to retrieve her. Will followed Elsif, and Jazzy sat alone at a table, while she waited for the girls to come back.

The ball quickly filled with people, and Elsif lost sight of Ruth. After several minutes, Elsif gave up her search and walked back to the table with Will. But once she had arrived, Jazzy was gone as well. In the first ten minutes, Elsif had lost both the girls.

"Are they trying to get away from me?" Elsif questioned, as she and Will checked the balcony, but neither Jazzy nor Ruth were found.

"Or me," Will joked. "Maybe my name is on their blacklist next to Juniper's."

"It's not," Elsif assured. "Maybe Duke, but definitely not you."

He laughed. "Yeah, that guy should definitely be on the list. He's an arrogant stupid jerk."

"He wasn't," Elsif said earnestly. "Just a little overzealous. The girl he was with though, she was kind of a stupid jerk, herself."

"She didn't say anything that wasn't warranted."

"But still," Elsif said, trying to piece together the words because she was getting lost in the analogy. "I'm sure she has some regrets about the way she acted and wishes she and Duke could have figured things out instead of saying the things she did."

Silence filled the space between them, which made Elsif nervous. But Will's reply reassured her. "I'm sure Duke has more regrets about that night than she can imagine."

Sublime couldn't begin to describe the way Elsif felt. Everything was perfect. She was finally going to have a good memory associated with the Felix Finis Ball instead of her most dreaded one.

But the moment didn't last forever. It lasted exactly thirty seven seconds before Elsif spotted Ruth and Juniper dancing in the middle of the room. Elsif's blood boiled as she watched Ruth make the worst mistake of her life.

"I'll be right back," Elsif told Will and left to intervene on the dance floor.

Elsif couldn't believe the foolishness of Ruth. Actually she could believe it, because Ruth always lost all her brain cells whenever a boy was in a hundred mile vicinity. Ruth didn't care that he might have Malum's Staff, she didn't care that he was friends with Melissa, and she didn't care that he was only playing games with her!

But instead of causing a horrific scene on the dance floor, Elsif froze on the outskirts. She stopped and watched Ruth dance.

Ruth looked different to Elsif. She looked elegant in her gown, and older, more mature. She no longer looked like a child, but instead stood taller. Even Ruth's mannerisms were different. She wasn't flighty or giggly. She danced with Juniper with a smile on her face. But it wasn't her usual smile, it was something deeper.

As Ruth twirled around the room, she caught sight of Elsif. Her mischievous grin returned for a single second as she flashed Elsif a smirk. Elsif laughed as Ruth returned to her dance with Juniper.

A sad realization came over Elsif as she understood what she had to do. It was time to let Ruth go. Elsif couldn't protect her forever. Ruth was her own person, who had to make her own mistakes. Ruth was growing older, and Elsif couldn't get in the way of that.

As Elsif watched Ruth dance around the room, she knew it was time to take a step back. Elsif would always be right behind Ruth with plenty of advice and backup, but she couldn't stand in her way any longer.

Slowly and reluctantly, Elsif walked away from Ruth and made her way back to Will. He was standing where Elsif left him and he smiled when she returned.

"I thought you were going to stop them?" Will teased, glancing at Ruth and Juniper. The song had just stopped and the pair were walking off the dance floor and towards the balcony.

"No," Elsif said, watching them disappear through the back door. She turned back to Will and asked, "Would you like to dance?"

*****

"I swear," Ruth warned as she and Juniper walked onto the balcony. "If you suggest we go looking in the maze tonight then I'm going to kill you."

Juniper sauntered towards the stairs that lead to the gardens. "Why else would we spend any time together?" He asked dryly.

"You're joking," Ruth replied flatly as she followed him.

Juniper stopped on the stairs and faced Ruth, with a fraction of a smile. "Not at all."

Ruth hit him in the shoulder and continued walking down the stairs. "Are we seriously looking for Melissa's thing again? Is that the only way you can get me alone in the gardens with you?"

"We need to keep looking for it," Juniper confirmed. "But I guess we should check some other areas as well. We haven't thoroughly searched the east side, have we?"

Smirking, Ruth grabbed Juniper's hand and led the way. "I know the perfect place."

Many girls who are like Ruth have a special place that they keep secret from others. Not secret as in location, but secret as in importance. It's a place that means more to them than words could express. A place of serenity and peace that they share with no others. A place where they have dreamt of bringing someone special for their entire lives. Even when they didn't know who that person would be, they knew that they would bring them to this place.

That place was Esmerelda's Fountain for Ruth. In Ruth's first year at Merlin, when she was six, her older cousin, David, showed her the gardens. At some point Ruth had wandered away from him, and stumbled upon Esmerelda. She didn't know how to get back to Merlin so she stayed with the fountain until David found her. Ever since then Ruth came into the garden to visit Esmerelda whenever she wanted some company.

The fountain herself was beautiful. Esmerelda had long, wavy hair with flowers intertwined, and wore a flowy dress that went down to her ankles. She held a jar loosely in her hands, and water poured from it, landing in a small pool around her ankles.

"Do you think I look like her?" Ruth asked. Ruth had always thought that Esmerelda was the prettiest woman in all of Fantasma, and she liked to think that they had similar features.

"No."

Ruth crossed her arms and shot a scowl at Juniper. "So you don't think I'm pretty."

"I didn't say that."

"So you *do* think I'm pretty?" Ruth said with a grin.

Rolling his eyes, Juniper changed the subject. "I'm surprised your supervisor let you attend the ball with me."

"Me too honestly," Ruth said. "But she's got a boyfriend now so that's been distracting her. I guess he's not her official boyfriend yet, but he did propose so I think they're serious."

Juniper flashed a startled expression, which surprised Ruth. "You never mentioned that."

Ruth had filled in Juniper a little on the Will situation, but mostly only gave him the highlights. "Well, that's the reason they were fighting," Ruth explained. "Why do you care?"

Juniper hesitated a moment before he answered. "Doesn't it seem a little convenient? He shows up right after Malum's Staff is stolen and you and your cousins start asking questions."

Ruth didn't understand Juniper's comment. "You think he knows Melissa or something?"

"Think about it," Juniper stated. "He shows up in the middle of your search for the Hat. Elsif also conveniently found the same Joseph Ellison in the book after he came around, even though all of you scoured that book and never saw that name."

Ruth frowned. "You think Will told Elsif the name and then Elsif lied about it? Not likely."

"How did she find it then and no one else?" Juniper continued. "And why would he propose to her so soon after meeting if he wasn't trying to ensure his presence in her life while you all are looking for the Hat?"

Ruth raised an eyebrow. "That's a stretch."

"Last September, right before Melissa stole the Staff she kept talking about this guy," Juniper continued. "A guy that was like a brother to her. She never shared his name but she did bring him up a lot when she talked about stealing Malum's Staff. He was the one trying to convince her to take it. This Will guy could be the same guy."

Ruth thought Juniper was crazy. Insane for thinking up the conspiracy theory. But in the back of her mind, the theory made some sense. "You really think Melissa would go to all those lengths?"

"I'd be shocked if she didn't," Juniper said. "I had a bad feeling when I first saw him and everything you've told me has increased my suspicions."

"Elsif is kind of shy," Ruth mumbled to herself more than saying it to Juniper. "I thought it was a little unbelievable when she eventually told us that she met a guy in Silvia."

"You need to be careful around him," Juniper urged.

Ruth looked up at Juniper who was looking at her with a serious expression. She knew that she should be heeding his words, but all Ruth could think about was the fact that he cared about her. He wanted her to be careful! First, he doesn't deny that she's pretty and now he wants her to be safe. Ruth's heart swelled as she met Juniper's eyes.

"I will," Ruth confirmed. "I promise."

"I don't want you around him without me."

Ruth thought she might pass away from too much love in her heart. "I don't want to be around anyone but you."

A real smile finally crept onto Juniper's face, but it didn't stay there for long because Ruth refused to waste her perfect evening by not kissing the love of her life.

*****

"Oh my," a voice said behind Jazzy.

Jazzy found Melissa standing behind her, with her standard smile plastered on her face. She was wearing a stunning emerald green gown

that complimented her light olive green skin nicely.

"Hello," Jazzy greeted, even though she was unsure if she was supposed to be talking to Melissa. Especially since she might be a potential evil villain, according to the other girls.

"I've never seen you without your cousins before," Melissa drawled.

"Oh," Jazzy replied in a friendly tone. "I'm not related to the girls."

"Really?" Melissa said with shock. "I didn't know they let outsiders into their little club. I suppose you must be the lucky exception.

Jazzy smiled but didn't know how to respond. Luckily Melissa kept talking. "Does the rest of your family go to Merlin?"

"I don't have any living family," Jazzy explained, trying to keep her tone light. "My parents passed away when I was young and I don't have any other family."

"That makes two of us then," Melissa said, taking a seat next to Jazzy. "We had to learn to fend for ourselves."

"I never had to fend for myself," Jazzy replied.

Melissa's expression slowly turned sympathetic. "I used to think that way. But you'll realize one day, family takes care of their own, and no one else. It's best that way, you never know who you truly are until you know your family."

"Well," Jazzy said hesitantly. "We know who we are despite not having family."

"I do, but that's because I found my family."

"What do you mean?" Jazzy asked, her confusion growing. "You said they passed away."

Melissa's smile grew deviously. "Just because they're dead, doesn't mean they can't be found." Jazzy's mouth hung open but couldn't come up with a response to Melissa's riddles. "I was going to take a stroll in the gardens, would you like to join me?" Melissa invited.

"Well." Jazzy looked around for Elsif or Ruth, but she couldn't see either of the girls. Jazzy wanted to keep her promise to stay with the girls, but Melissa's words were echoing inside her. "Sure, I'd love to."

Jazzy and Melissa left the ballroom and strolled into the gardens. They began in the east section and walked towards the back. As they walked through the flower patches, Melissa eventually spoke about the subject that was on Jazzy's mind. "Family is a very important thing."

"I think I'm starting to understand that," Jazzy replied as they crossed the bridge that led to the maze.

"Family gives you a purpose," Melissa explained. "It gives you perspective. For most of my life I thought my family was gone. I was three years old when they brought me to Merlin so I had no memories of them."

"Why didn't you visit home? Or write?"

Melissa looked down at Jazzy with pity in her eyes. "There's a lot you don't know about the world."

Her words stung Jazzy, even though she knew they were true.

"This year was different," Melissa continued. "I found my family, and now I finally know who I am. I'm not alone anymore."

"Just because a person doesn't have a family, doesn't mean they're alone." Jazzy remembered how Mellberg always took care of her, and everyone in the village. If someone needed a job, then a job was found. If a person was sick, they were cared for. If a girl became orphaned, then food and housing were always provided.

"It might appear that way for a while," Melissa warned. "But eventually people are always drawn to their pasts. It's an inevitable fate. But when you don't have a past, that's when you lose perspective. And if you lose perspective, then you lose yourself and are left with nothing."

Jazzy remained silent as she soaked in Melissa's words, which made her feel troubled.

"You don't know *anything* about your family?" Melissa asked. It might have been Jazzy's imagination but she almost heard a hint of desperation in Melissa's tone.

"No. My parents didn't leave much behind."

"Odd," Melissa insisted. "Nothing? You've checked?"

"I mean-" Jazzy felt self conscious. "I live in the same house that my parents did, but I've never found anything from them. It's like they never lived there at all."

"Odd," Melissa repeated.

"How did you find your family?" Jazzy asked hurriedly.

Melissa glanced around before she answered. "I went home. To the region of Scelus in Versario. I met a *friend* who helped me find my mom. She told me everything about me, my family, and my past. She went to Merlin too but was kicked out. Ever since I visited my childhood home, in Moorville, my life has been changed. My perspective is fresh and I have a purpose."

Jazzy desperately took in every word that Melissa shared. It was as if Melissa had found the fountain of youth and Jazzy gravely needed a sip. For the first time, Jazzy realized she was missing something in her life.

"I have to go," Jazzy said suddenly. She turned around and began scurrying haphazardly through the maze.

"Wait!" Melissa called. "I need to show you something!"

But Jazzy had already stopped listening. The only thing she could think about was getting back to Melberg and finding her purpose. Her heart ached and longed for her parents who she had never known. Sorrow filled Jazzy's soul like never before.

There was no doubt that Jazzy was now different. But she didn't change for the better like Melissa had, instead she was now aware that she was all alone in the world. She was no longer the ignorant, happy girl she had once been. Her eyes had been opened to the harsh reality of the world, and would never be able to return to the way things once were.

*****

Milly couldn't find Rose, which wasn't surprising but still concerning. Usually Milly didn't care about Rose's antics but unfortunately she was the only one on Rose watch that night.

She checked all of Rose's favorite places: the dining chambers, the one painting of an old man that Rose strangely liked, the nurse's chambers, several classrooms, the elixir closet, and their chambers.

The only other place Rose liked was the weaponry but that room had been heavily locked up since the weapons had been stolen- Milly scolded herself for being so dumb. Rose couldn't get into the Academy's weaponry but she did have her own personal weaponry.

Milly climbed down in Rose's dungeon and found her pesky younger cousin. "Rose! I've been looking everywhere for you!"

Rose sighed loudly as she sat in the middle of the room while staring longingly at her chain whips. "When we stole these dangerous weapons, I thought we were going to be using them all the time. I thought we'd have secret meetings down here every other day and fight people on the other days. But it turns out we're just a bunch of losers who chase after boys and ignore our cool weapons."

"I'm not chasing after boys," Milly clarified. "But yeah, Elsif and Ruth are losers."

"The weapons are being wasted! We have to do something!"

"Yeah," Milly agreed. "We should probably return them."

"NO!" Rose exclaimed, throwing herself in front of the weapons. "We need to *use* them! It's an injustice for these beautiful weapons to sit on a shelf and collect dust. We need to go stop evil super villains or raid a village. Either one will do!"

Milly thought for a moment before replying, "Maybe we could *train* with the weapons. As a cautionary measure, of course. The whole point in borrowing the weapons was to protect ourselves from Malum's Staff."

"YES!" Rose began cheering and leaping around the small room. "YES! We should practice right now. Put a dagger in each of your hands and I'll start flinging my chain whips at you."

Milly shot two daggers into her hands from her contraption. She had started wearing it around her forearm every day since the kraken incident.

They sparred for a few minutes before they realized the room was too small. There was not enough range of motion to do any real practicing.

"Where else could we go?" Rose asked, putting her whips down.

"We'll have to go off property," Milly commented. "We can't risk the school catching us."

"And it has to be somewhere with plenty of space," Rose said eagerly. "So we can test the full abilities of our weapons."

Milly nodded in agreement. "We'll need more people too. Ruth will definitely join us and Jazzy can be easily convinced. Elsif is the one who will have objections."

"Ruth is Elsif's little puppet," Rose argued. "She'll do whatever Elsif tells her."

"But Ruth likes fighting," Milly countered. "She went to those archery camps when she was younger. I'm sure she'll join us especially if Elsif doesn't specifically tell her not to. But we would have to find some arrows, and I don't know where we would get those."

"So we need to keep it a secret from Elsif?" Rose asked. "I can do that. I keep so many secrets from her. Like how I cut a millimeter of her hair each night and I keep it in a secret bag for later."

"Okay," Milly said, pushing Rose's disturbing comment aside. "We'll figure out logistics later."

*****

Jazzy ran all the way back to the ball, as fireworks went off above her head. As she weaved through the crowded balcony, Jazzy desperately tried to find either Elsif or Ruth. As the fireworks boomed in the sky and the crowd watched from the ground, Jazzy stood helplessly with tears in her eyes.

She longed to go home, to find her past, and to connect with her parents. Jazzy had never felt more alone in her life as she stood in the darkness of the crowd with only moments of light flashing over her.

"Jazzy?" A familiar voice said. Jazzy spun around and saw Ruth walking towards her with Juniper behind her. "What's wrong?"

"Nothing," Jazzy said, trying not to lose control of her tears. "I just need to go home."

"To the chambers?" Ruth asked.

"No," Jazzy said, her voice cracking. "I need to go back home."

"What?" Ruth questioned, having trouble hearing from the sounds of the fireworks.

"I need to-"

"Jazzy?" Elsif walked up from behind Jazzy, with Will beside her. She had seen Jazzy and Ruth from across the balcony and noticed Jazzy's distressed expression. "Are you alright?"

"I need to go home," Jazzy said as sobs overcame her. Elsif wrapped her arms around Jazzy and led her out of the ball.

"I didn't do anything," Ruth clarified as they left.

"Really?" Elsif replied sarcastically. "I thought you socked her in the eye or something."

The girls walked back to their chambers while Juniper and Will walked slowly behind them. An awkward silence passed between the boys as they followed the girls.

Once the girls had arrived at their chambers, Elsif and Ruth took Jazzy inside and had her sit down on the couch. Ruth sat beside her as Elsif grabbed her a glass of water. Juniper and Will stood, lingering in the doorway. Milly and Rose came out of their bedroom when they heard the others arrived.

"Why are there boys in here!" Rose yelled.

"Stop," Elsif chided as she gave Jazzy the water. "Jazzy's upset."

"Probably because there's boys in here!" Rose complained loudly. "Right Jazzy?"

Jazzy was not able to talk since her crying took up all the space in her lungs. Ruth and Elsif sat with Jazzy and tried to comfort her while Milly and Rose stood by helplessly.

"Uh," Milly eventually interrupted. "Should we be doing something?"

Jazzy shook her head sheepishly. "No, I'm fine," she squeaked between sobs.

"We could entertain you," Rose suggested. "Milly come on."

Rose disappeared into her room and came back with a few of Milly's daggers. Rose and Milly then pushed back the adjacent couch and coffee table so they had plenty of room behind Elsif. They began to juggle the daggers between the two of them. Well, juggling was a loose term. It was more of one of them would throw the dagger underhand and the other one would dodge.

While that whole scene played in the background, Elsif asked Jazzy, "Did something happen? I know we both lost you during the ball. Did that upset you?"

"No, I went out to the maze with-" Jazzy's sniffles cut her off before she revealed Melissa's name. But when she composed herself once more, she decided to not share the name after all. "I just started thinking and became upset. I'm sorry for making you girls leave the ball early?"

"You don't have to be sorry," Elsif insisted. "Of course we'd leave for you."

"The ball gets lame if you stay too long anyway," Ruth insisted.

Elsif gently stroked Jazzy's hands. "You said you wanted to go home. Did you mean Mellberg? I thought you wanted to come to Gelida with me for August break. Do you want to go to Mellberg instead?"

Jazzy nodded frantically. "I know it sounds silly but I really miss my parents. I don't know anything about them so I want to go home and try to figure out who they were."

"That's not silly," Elsif assured.

"Sounds fun," Ruth added cheerfully. "You'll be like a detective."

"Do you want us to come with you to Koronia?" Elsif asked.

Jazzy's eyes grew wide. "You'd do that?"

"Duh," Ruth answered. "We'd love to!"

"Yeah, we'll all come," Elsif said and gestured to Milly and Rose. Once Elsif looked behind her and saw the dangerous entertainment the girls were doing, she immediately put a stop to it. "Don't ever do that again," she warned when the girls put down the daggers.

"I think I nicked myself," Milly commented, looking at her hand.

Rose rolled her eyes. "You're a baby. And really bad at dodging daggers."

Milly and Rose put all the furniture back in its place, and then sat across from Jazzy.

"I've always wanted to go to Koronia," Rose said with excitement. "I think they'll be the easiest district to persuade to join my new democracy."

"I'm always up for traveling," Milly said.

"Thank you," Jazzy said earnestly. "I would love the company."

"When do you want to leave?" Elsif asked.

"Now? Tonight? I want to leave as soon as possible."

The girls had almost forgotten that they had two boys in their chambers, until Will chimed into the conversation. "I don't want to impose but I know my way around Koronia, if you could use the help?"

"That would be lovely," Jazzy said before Elsif could interject.

"If he's going," Juniper said, stepping into the discussion. "I'm going."

Elsif shook her head. "I don't think that's a good idea-"

"It's fine," Jazzy insisted. "The more the merrier."

"But," Elsif told Jazzy. "You don't know either of them."

Jazzy shrugged timidly. "You were once a stranger. I'm grateful for anyone that wants to help me."

Elsif wanted to object but decided to concede to Jazzy's wishes. "Okay," Elsif said. "But the last carriages leave Merlin at midnight, so we've got twenty minutes to get down there."

Everyone, but mostly Ruth, began rushing around and packing for their next adventure. Juniper went back to his chambers to grab a few things, and Will's belongings were at an inn in the next town over so the carriage would have to make one small stop.

Before long everyone was ready and the gang walked out to the carriages. Rose and Milly carefully carried their bags because they had snuck several weapons in their luggage and didn't want Elsif to find out.

A carriage was assigned to them and they began to load up their belongings. Elsif was about to board when Will stopped her. "You should arrange for a carriage to pick you guys up in Mellberg. Koronia doesn't have their own carriages."

"We'll send a letter when we're ready," Elsif suggested.

"Koronia's mail system isn't the same as the rest of Fantasma," Will explained. "It'll take longer."

"What do you mean?" Elsif questioned.

"Oh yeah," Jazzy added since she overheard the conversation. "We have a physical mail system, not a magical one. I always arrange all my carriages before I go home."

Elsif was thoroughly shocked by the news, but happy that she learned it there and not when she was stranded in Melberg. Elsif set up the carriage ride for the end of August and also sent a quick letter to her parents explaining her absence for the month.

"Hey," Elsif said to Will as they boarded the carriage. "Are you okay with traveling by carriage? I know you're more of a walker."

"I'll make an exception," Will said with his charming smile.

After they were in the carriage, the only couple left was Ruth and Juniper. Ruth was smiling from ear to ear, overjoyed that Juniper was going to spend the break with her. Juniper kept glancing over his shoulder.

"Are you excited?" Ruth asked in a quiet but chipper tone. "First time traveling since you were nine."

Juniper did another double take over his shoulder. "Let's just get in the carriage before someone sees."

"Who would see?" Ruth questioned.

"I don't know," Juniper admitted as they joined the others in the carriage.

The gang set off for Mellberg right before the strike of midnight.

Chapter 19: Wow, Another Boy, How Original

The girls (plus Juniper and Will) traveled seven hours in the carriage to the village of Mellberg. For every single minute of the ride, Elsif thought she was going to have a mental breakdown.

It was strange for Elsif to watch Will interact with her cousins. Elsif had kept Will as a secret for so long, and she didn't realize it would be so hard to finally share him with the girls. But the younger cousins weren't making it any easier with their odd topics of conversation such as krakens or best explosive materials.

Another reason the carriage ride was torturous for Elsif was because of Juniper's presence. He didn't speak the whole time except a whisper to Ruth here and there. He also had a permanent glare across his face that was mostly directed at Will, so that made Elsif's dislike for him grow even more.

The carriage eventually stopped on a dirt road in front of a small house that stood in the middle of a small village. There were only about twenty five buildings in the whole town, and half of them were the size of the girls' chambers at Merlin.

Jazzy owned a modest two story home. The house had a small living room, kitchen, and bathroom on the first floor, and two small bedrooms on the second floor.

They arrived around seven in the morning and began scouring the residence for clues to Jazzy's past. Jazzy, Elsif, Milly, and Will started with the four storage boxes that Jazzy kept in the spare bedroom, while Ruth, Rose, and Juniper looked through the three bookshelves in the living room.

The house was a little cramped with seven people. There was only one couch and one chair for a small desk, so half the gang had to sit on the floor while they worked. The first day of work was light and mostly organized. Most of the day was spent with Jazzy sharing the memories she had of her mom and her childhood in Mellberg.

As the girls listened they realized there was another side of Jazzy that they hadn't known before. They talked about their family or Merlin a lot, but not about Jazzy's personal life outside of school. It was incredible hearing about how she was raised by the whole village, and not just one family.

After a long day of stories, organizing, and multiple trips into town for food, the sun began to set and the house grew dark.

"Can someone turn the lights on?" Ruth asked.

"Sure," Jazzy said, standing up. But instead of going to a light switch or lamp, she went to her desk drawer and pulled out a couple of candles and matches. "It looks like I only have two."

Confused glances were shared as Will answered what everyone was thinking. "Koronia doesn't use electricity like the rest of Fantasma."

"Why?" Rose demanded. "Do they have something against seeing?"

"There's a magic current in electricity," Will answered. "Koronia doesn't use magic."

Elsif had never heard of magic being in electricity before, but she didn't understand most things that happened in her magical science classes. Magic was a confusing subject, even at Merlin, so she found it best to focus on subjects that were more concrete, like history.

"Maybe we should call it an early night then," Elsif said.

"I agree," Milly agreed. "I didn't sleep at all in the carriage."

"I slept great," Rose announced.

"We were all very aware," Ruth muttered.

The group decided that the boys would sleep in the living room and the girls would divide the two bedrooms upstairs. Once the girls were upstairs, Elsif shut the door that was at the top of the stairs and began threatening Ruth.

"This door will remain shut from sundown until sunrise, and will only open if two other girls are awake," Elsif warned. "You will not have any midnight visits, strolls, or whatever other little ideas are floating around in your head."

Ruth crossed her arms and frowned. "Why am I the only one getting this lecture?"

"I'm pretty sure the rest of us aren't secretly in love with Juniper," Elsif told Ruth.

"Secretly?" Milly muttered.

"You don't know that!" Ruth accused, her anger growing from the snide comment. "I saw Milly sharing some glances with Will!"

"Oh yeah," Milly replied dryly. "There was a lot of tension when I asked him to pass the scissors."

"I saw your hands lingering!" Rose agreed. "Milly and Elsif must duel!"

Elsif ignored Ruth and turned to Jazzy. "Is there a key for this lock?"

"I think so," Jazzy thought. She walked into her bedroom and opened the drawer in her bedside table. She returned with a key a few seconds later. "Here you go."

"Thank you," Elsif said and locked the door. She then strung the key in the chain of her necklace. "No one goes in or out of this door without me knowing."

"What if we have to use the bathroom?" Milly asked.

"Then you'll wake me up," Elsif answered. "And depending on the person, I will accompany them to the bathroom and back."

"I'd like to request an amendment to that rule," Rose announced. "If you're making us be escorted to the bathroom then you must also give us piggy back rides."

Ruth scoffed in disbelief. "Are you serious? Do you not have an ounce of trust for me?"

"Do I trust you, yes," Elsif confirmed. "Do I trust Juniper, no. Do I trust your underdeveloped brain, no. Do I trust your decision making skills while you are love sick for that stupid guy, no."

"You're two years older than me," Ruth argued. "You have the same underdeveloped brain."

"Physically I might only be two years older than you," Elsif countered. "But mentally I've aged thirty years from taking care of all of you my entire life."

Ruth groaned, "You're insane."

"She is," Rose confirmed. "I should know."

"Now we just need to divide up to sleep," Elsif said. "I'll be sleeping next to Ruth."

Ruth rolled her eyes. "You better watch out. You might wake up smothered."

"I call not sleeping next to Elsif," Rose said.

"I'll sacrifice myself and share a bed with Rose," Milly said. "I'm semi used to her strange sleeping habits."

"I think," Jazzy began. "I'd like to join Ruth and Elsif."

The girls went to their respective bedrooms for the night. Elsif, Ruth, and Jazzy in Jazzy's bedroom to the left, and Milly and Rose in the guest bedroom to the right. The familiar sleeping arrangements brought on a pleasant night for that first sleep, but that could not be said for the rest of the trip.

*****

A week went by with no luck with Jazzy's parents. The gang went through every photo, note, book, box, and item in Jazzy's house but it didn't seem like Jazzy's parents left a single personal item. It was as if they had never existed.

"Some of us could start asking the other villagers about Jazzy's parents," Elsif suggested. She was currently sitting on the floor with all of Jazzy's books, trying to piece together some common interests that Jazzy's parents may have had. But the few books in the house were very generic and didn't create any patterns of interest.

"I'll go!" Rose bounded to her feet. "And Milly will come too!"

"I'm busy," Milly called from the kitchen.

"*You are not busy!*" Rose insisted in her most suspicious tone.

Milly realized what Rose was not-so-slyly communicating and came into the living room. "Oh yes," she said in a forcefully casual way. "I'm not busy. I can go."

"Let me run upstairs real quick and we'll go!" Rose exclaimed and ran up the stairs.

Elsif ignored her cousin's odd behavior, because frankly, not acting weird would be the real cause for suspicion. "You two should take a third?" Elsif said and looked around to see who was available. "Will, do you want to go with them?"

"Sure," Will said energetically.

Ruth and Juniper exchanged a quick, concerned glance.

"We're fine," Milly insisted, her eyes growing wide as she looked from the stairs to Elsif.

"You'll talk to more people with three," Elsif countered. "And Will's good at talking with people. You'll need someone normal if Rose is going."

"I'm normal enough," Milly claimed.

"Not enough to counteract Rose."

Rose glided down the banister with a giant backpack and replied, "Who is trying to counteract me? I'll conquer them in a mighty battle!"

"They want Will to come with us," Milly told Rose with concern.

"NO!" Rose yelled. "Milly and I want to go alone!"

"Stop it," Elsif warned with her annoyingly stern face that her cousins always hated. "He's going."

Rose crossed her arms while Milly reluctantly said, "Okay."

Will stood up to join the girls but Juniper also jumped to his feet. "I'll go too," he said. Before anyone could argue, Juniper walked out the door.

Rose shrugged, then gestured at the door. "I'd rather have him," she then pointed an accusatory finger at Will, "than him."

Elsif gave an encouraging smile to Will as he followed the girls and Juniper out the door. "Grab some food while you're in town!" Elsif yelled after the group.

After several yards, Rose took the lead and began trekking in the wrong direction. "We're going to the woods," she stated with no further explanation.

"Why?" Will asked with hesitation.

"Because there aren't any people there," Rose said matter of factly.

"Isn't that the opposite of what we're supposed to be doing?"

Rose skipped along the path. "It's the opposite of the supposed doing but not the opposite of the actual doing. So all is fine."

"What?" Milly asked.

"We are going to the woods!" Rose announced loudly. "No more questions! No more detours!"

"But *why* are we going to the woods?" Will questioned.

Rose groaned impatiently. "To get away from people! Haven't you been listening?"

Will had no idea what was going on. "Why do we need to get away from people?"

"So our weapons," Rose said, gesturing to her backpack. "Don't accidentally kill anyone. Duh!"

"Why do we have weapons?"

Rose was beginning to lose all her patience with Will. "To play with," she answered through gritted teeth.

Milly placed a hand on Rose's shoulder in an attempt to calm her down. "We want to practice with them," Milly explained.

"Understand now?" Rose questioned Will. When he slowly nodded, Rose continued, "Amazing, now let's go."

The girls continued to walk while Will turned to Juniper. "We shouldn't be going along with this."

Juniper ignored Will and kept following the girls.

"Point for Juniper," Rose declared. "Will, if you want a point then you can't tell Elsif. She's lame and doesn't know how to have a good time."

"We shouldn't be keeping secrets from each other," Will stated.

Juniper scoffed under his breath while Rose whirled around to face Will. "Then become mute for the next twenty-seven years. Or only speak every third word so Elsif won't understand you. I don't care what you have to do but you better not rat us out."

"Fine," Will said, raising his hands in defeat. "Obviously I'm outnumbered so let's go to the woods."

*****

Jazzy sifted through a pile of pictures. There were four. Only four total pictures were found in her home. Three were pictures that Jazzy had collected throughout her life. One picture was from her parents.

The first picture was taken when she was around twelve years old. In the photo she was covered with mud from the creek because she had tried to jump across it unsuccessfully. Her older friend, Lauria, had found Jazzy's appearance so amusing that she borrowed her uncle's camera and took a picture of Jazzy. A couple years later Lauria gifted Jazzy the photo since she was moving to another village in Koronia and getting married.

The second photo was of a Mellberg sunset that Jazzy had bought in the market when she was around fourteen. Her house was in the left corner and Jazzy loved how the orange and pink sky settled behind it. Jazzy used to look at it often but she forgot about it in recent years.

The third photo was another picture of Jazzy that was taken only a few months before she left for Merlin. Mrs. Thompson, Jazzy's neighbor, had insisted that she needed a portrait of herself. At the time Jazzy thought it was an odd request but Mrs. Thompson was one of the lovely ladies that helped raise Jazzy, so she obliged. Later she found out that Mrs. Thompson's intention was for Jazzy to give the portrait to Kent, the Baker's son who later proposed to her.

And the last and final photo that Jazzy owned was from her parents. The only photo that Jazzy had not acquired herself. One of Jazzy's most personal and puzzling possessions. It was a photo of the clouds. Big white fluffy clouds. That was it. No photos of her parents. No photos of herself as a baby. Just the clouds. The only thing that Jazzy had from her parents.

Jazzy pushed the photos aside as sorrow filled her heart. Her parents had left no trace for her to find. It was as if they didn't want to be known by their own daughter. Loneliness once again overtook her.

Ruth and Elsif were upstairs in Jazzy's bedroom going through her drawers and shelves to see if there was anything interesting.

"What do you think the guys are doing?" Ruth asked nonchalantly for the seventh time.

"Talking to people," Elsif repeated. "Or they should be."

"Rose is going to embarrass us," Ruth stated with agitation. "We shouldn't have let her out of our sight."

Elsif rolled her eyes as she folded Jazzy's blouses. "Rose has already embarrassed me in front of Will more times than I can count. It's just a part of life and we have to accept that."

"Why do you think Juniper and Will came?"

"Because Mellberg is a cool place," Elsif replied with sarcasm.

Ruth didn't appreciate the joke and let Elsif know by throwing a pillow at her head. "Be serious! I can't believe Juniper came."

"I wish he hadn't," Elsif snapped. "I wish neither of them came."

"Boohoo," Ruth mocked. "A boy wants to spend time with you. You poor thing."

"I'm not obsessed with the male species like you," Elsif retorted. "I don't feel the need to leave home and marry the first man that can stand to be with me for more than five minutes."

"You're so defensive," Ruth said bitterly. "You can insult me all you want, but I don't care. I'm marrying Juniper the first chance I get."

Elsif stopped mid-fold and gave Ruth a cold hard stare. "You are *not* marrying him."

Ruth smiled in return. "Yes, I am. Then me and you can go on double dates while we leave all the single losers at home."

"I would rather Rose stab me a thousand times with her chain whips than ever go on a date with you."

"You'd be so lucky," Ruth teased. "I'm so out of your league."

*****

"I don't think that's how you're supposed to use them!" Will yelled as he dodged out of the way of Rose's fatal swing.

"It slipped!" Rose shouted back as she regained her grip on her chain whips.

Milly winced at the narrow miss. "Maybe Elsif was right-"

"She's fine," Juniper interjected beside Milly. "Will just doesn't know what he's doing."

"I don't know," Milly said as she covered her eyes as Rose almost hit Will again. "Maybe we should switch to swords."

Will nodded. "Yeah, let's do anything but this." He fell to the ground as the whip flew above his head.

"Fine," Rose grumbled as she traded her whips for a sword.

Milly quickly grabbed the weapon out of Rose's hands. "You should take a break. I'll duel Will."

Milly gave the sword to Will, and picked up her own blade, *Tuccley*. "How are you with a blade?"

"Well," Will paused. "I'm more of a throw random object in defense kind of guy, but I'll try it out."

Milly and Will raised their swords and began their duel. Milly took it easy on Will as she slowly slashed and parried her weapon. Will was a little sloppy at first but picked up the rhythm quickly. After a few lunges and blocks, Juniper became impatient and interrupted the duel.

"My turn," Juniper stated, walking between the two.

"Great," Will muttered.

Juniper ignored Will and took Milly's sword.

"Be careful," Milly warned, letting go of her weapon reluctantly. "That one's my favorite."

"This will be quick," Juniper assured.

Will rolled his eyes and faced Juniper's coming attack. Rose and Milly stood on the sidelines and watched, their faces quickly turned from entertained to horror. Before Will could blink, Juniper lunged at Will's chest. Will jumped out of the way but wasn't quick enough and Juniper slashed his arm.

"What was that?" Will demanded as he dropped his sword and clutched his upper arm.

"You should have blocked that," Juniper stated bluntly.

"I've got bandages," Milly said, reaching for her bag. "I anticipated Rose doing a lot of damage."

Rose crossed her arms. "You have no faith in me!"

Milly rolled her eyes as she helped bandage Will's arm. "Maybe we should call it a day. We can head into town to talk to a couple people so we aren't complete liars when we return home."

"Fine with me," Will mumbled as he eyed Juniper.

"Whatever," Juniper said.

"Let's continue the fun," Rose said as she bounded towards the village.

*****

Rose, Milly, Juniper, and Will walked back to Jazzy's house in the late afternoon and intentionally 'forgot' to mention their previous activities. Everyone except Will, who broke as soon as Elsif noticed the red stain on Will's sleeve.

"Rose can be persuasive," Elsif said. "Most people aren't able to resist her powers of coercion."

"I tried," Will insisted.

Elsif laughed. "Well I'm sorry Rose nicked you."

"Actually," Will admitted. "It happened when Juniper and I dueled."

Elsif's eyes grew wide. "Juniper stabbed you?"

"It's just a scratch," Will assured.

As Elsif and Will continued to discuss the events of that day, Ruth and Juniper discussed the same subject in the kitchen.

"You *had* to injure him?" Ruth questioned. "Elsif is going to hate you forever now."

"I don't care," Juniper stated. "I know how to handle Melissa and her friends. You need to intimidate them."

"Yeah," Ruth said wryly. "I'm sure the papercut you gave him caused him a real scare."

"What did you want me to do? Cut off his head?"

"Just saying," Ruth replied. "If you wanted to intimidate someone, then maybe they shouldn't walk away so easily."

"Weren't you just lecturing me about injuring him?"

"I'm a complicated person," Ruth said with a smile. "Keep up."

Milly and Rose were in the guest bedroom, reenacting the epic Juniper and Will fight.

"Juniper did not have Will in a choke hold," Milly complained.

"Quiet you," Rose said as she adjusted her grip. "I'm improvising."

Jazzy was alone in her old bedroom. Even though technically, it was still her bedroom, it didn't feel like hers anymore. Her home didn't feel like hers anymore. It was colder than Jazzy remembered and impersonal.

Anyone could walk in and have no idea who she was. Jazzy had unconsciously left the house like her parents had. No personal touches or mementos to help point someone to her. She hadn't realized how abnormal that way of living was until she experienced a real family.

Merlin had seemed like the perfect home and Jazzy had loved her first year there, but now she was dreading going back. She knew that she would feel lonely at Merlin this coming year, and she didn't know how to stop the feeling. The dreadful loneliness was consuming her, drowning her, and she didn't know how to swim out.

She heard laughter from other parts of the house. Jazzy couldn't tell who it was, but it could have been anyone. Everyone had someone. Everyone but her. They were happy and content, while Jazzy would never be again.

Of course they should be, Jazzy thought to herself. *They all have families. None of them are alone.*

Jazzy began to wish she had never gone to Merlin, never met any of the girls. Before she had no idea what a family was meant to be. But now she knew, and she would never be able to erase those ideal ideas.

A ruckus of noise came from Jazzy's window, which startled her out of her thoughts. She stood up and looked over to see the window opening on its own. Before she knew it, a man was climbing into her bedroom.

"Hello," Jazzy greeted as she watched the man stand up and brush off his clothes. He looked up and met Jazzy's gaze with blood-shot eyes. He stood in her room casually, like it was Jazzy who was intruding.

The stranger was young, not much older than Jazzy. He had messy, dark hair and appeared like he hadn't slept in days. He didn't speak to Jazzy nor broke eye contact. Through the red veins Jazzy could see that his eyes were grey.

"Did you," Jazzy asked slowly. "Climb the tree? The window is awfully high up. You could have fallen and gotten hurt."

The man's head tilted slightly. "You should be concerned about other things besides an intruder falling."

"But there's no bushes or anything to break your fall," Jazzy countered. "It's dangerous."

He didn't change his expression as he continued in a complete monotone voice. "You're not going to ask why I climbed into your room? When you were alone?"

"Oh I'm sorry," Jazzy said apologetically. "Did you need something?"

He extended his hand that held a note, and Jazzy took it. She read the address on top.

To: Jasmine Arabella Thomas
From: Dylan

"Your name is Dylan?" Jazzy asked as she looked up. "It's nice to meet you-" She trailed off when she saw he was already gone, with the window closed behind him.

Jazzy rushed over to the window and peered out. She saw him descending the tree, so she opened the window and called down. "In the future, you should go through the front door."

He glanced up at Jazzy for a half second, before he disappeared into the darkness. Jazzy closed the window, and opened the note. She wondered how he knew her name, or at least a version of her name. Elsif had made up the name Thomas but she had never seen the name Arabella before.

Meet me at the town fountain at midnight tomorrow night. Tell no one.

Jazzy reread the note a dozen times. She didn't understand anything about the interaction or the note. There was no logic in any of it. Jazzy knew she probably shouldn't meet him. It would be a foolish thing to do. But for the few minutes that the stranger had been with Jazzy, she had felt less alone.

*****

Jazzy stared at the clock on the wall as she laid next to Ruth, with Elsif on the far side of the bed. Jazzy glanced at the clock and read 11:47, then looked at the window. She hadn't told the girls about Dylan, even though she probably should have. But Jazzy knew she shouldn't meet a stranger in the middle of the night, so there was no reason to tell the others. And of course Dylan told Jazzy not to tell anyone, and Jazzy didn't want to betray his trust even though she hardly knew him.

No, Jazzy was not leaving her house that night. But as Jazzy tossed and turned she couldn't forget the feelings she had when he was with her for only a few seconds.

But even if she wanted to leave, Jazzy couldn't without waking Elsif and asking for the key to unlock the door that led downstairs. Her eyes once again found the window. Jazzy had climbed that tree once. She was feeling adventurous as a preteen one day and decided to climb instead of walk out of her house. Jazzy had fallen and broken her arm. The climb was thrilling, but Jazzy felt foolish afterwards so she never left that way again.

The stranger had climbed the tree easily, and Jazzy knew she was steadier on her feet as an adult. The mystery and questions were knocking on her mind, and Jazzy was itching for answers.

Slowly and quietly, Jazzy rose from the bed and made her way to the window. She gently opened it and maneuvered her way out. She grabbed a tree branch and pulled herself out. The air was brisk but Jazzy didn't mind. She was exhilarated for the first time in a long time.

Jazzy was at the fountain before she knew it, running almost the whole way. She didn't know what filled her with excitement more, the mystery boy or that she hadn't fallen out of the tree.

The village clock struck midnight right as Jazzy arrived. The village square was empty except for a couple of crickets, owls, and Dylan. He stood at the fountain and watched Jazzy approach. He didn't say anything to her, but that didn't stop Jazzy's stomach from twisting and turning.

"Hi," Jazzy said with a smile. "How are you?"

"You want to know about your family," He stated without answering Jazzy. "I can give you that, but you have to make me a promise first."

"What is it?"

Dylan's face held a serious expression. "You can't tell anybody about me or what I tell you."

Jazzy's brow knitted in confusion. "Why not? My friends are also trying to help me find out more about my family. They could help us?"

"No. You can't involve anyone else. This is the deal."

Jazzy should have hesitated, but she didn't. "Okay, I'll welcome all the help I can get."

"Good. You can consider this a life lesson."

"But why are you helping me?" Jazzy asked.

Dylan considered his response for a few moments. "A *friend* asked me."

"Who?" Jazzy thought about everyone that knew about her current situation. "Melissa?"

"Who knows?"

"I would hope you?"

Dylan ignored Jazzy's words and continued. "You'll be hearing from me soon."

He turned to walk away, as Jazzy tried to stop him "Wait!" She called after him but he once again disappeared into the dark.

*****

Elsif rolled over in the bed and readjusted her pillow. As she turned she glanced at the girls, and noticed there was only one lump next to her instead of two. Elsif's head snapped up as she reached for her glasses. She checked the bed again, but only one girl was present.

Elsif jumped out of the bed and raced out of the room. She swiftly unlocked the door and sprinted down the stairs. But when she arrived in the living she found Juniper asleep on the couch, and no Ruth.

Looking around Elsif found herself puzzled. The door was locked when she came down, Juniper was asleep, but Ruth was gone. Something didn't add up.

Elsif walked around Will, who was sleeping on the floor, and hovered over Juniper. "Where's Ruth?" She asked and shook Juniper.

Juniper mumbled something but didn't wake up.

Elsif grabbed the pillow from under Juniper's head and began hitting him with it. "Where is Ruth!"

Juniper jolted awake. "What is going on!" He demanded as he defended himself from the pillow attack.

"Ruth is gone," Elsif said, throwing the pillow on the ground. "Where is she?"

Will rustled on the floor as he woke up from the noise. "Elsif?"

"What do you mean?" Juniper questioned with annoyance as he sat up. "She's upstairs."

"No, she's not!" Elsif exclaimed with impatience. "I woke up and she was gone." Juniper stood up and walked past Elsif as she continued. "So she's obviously trying to meet you somewhere?" Juniper rushed to the bathroom and then the kitchen, looking around. "What are you doing?" Elsif demanded.

"Looking for Ruth!" Juniper yelled back as he frantically looked through all the windows.

"What's happening?" Will asked, standing up.

"Uh," Elsif said as she looked from Juniper to Will with confusion. "I woke up and Ruth wasn't there so I thought- Juniper, seriously, where's Ruth?"

"I'm looking," Juniper snapped as he opened the front door. He walked outside for half a minute before he came back in. "Is she in the other bedroom?"

"I don't know," Elsif admitted. "I'll check." She ran up the stairs and went into Milly and Rose's room. Elsif only found the two girls, but she woke them up anyway.

"Guys," Elsif said, shaking the pair. "Have you seen Ruth?"

"Not in my dreams," Rose mumbled.

Milly rubbed her eyes as she sat up. "She's not in your room?"

"No," Elsif replied, concern growing in her voice. "And she's not with Juniper either."

"Okay," Milly said, as she pushed back the covers. "I'm sure she's around somewhere. Rose, come help look."

Though she grumbled, Rose sat up and went downstairs with Milly and Elsif. The girls found both boys looking around the small house. Will was looking out the front window and Juniper was looking in the cupboards.

"I don't think Ruth would fit in there," Rose mumbled.

Juniper ignored the comment and came into the living room. "Are you sure Ruth isn't in *your* room?"

"Yes," Elsif stated. "It's only Jazzy up there."

"Does Jazzy know anything?" Juniper asked, his tone stressed.

"I'm sure she doesn't," Elsif said. "She would have told me."

Juniper started walking towards the stairs. "We need to ask her."

"We shouldn't wake her," Elsif said, attempting to stop Juniper. "She's been going through a lot recently."

"Ruth's missing," Juniper said, shoving past Elsif. "We have to ask everyone."

"Don't push her," Will said as he came beside Elsif. "If she doesn't want to wake Jazzy, then that's her choice."

"We don't need to worry her too," Elsif insisted.

Juniper ignored both comments and barged up the stairs. Elsif and Will ran after him, and Elsif cut off Juniper right before he opened Jazzy's bedroom door.

"Fine," Elsif conceded. "But *I'll* ask her. You two can wait here."

Elsif slipped inside while Juniper and Will waited outside the door. As Elsif made her way to the opposite side of the bed, she realized her mistake. Both girls were in the bed.

"Ruth?" Elsif reached over Jazzy and tapped Ruth. "Were you here the whole time?"

Ruth rolled over and mumbled, "What?"

The door opened and Rose walked in, as Milly, Juniper, and Will stood behind her. "RUTH! WHY ARE YOU NOT KIDNAPPED!"

Ruth and Jazzy both woke up and looked around. Ruth frowned as she saw all the commotion, and Jazzy covered her face.

"What are you talking about?" Ruth demanded. "What's everyone doing in here?"

Juniper walked into the room. "Did you leave the house tonight?"

Ruth shook her head. "I've been sleeping."

Juniper shot a look at Elsif then left to return to the couch downstairs.

"I'm glad everyone's safe," Will said and waved goodnight to Elsif.

"Elsif," Milly said. "You need to make sure the unaccounted party is *actually* missing next time."

"Yeah," Rose agreed. "I was dreaming about marrying a block of cheese before you interrupted."

Elsif's face dropped. "Sorry."

The two girls returned to bed and Elsif locked the upstairs door before returning to her own. She turned to face Ruth. "Tell me the truth," she said sternly. "Did you ever leave the bed?"

"I didn't," Ruth said as she closed her eyes. "You're going crazy."

Elsif sighed and closed her own eyes. "Maybe I am."

Jazzy kept her eyes open as guilt washed over her.

Chapter 20: Be Careful Who You Make Deals With

The new school year had officially started and the girls were deep in their studies. Elsif finally started her advanced program for teaching while the rest of the girls continued their normal classes. The year began in a normal manner and it seemed as if maybe the craziness and adventure from the previous year would be a one time occurrence. It was not.

Elsif was ready and prepared for the school year, anticipating a heavy course load. She knew that she wouldn't have much free time for treasure hunting or traveling across Fantasma, but she was fine with that. Her dreams were finally in reach so she wanted to dedicate all her energy to her classes. The only distraction that Elsif would allow was Will. She initially was against it, but eventually she caved and agreed for Will to visit her in October.

Jazzy had left Mellberg with conflicting feelings but she was hoping Merlin would brighten her spirits, or at least distract her from her emotions. She didn't understand her feelings half the time, but Jazzy knew she didn't like them. Merlin had been a source of joy for Jazzy the past year, and she wished for that time again. A time before she felt alone and missed a family she never had. But ultimately, she anticipated the moment that Dylan would appear again.

Ruth was optimistic about the school year. She had a 'kind of' boyfriend, a schedule full of animal care classes, and she hadn't seen Melissa the first few days back, so there was a chance she was gone. The year was looking good for Ruth.

Milly had extensive goals for the academic year that included properly training her kraken, becoming a full time captain for one of Merlin's ships, and to not be brutally maimed by one of Rose's pranks. The first two tasks were fairly attainable, but the third would take a miracle.

Rose had one thought on her mind for the year: *CHAOS*. She was going to create glitter bombs, torture Elsif, trick people into eating magical food, wield her destructive weapons, and drive everyone completely mad.

After the first day of lessons, all the students were instructed to go to the auditorium for a mandatory school wide announcement. Since this was not a normal occurrence, the girls found the timing a little strange and extremely inconvenient since they would have to eat dinner at a later time.

As the last students found their seats, the President of Merlin stepped up to the podium. "This academic year will be one of great precedent but only if we heed-"

Elsif stopped listening after the President's first sentence. She became distracted when she saw Libi sitting a few rows in front of her. The first thought that crossed her mind was if Libi was taking advanced classes to become an Oceanic Navyicus. That's what she always talked about when they were younger.

It was hard for Elsif not to hate her. She wanted to hate her, but she also didn't. Her feelings toward Libi were complicated and she didn't fully understand them. But despite all that, Elsif had a great year without her. She had survived without Libi. But she still missed her old friend nonetheless.

"Safety is not just a priority here at Merlin," the President continued as Elsif grasped for her attention. "It is our chief concern this academic year. I hope you all take these words and use them to guide yourselves as you navigate your year and excel in your academics. You may all be dismissed."

The girls stood up and shuffled out of the auditorium with the crowd. As they made their way to the dining chambers, Ruth leaned over and said, "So Malum's Staff was returned."

"What?" Elsif questioned with surprise.

"He said everything that was stolen last year was returned."

Elsif frowned. "Oh. I wasn't listening."

"Me either," Rose claimed proudly. "He was boring. I can't believe no one tried to stab him."

"I can't believe he would announce that to everyone," Elsif commented offhandedly.

"He didn't say that word for word," Milly clarified. "He said something about the breaking of trust last year but it's been restored now. He then said something about all the items at Merlin had been returned to their rightful places. He also threw in stuff about safety is something we don't need to worry about and it never was. If you read between the lines it seemed like he was talking about Malum's Staff."

"So," Ruth interjected. "Melissa doesn't have the Staff, and she hasn't been around. So she was probably expelled or arrested."

"That would be a little sad," Jazzy mentioned. "It was her last year. She was so close to graduating."

Ruth scoffed, "It's Melissa. She didn't deserve to graduate after stealing Malum's Staff!"

Juniper walked up behind Ruth as she exclaimed her last sentence. "How about you talk louder so the whole school can hear you?"

Ruth scrunched her nose in annoyance. "Yes, because we are so popular and everyone is dying to hear every word we say. Honestly, we could start talking about how we're going to kill the President of Merlin and not a single student would pay attention to us."

Elsif whipped her head around with sudden paranoia. She knew a certain friend group that would love to hear every word they said. Elsif's suspicions were either right or it was a crazy coincidence that Bernard was walking a few paces behind them with his head down.

"So Melissa was expelled?" Ruth asked Juniper.

He shrugged in response. "I haven't seen her but that doesn't mean much."

"I don't think she was," Milly countered. "I think he was lying about Malum's Staff being returned."

Ruth shot Milly a skeptical look. "Why would he lie?"

"He said *everything* was returned to its rightful place," Milly stated, then lowered her voice. "But *we* still have our weapons."

"Shoot," Ruth groaned through gritted teeth. "Are we sure we still have all the weapons?"

"Yup," Rose confirmed. "All my children are accounted for as of this morning."

Elsif looked at Rose. "We need to keep a closer eye on you."

Rose stuck her tongue out at Elsif and said, "Of course you do, but the real person we should be keeping an eye on is the President. He looked *weird*."

"What do you mean, *weird*?" Milly asked.

"You know," Rose made a vague gesture towards her face. "*Weird.* He's like sick or possessed or something."

Ruth rolled her eyes in exasperation. "We're straying off topic! We need to find out if Melissa is expelled or not."

"I haven't seen her either," Jazzy said softly. She had been looking for Melissa since she had stepped back onto Merlin property. Jazzy was beginning to grow concerned that the girls were right and Melissa was gone.

"We'll find out sooner or later," Juniper stated.

Since no one could think of a better solution, the gang accepted Juniper's conclusion and walked to the dining chambers. Elsif and Rose were last to the table.

"When did Juniper join our group?" Elsif grumbled to Rose.

"He's better than that loser Will," Rose countered. "You have pathetic taste in men."

"Thanks," Elsif muttered as they sat down.

Dinner on the first night of the school year was usually a terrific meal, but for some unknown reason the sight of the glazed vish ham made Jazzy's stomach ache. The others ate, chatted, and laughed, but Jazzy didn't join them. Even Juniper seemed to enjoy himself.

Jazzy sat on the outskirts of the conversation as she watched but did not participate. Everyone knew what to say and how to make the others laugh. Jazzy noticed a lot more inside jokes, stories, or other topics that she didn't know. Another wave of loneliness washed over Jazzy as she watched the others belong together but not with her. Jazzy had no desire to stay so she stood up once there was a break in the conversation.

"I'm a little tired," Jazzy explained, hoping her smile would convey that nothing was wrong. "I think I'll retire early."

"You're sounding like Elsif," Rose laughed.

"Have a good night's sleep," Ruth said.

"We'll be quiet when we come back to the chambers," Milly promised.

"You didn't eat much," Elsif said. "Do you want us to bring you back something?"

Jazzy shook her head. "I'm not hungry."

She left the dining chambers but Jazzy did not return to the girls' wing. Instead, she wandered outside and into the gardens. Jazzy didn't have a particular destination in mind, other than a place that would help her forget her current situation.

She strolled in the butterfly grove, but most of the insects were asleep. Jazzy walked by the waterfalls, but the sound of the rippling water did not comfort her. She contemplated wandering through the maze for a moment, as she lingered by the entrance. But she thought better of the idea at the last second and walked across the bridge that led back to the school. Jazzy knew if she began wandering in the maze then she may never leave.

"Hi Jazzy," a voice came from behind.

Jazzy turned around and found the person she had been looking for. "Melissa, where have you been?"

"Around," Melissa said casually as she joined Jazzy on the bridge.

"I haven't seen you in the hallways or the girls' wing," Jazzy explained. "Not even at the assembly. I was starting to worry that you weren't here anymore."

Melissa put a comforting hand on Jazzy's shoulder. "Oh Jazzy," she told her. "There's thousands of students here. It's hard to pinpoint a needle in a haystack."

"Yes, I suppose you're right."

"How was your August break?" Melissa asked with a knowing smile.

"I went to Mellberg," Jazzy replied, excitement filling her after a dreary day. "And I met-" Jazzy hesitated. It was unlikely anyone else could have been the *friend* Dylan mentioned, but Jazzy also didn't want to appear foolish. "And I met someone who, um, is going to help me find my family."

Melissa's devious smile appeared. "Sounds like a miracle. I wouldn't take him for granted if I were you."

"I won't," Jazzy assured. "I'm very grateful for him."

"As you should be," Melissa stated.

"Yes," Jazzy agreed, taking a few steps back. "I should head back to my chamber. I want to be back before the girls get there."

"See you later then," Melissa said. "If you need anything, I'm around."

"Thank you."

*****

The next morning as the girls got ready for classes, Jazzy felt guilty for not mentioning something sooner.

"I saw Melissa," she mentioned as she packed her book bag in the living room while the girls walked around. Each girl stopped in their tracks.

"Where?" Ruth demanded. "Was it actually her? Could it have been someone that only looked like her? Does anyone else in the school have green tones in their skin?"

"It was her," Jazzy confirmed. "I ran into her on my way back to the room last night." The statement wasn't a lie, but it still created a knotted feeling in Jazzy's gut.

"Did you talk to her?" Milly asked.

"A little," Jazzy admitted, avoiding eye contact. "Only pleasantries."

Rose's head tilted to one side. "Why would you talk about birds?"

"No," Milly corrected. "Those are pheasants."

"Oh!" Rose said dramatically. "They were talking about the people that are beneath me."

"No!" Milly groaned with exasperation. "That's peasants! Do you not know words?"

"This isn't good," Ruth said, pulling the conversation back to the original topic.

"It doesn't really matter to any of us anyway," Elsif commented. "We have more important things to do than obsess over Melissa. We're about to be late for class."

Ruth frowned. "We have half an hour."

"If you're not early," Elsif said as she grabbed her bag and strolled out the door. "Then you're late."

Elsif loved her advanced program schedule. She was only in classes a quarter of the time and she was able to independently study the rest of the day. After two classes Elsif went to the library, a place that had once again become her favorite. She had decided it was silly to be concerned about the lack of authors. Merlin only wanted the best, and Elsif shouldn't complain about that. She was thoroughly educated and that is what mattered.

She sat at a long table with dozens of books about the topic of human slavery under Elven rule. She had a twenty-five page paper due at the end of the month so she flipped through her favorite books on the subject.

As she was writing down notes, Elsif's eyes strayed to someone sitting a few tables away. The library was pretty empty during the day since most students were in class so Bernard didn't have anywhere to hide. Which was bad news for him.

Something inside Elsif snapped as she saw him sitting casually at the table. She hated that he or Paisley or Piper were always around a corner, wherever she was. She and her cousins weren't bothering with the Staff or the Hat or even Melissa anymore. Why did they have to insist on following every step of her day? Elsif had enough.

"You need to stop," she demanded as she marched up to Bernard.

He looked up from where he had been staring at the floor. "What do you want, Frosty?"

"Don't act like a fool," Elsif warned. "You need to leave me and my cousins alone. That goes for your friends too. I never want to see you ten yards behind me *ever* again."

Bernard laughed. "I have no idea what you're talking abou-"

"Stop it!" Elsif yelled at him. She didn't know where her bravery came from but it was spilling over. Elsif was lucky that no librarians were currently around or she probably would have been kicked out. "I never want to see you or the others following me again or you'll regret it."

"What could you possibly do to me?" Bernard taunted while he continued to laugh. "Freeze my head off? Create a snow storm in my room?"

"I'll get you expelled." Elsif had no idea where that plan came from but once she said it, she fully committed. "I'm one of the best students that this Academy has. I come from a long and honorable family of alumni. All the faculty love and trust me. I can get you kicked out of here faster than you can spell the word *disgraced*. I'll have you, and anyone else that tries to mess with my family, sent back to Versario in a blink of an eye."

Bernard stood up and looked down at Elsif. In return Elsif crossed her arms and stared up at him. "You leave me and my family alone and I'll leave you alone. Deal?"

He didn't respond for what felt like an eternity. Elsif tried to hold her confident stare but her nerves were waning and anxiety was snaking up her body. But before she broke, Bernard extended his hand.

"Deal."

Elsif didn't shake his hand. Instead she walked back to her table. She began studying as if nothing had transpired with the student across the room from her.

Chapter 21: A Dark Night's Sky

After the last day of classes in September, Jazzy walked back to her chambers, and ran into Melissa in the hallway.

"Hey Jazzy," Melissa said with her well-practiced smile. "How are you?"

"Good," Jazzy answered. "And you?"

"Fine," Melissa said while pulling a note from her pocket. "This is for you."

When Jazzy saw who the note was from, she opened her mouth to ask a million questions, but Melissa pressed her finger to her lips. Jazzy closed her jaw, and Melissa walked away.

Jazzy was right outside of her own chambers, but didn't want to open the note in front of the girls. She didn't have a good explanation for the mysteries behind the note, so Jazzy decided to find a private place to be alone. She found a nearby storage closet, and ducked inside to read the letter.

To: Jasmine Arabella Thomas

From: Dylan

Her heart raced as she carefully opened the paper. She was filled with excitement as she saw more words with his handwriting.

Docks at midnight. Pack for seven days.

No unnecessary baggage. Tell no one.

Jazzy read the note a million times. Studied it. Memorized the few words. She was going somewhere with Dylan. Somewhere else in Fantasma maybe? Was she going to be alone with him? That probably wasn't the safest decision. But he was Melissa's friend and she had been nothing but nice to Jazzy. Melissa wouldn't put her in danger, and Jazzy really wanted to know more about her family.

There was no longer any hesitation inside Jazzy. She was determined to go with Dylan and find her purpose. Her new perspective. Once she found her past, everything would become clear and Jazzy would know exactly who she was.

There was one problem though. Jazzy was supposed to go to Bellator with Ruth for October break. She needed an adequate excuse so she didn't hurt Ruth's feelings. As Jazzy thought about possible reasons, the closet door opened in front of her.

"Why are you in a closet, child?" Ms. Princey asked as she stared down at Jazzy.

Jazzy held the note tightly to her chest as her mouth ran dry. She had not seen the woman who had convinced her to attend Merlin Academy since coming to the school, and Jazzy had not imagined that this would be their second meeting.

"To," Jazzy desperately attempted to think of an excuse. "Help me- concentrate on my studies."

Ms. Princey looked at Jazzy with a suspicious eye. "I would think you could do that somewhere else."

"Yes ma'am," Jazzy nodded frantically. "I could."

"Then I suggest you go find that other place," Ms. Princey said forcefully. "Now."

Jazzy scurried away as she heard Ms. Princey mutter under her breath. She went back to her room and packed for her adventure. After several minutes the other girls walked into the chamber.

Rose and Milly were in a huge debate about who would win in a fight, Milly's kraken or Rose. Milly argued that Rose wouldn't last two seconds, and Rose said the same thing about the kraken. Ruth and Elsif walked in next and joined Jazzy.

"Why weren't you at dinner?" Ruth asked.

"Oh." Jazzy forgot she was supposed to go to dinner with them that night. "I had a sudden feeling," Jazzy prepared her lie. "That I wanted to go back to Mellberg for October break. I'm sorry Ruth, but I think it'll be good for me."

"Really?" Ruth asked. "But I'll be so bored in Bellator without you."

"What about your cute neighbor?" Elsif suggested.

"You hate my neighbor."

"I hate him less than Juniper," Elsif replied, then turned to Jazzy. "Do you want me to go to Mellberg with you?"

"No," Jazzy insisted. "You were so excited about staying at Merlin and studying. I'll be fine."

"Alright," Elsif said with skepticism. "But if you don't want to spend the whole break in Mellberg then you can always come back to Merlin early. We could study together."

"That would be nice," Jazzy said.

*****

Ruth, Milly, Rose, and Jazzy said their goodbyes to Elsif as they headed to the carriages. Since Jazzy was the only student who lived in Koronia she was able to decide exactly when her carriage left, and it conveniently left after the other girls' carriages.

Once the girls arrived at the carriages, Ruth gave them a blunt, "Goodbye!" before walking over to Juniper, who she chatted with until she left.

"I have to say goodbye to Elwin," Milly said.

"Who the heck is Elwin?" Rose asked.

Milly gestured toward the sea. "My kraken."

"Since when did it have a name?"

"Since I tamed him."

"How was I supposed to remember that? That was ages ago!"

"Go bother someone else until I get back," Milly said as she walked towards the water. "But not Jazzy!"

"Who then!" Rose called to Milly.

"I don't know!" Milly yelled. "The next unfortunate person to walk by!"

Rose pouted for a moment but then a tall, gangly boy around her age walked by carrying a big stack of books. Rose knew he was her perfect victim so she pounced at once.

"If you were only four inches taller, then you would be able to reach the top shelf in the potions closet and we would be able to make the perfect magical bomb," Rose told the boy as she jumped in front of him.

The startled boy abruptly stopped walking, and looked around to see who Rose was talking to. Once he realized Rose was addressing him, he nervously fixed his glasses, which caused him to almost drop his books. "I'm Kenneth," he said, straightening up. "Kenneth Fredrickson III."

"That is the most boring name that I have ever heard in my life," Rose stated. "You're now Kfred."

"Okay," he said, shifting his gangly weight from side to side.

"Are you planning on growing any more?" Rose asked, examining Kfred's stature.

He shrugged nervously. "I was hoping I would."

"How many inches exactly?"

"One of my brothers is six inches taller than me," Kfred mentioned. "The other is five inches taller."

Rose smiled up at him. "Kfred, you are my new best friend."

*****

Jazzy waved goodbye to Milly who was the last to leave Merlin Academy. She then canceled her carriage and found a place to sit that was blocked by trees so Elsif couldn't see her from the school. She sat there for three hours as she waited for Dylan, but it felt closer to three minutes because of how consumed she was with excitement.

At midnight, Jazzy walked over to the docks and found Dylan waiting in a boat. As she approached, he saw her but didn't say a word.

"Hello," she said, beaming at him. "Where are we going?"

"Get on," he instructed, with a tilt of his head and tap of his foot.

Jazzy obeyed and climbed onto the small boat. "Are we sailing somewhere?" She asked with eagerness.

"Obviously," he muttered, not taking his eyes off her.

Jazzy broke eye contact first. "Where are we going?" He didn't respond, but instead started the engine and pulled the boat away from the docks. "Can I guess?" Jazzy suggested.

"No," he replied rudely. Jazzy looked over at him and could see a hundred little red veins in his eyes. She grew concerned that he hadn't slept recently.

As the boat cruised through the starless night, Jazzy sat at the front of the boat and watched the water as they headed north. Whenever Jazzy looked behind her she saw Dylan watching her. She found it a little unnerving but she also enjoyed it at the same time.

Jazzy didn't know when she fell asleep but when she opened her eyes she saw the sun rising in the distance. They were still sailing but Jazzy couldn't see any land around them. Since Jazzy wasn't used to being on the water, she wasn't sure what direction they were going.

After Jazzy sat up and stretched, Dylan tossed her a small brown bag from where he stood at the steering wheel. Jazzy opened the bag and found an apple, some pieces of cheese, and a small loaf of bread.

"Thank you," Jazzy said to Dylan. As Jazzy ate her breakfast, she wondered if Dylan had slept at all last night. He looked the same as last night, bloodshot eyes and unkempt hair. She noticed that Dylan didn't seem to have a map or compass so she wondered how he knew where they were going.

Jazzy also noticed that the boat didn't seem to be going in a straight path, but instead was traveling in wide turns that eventually turned into circles. She hoped that Dylan knew what he was doing and that they weren't lost at sea.

"Dylan," Jazzy spoke up. "Do you know when we'll arrive?"

"Yes."

"When?"

"You don't need to know."

Jazzy slouched into her seat. Worry nipped at her, until she finally saw hazy land in the distance.

"We're here," Jazzy smiled back at Dylan. "How exciting!"

Dylan steered the boat to a busy port full of boats, ships, people, crates, barrels, and animals. Even though the day had just begun, the docks were alive and bustling in the new region that Jazzy was unfamiliar with. Dylan docked the boat between two very large ships that reminded Jazzy of the ones that Milly liked to sail at Merlin.

Dylan tied the boat, jumped out, and walked into town. Jazzy quickly ran after him and weaved through the crowd. When Jazzy caught up, she made sure to stay close to him.

There was a large flag flying on a high tower and Jazzy recognized it from Milly's bedroom. Dylan must have brought Jazzy to Navisia. The only things that Jazzy knew about Navisia was that there were a lot of pirates, ships, and swords, and Milly was nice, so everyone else must be too!

As Jazzy walked through the port, she kept accidentally colliding with different people, which did not make the locals happy. They usually pushed Jazzy off them or said a few nasty words. One woman drew her sword, and Jazzy had to duck away quickly.

Dylan walked down the road until he came to a restaurant with several rowdy patrons. Jazzy carefully followed Dylan as they swerved around crowds of people shouting, fighting, and drinking. Dylan walked up to a rough looking bartender who wore an eye patch.

"Time to go Stitch," Dylan said.

"Go where?" Stitch grumbled. "I said I'd give you the name. Nothing else."

"I already know the name," Dylan spat. "I need you to take us to him."

Stitch shook his head. "Mariano told me that you needed the name. He never mentioned taking you somewhere."

"Mariano lied," Dylan stated. "If you don't take us now, the deal's off."

Stitch thought about it and grudgingly said, "Fine."

He set down the glass and walked through a door behind the bar. Jazzy had to sprint to catch up with Dylan, who was close behind Stitch. Dylan and Jazzy followed Stitch through the kitchen, which was far beneath the average health code, and came to a carriage pulled by a horse in the alley behind the restaurant.

Stitch, Dylan, and Jazzy squeezed onto the small two-bench carriage, and began slowly rolling through the streets. As the carriage drove through pothole-filled alleys, the crowds thinned as they went further from the shore.

At one point, the carriage pulled up to a bridge and they were stopped by several men with swords and guns. Jazzy shivered with nerves, and scooted closer to Dylan. Once their carriage pulled up, Stitch handed the guards a small bag and they were on their way.

"Why aren't the guards wearing uniforms?" Jazzy asked Dylan in a low whisper after they passed the bridge.

"They aren't guards," Dylan replied. "They're gangs."

"Oh," Jazzy mumbled. She hoped Milly didn't live anywhere near that bridge.

After a while, they arrived at a large building with large pillars and windows. There was a sign in front that read *Rossio's Revenge Marriage Courthouse*.

"Get off," Stitch commanded. Dylan hopped off the carriage and headed inside without waiting for Jazzy.

"Thank you," Jazzy said as she climbed down from the carriage and hurried after Dylan. Stitch and his carriage disappeared down the street before Jazzy walked inside. Once Jazzy walked in, she found Dylan arguing with the receptionist.

"Melton Hairville is not available," the lady insisted. "There's plenty of other attorneys that are able to assist you."

"Unless their names are Melton Hairville," Dylan snapped. "I'm not interested. Tell him *Dylan* is waiting."

The lady sighed as she left the front desk. A few minutes later a short, greasy man came into the room and approached Dylan in a haphazard manor.

"I already told you," the man insisted as he squirmed behind the desk. "There are no names under Arabella here. We don't want anything to do with any Versario dealings here. Try another courthouse. There's a lot more along both coasts. They could have gotten married anywhere in Navisia, there's nothing special about this courthouse."

Dylan leaned against the desk while staring down Melton. "I know it's here. You're going to want to show me the names instead of someone else."

Melton gulped a big breath of air. "I don't want any more of you coming into this courthouse. This is a legitimate business. I most certainly don't want anyone like Stone stepping foot in here."

"Then show us the names."

Melton bawled up his fists and scrunched his nose. "You have two minutes. Two!" He ushered them to another room full of wooden chests. He began pulling out papers of a chest labeled AN-AZ. He pulled out one scroll and laid it on the table. Melvin glanced at Dylan in a sheepish manner and repeated his warning, "Two minutes." He then walked out of the room quickly.

Dylan scanned the scroll while Jazzy looked at the paper over his shoulder. After a few seconds, Dylan pointed at two names, *Louis & Charlotte Arabella.*

"Your parents."

"What?" Jazzy asked frantically as she took a closer look at the scroll. "These are my parents? That's them?"

"That's what I said."

Jazzy stared at the names in shock. She was mesmerized by the letters, as she traced her fingers across the words. She cherished the moment. "I only knew my mothers name, Charlotte. No one in the village knew my father's name, or my last name."

"They're fake names," Dylan stated. "No one marries in Navisia unless they have something to hide. This region has very loose marriage laws. You can show up at any marriage courthouse and get married within ten minutes with no identification or papers. You just need money. Most of the laws here fall in a gray area, if you're willing to pay."

"Hide?" Jazzy questioned. "What would they be hiding?"

"That's what we're trying to find out."

Jazzy looked at the names again. She didn't care if they were fake, those names were her parents. *Her parents.*

"The other paperwork tells us they came here about twenty years ago give or take a year, but there's no other information," Dylan said. "And Melton is going to have an aneurysm if I ask to see anything else."

"Why doesn't he like you?" Jazzy asked.

"He didn't appreciate my friends who came before me."

"What does that-" Jazzy started but Dylan turned to walk out of the room. "Where are you going?"

"It's been two minutes," Dylan replied as he closed the door behind him.

Jazzy desperately wanted to stay with her parent's names, but she knew it would be foolish to separate herself from Dylan. She glanced at the names one last time, then rushed after Dylan.

Once Jazzy found Dylan outside the courthouse, she grabbed Dylan's arm, and stopped him. "There has to be more," Jazzy pleaded. "Maybe I could talk to

Melton, or we could sneak in when he leaves. There has to be more information about them."

"We're done," Dylan said. "You'll have to wait until I find out more."

"But when will that be?" Jazzy pressed. "How will you find more? I can't wait!"

Dylan whipped his arm from Jazzy's clutch and grabbed her arm instead. "You really don't know?" He snapped harshly.

With shaking hesitation, Jazzy replied, "What?"

Dylan shook his head and let go of Jazzy. "Don't act like you don't know what's going on here."

"You're helping me," Jazzy said softly, still startled from before. "Because you're friends with Melissa?"

Dylan stared at Jazzy for a long moment before responding. "Yeah," he said, his face portraying a single second of regret. "That's what's happening."

Chapter 22: I Feel Destined

"I'm just going to say it," Elsif announced one day at dinner. "I don't think Juniper should be allowed to sit with us."

"Wow," Milly said with no amusement. "What a surprising opinion."

"You don't have to say it every day," Ruth stated.

"Elsif, stop complaining and do something about it," Rose demanded. "You're all talk and no action!"

"What do you want me to do?" Elsif asked with annoyance. "Stab him?"

"Yes! Perfect! Stop grumbling and stab him!" Rose exclaimed then turned to Juniper. "You wouldn't mind, would you?"

"Not if it gets Elsif to shut up," Juniper muttered.

A loud clang was heard as Elsif's knife hit her plate.

Jazzy leaned over to Juniper. "Elsif doesn't like that phrase."

Crossing her arms Elsif said, "Why don't you hang out with your own friends?"

Ruth punched Elsif in the arm. "You're so mean!"

"He told me to shut up," Elsif defended herself. "And he doesn't have to sit with us for every meal."

Ruth shook her head in disbelief. "You're a jerk whenever Will isn't around."

"I'm the exact same person whether Will is here or not."

"Maybe Elsif is just a mean person," Milly commented. "But we never noticed before."

"I agree," Rose nodded. "Juniper, I'm sorry she's hurting your feelings."

"I'll get over it."

Rose wore a sympathetic expression on her face. "If you need to cry it's alright."

"I'm good."

"Look what you did Elsif," Rose said with an accusatory finger pointed at Elsif. "Another man who has to suppress his emotions all because of you."

"Oh no, I feel terr-" Elsif was cut off when a student began yelling on the other side of the dining chambers.

The group turned their heads towards the commotion and saw a student standing on one of the tables. The girls recognized him as one of Michael's friends, Iray. He was also in one of Elsif's classes, Region Relations. It was hard to hear him at first but once the student body turned their attention to Iray, the room fell silent and only his words could be heard.

"Versario is coming!" He warned with a shout. "But why shouldn't they? Magicis has ruined them! They have nothing to lose and everything to take! Versario is coming with righteous vengeance! How will we pay for the sins of our ancestors-"

He was pulled off the table by several professors. Iray fought back and yelled as he struggled. The girls lost sight of him as commotion filled the room and everyone stood up to watch. The girls jumped to their feet as well, but the crowd was too thick to get a good view.

"What is he saying?" Ruth said, as she stood on her tiptoes.

"He's probably still talking about how Versario declared war on Magicis this morning," Juniper said from his seat. He was the only one in the whole room that didn't stand up.

The girls looked at Juniper with shocked expressions.

"What do you mean?" Milly asked.

"They do it every other month," Juniper said as he continued to eat his food. His demeanor showed that he was unimpressed by Iray's words.

Elsif glanced at the crowd that was still buzzing from Iray's speech. "What if they mean it this time? Region relations is what Iray's studying and he's a pretty smart guy." "It wouldn't be possible for Versario to conduct a full fledged war on another region," Juniper insisted. "They don't have a unified government. Every town fends for themselves. Some of the bigger cities have local governments but they're dysfunctional."

Silence fell over the room, and the girls stopped their chattering as well when they saw who entered the dining chambers. The President of Merlin walked in with several people following close behind.

"Attention everyone!" He announced. "Please report back to your chambers immediately. Curfew will be early tonight, in fifteen minutes. Classes will resume as usual in the morning. Thank you."

He walked out of the room with his entourage, and the students were left perplexed. After a minute, everyone began shuffling out of the room.

"Why would the President come?" Milly asked the others as she grabbed her backpack. "And he's sending us to our chambers? Just because some guy was talking about Versario?"

"It's because he's suspicious," Rose stated. "I tried to warn you all but no one listened."

"More likely," Ruth interjected. "He didn't want to cause a panic for people like Elsif."

Elsif shot a glare at Ruth as she packed up her study material. "I wasn't panicking. I was thinking cautiously."

"You know," Milly commented in a low voice. "There's one thing that might be different from the other times Versario declared war. They might have the Staff now."

Tension coursed through the group as some professors walked by and warned the students that they only had ten minutes until curfew.

"But it's been missing for a year," Ruth countered. "If Melissa was planning something, wouldn't it have happened already?"

"Maybe Melissa was only able to get the Staff back to Versario in the last month," Milly suggested. "Or maybe they've been planning this attack for a year."

Rose cracked her knuckles. "I'd like to see them try to wage a war against me and my chain whips."

Ruth tugged nervously on Juniper's sleeve. "You don't think that Versario has the Staff, do you?"

Juniper's unfeeling expression remained stoic during the conversation, but hesitated for a moment before replying to Ruth. "Versario isn't anything to worry about."

"It's not our problem anyway," Elsif stated. "We need to get back to our chambers."

The group left the dining chambers with the last few stragglers who had tried to finish their meals before returning to their rooms. Ruth said goodbye to Juniper outside the dining chambers, and the girls left.

Ruth suddenly stopped walking right before the stairs to the second level. "Wait," she said urgently. "We were going to go to the gardens."

The girls had decided earlier that week that they wanted to spend some time in the gardens on Saturday night after dinner since they were so busy and there was no other time to go.

"We can't anymore," Elsif said. She turned to walk up the stairs but Milly and Rose stopped as well.

"Shoot," Milly muttered. "We *were* supposed to go to the gardens. I forgot after the Versario speech."

"We can still go," Rose insisted. "Who's going to stop us?"

"Our monitor," Elsif stated.

"Sabrina won't care," Rose countered

"Do you think we'd be caught?" Ruth wondered out loud.

"I don't know," Milly replied. "I think the President sounded serious."

"Darn," Ruth muttered. "Maybe one of us can run to the gardens real fast and make it back in time. Who's the fastest?"

Rose shot her arm in the air. "ME!"

"You'll get side tracked," Milly told Rose. "I'm the second fastest. I'll be quick."

"Why do you need to go to the gardens so desperately?" Elsif questioned.

"Uh," Milly stuttered. "To- touch grass. I'll bring some back for everyone. Bye!"

Elsif rolled her eyes at the odd behavior and walked up the stairs. As the girls made their way to their chambers, Elsif noticed Jazzy walking silently next to her. "You've been really quiet today."

Jazzy perked up once she realized Elsif was talking to her. "Oh, have I? I guess I've just been thinking."

"Leave Jazzy alone," Ruth said from behind them. "Sometimes she's quiet. She likes thinking instead of saying every word that pops up in her brain like some people." Ruth gave Rose a side eye.

"I was just wondering if anything was wrong," Elsif stated.

"Jazzy will let us know if anything is bothering her," Ruth said. "We don't need to interrupt her peaceful thoughts."

"I'm fine," Jazzy assured Elsif. "Just lost in thought today."

The girls arrived at their chambers and tried to find things to entertain themselves for their early night in. After a few minutes Milly came running into the room, completely out of breath.

"I think," she said between gasps of air. "I made it."

"Where's the grass?" Elsif asked when she noticed Milly's empty hands.

Milly, who was trying to catch her breath while bent over, stared at Elsif with wide eyes. "I forgot it."

Elsif shook her head, immune to weird behavior at that point in her life. She sat down on the couch and read her book, *History of the Mimpius People and Everyone's Hatred for Them*. Jazzy had gone to bed early, while the other three girls were playing a round of *Magic Goblins*.

After a while, a tap was heard on the balcony window. Well, it was heard by everyone except for Elsif who was engrossed in her book. After several taps, which progressively grew louder, Elsif muttered while still reading, "Knock it off, Rose."

Rose bounded across the couch and ripped the book from Elsif's hands. "I'm not doing anything!"

There was another loud tap and Elsif realized it was coming from the balcony. "My bad," she said, then grabbed the book back from Rose.

"Aren't you going to check it?" Rose demanded.

"Why me?" Elsif questioned. "You're closer."

"Could you just check it, Elsif?" Ruth asked.

"Yeah," Milly agreed. "You're the oldest. And the wisest. It should be you."

Elsif eyed the girls suspiciously, but conceded. She stood up, placed her book on the table, and went to open the curtains of the balcony. She found the culprit of the tapping and quickly opened the door with a smile.

"Why are you so obsessed with climbing my balcony?" Elsif asked, taking a step outside. She closed the door behind her, and stood in the chilly November night air with Will.

"I couldn't resist," Will teased. "I was supposed to surprise you in the garden, but apparently there was an early curfew because of Versario or something. Milly talked really fast and then ran away from me before I could understand the full story."

Elsif told Will about the announcement that Iray shared in the dining chambers. "So now we're stuck in our chambers," Elsif explained, while twirling the snowflake necklace that Will had given her a few months previously, that she never took off. "And I'm not sure if you should stick around tonight. I have a feeling the monitors will keep a close eye on everyone."

"Then I'll get going," Will said with understanding. "But I'll be back tomorrow so I can help you study."

"Thanks," Elsif replied with a smile.

Will climbed over the railing but before he descended he pulled out a small package from his coat. "I almost forgot," he said, handing the parcel to Elsif. "Happy birthday."

"My birthday's on Thursday," Elsif said, taking the package.

"I know," Will assured. "But you have a test on Friday so you'll be busy studying on Thursday. So I thought today could be your birthday instead." He leaned over the railing and placed a kiss on Elsif's cheek. "See you tomorrow, love."

Will climbed to the ground as Elsif felt her face grow warm because she forgot to close the curtain of the balcony. She knew her cousins were watching her, and she gritted her teeth as she turned around.

Milly wasn't paying her any attention, Rose was shaking her head and crossing her arms with disappointment, and Ruth was blowing air kisses in a mocking manner.

Elsif went straight to her room and ignored her cousins. She opened her package and cherished the gift from Will. Elsif hid the present in her dresser so her cousins wouldn't find it, and went to bed. She enjoyed having something special that no one knew about. No one except Will.

*****

Jazzy woke up late the next morning. She walked into the living room and found only Milly. "Good morning," Jazzy said as she found the last boysenberry muffin from the batch she had made earlier that week.

"Morning," Milly replied while she worked on homework.

"Where's Elsif?" Jazzy asked.

"With Will in the library," Milly stated.

"Ruth?"

"With Juniper in the garden."

"Rose?"

"With-" Milly paused then sighed. "I don't know but I should probably find out." She began putting away her homework.

Ruth walked into the chambers as Milly was getting ready to leave to find Rose. "Hey," Milly said to Ruth. "Do you know where Rose is?"

"No," Ruth said. "Who's weekend is it to watch her?"

"I'll check the list," Jazzy said as she looked at the note on the refrigerator that outlined an organized time schedule of who was in charge of watching Rose. "It's Elsif's weekend."

"She's obviously not watching her," Ruth commented.

Milly grumbled as she grabbed a jacket. "She owes me a weekend then. Hopefully Rose hasn't done too much damage yet." She left in a hurry out the front door and began scouring Merlin Academy.

After Milly left, Ruth turned to Jazzy. "Do you want to get lunch together?"

"Um," Jazzy hesitated. "I'm alright. I have a muffin."

"A muffin isn't a meal," Ruth stated. "Juniper said he has too much homework so I don't have anyone to eat with."

Jazzy smiled, and put down her muffin. "Sure, I'd love to join you."

The girls walked to the dining chambers and ate roasted turkey, mashed potatoes, carrots, and chocolate fairy cookies. Jazzy felt better once she was out of the chambers and eating with only one other person. Less pressure to join a conversation but instead have a meaningful connection.

"I forgot to ask you," Ruth said. "How was Mellberg?"

"Nice," Jazzy said without providing details. "I really like the turkey."

"Did you find anything?" Ruth continued.

Jazzy stared at her food very intently. "Nothing much."

"Do you ever imagine what they were like?" Ruth wondered.

"Sometimes," Jazzy answered softly.

In the last couple weeks Jazzy had imagined what her parents were like for hours every day. Her mother was a lot like her, with the same physique and meekness, while her father was tall and shared her eyes. Her father was the funniest person that her mother had ever met, and his personality contrasted with her shyness. She hated oranges, and he pretended to be allergic to them for the longest time. He didn't tell her the truth until after they were married. Her mother thought it was the sweetest thing in the world.

Jazzy shook off her thoughts. "But you can't tell much from only the names."

"Names?" Ruth questioned. "I thought you only knew your mom's name, Charlotte."

"Well-" Jazzy hesitated. "That's correct. I only know my mothers name. I don't know why I said *names*."

Ruth leaned forward. "Did you find your dad's name?"

Jazzy frantically shook her head. "No. No I didn't."

Ruth laughed. "Why are you lying to me?"

"Uh, uh," Jazzy stuttered nervously. "I don't know."

"It's fine if you want to have a few secrets," Ruth said with a smile. "I'm just extremely nosey and really want to know his name."

Jazzy nodded slowly. "I'll tell you but please promise to not tell the others. I wanted to keep a few things private, just for now."

"Of course," Ruth said.

"His name was Louis," Jazzy said. "And our last name is Arabella. But actually that might be a fake last name. But I'm pretty sure their first names were Charlotte and Louis."

"That's amazing," Ruth beamed.

Jazzy smiled back, happy that she had another person to share the secret with.

*****

"Rose, what on earth are you doing!" Milly exclaimed.

Rose stood in a random empty room with a baby elephant, small mouse, and several fireworks in her hand. "Before you say anything, this is exactly what it looks like."

"Where did you get the animals?" Milly questioned.

"I borrowed them from Merlin's farm."

"They shouldn't be inside the school," Milly insisted. "And fireworks are definitely not allowed!"

Rose laughed. "Give me five more minutes and I will be executing the greatest prank of all time."

"Rose no-"

"Okay, maybe it could have been slightly better executed," Rose admitted. "I wanted a full circus in a classroom, but Kfred was busy with homework, and I needed someone with height."

"I'm pretty sure Kfred is a fake person and this isn't a classroom," Milly corrected. "This is the prophecy room, and we'll be in tons of trouble if we're caught."

"How was I supposed to know this was the prophecy room?"

"The big words that say PROPHECY ROOM on the door, or the big cauldron, or the inspirational poster that has the cat hanging from the tree and says, '*Prophecies don't define you, they guide you.*'"

Rose raised her hands in defeat. "I'm sorry that I'm not perfect. Let's get a prophecy though." Rose walked over to the cauldron and looked inside. It was boiling, smoking, and changing colors. "How do we get one?"

"I don't think we can *get* one," Milly answered, coming beside her. "I think one appears if you're destined or something."

"I feel destined!" Rose exclaimed. They both stood at the large cauldron looking into the swirls for several minutes.

"Hey, why would you shoot off fireworks around animals?" Milly asked. "That seems mean?"

"They're silent," Rose assured. "And they explode colorful grass that the elephant can eat."

"Oh," Milly said with surprise. "That's nice."

"Yeah, I think it would have been one of my better pranks-"

The cauldron began to bubble and steam spilled out, spreading across the room. The colors became more vivid and flashed with urgency. Suddenly a glass orb emerged from the boiling water.

"Rose, if we die then I'm going to kill you."

Rose picked up the orb and there was a message inside.

Five have been chosen,
With marks on their backs.
Five have been gifted,
With powers without lack.
Five will fight,
To bring peace and war.
Five will quest,
To bring balance and more.
Five will all die or all live alike,
together without holding a single one.
Five are deemed to vanquish evil,
If their plights have failed then darkness has won.

"That's not ominous," Milly muttered.

Chapter 23: I'm Not Colorblind! The Tree Is Colorblind!

December arrived rapidly and the girls found themselves traveling to Stellae for their annual family vacation to celebrate Grandpa Henry's birthday. Jazzy was hesitant to join, hoping that Dylan would contact her again, but sadly there had been no word from him since their trip to Navisia. Since she had no other plans, Jazzy accepted their invitation.

A feeling of sorrowful deja vu washed over Jazzy as she once again entered the Walker family home. Seeing and hearing a happy family made the pit in Jazzy's stomach grow a million times larger. She quickly excused herself to the guest chambers.

The girls joined Jazzy a few minutes later to unpack their luggage.

"So the elephant prophesied that we would all die?" Elsif questioned after Milly and Rose retold the prophecy room story for the twelfth time.

Milly sighed. "No, the elephant had nothing to do with the prophecy."

"Then why do you keep bringing up the elephant?" Elsif demanded.

"Because!" Rose shouted as if she was in agony. "It's a fun little detail!" "I'm also confused about the elephant," Jazzy commented.

"Wait," Ruth dropped her clothes and grabbed Rose's arm. "You didn't take the elephant from Merlin's sanctuary did you? Was it Penelope? Or Daphne? Did you return her!"

Rose smirked down at Ruth (since Rose recently had a growth spurt and was half a foot taller than Ruth.) "She is now in my personal habitat, happy as a clam."

"Guys," Milly wrangled the conversation back. "A prophecy was presented to Rose and I. Do you know how big of a deal this is?"

"Why were you in the prophecy room again?" Elsif asked.

"So we're just going to ignore the fact that Rose kidnapped one of Merlin's elephants?" Ruth questioned while crossing her arms.

"FORGET ABOUT THE ELEPHANT!" Milly yelled. "We could be destined to save Fantasma and you're worried about an elephant!"

Ruth scoffed. "Everyone loves elephants."

"That's true," Elsif pointed out. "Everyone besides my mom. She really doesn't like elephants-"

"People!" Milly begged, snapping her fingers. "Stay on topic! Please! We need to figure out what this prophecy means!"

Jazzy read the paper that Milly had scribbled the prophecy on. "Why do you think it's about us?" She asked.

"It was presented to Rose and I," Milly stated. "And there's five of us. One, two, three, four, five." She pointed to each girl.

Ruth sat on her bed, unimpressed by Milly's argument. "I think there's more to being a member of a prophecy than meeting a quota."

"Historically," Elsif began, which caused the others to groan because they knew a history lesson was coming. "Prophecies have very specific language, or otherwise known as identification language. Marked and gifted are the identification language in this prophecy. Marked means something physical, usually a birthmark or some type of scar, and it has to match somehow with everyone involved in the prophecy. Gifted is any type of magic. And I'm not aware of any of us having birthmarks or scars, and I'm the only one with powers."

Milly frowned. "Those are minor details."

"We could be destined to rule the world!" Rose exclaimed.

"You can't change history," Elsif said standing up. "I'm going to go make oy-oy puffs."

"I'll join," Jazzy said, and the pair left for the kitchen. Milly and Rose ran after them to continue arguing their points.

Instead of joining the chaos downstairs, Ruth resumed unpacking. As she hung up her dresses in the closet, Ruth tripped on the floor.

A bit of the carpet had turned up, and curiosity came over Ruth along with a little deja vu. She imagined something extraordinary was hidden under the floor, like there had been in Juniper's room all those months ago. Maybe someone had planted something like Melissa had planted the bag. Ruth wondered about different things that could be under the carpet. A box full of Pecuun bills? Fake IDs? A bloody knife?

Before Ruth could regret her decisions, she was on her hands and knees, tearing up the carpet in the closet. The carpet didn't pull easily, but after a few yanks, a big square dislodged into Ruth's hands. There was no loose floorboard, but there was a large piece of paper with some drawings. On closer inspection, Ruth saw a map within the scribbles.

While she rushed down the stairs to tell the others, Ruth accidentally ran into Uncle Earnest and dropped her map. "Sorry," she stammered as she quickly grabbed the paper from the ground.

"Looks like you're in a hurry," Uncle Earnest mentioned. "If it's for the oy-oy puffs, I wouldn't get your hopes up. There's a burnt smell coming from the kitchen."

"No," Ruth said casually. "I was just- actually I have a question. Do you know whose room our chambers used to be?"

Uncle Earnest thought for a moment. "I think it's always been a guest room."

"Interesting," Ruth mumbled, as she continued down the stairs. That meant the map could be anyone's.

Ruth walked into the kitchen to find Elsif fanning the smoke out of the window, Jazzy eating a burnt puff, Milly mixing up a new batch, and Rose juggling four bowls.

"You all must follow me right now," Ruth demanded, while waving the map. "We have an adventure to go on."

*****

"You're reading it wrong," Milly insisted, as she tried to grab the map from Ruth.

Ruth fended off Milly with one hand while she read the map in the other. "No, I'm not. I found it so I lead."

"We're supposed to be going north of the triangle building," Milly stated. "You're *leading* us east."

With a sigh, Ruth handed the map to Milly. The map was complicated, but eventually the girls found the right path. Once they navigated their way through a series of tunnels, bridges, buildings, and walkways the girls found a very small secluded forest in the middle of the bustling city. There was a small stone path through the forest and the map showed that the trail would lead them to their final destination.

After a few minutes of walking through the dense small forest, the girls arrived at a clearing with one large tree in the middle. The tree was in full bloom, with millions of stunning flowers.

"It's beautiful," Elsif whispered as she stared at the mesmerizing blue flowers. It was a light blue that matched her eyes.

"There should be more trees with my favorite color," Rose stated, also staring at the tree in awe. "When I'm dictator of Fantasma, all trees will be like this tree."

"White is a weird favorite color to have," Milly mentioned.

Rose frowned at Milly. "It's not, but thanks for contributing to the conversation."

"I thought your favorite color was yellow," Elsif said. "The same color as your favorite type of fire."

"Yes," Rose said with exaggeration. "It is."

"Girl," Ruth interjected. "The tree isn't yellow."

Rose looked at the tree then at the girls. "*Yes, it is.*"

Milly shook her head. "No it's not."

"What?" Rose demanded and turned to Jazzy who replied in a small nod. "The tree is yellow!"

"Are you color blind?" Elsif asked.

"No!" Rose replied with panic in her voice. "I can see color! I'm not color blind! The tree is color blind!"

Milly pointed at the tree. "It's clearly white, with little specks of red. Even if you are color blind, how do you not see white?"

"Um," Jazzy added to the confusing conversation. "I don't see white or yellow. I see purple flowers."

"Are you guys joking?" Ruth asked. "It's pink."

Elsif laughed. "I think we're all hallucinating, because I'm seeing blue. Or Rose paid you all to prank me."

"I like money too much to pay people," Rose stated.

"This is weird," Milly said. "Do you think anyone in the family knows something about the tree?"

"Obviously someone does," Ruth said. "*Someone* drew the map."

"Why would someone want a map to a color confused tree?" Rose questioned.

Jazzy smiled up at the lovely purple petals. "It's quite pretty."

Ruth walked towards the tree. "Let's pick some flowers and find out the colors that the rest of the family sees."

"If this is someone's property," Elsif commented. "Then we'll be stealing if we pick the flowers."

"It's nature," Ruth said as she climbed the tree. "It belongs to the world."

Milly shook her head. "I don't think that's how it works."

Ruth ignored the opposition and continued to pull herself higher and higher. The flowers were significantly high on the tree, and Ruth was thankful that she had taken such an interest in pole climbing at a young age. Eventually she reached the first branch with a bloom, and she carefully plucked the nearest one. As soon as the flower was disconnected from the tree, the color drained from the flower. It turned to a sad grey and wilted instantly.

"Darn it," Ruth muttered. She dropped the flower, and continued to climb to see if other branches would give her any luck. Branch after branch produced flower after flower that wilted and greyed the same way as the first.

With disappointment, Ruth began to descend the tree. As she climbed down the branches, she noticed a hollow opening in the trunk in between a few branches. Ruth took a peek in the hole because she knew bats sometimes hid in tree trunks and she was not going to pass up the chance to see a wild one.

But unfortunately there was no bat or any animal for that matter. Ruth turned to continue her descent, but a glint caught the corner of her eye. Looking back into the hole, Ruth saw something under the leaves and dirt. Carefully reaching in, Ruth grasped a solid object and brought it out. A very dirty book was in her hands.

Dusting off the grime, Ruth opened the book. She found a journal with many scribbles and words inside. It was completely full. Whoever the journal belonged to, had a *lot* to say. Ruth glanced at some of the pages, until two words caught her eyes.

Charlotte Arabella, was written several times on the page that Ruth had flipped to. Ruth knew the name could not be a coincidence. Her heart beat hard and fast in her chest, as she tried to scan the rest of the page.

"Ruth!" Rose yelled, which made Ruth almost drop the journal. "Hurry up!"

Ruth snapped the book closed and shoved it under her blouse, not caring about the dirt. She didn't want anyone else to see the journal until she had time to understand why that particular name was in it.

"Coming!" Ruth shouted back and climbed down the tree.

*****

The girls returned to their grandparent's house an hour later with lots of questions. They had decided to ask their Grandpa Henry about the tree, because he had lived in Stellae the longest. If anyone knew anything about the tree, it would be him. Ruth decided to skip the interview and head up to the room for an early night.

Grandpa Henry had heard of the tree the girls described but had never seen it himself. He said it was a mythical tree that the people of Stellae often told tall tales about. Some people called it the Tree of Life, and many different stories had been created about its magical abilities. The truth was that no one knew for sure if it was magical or not. Some theorized it was a type of ancient technology. The most famous story about the tree was that the humans that founded Stellae cut down all the trees in the region to make way for buildings, but that was the one tree that no one could uproot. So it's the last original tree in all of Stellae.

While the girls spoke to Grandpa Henry, Ruth rushed up the stairs, and once again ran into Uncle Earnest.

"Deja vu," Uncle Earnest joked as he walked down.

Ruth continued her sprint up the stairs, but stopped after a couple feet. She had a dreadful feeling that wouldn't subside. "Did you lie to me before? About the room?"

Uncle Earnest stopped walking down and turned around to face Ruth. "Partially."

"It was Uncle Louis' room," Ruth said quietly because she knew the unspoken rule of saying his name.

"Yes," Uncle Earnest replied, sorrow behind his eyes. "Sometimes it's easier not to say his name."

Nodding, Ruth continued her way to Uncle Louis' old room. She locked the door so no one would disturb her. Ruth pulled the old journal from her blouse, sat on her bed, and began dissecting the contents.

Nothing could have prepared Ruth for the shocking truth that was hidden between those pages.

Chapter 24: A Blast From The Past

Louis tried his best to sketch in his journal but the carriage ride to Merlin was particularly bumpy. Though drawing in a carriage with five siblings was already a challenge because there was not a moment of peace during the fifteen-hour ride from Stellae. Louis was punched, shoved, mocked, and bullied dozens of times during the trip, which distracted him from his sketching. But it didn't bother him too much because he enjoyed retaliating.

"What do you know about Mirabilis?" Earnest asked Louis, leaning over his journal so Louis couldn't see his drawing.

Earnest was Louis' best friend, and his little brother by eleven months. The two of them bonded over being the runts of the family. They weren't as smart as Mary-Anne or Poppy-May, and they weren't as athletic as Oliver or Benjamin. Earnest and Louis were also the only siblings not in advanced classes, though they were expected to continue their education at Merlin once they graduated.

The two of them certainly didn't live up to their parents either. Their father was an important senator in Stellae and their mother was a lawyer who represented Magicis clients in Stellae. They were the forgotten and borderline failures of the family, but it was alright, because they had each other.

"They're all insane and like weird food," Louis replied, putting down his sketches. "Like you. You'd fit right in."

Earnest grabbed a scrap of paper and fervently scribbled down the pitiful information that Louis provided. "I'm going to fail my Mirabilis Culture class."

"Get a tutor," Louis said. "You'll be fine."

"Has that ever worked for you?"

Louis snorted. "No."

Earnest rolled his eyes. "I know one girl from Mirabilis that's in my class. Maybe she'll help me."

"Rainbow?" Louis asked. "She's pretty. She'll never help you."

"Shut up," Earnest laughed, but was hit in the head a moment later.

Poppy-May glared at Earnest. "That's rude." Poppy-May was practically a second mother to the four boys.

"He started it," Ernest defended.

"Louis?" Mary-Anne questioned with sarcasm. "Never. He's an angel."

Oliver laughed. "I don't think we have the same brother."

"I think we do," Benjamin stated, gesturing to Earnest. "He's right here."

"No, the other one," Oliver replied.

"Me?" Benjamin questioned. "I'm the angel?"

Louis interjected, "Definitely not. I'm clearly the angel of the family."

Mary-Anne looked out the window. "We're pulling up," She announced as everyone gathered their things. Mary-Anne was the first to leave the carriage. "Boys, none of you are allowed to talk to me until October break."

Poppy-May followed Mary-Anne out of the carriage. "I'll talk to you boys anytime."

Benjamin and Oliver left next without a goodbye. Louis and Earnest took their time leaving the carriage and strolling up to the entrance of Merlin. Crowds of students arrived for the first day of classes and filled the front lawn. Through the crowd, Earnest spotted Rainbow by the water.

"I'll see you later," Earnest told Louis then ran off. Louis rolled his eyes as he watched his younger brother leave to make a fool of himself.

Louis dropped his bags off at his chambers, and went to the gardens to finish his sketch. Over August break in Stellae he had discovered a cool tree, but it was very hard to find so Louis was drawing a map. He wanted to finish the drawing by the end of the day so he didn't forget any details.

He walked through the gardens and headed in the direction of his favorite bench that overlooked a stream and was shaded by the willow trees. But to Louis' surprise when he arrived, the bench was already occupied by the prettiest girl that he had ever seen.

*****

"Dia," The strange woman said in a warning tone as she loomed over the small girl. "Get in this carriage *now*."

Struggling under the woman's firm grip, Dia looked up with pleading eyes. "Please, I don't want to go."

"Your parents signed the papers," the woman replied with a stern finger in Dia's face. "You legally have to come with me. Your sister had no trouble following directions."

"My sister," Dia spat as she tried to free her arm. "Is too young to understand that she's signing her life away."

Dia's sister Cent was only a few years younger, but Dia had done her best to shield her from the harsh realities of Versario. It was because of these foolish actions that Cent had no idea about the dangers of getting into carriages from Magicis.

The woman sighed as she seized Dia's arm with her second hand. "You don't want to stay here."

"Yes I do," Dia argued with shaky words. "You can't take me away!"

"I can actually," The woman replied, while releasing Dia from her grip. Dia turned to run but an invisible force caught her and dragged her into the carriage.

"Stop!" She screamed, kicked, and fought against her secret captor. "Mom! Dad! Please don't let them take me!" Dia yelled toward her home as she saw the curtains close. They didn't care about Dia or Cent being taken away, especially since they had deep pockets now to fill the void.

Dia continued her fight as the carriage door slammed behind her. She would have fought for the rest of her life if it wasn't for Cent's fear filled face. Dia stopped, she gave up her fight and replaced her expression with an emotionless one. No tears, no pain. She reached out and stroked a tear away from her younger sister's cheek.

"Everything is alright," Dia insisted coolly. "I only forgot my favorite book inside. They didn't let me retrieve it. But that's alright because Merlin will have so many new wonderful books."

"You can get it when we come back home," Cent replied, her smile returning. *Oh sweetie,* Dia thought. *We're never coming home.*

The whole thing was Dia's fault. She shouldn't have tried so hard in school, and encouraged her sister to do the same. If only she hadn't been top of her class. If only she hadn't been so proactive and volunteered in her community. If only Dia had flown under the radar like every other smart kid. If only she had listened to the whispered warnings. If only Dia hadn't been so vain to think she could shine in school but still avoid the attention of Magicis. If Dia had been wise then she wouldn't have been in a carriage that was taking her away.

"You two will need new names when we arrive," the woman said as she sat across from Dia and Cent. "Your current ones are too Versarian. You don't want to be associated with *that* any longer."

As the carriage pulled away, Dia glanced out the window and took in the last glimpse of her home. Moorville was violent, poor, and dangerous, but it was the place that raised her and for that she would be eternally grateful.

The woman drew the curtain closed with a forceful pull. "Horrid place. I'm happy we can save a few poor souls from it."

Dia would have snapped if it wasn't for Cent who sat blissfully unaware beside her.

"Are you excited to attend Merlin Academy?" Cent asked Dia cheerfully.

Dia swallowed her truthful response. "Yes. Yes I am."

*****

"Excuse me." Dia looked up to see a boy holding a journal and a pencil in front of her. "I think you're in my seat."

Dia looked down at the bench then back up. "I'm sorry," she replied in a nice manner. "I didn't know you owned this bench."

"I don't *technically* own it." The boy exaggerated his words. "But I have a very important task to accomplish and I won't be able to concentrate unless I can sit on that particular bench."

"Well," Dia countered. "*I'm* in the middle of a very important sewing project and if I can't concentrate by sitting on this bench then I won't have anything to wear for the first day of classes tomorrow."

The boy scratched his chin in thought. "This is a predicament."

"It appears so."

"I guess we'll have to share the bench," the boy sighed dramatically. "There's no other viable options."

Dia scooted to one side. "If that's the only way."

He sat down quickly beside her. "I'm Louis."

"Charlotte," Dia responded.

"Okay Charlotte," Louis stated. "I desperately need to concentrate so under no circumstances should you distract me."

"Understood."

Louis turned to his sketchbook, but was only able to remain silent for thirty seconds. "So where are you from?" Dia laughed as they began chatting and never stopped.

They talked about almost everything under the sun. Dia told him that she was from Currus and had been at Merlin for about a year. Louis talked about how he was from Stellae, attended Merlin since he was three, and had the craziest family in Fantasma.

The two stayed in the gardens for hours that day, and only left when a professor told them it was curfew.

*****

"I'm from Versario," Dia said.

That secret had been locked safely away in the deepest parts of Dia's mind, but she felt free for the first time in three years confessing the truth to Louis. He was her saving grace at Merlin. They had not gone a day without speaking since their first meeting. The two had become quick friends, to something more, to officially dating within weeks.

Dia never imagined she would be happy again after being taken away from her life, but meeting Louis made her almost glad she came to Merlin. It was a confusing feeling for Dia. On one hand Merlin was wonderful, gave her opportunities, treated her well, and introduced her to Louis. While Moorville would have killed her one way or another. But it was her home, a part of who she was. Maybe it would have been easier to live her life if she had chosen to go with Ms. Princey, not dragged.

It was a year and a half later and Dia's hand was intertwined with Louis's in the empty library. She didn't know if she loved or hated Merlin, wanted to go home or stay far away and never return. The only thing she knew was that she loved Louis, and she wanted him to love the true Dia. She needed him like she needed air to breathe. Dia could only hope that he would still love her when he learned the truth, and would help her with the impending doom she knew was looming overhead.

"What?" Louis looked up at Dia suddenly, closing the book he was reading. "What are you talking about?"

"Don't look alarmed," Dia told Louis in a whisper. "They might be watching us."

Louis' brow scrunched in confusion. "Who?"

Dia ignored the question and said the monologue she had been practicing for months. "When I was fifteen I was taken from my home in Moorville with my sister. Merlin does that sometimes. They take the smart children from Versario and force them to go to Merlin and abandon their old lives. I used to be Dia but they changed my name to Charlotte. I'm not from Currus, my parents didn't die in a factory accident, and my whole past is a lie."

Louis listened with wide eyes. "Are you joking?" He asked but he knew the answer from Dia's tone.

"No," Dia stated.

"Why-" Louis stumbled over his words. "Who forced you?"

"Ms. Princey at the time," Dia explained. "But it was really the whole institution of Merlin."

"Why didn't you tell me before?"

"Because," Dia said as she scanned the room again. "I wasn't allowed to. I had to abandon Dia in Moorville and start a new life. I couldn't have any ties to my old life, my old family. And for good reasons."

Louis' confusion turned to concern. "What's up with your family?"

"I don't know," Dia admitted. "I have no idea what they've done since I've been gone, and even when I was home, I tried so hard to stay on the right path that I hardly knew them. I couldn't believe my ears when I heard they sold me to Merlin Academy."

"They sold you!" Louis yelled.

"Quiet!" Dia insisted, looking over her shoulder again.

Louis breathed for a moment to calm down. "Sorry, but what do you mean they sold you?"

Dia shook her head. "Merlin gets the children they want one way or another, even if they have to steal, bribe, or trick the parents. But none of that matters at this point. What matters is what my family is doing now. Cent lied about where she went last December break and she found a way to Versario. Now she's talking like a crazy person. She apparently found my family and they must have corrupted her or something. She keeps saying that she's going to burn Merlin Academy to the ground, and if I don't help her then she is going to burn me down with it."

"You mean May?" Louis questioned. "Who's Cent?"

"Cent was her old name," Dia explained. "But I don't know what to do."

Louis squeezed Dia's hand that he never let go of throughout the whole conversation. "Everything is going to be alright. We'll figure out what to do with your sister and family."

Dia breathed fully for the first time in awhile. The nerves and anxiety that usually encapsulated her melted away as she pictured a brighter future.

*****

Louis held Dia as she wiped tears from her face. They stood on the front lawn of Merlin and watched a carriage roll away. A carriage that contained Dia's younger sister who was kicked out of Merlin because of Dia's actions.

"You did the right thing," Louis told Dia as he rubbed her arm. "You *had* to do it."

"I didn't want to," Dia replied quietly on Louis' shoulder.

The carriage was so far away that it was only a dot on the horizon. Dia's stomach constricted as she watched the carriage completely disappear. There was no going back now.

Dia begged and pleaded with her sister. Tried to explain the memories of Versario and of her family that Cent had were clouded with Dia's protection. Cent didn't know the true horrors of her past.

But nothing worked. No words could convince Cent that her current path would lead to nothing but destruction and sorrow. Dia was scared of the things Cent said. She feared for Merlin and her own life. Cent left Dia with no choice but to tell the administration of the school about what Cent was planning.

Cent was put into a carriage and sent back to Versario twenty minutes later. Dia knew what would happen but it still broke her heart. No matter what happened to Dia, she had always had her sister by her side. But now she didn't even have that.

"Louis," Dia said, leaning back so she could look at him. "I'm scared."

"It's alright," Louis reassured Dia. "Cent can't hurt you while you're at Merlin."

Dia shook her head. "I don't think that's true. I want to go somewhere where my family can't find me. Ever."

"Then let's find that place," Louis said.

*****

"We're leaving!" Louis stormed out of his house, Dia beside him. "Consider me dead because I never want to see any of you again!" He said as he slammed the front door behind him.

Nothing went according to plan. After Cent got kicked out of school, Dia and Louis tried to come up with a plan to keep themselves safe after graduation. But graduation never came because Dia was also expelled from the school for unknown reasons a few weeks later. Louis stormed the President's office completely enraged, which resulted in his expulsion as well. The pair had no protection now that Merlin had turned their backs on them.

The two went to Stellae and turned to Louis' family for help. They decided to tell Louis' family everything, the whole truth, which was a grave mistake.

"What are we going to do now?" Dia asked, as they stood on a random street in Stellae.

Louis fumed beside Dia. "We don't need them. We'll disappear, get married, and never see our families again."

"I don't want to be the reason you lose your family too," Dia replied, looking down to hide the tears that were forming.

"You're my family Dia," Louis stated, lifting Dia's chin up. "I love you and you're the only thing I care about."

Dia smiled through the pain. "I love you. But I'm scared."

"We'll burn all our belongings," Louis said. "Use fake names, and move around until we find the place where they'll never find us."

"I don't want to burn everything," Dia said, more tears forming. "I want our memories."

Louis wiped away Dia's tears. "We'll hide them then. I know just the place."

*****

"Do you think they know where we are?" Dia asked, frightened, holding her newborn baby in one arm and the local paper in the other.

"They don't know," Louis insisted. "It was a mistake telling Earnest we were in Regium, but he doesn't know exactly where we are."

Dia and Louis stared at a small message that was in the announcements section of the local paper. It read: **Dear Louis, We are concerned about you. We have received some concerning messages. Please come home. -Earnest**. Apparently the message had been printed in every newspaper in Regium.

No one in Mellberg knew that the message was for Dia and Louis because they had been careful to not share Louis' real name. But Dia and Louis knew it was for them, there was no doubt.

Louis had a moment of weakness a year or two earlier when he felt immensely homesick, specifically for his brother Earnest. He sent him a short letter to make sure he was alright, nothing more. Louis told Earnest they were in Regium, but didn't say the town or the district. And now he was trying to contact them.

"What if my family does know?" Dia asked with worry. "What if that's what Earnest is concerned about. What if it's a warning?"

Louis thought about the possibilities over and over again, and came to a decision. "I'll go to Stellae and figure out what's going on. I'll be gone for two days, three at most. I'll talk to Earnest and then come straight home."

Dia had known fear before, lived with it most days. She was scared when she and Louis went to Navisia to get married in a rough part of the region. She was scared when they lived in the remote jungles of Andorae. She was scared when they moved to Struth without a single coin. She was especially scared when she became pregnant in Mellberg, the quietest village Dia had ever known. But a day without Louis, surpassed the worst day that Dia had ever lived. That fear grew every day that he didn't come home.

Dia was completely consumed by grief when she gave up hope that Louis would ever return.

Five years later, Dia couldn't go another day without knowing what happened to Louis. She had to go to Stellae and find out.

"Goodbye Jasmine." Dia kissed her little girl's head, and blinked away tears. "I'll see you in a few days. I love you, my sweet girl."

"Bye Momma." Jasmine smiled, barely five years old.

It broke Dia's heart when she left the Smeeth's house, the family that agreed to watch Jazzy. Dia didn't want to leave her baby, but she needed to find out why Louis disappeared, and make sure no one was coming to harm her daughter.

Dia never made it to Stellae, similar to how Louis had never made it to Stellae five years earlier. They were both found in similar spots, a ditch on the outskirts of Stellae, and later identified by the Walker family. The two incidents were five years apart but oddly similar. They were reunited in death, to never be separated again.

–From the journal entries of Louis Walker and the accounts of Earnest, Poppy-May, and Benjamin Walker.

Chapter 25: Winter Games And Weird Conversations

The month of January passed with minimal craziness, only a few existential crises. Ruth hadn't told anyone what she found in the tree back in Stellae. She didn't know how or even if she should tell anyone. How do you tell your best friend that your own family covered up the past and death of her parents. It was quite the scandal and Ruth was not equipped to handle the drama, emotions, or the delicate nature of it.

Ruth decided to keep the secret from everyone for the time being. Since Ruth had a big mouth, she kept her distance from everyone, even Juniper. The Winter Games were a few days away and Ruth hoped it would be a nice distraction from her heavy thoughts.

"I'm not doing the maze race," Elsif stated, folding her arms as the girls waited for the list to be posted.

Rose shook Elsif's shoulders from behind. "You are the lamest person in Fantasma!"

Elsif pushed Rose away. "I don't want to waste time doing something I'm horrible at."

"And she doesn't want to spend a single second away from Will while he's here," Ruth added with a tease.

"If I ever give up good ole quality time with my cousins for a stupid boy, then someone needs to stab me because that's not me!" Rose declared

Milly moved in front of the girls. "They're bringing out the list."

"I hope they have a sewing competition," Jazzy commented, standing on her tiptoes. "My class this year has taught me so much."

"I hope nobody almost dies," Elsif mumbled, moving towards the list along with the rest of the girls.

Winter Games Events

Archery   February 3rd

Sword Dueling   February 5th

Magic Dueling   February 7th

Ship Racing   February 10th

Contemporary Dance   February 12th

Tapestry Making   February 13th

Pole Climbing   February 15th

Hand-to-Hand Combat   February 18th

Synchronized Flying   February 20th

Canon Shooting   February 23rd

Maze Race   February 25th

"They finally have pole climbing," Juniper said from behind Ruth, which made her jump. She hadn't noticed that he had walked up behind her, which was weird because Ruth usually knew if Juniper was within a hundred feet of her.

She'd been forced to avoid him at all costs. Ruth knew that she would tell Juniper everything in a heartbeat if the choice was up to her. But it wasn't. Jazzy's whole life was at stake so it wasn't up to Ruth. Jazzy needed to know first, if Ruth ever had the courage to share.

"I thought you liked pole climbing?" Juniper said.

Ruth blinked and realized she had been staring at Juniper with a concerned expression on her face. "I do, I mean- I'm excited- I uh, I'm signing up now."

Milly had finished signing up and was passing the pen to Rose, when Ruth intercepted. She quickly signed up for several events while Rose protested beside her. Once she was done, Rose snatched the pen back, and Ruth was forced to face Juniper.

She opened her mouth to say something but no words came out. Ruth was afraid that if she said anything, then the words would form into her terrible secret. She began to squirm under Juniper's gaze.

"You've been acting weird," Juniper said. "You *are* acting weird."

Ruth crossed her arms and argued, "No I haven't."

"Yes, you have," Juniper insisted. "I hardly saw you last month."

Ruth didn't want to argue, but she felt like she didn't have a choice. "Just because I haven't been at your beck and call every minute of the day doesn't mean I've been acting weird. I have a life you know."

Juniper stood unfazed by Ruth's words. "You seem different."

Ruth wanted to tell him. She desperately wanted to tell him. Her mouth trembled and the words were on the tip of her tongue. She was no longer able to control her mouth.

But fortunately, Ruth could still control her feet, so she ran as fast as she could away from Juniper.

Juniper and the girls watched Ruth sprint away.

"What's going on with her?" Juniper asked.

"Maybe she's finally gotten some common sense," Elsif muttered.

Jazzy finished signing up for her events and handed the pen to Elsif, who was forced to sign up for the maze race. After Jazzy passed the pen, she walked up to Juniper.

"It's not only you," Jazzy said in a low voice. "She's been avoiding me too. She's been avoiding everyone I think."

Juniper heard Jazzy but didn't acknowledge her words. He instead disappeared in the crowd.

*****

Ruth woke early on the third of February. It was the first day of competition and she was supposed to be competing in archery that day. Usually Ruth loved archery. It reminded her of her childhood when she attended camp in Bellator, but today was different. She woke up with a gnawing feeling in her gut again and she couldn't think of anything else but Uncle Louis and Jazzy.

Jazzy was her cousin. Jazzy was a part of the Walker family. Jazzy's parents were ostracised by her own family-

Ruth jumped out of bed and got ready for the day. She refused to be consumed by her thoughts. Ruth knew she couldn't think if she kept busy, so she distracted herself. After she was ready, Ruth went to her favorite place at Merlin. She couldn't be upset as long as she was near her beloved fountain.

Hours passed while Ruth sat, walked, and stared at the fountain. It was the only place that provided peace for Ruth since she learned the secret.

"You're going to be late for archery."

And within seconds, Ruth's peace was gone and she was back to worrying about spilling all her secrets to Juniper.

"I have time," Ruth said, looking in the opposite direction. "I think," she added when she overheard the noises from the crowd on the other side of the garden.

"Thirty minutes," Juniper clarified.

"I should go then." She stood up to walk away but Juniper grabbed her arm.

"What's going on?" Juniper demanded. "You're avoiding me, your cousins, and acting weird. Are you in trouble?"

"No!" Ruth shouted. "Of course not. I would have told you."

"Well you're not telling me *something*," Juniper stated. "What is it? Is there some other guy you're running around with?"

"No!" Ruth repeated even louder. "I'm not sneaking around with anyone. I've been wanting to be alone. Why?" A sudden smile crept onto Ruth's face. "Are you jealous?"

"Just tell me what's going on."

"Fine," Ruth bluffed. "Let me go and I'll tell you everything."

"So you can run away again?"

Ruth frowned. "Maybe."

Juniper waited for a response, while Ruth frantically attempted to think of a fake secret that would explain her odd behavior. She hated how he stared at her. Hated his stupid green eyes and his stupid dark hair and his stupid height that towered over her.

It was cruel and unusual torture, that Ruth could endure no longer.

"I can't tell you," Ruth pleaded. "But I want to. I want to tell you everything and be released from this burden. I know a secret that I need to tell the girls, one girl specifically. I can't tell anyone until I tell her, but I don't know if I'll ever be able to. But I can't be around you without telling you everything. So if I ever begin to share the secret, you need to stop me. Promise me you won't let me tell you anything without telling her first."

Juniper nodded, his expression growing serious. "I promise. But next time don't avoid me."

"I won't," Ruth agreed, her spirit lifting. "Ever again."

*****

"The competition's been good this year," Elsif told Will as they stood in the crowd that had gathered for the maze race. "Usually the Winter Games aren't as good as the Summer Games but it's been fun to watch this year. Especially since the girls have been doing well."

That year's Winter Games might have been the best games the girls had ever competed in. The best scores were Milly in 2nd for ship racing, Ruth in 6th for pole climbing, and Jazzy in 1st for tapestry making. Rose 'surprisingly' was disqualified from all her events from either bombs, knives, or threats.

"That canon shooting event was crazy," Will said. "Merlin must have lost eight ships."

"Yeah," Elsif replied. "Milly was so upset- Rose stop it. You're going to crack open your skull."

Rose was beside Elsif and Will, but was not participating in the conversation because she was too busy repeatedly bashing her head against a tree.

"I can't," Rose said between bashes. "This is the only way I can stand Will's irritating voice."

"You could have come with the others," Elsif said. Elsif had left the chambers early to meet Will while Ruth, Milly, and Jazzy were arriving later.

Rose eyed Elsif. "I can't let you out of my sight. You might try to back out of the race."

"I *am* backing out," Elsif told Rose. "I never wanted to be in it."

"You signed your name! You're contractually obligated!"

"You made me sign it," Elsif defended. "I was under duress."

Elsif and Rose continued their argument when the other girls eventually joined them, bringing Juniper with them.

"Are you serious Elsif?" Ruth said, joining the conversation. "You aren't participating?"

Elsif crossed her arms. "I don't want to."

"You haven't competed in anything yet," Milly said. "You can't miss all the events."

"I'm going to walk," Jazzy said. "We could be a team?"

"No," Rose interjected. "Elsif's on my team. I've already claimed her!"

As the gang continued to chat and argue before the race, an abnormal occurrence happened. A deafening siren began to wail throughout the gardens that the girls had never heard before. The sound rang so loud that it might have reached all of Magicis.

"What's going on?" Milly tried to yell above the siren.

"What!" Rose screamed back.

"What's going on!" Milly yelled louder.

Rose smiled. "Wartime in the valley!"

Milly shot Rose a confused expression. "Merlin isn't in a valley!"

"There's a war?" Jazzy questioned loudly, with a fear filled face.

Elsif shook her head. "There's no war!"

Ruth turned to Juniper. "Should we be concerned!"

"I don't know!" Juniper shouted over the siren. "I've never heard this alarm!"

"We should go inside!" Will yelled, pointing at the hundreds of students who were filing inside Merlin.

Since no one had any better ideas, (besides Rose who wanted to strike first with Milly's kraken) they followed the crowd into Merlin and eventually the basement.

The basement of Merlin was not like the rest of the school. It was dingy, small, and dark. The basement was primarily used for storage so students never went down there. It was mostly one large room that was directly below the dining chambers and was about the same size. The room contained things like extra desks, extra potion supplies, extra wands, extra door portals, and things like that. Along the walls of the basement there were several doors that only administration had keys to, which contained the more valuable storage items.

The students felt cramped as they waited. An hour passed with the faint siren still going off overhead. There was no explanation from the professors about the alarm or the reason they were ushered to the basement.

The inconvenience was annoying, but no one was overly concerned. If anything, the students assumed they were in the basement so they wouldn't have to hear the piercing alarm, and they would be able to leave as soon as someone turned it off.

Theories went through the crowd that some random intern accidentally hit the alarm in the capital of Magicis, and no one knew how to turn it off since it had never been needed before.

The girls assumed the same thing, that the siren wasn't anything important and they talked about inconsequential things while they waited. No one in the basement of Merlin could have guessed the dire significance of that siren.

Eventually the alarm stopped and everyone shuffled out of the basement and back to the gardens. Everything went back to normal. The maze race continued. Everyone laughed. Everyone had fun.

Elsif was forced to partner with Rose while Will watched from the sideline. They finished dead last. Milly raced with Jazzy and helped bring out her competitive side, and finished in the top fifty. Ruth walked with Juniper, and breathed easy for the first time in a month.

It was a great day for the girls, especially because they had no idea about the horrors that were occurring at the Magicis border.

*****

"I got a letter from Jerry!" Milly cheered as she ran around the chambers, with Rose-level excitement. "I got a letter from Jerry!"

Ruth gasped, and stood instantly from her chair. "You're writing to a boy!"

"I think," Jazzy corrected gently. "That Milly is talking about the older gentleman that we met in Viverra."

"Ew," Ruth said. "Milly raise your standards."

"Don't judge her," Rose sneered. "In a couple years she'll get all his money."

Milly stood in front of the group, pleading with them to be serious. "This could be about the Warlock's Hat!"

Rose waved off Milly. "I have enough hats."

"Do you have enough hats with an infinite amount of power?" Milly asked.

"I do," Rose stated. "But I could use a spare."

The left bedroom door opened. "Guys," Elsif complained as she emerged from her sleepy state. "You're so loud."

"Elsif it's noon," Milly said with disappointment as she ripped the letter open, and began reading. "He wants to talk to us!" She said with excitement and continued to scan her eyes across the paper. "He wants to meet us at Carroll's Eatery in Mirabilis on April 2nd." She paused before reading the last line. "He says the topic is dangerous and could cost us our lives so we must think carefully before deciding to come." Milly lowered the letter. "I can't wait!"

Chapter 26: Life Or Death Or Just Being Dramatic

"**I**'m almost home," Rose announced, as the girls and Will sat in a carriage on the edge of Merlin property. "And I'm almost free."

"And if we leave you in Mirabilis," Elsif suggested. "We'll all almost be at peace."

Ruth scoffed, "Elsif you're definitely the meanest among us. Everyone thinks it's Rose, but it's you."

"Yeah," Will agreed with a smile. "She bullies me all the time."

"Quiet you!" Rose chided, pointing her finger. "You haven't earned your right to make jokes yet."

Milly slapped Rose's finger away from Will. "Stop it or Ruth is going to promote you to the meanest cousin."

"Do I have that power?" Ruth asked with delight. "Am I the authority figure for meanness?"

"I don't think any of us are mean," Jazzy commented.

Rose shot a look at Jazzy. "Jazzy you *have* to be from another planet or alternate dimension."

"Maybe she's from that Menkensma place that David told us about," Milly suggested.

"Except," Elsif replied. "That place doesn't exist and Jazzy does- Someone's excessively late." Elsif interjected with her insult when Juniper opened the carriage door.

Juniper was concerned about leaving Merlin this time around so he insisted on slipping out in the middle of the night and meeting the carriage away from the entrance of the school.

"See," Ruth said, gesturing to Elsif. "Mean."

Juniper closed the carriage door behind him. "I went into the garden and maze area in case someone was following me."

Elsif rolled her eyes. She didn't believe that students from Versario weren't allowed to leave Merlin, and she didn't think someone cared enough about Juniper to follow him. "Let's just go," Elsif announced and a moment later the gang felt the carriage move beneath them

*****

The carriage ride was only about six hours, so when they arrived it was about five in the morning, which was a very bad time to roll into Mirabilis. Mostly because it was far too early to deal with the craziness of the region. The only comforting thing about going to Mirabilis was that it explained Rose's general personality enough where it began to make sense.

The trees looked wonky and the trunks were never straight up and down. The flowers swayed back and forth but not from the wind, it was more like they were dancing. Things always seemed to be out of proportion like giant mushrooms or horses that could fit in the palm of your hand. Many things also appeared backwards such as signs with backward words or clocks with numbers on the wrong side.

But the people were another story. Before the carriage arrived at Carrol's Eatery, it was flagged down by a random man standing in the middle of the roadway. When the carriage stopped, Rose popped her head out and the two had a very loud conversation about tickets, tea, and truth. After three minutes the two came to an agreement that time was upside down today, and the carriage moved on. The man continued to talk to a rhinoceros dressed in a suit and tie as the carriage rolled away.

The girls knew about Loquanims and that most of their population lived in Mirabilis, but it was still a little odd to see a community with more talking animals than humans.

A lot of nonsensical conversations filled the air alongside a lot of thrown objects. It wasn't uncommon to have to duck or dodge something every couple minutes. Speaking in riddles also seemed to be a common conversation style, which left the gang confused after every interaction.

By six the group found Carroll's Eatery, and it had just opened its doors. Jerry didn't specify a time so the gang decided it would be best to get there early. Most of them slept in the carriage, so they were prepared for the day, but the six hour ride was not nearly enough sleep for Elsif.

"Just coffee," Elsif told the waitress when the group found a seat near the entrance.

"You hate coffee," Ruth said once the waitress had walked away with their breakfast orders.

"I hate being tired more," Elsif retorted.

"When do you think Jerry will get here?" Milly asked, watching the door.

Rose shrugged. "People get lost here all the time, so maybe in fifteen million hours."

"I'm sure it won't be long," Jazzy said with a smile.

"I hope not," Will agreed.

Rose frowned. "Do you have a better place to be?"

"No," Will replied with a light tone. "I just don't think Elsif can hang in much longer before falling asleep."

Rose rolled her eyes. "Kiss up."

Several hours passed with no sign of Jerry. There was only so much food to eat and conversation to make before the group grew bored. The only source of entertainment was people watching, because the Mirabilians were quite an interesting bunch.

"The ground is too soft!" An owl in a dress said as she walked in. "I hate days where the flowers are asleep."

"I hear you!" Rose cheered back.

Milly groaned. "Why hasn't Jerry come yet?"

"Doesn't Jerry have a different name?" Jazzy asked. "I thought that was his nickname."

"It is," Elsif agreed. "But I don't remember his actual name."

Ruth tapped the table. "It's on the tip of my tongue."

"I don't see a problem with calling him Jerry," Rose commented. "It's a very flattering name. Way more flattering than whatever his old geezer name was."

Juniper turned to Will. "Didn't you get his name?"

"*I* didn't," Will clarified. "My friend Byron did. *He* would definitely remember his name?"

"So you don't remember?" Milly asked.

Will replied hesitantly, "No."

Rose groaned while leaning precariously back in her chair. "Darn it! Why didn't you bring Byron with you, idiot!"

Elsif jabbed Rose's ribs which made her crash to the floor. "Don't say- oh sorry- but please don't call people idiots. It's rude."

"Milly," Jazzy said. "Didn't Jerry say his true name in the letter."

"No," Milly replied, shaking her head.

"*No?*" Ruth questioned with wide eyes and a tilted head. "How do you know that he's the one we're meeting? Maybe we're meeting some other random old man?"

"Because he said the meeting was about the Warlock's Hat," Milly defended herself. "And I gave him our address when we met him in Viverra. Who else could it be?"

"A murderer," Elsif suggested.

Rose jumped up out of her chair. "Or it's me pulling a prank because you all refuse to come to Mirabilis, the best region in Fantasma!"

"Rose," Milly said in a warning tone. "I'm going to kill you."

"I didn't send the letter," Rose said glumly while sitting back down. "But it would have been really funny if I had."

"Why can Milly say kill but Rose can't say idiot?" Ruth questioned Elsif. "Your bad language radar isn't accurate."

Elsif frowned. "That doesn't matter right now because we could be meeting with a murderer any minute."

"I don't think a murderer would ask to meet us in a restaurant," Will added.

"You don't know that," Elsif insisted. "I thought you were a murderer for a while. You still could be. I'm not sure."

"He is, Elsif!" Rose shouted while banging the table. "Break up with him!"

"It could be someone Melissa sent," Juniper added gravely.

Silence filled the table as the realization hit each person. Melissa knew about the Warlock's Hat and also knew where the girls lived. They could be waiting for someone that she sent, and they could be in a lot of trouble very soon.

"I hate Melissa," Ruth groaned.

"Don't say hate," Elsif mentioned out of habit.

Ruth scowled. "Should we leave?"

Milly crossed her arms. "I'm not leaving until I see Jerry."

"Are you youths still calling me that?" An angry voice barked at the group, which made several of them jump, two of them gasp, and one of them scream a little.

There was a moment of awkward silence as the group stared at Jerry in surprise, but after several seconds Milly sprung to her feet and shook Jerry's hand. "Nice to see you sir. Please sit down. Right here. I saved you a seat."

Milly made sure to have an empty chair right next to her and wouldn't let anyone else sit in it, and even made sure there were no other empty chairs at the table.

He sat down reluctantly as if he was being taken hostage into the conversation. His grumpy expression was displayed evidently on his face. "I didn't say you could bring extra people," He said, scowling at Juniper and Will.

"They're cool," Ruth assured. "They're with us."

Jerry rolled his eyes. "Obviously they're *with* you," he snapped. "But that doesn't mean I can trust them." He shook his head and mumbled to himself. "This was a mistake. I shouldn't be here. I shouldn't trust a bunch of kids."

He began to stand up but Milly stood up faster and blocked his chair from sliding out. "No you can trust us!" she begged. "We're trustworthy! I promise you that we want the same thing!"

Jerry eyed Milly with contempt. "And what do we both want?"

Milly took a few breaths, and scrambled for an answer. "To do the right thing."

A moment of stillness passed between Jerry and Milly, but eventually Jerry grunted and pulled his chair back towards the table. "You're lucky that I'm desperate and have no other choice."

As Milly sat back down Elsif leaned over to Rose and whispered, "That was the most generic reason I've ever heard."

"Old people eat that up," Rose whispered back. "It reminds them of a simpler time when Elves and Dwarves roamed Fantasma and no one used complicated words like establishment or literally."

"Do you know how to talk normally?" Elsif muttered.

Once Milly sat down she bombarded Jerry with questions. "What do you need? Why don't you have anyone else to help you? What do you need our help for? Do you need *all* of our help? Because if you only need one person then *I* can definitely help you."

Jerry held his hand up to stop the interrogation. "I'll tell you what I need to tell you."

Milly nodded. "Yes sir."

Ruth chuckled to herself. "*Sir?* Someone else is a kiss up too."

"You should all listen to what I have to say," Jerry said sternly, shooting a look at Ruth. "This will affect all of you. It will affect all of Fantasma."

Ruth squirmed in her seat. "I wasn't the only one whispering," She mumbled.

Jazzy placed a hand on Ruth's arm. "We all promise to listen very carefully, Mr. Jerry."

Jerry sighed while his expression relented. "I want you kids to know-" He hesitated for a moment, either not knowing his next words or not wanting to say them. "You don't have to do what I'm asking you all to do. It's your choice, and you shouldn't make it lightly."

Milly nodded vigorously while leaning forward in her chair. "We understand," She answered breathlessly. The rest of the group weren't quite as enthusiastic as Milly, but they nodded as well.

Reaching into his bag, Jerry pulled out an old, rusty, metal box about the size of his hand and placed it on the table. "I can't hold on to this much longer. I've been trying to find someone to give it to for over two years. Meeting someone at a different location every month or so, but I haven't been able to find anyone I trust. If I wait much longer, I don't know who's going to end up with it."

"What is it?" Rose asked, poking the unimpressive block.

"Careful," Jerry retorted, looking over his shoulder. Once he was satisfied with his scan of the room, he slowly turned back and answered Rose in a low voice. "This is a tracker for the Warlock's Hat, made by Xen Siid, the great warlock himself."

Several gasps sounded from around the table but others in the group were sceptical. "If you have a tracker then why haven't you found the Hat?" Elsif asked, unimpressed.

With a frown, Jerry explained, "I was given this tracker about thirty years ago by a-" He hesitated. "*Friend*. The tracker wasn't safe for him so he was forced to give it to me. But we agreed that I would never search for the Hat because it's too powerful. I kept my promise. And I stopped every fool and idiot I could from finding the blasted thing."

Jerry's tone and face grew increasingly somber with every word he said. "Recently I've heard some chatter which has worried me about the safety of the Hat. It's going to be found soon whether this tracker is involved or not. And I can't in good conscience let it fall into the wrong hands."

"Like Melissa," Ruth interrupted, which was met with resounding shushes from the table.

With a quick side eye, Jerry continued speaking. "I can't go looking for myself. There's too many people who have an invested interest in me and I'll be followed if I go anywhere near Andorae."

"The Hat's in Andorae?" Milly gasped with a hand to her mouth.

"No," Jerry chided. "The powersource for the tracker is in Andorae, and there's too many people that know that. So if I go to Andorae then I'll be followed until I find the Hat, and then I'll be ambushed, killed, and thrown in a ditch while the Hat is taken to the worst people in Fantasma. I need someone else to go to Andorae. People that aren't on any kind of radar and aren't corrupted by the world. I wouldn't be asking this of you if I had any other choice. Trust me there's no one left in any of these regions with any moral backing."

"You can trust us," Milly repeated her words from earlier.

Jerry sighed deeply, the wrinkles around his eyes becoming more pronounced. "I trust that you all are naive children that no one will look at twice. I also trust none of you have a secret agenda."

Milly nodded. "What should we do with the Hat once we get it?"

"Are you insane?" Jerry questioned. "You will be going nowhere near the Hat! At any time! All I need from you all is to go to Andorae, find an adequate powersource, then keep the tracker until I have a chance to retrieve it."

"We can do that," Milly said while trying to hide her disappointment. "What's the power source?"

"Meliocordian," Jerry said. "It's a type of condensed plant that is old and rare to find these days. I can't tell you where to look for it, because you might attract suspicion. You'll need to go to Andorae yourselves and act like it's some type of school project, and find the meliocordian on your own. I'm sure it won't take you more than a couple days to find someone that will sell you some."

Jerry slid the tracker over to Milly. "You'll take this for now, just to make sure you find the right power source. Under no circumstance will any of you try to find the Hat yourself. Understand? Once you procure the meliocordian then I'll contact you to get the tracker back. It might be a few months or a few years. Keeping you all safe and away from scheming eyes will be my number one priority."

"Thank you for trusting us with this, we won't take it lightly," Milly said. "But we could help you more than just getting the meliocordian. I know you haven't said it out right, but you're hinting at something happening in Fantasma. Something grave and end of the world-ish. We can help you. I think we're supposed to help you. We've been presented with a prophecy, and it sounds serious."

Jerry appeared skeptical. "Well let's hear it then."

Milly recited the words to Jerry in a low whisper.

"It's not about any of you," Jerry said with no hesitation.

Milly stumbled over her words, "What- how, how do you know?"

"There's seven of you."

Rose interjected, "It's only about the girls. It's a sexist prophecy."

"Also it uses the words marked and gifted which is very specific language for prophecies," Jerry continued. "Unless all five of you have prominent birthmarks and powerful magic then it's about five others."

"Then why was it presented to us?" Milly argued.

Jerry shrugged. "A plethora of reasons. You might meet the five individuals in the future, they might be your descendents, or you were in the right place at the right time. This prophecy might not come to fruition for another five thousand years."

"But it can't be a coincidence that the prophecy is talking about five people and there's five of us," Milly insisted. "Maybe we'll develop powers and marks will appear one day!"

Scoffing, Jerry stood up. "I don't have time to explain the complexities of ancient Elven prophecies to children. We'll be in contact once you get the powersource."

Milly protested but Jerry walked out of the restaurant without stalling.

"Well, that was interesting," Elsif said with a laugh. "He's crazier than last time. Now he thinks people are after him and that Elves have something to do with prophecies. I took advanced prophecy formation, so I think I know a thing or two about prophecies."

"Yes," Rose said with exaggeration. "You're smart. We know!"

"So when are we going to Andorae?" Ruth asked. "If we go now then we don't have to spend the rest of our break in Mirabilis with all these psychos."

Elsif shook her head. "We're not going to Andorae."

"Yes we are," Milly protested.

Jazzy shifted in her seat. "It sounded dangerous."

"I agree," Will added. "If Jerry has people that want to hurt him then maybe we don't want to get involved."

"Of course you'd say that," Juniper said, shooting a suspicious eye at Will. "Obviously the Hat needs to be found soon or the wrong hands are going to find it."

"That's not our problem," Elsif argued. "We shouldn't get involved in Jerry's drama."

"We're going to Andorae," Milly said absolutely. "And we're finding the meliocordian. I'm in charge of searching for the Warlock's Hat so this is my call."

"Who put you in charge?" Ruth questioned.

Milly gestured across the table. "Elsif."

"I have no recollection of that."

"Well you did," Milly said while crossing her arms. "And I am. So we're doing this!"

Elsif rolled her eyes. "Whatever, we'll see what happens."

"Yeah," Milly agreed, stubbornness filling her. "We will."

"Joseph Ellison!" Ruth said out of the blue.

"What?" Elsif questioned.

Ruth smiled. "I remembered his name."

Chapter 27: A Declaration of Love

"**T**orture is not a sport," Milly stated.

"Torture is my favorite sport!" Rose exclaimed. "Me and the boys play every Tuesday night."

Elsif walked out of her bedroom. "Can you guys keep it down? I'm writing a paper for my Teaching the Ancient Age class and I need to concentrate."

Rose frowned. "Is it due tomorrow?"

"No."

"Is it due this week?" Milly asked.

Elsif hesitated at her repeated response. "No."

"Then take a seat Elsif," Rose said with a mischievous smile. "And you can help me decide on how to best torture Bernard."

"Bernard?" Elsif asked with concern. "Melissa's friend? The one with the red hair? Bernard John?"

"Yup," Milly confirmed. "Rose is claiming he stole her notes from her Monstrum Region's class."

"He did!" Rose announced, hitting the arm of her chair. "He did! I saw him following me out of class and then later my notes were missing from my bag. He's guilty!"

"Or," Milly proposed. "He happened to be taking the same path as you after class and you lost your notes yourself. As you often do."

Elsif sat beside Rose. "How do you know he was following you?"

Milly groaned. "Elsif don't feed into her delusions. I can't be the only rational one around here."

Rose shushed Milly and continued. "I was wandering around the school for half an hour. He was always thirty feet behind me. How could he not be following me? I was walking in the most random pattern!"

"Maybe he was wandering too," Milly said nonchalantly.

Rose groaned as well. "How do you explain the missing notes then, Millicent?"

"Have you checked under your bed?" Milly questioned. "You shove everything under there and then you later claim it's lost."

"The items under my bed are between me and the government."

Milly rolled her eyes. "Why is Bernard even in your class? He's supposed to be an advanced student."

"*Because*," Rose exaggerated. "He's dumb as a doornail. Which is an insult to doornails!"

As Milly and Rose argued, Elsif's mind raced. Bernard may have not been bothering Elsif anymore, but he had moved onto one of her cousins. He broke their deal. And Elsif wasn't one to forgive her foes quickly.

"What if we steal your notes back," Elsif suggested, while scheming a different plan in her head.

Rose perked up. "Elsif you're singing sweet music to my ears."

"I give up," Milly said with a slouch.

"We can sneak into his room and look for your notes," Elsif said. "We can do it tomorrow during dinner. The dining chambers always serves the best meals on Friday night so the boys' wing will be empty."

"Yes!" Rose agreed with anticipation. "And we'll wear gloves and masks to protect our identities. If we're caught then we'll pretend to be pirates from Navisia."

"That's offensive," Milly said. "And if you really want to check if Bernard has your notes then ask Ruth to ask Juniper to check his chambers."

"Too many middle men," Rose snapped. "Elsif and I know how to get things done."

"Yeah," Elsif agreed, the edge of her voice revealing the slightest hesitation. "We do."

*****

Milly left Elsif and Rose to their scheming and walked to the library. There were only a few hours before curfew, and Milly wanted to spend some time researching the meliocordian. The sooner the girls could pinpoint exactly where to buy it in Andorae, the sooner they could turn on the tracker, and the sooner the Warlock's Hat could be found. Whether it was found by Milly or not, the Hat needed to be located.

Ruth was already in the library with several books strewn along the table about Andorae. She was scribbling notes down when Milly walked over.

"Any new information?" Milly asked.

"Not really," Ruth said. "It still looks like Reuter is still the best option. But it seems like we're going to have to ask a local once we get there."

So far the girls had gathered that the meliocordian was a condensed flower that was native to only Andorae. It was powerful but was mainly used in the Ancient Ages, and modern day magic had made it mostly obsolete. The remaining meliocordian was far and few between.

Reuter was the largest 'city' in Andorae so that would be the most likely place to find someone selling it. City is also a very loose term because Andorae didn't really have buildings like other regions. Their whole region was a big jungle and a lot of their buildings were in the trees.

The other little snag in the plan was that the meliocordian was going to be expensive, and Andorae didn't use the same currency as the rest of Fantasma. They preferred trading items that were useful to them.

Milly had talked to a girl from Andorae, Igia, about the meliocordian but she wasn't very helpful. Apparently, all the students from Andorae hadn't been back since they were young children and didn't have many answers. The one thing Igia suggested was that the girls use gold to buy the meliocordian. She had no idea how much or where to buy it, but gold was the only thing she could think of that the girls might be able to obtain. Gold was a hot commodity in Andorae because people liked to melt it down and use it for jewelry or to coat their *decorative* weapons.

"Let's find a map of Reuter and maybe we can pinpoint some shops," Milly suggested.

The girls walked over to the mapping shelves and found several maps for Reuter. They started mapping their route and planning their trip to Andorae.

"Do you think Jerry was telling the truth?" Ruth asked as she wrote down information. "About this being dangerous?"

"Yes," Milly said cautiously. "I believe him."

"Are you scared?"

"No," Milly answered immediately. Then she added with a little more hesitation, "Are you?"

Ruth shook her head and answered quickly, "No. Of course not. Why would you ask such a thing?" The girls continued to gather data about the town of Reuter, but after a moment Ruth added in a softer tone, "Maybe a little."

Milly nodded. "Me too."

*****

Jazzy sat on a bench in the garden and practiced her sewing. The sun was setting and darkness began to surround her. Although it was dark and it was hard to see the needle and the skirt, Jazzy didn't stop. She poked the skirt and pulled out the needle over and over again, without her normal attention to detail.

The skirt was coming out sloppy, but Jazzy didn't care. She was mesmerized by the rhythmic motion. She was stuck in that movement, unable to stop. It was comforting to her, even though the skirt would not end up satisfactory.

In the distance students walked through the garden, but Jazzy paid little attention to them, until someone passed by that caught her eye. His saunter was unmistakable and his presence was out of place at Merlin.

Dylan was one of those people that you couldn't describe. Even in that moment Jazzy couldn't capture who he was in her mind. All Jazzy knew about him was that he would never leave the center of her thoughts.

His indescribable and baffling demeanor almost distracted Jazzy from noticing his companion. A beautiful girl with subtle olive-green skin and dark hair. Melissa walked by his side with effortless long strides and a smirk that would stop any boy in his tracks.

Disdain dropped to the pit of Jazzy's stomach. It sat for a moment, brewing, as she watched the pair walk with their backs towards her and into the maze. Jealousy swirled inside her when she saw Dylan look at Melissa. The jealousy spun and churned inside her, clashing with her disdain. Her feelings fought inside her until the storm was too much and it burst upward into her heart. Hatred was a bitter taste that Jazzy never wanted to get used to.

They disappeared behind the perfect green shrubbery that made up the walls of the maze. Jazzy's hands had finally stopped the repetitive motion and her eyes were glued to the last spot the pair had been seen.

Her jealousy slowly fizzled out and her pit of disdain lightened. A moment later Jazzy's hatred turned into shame. She shouldn't feel those things towards another person. Especially Melissa who had been so helpful to Jazzy.

Melissa and Dylan were friends first, and Dylan had been very kind to agree to help Jazzy. She wasn't owed anything by either of them. Jazzy hoped those emotions would never surface again.

Jazzy decided she should leave and go to dinner. She stood up, put away her sewing materials, and took a few steps towards the school. But once her mind started racing again, she found her feet turning around and walking into the maze instead.

*****

Elsif and Rose strolled over to the boys' wing with quiet feet and watchful eyes. Elsif wore her regular clothes, planning to say she accidentally wandered too far west if she was caught. Rose took a different approach. She was dressed head to toe in black, with a black mask that showed only her eyes and mouth. If they were caught Rose planned to claim she was a spy and it was for national security's sake that she had to break into Bernard John's room. Elsif didn't think they would run into anyone, so she didn't care what Rose did.

Girls were technically never allowed in the boys' wing, but over the last year and a half, the girls discovered that there was a lot more leeway in security then they had previously thought. Before, they were led to believe that magic would somehow inform the authorities as soon as anyone put one foot out of place, but obviously from their former schemes, that wasn't the case.

"Do you remember which chamber it is?" Elsif asked.

"I remember everything," Rose said as she confidently walked up to a door and proceeded to open it. She poked her head into the chamber then immediately shut the door. "Nope, too clean," She said to Elsif then moved on to the next door.

"We can't go into every single room," Elsif snapped.

"We're not," Rose fumed as she quickly opened two more doors. "We're going into *this one*. Relax."

Rose walked into the third door, and Elsif reluctantly followed. But once Elsif crossed the threshold she knew it was Juniper and Bernard's room. It was eerily familiar and the mess was remarkably the same.

"Why does no one lock their chambers?" Elsif questioned as she closed the door behind her.

"We don't lock our chambers," Rose pointed out

Elsif frowned. "We should. Now that we know there's no magic to keep people out."

The girls entered the second bedroom to the left, the room they knew belonged to Bernard. It was far messier than the rest of the chamber, and there was trash, paper, textbooks, and clothes everywhere.

"Okay," Elsif said, moving stuff around with her foot because she didn't want to touch anything. "Let's find your notes quickly and get out of here."

The search would be difficult because of the lack of organization, but Elsif was determined to know for certain if Bernard had stolen Rose's notes. The outcome of the search would determine her next actions, and she couldn't afford to be wrong.

"Do you ever think about what life would be like if we were pufferfish?" Rose asked randomly as the girls sifted through the room.

"No," Elsif answered as she picked up a large stack of papers.

Rose groaned. "Elsif, you're the worst conversationalist ever."

Elsif ignored Rose as she took a closer look at the papers. They were all letters from the same person, and the name seemed oddly familiar. "Do you know an E. Stone?"

"I know lots of stones," Rose said, walking over to Elsif. "But I usually name my pet rocks something a little more clever than E. Bernard is very unoriginal."

"This guy has written almost a hundred letters to Bernard just this month," Elsif said. "And it looks like Bernard has been responding a lot too. Who do you write hundreds of letters to each month?"

"My weapons dealer," Rose grinned.

Elsif flipped through the pages. She knew she shouldn't snoop, but she wanted to figure out why the name was familiar. "Here it says his full name is Everette. Everett Stone. I've heard that name before."

"Maybe it's his dad," Rose said, bored of the topic.

"But they have different last names," Elsif argued.

"I'm not his mother," Rose pouted. "So it's not my business."

Elsif scratched her head. "But why would I know Bernard's dad?"

"I don't know," Rose replied. "But you do have questionable taste in men."

"But who writes to their parents five times a day?"

"Who cares!" Rose said exasperated. "I'm bored, let's go."

Elsif put down the letters. "We haven't found your notes yet."

"Oh," Rose said in a light hearted tone, that Elsif knew to fear. "I forgot to mention that I found them this morning. Or Milly found them on my messy desk this morning."

Elsif frowned. "And you didn't think to mention that?"

"Of course not," Rose said with a smile. "Because then we wouldn't be having this fun quality cousin time."

Elsif side-eyed Rose. "Fine, let's go then."

Rose bounded out of the room, but Elsif lagged behind for a moment. Once Rose was out of eye line, Elsif snatched a pen and a small piece of paper. She scribbled down some quick words and left the note in a noticeable spot. Elsif glanced at the note one last time, before leaving.

You broke our deal -EM

Elsif walked out of Bernard's room, and wondered if she made the right decision. But even if she hadn't, there was no going back.

"Let's go," Elsif said.

"Do you think we'll make it back in time for din-" Rose stopped mid word when the chamber door opened in front of them.

Juniper walked in his living room to find Elsif and Rose staring at him in horror. He was less horrified but definitely annoyed.

"We can explain ourselves," Elsif began.

"I don't care," Juniper said plainly. "Get out."

"We were just- uh- um," Elsif stuttered. "Rose?"

Rose looked from Elsif to Juniper, then pointed at Elsif. "She's in love with you!"

"No way!" Elsif yelled back. "Rose is the one in love with you!"

"She was planning to steal your hair from your pillow and make a love potion!"

"Rose stole all your left socks and a couple of your combs!"

"Elsif named her favorite book after you!"

"Rose hops on one foot through doorways because she heard it brings good luck for relationships with guys named Juniper!"

"That doesn't even make sense," Rose told Elsif.

"We were saying random things! Why are you judging?"

Juniper swung the door wide open. "Get out."

Elsif quickly walked out the door, and Rose followed while hopping on one foot. "We're both in love with you and we'll duel for your hand in one fortnight," Rose called as she went out the door.

The girls walked out of the boys' wing before anyone else caught them, but at the edge of the hallway the girls ran into another unwelcome person. Bernard sneered as he passed the girls.

"Hey Frosty."

Elsif frowned and didn't respond. She knew that she wouldn't have to deal with him much longer.

*****

Jazzy wandered through the maze but never came across Melissa or Dylan. It was dark and the wind grew brisk, but Jazzy kept walking. She was lost. In a physical sense but also in a metaphorical one. Jazzy no longer knew where she was or who she was, and she didn't know how to figure either one out.

She placed her right hand on the wall and brushed the bushes as she walked. Her logical side thought that if she never took her hand off the wall and always turned right then she would eventually find her way out. Though a part of her didn't want to escape the maze. If she did then she would have to continue to face her life.

Walking for almost an hour, Jazzy thought it was odd that she hadn't come across any other students. She wondered if it was already past curfew and if a teacher would find her soon.

While she was lost in thought, a strange thing happened. As Jazzy's hand brushed up on part of the wall, it moved away from her fingertips. Stepping back in shock, Jazzy saw the wall open as if it was a door. In its place was a dark entrance that opened into a clearing. The only thing she could see was a faint green light.

Jazzy was reluctant to go into the ominous opening, but she had always been a curious girl.

She stepped cautiously through the dark abyss. Once she was over the threshold of the hedge, the bush door slid back into place, and left a perfect wall behind her. She was now in a dark circular clearing that was closed off from the rest of the world. The only thing Jazzy could see was a shadowy object in the middle, with a small amount of green light emanating from the top left.

As Jazzy walked toward the large object, light suddenly flooded around her. Green-fire torches lit one by one all around the edge of the clearing. Jazzy jumped in fright, but once her nerves were calmed, she looked up at the towering object that was now perfectly illuminated.

It was a statue, like several others in the garden, but this one appeared different to Jazzy. The statue was of a woman, not much older than herself. She had long hair that fell out of the hood of her cloak that she clutched with a fist in one hand, close to her neck. In the other, she held a long scepter that was taller than her. The top of the scepter was the home of the green light that grew brighter each second.

The woman's face caught Jazzy's attention. She wasn't quite smiling but she looked kind. She didn't have a happy expression but it wasn't sad either. It was accepting.

The other statues and fountains in the garden were grand and modeled after powerful individuals. They were to show honor and respect for great people. This woman didn't appear great or powerful. She looked like Jazzy. No one special, but she was still welcomed here at Merlin.

Jazzy's heart filled with warmth for the first time in a long time. She didn't want to leave that place in fear of losing the feeling. It felt peaceful. It felt like what Jazzy pictured as the perfect home feeling. Jazzy forgot about Dylan, Melissa, and her loneliness at that moment. She had found her tranquility.

A voice yelled from a distance. Jazzy backed away from the statue. She instantly wanted to keep the place hidden. The woman had been a secret up until then and Jazzy felt as if she was invited into a special place. So Jazzy would honor the woman and keep her a secret.

Walking up to the wall that had once opened up, Jazzy extended her hand and brushed the branches like she did before. The bush opened up, and Jazzy snuck back into the maze.

She walked around a corner and found a guard. "What are you doing out here?" He demanded. "Curfew is in fifteen minutes."

"I uh-," Jazzy stuttered. "I got lost."

The guard shook his head. "Students aren't competent anymore."

Jazzy followed the guard back to the school and thanked him for his help. She went back to her chambers to find the girls in the middle of an elaborate story.

"Jazzy, where were you?" Elsif asked with concern, stopping her account of the previous activities. "It's past curfew."

"I was sewing in the garden," Jazzy answered, placing a smile on her face. "Then I went into the maze for a stroll and I got terribly lost. A nice guard found me and walked me back."

"Was he a cute guard?" Ruth asked.

"This is why you should never go in the maze without me as your personal guide," Rose said with disappointment.

"Where's your sewing?" Milly questioned, noticing Jazzy's empty hands and no bag.

Jazzy fiddled with her hands once she realized she had left her sewing on the bench outside the maze. "I forgot it. But it wasn't very good anyways."

"I'm sure that's not true," Elsif assured. "All your sewing is so beautiful."

"This one wasn't," Jazzy stated. "But that's alright because my next one will be." She smiled to herself and retreated to her bedroom.

"Ok now that we know Jazzy's not dead," Ruth said. "Continue the story."

Rose jumped onto the table. "And then we both declared our undying love for Juniper!"

"No we didn't!" Elsif quickly corrected.

"What?" Milly questioned.

"What!" Ruth screamed.

Rose threw her arms in the air. "We obviously needed a cover on why we were in his chambers. Being in love with him was the easiest solution."

"So," Milly said to Elsif with a laugh. "Are you, Will, and Juniper going to be some kind of weird love triangle now."

Elsif frowned. "No."

"NO!" Ruth yelled with a fist in the air towards Elsif. "Juniper is mine!"

"Calm down, you can have him," Elsif replied.

Rose twirled on the table. "I'm the one that's going to be having a love triangle with Will and Juniper. First I will kill Will -the only reasonable option- then I will marry Juniper, take all his money, then kill him too. Then I will live the rest of my life in luxury on Numterram."

Ruth pouted in her chair. "I can't believe you both told Juniper you loved him, before I told him I loved him."

Milly shot Ruth a confused look. "You haven't told him? You tell *us* every day that you're in love with him."

"Don't judge me," Ruth snapped. "I'm waiting for the perfect moment."

"Yeah," Rose mocked. "She's waiting for a perfect moment like Juniper and I just had."

*****

It was early the next morning when Elsif woke up. The sun was just beginning to peak over the horizon, as Elsif tiptoed around her room. None of the girls were awake yet, and Elsif wanted to slip out before anyone could question her.

She dressed quietly and crept into the living room silently. Light snores were heard as Elsif left the chambers. Saturday morning was usually a ghost town at Merlin since all the students and staff slept in.

Elsif went down two flights of stairs and walked to the school's office on the first floor. The secretary had just arrived and was unpacking her bag for the day.

Elsif hesitated at the door. She hadn't been seen yet so she still had the chance to change her mind. She didn't have to go through with her threat. Her empty threat, she never thought she would be cashing in. But a voice inside Elsif convinced her that the next actions were a necessity. It was for her family's safety. The voice wasn't Elsif's usual reasonable inner dialogue, it was a different one that made its first appearance.

"Excuse me," Elsif said as she walked into the office.

"Hello," the secretary said without looking up. "How can I help you?"

Hesitation once again filled Elsif, but the inner voice urged her to take another step. "I'm not really sure how to do this, but I need to file a complaint."

The secretary looked up with surprise. "About a professor?"

"No, of course not," Elsif assured. "It's actually about another student. Bernard John."

"Ok," The secretary said, finding a pen and a form. "What is your complaint?"

"He's been following me around."

"Following you?" She asked with skepticism.

"Um well," Elsif said, then her inner voice took over. "For the last year he's become a little obsessed with me. Everywhere I go, he's right behind me. Every single day. I'll be outside by the docks and I turn around and he's there twenty yards away, watching me. I walk to class and he always walks behind me on the same path even though I found out his classes are on the other side of the school. Now my cousins are saying he's following them too. He's also made several threats."

"Threats?" The secretary asked with concern.

"Not threats," Elsif quickly corrected. "More like suggestive comments that made me really uncomfortable. I don't say this lightly but he's been harassing me for a long time. He even followed me to Struth one month when I was on vacation with my family. He was following me *in Struth*. I'm not trying to be mean but he's also from Versario so I might be in danger or something. I mean, stalking and threatening are serious offenses that shouldn't be taken lightly. I think the administration needs to get involved."

The secretary nodded as she scribbled vigorously on her form. "Of course, I'm glad you came here this morning. I'm so sorry that you have dealt with this behavior and he will be handled right away."

Elsif smiled. "Thank you."

After a few more questions, Elsif walked out of the office with mixed feelings. But she stuffed them down and walked to the front lawn of Merlin and found a bench by the water to do some studying. She watched the end of the sunrise as she waited for her plan to become complete.

She didn't wait long. After several minutes the front doors of Merlin opened and Bernard was being escorted out by several guards. Elsif stood up and walked a few paces towards them, so that Bernard could see her. The front lawn and docks were empty so it was easy to spot Elsif.

He saw her once he was halfway towards the carriages. He looked at her with a shocked expression. He thought she was bluffing, but to be fair, Elsif thought she was bluffing before too.

She forced her face to remain expressionless but waved at Bernard. She wasn't trying to taunt him, but she also wanted him to realize what had happened.

He waved back, a short wave of defeat. He was escorted all the way to the carriages with one bag of luggage. He rolled away from the Academy alone.

Elsif stood for a while, watching the place his carriage disappeared. She didn't feel regret, but she also didn't feel satisfied. But the little inner voice inside Elsif told her it was the right and necessary thing to do. Bernard brought it upon himself. If he hadn't been convinced by Melissa that she and her cousins had something to do with the Warlock's Hat then none of this would have happened. If he had only listened to Elsif then he wouldn't have been expelled. The inner voice won over Elsif, and she eventually listened to it.

Chapter 28: Wyvern Riding Part Two

"Here's the final plan," Milly said as she slid the piece of paper across to Ruth. "I don't know what's going to be more difficult, stealing the gold, riding wyverns, or convincing Elsif to go."

Ruth picked up the list and read off the items. "First we pack. Done. Then we secretly pack for Elsif. Done. Did you pack a few books for her so she won't be crabby in the carriage?"

"Yeah," Milly confirmed. "I packed something about the mass production of Loquanims in the classical age and then something about the Third Elven War."

"Good," Ruth said then continued. "Intercept Will before he comes to visit Elsif and convince him to come to Andorae with us." Ruth looked at a clock on the wall. "We'll need to leave soon to make sure we get to the carriages before he arrives." Ruth looked back at the list. "Then we'll borrow slash steal some gold from the treasury-"

"We're paying for it," Milly interrupted.

Ruth rolled her eyes and continued reading. "Then we go back to the chambers and we'll all be ready to go to Andorae. Elsif will be caught off guard and is peer pressured into coming with us slash Will wants to go so she'll want to go. If she still isn't convinced then we tell her we'll be missing the Summer Games."

"But we'll be back in time for the second half," Milly interjected. "I've never missed the Merlin Games in my life, but the Hat has to come first."

"Then we take a carriage to Andorae," Ruth resumed. "We'll go as far as the road goes, which is the edge of Reuter. Then we'll have to take some village wyverns to the heart of the town. There we'll ask a local where to buy meliocordian. We'll buy it with the previously mentioned gold. We'll fly back to the edge of town and find a place to stay or maybe take a carriage to Animalium and stay somewhere there. At the inn we'll attach the power source to the tracker then spend the night. The next day we'll head back to Merlin and participate in the rest of the Summer Games. Finally we will find the Hat and become famous, rich heroes."

"I didn't write that last part," Milly said.

"Don't worry I penciled it in."

*****

Ruth and Milly stood at the carriage drop off area on the front lawn of Merlin. It was the first day of June and Will had told Elsif that he would be arriving around noon that day.

Will was spotted fifteen minutes before noon, but he did not arrive in the expected way. Milly saw him walking on the path that came from the town to the west of Merlin. He was halfway down the path so the girls had to wait for him to actually arrive at Merlin.

"He would have been here an hour ago if he had just taken the carriage," Ruth complained.

"I think Elsif said something once about him preferring walking," Milly commented. "Maybe he has something against it. Like you hear about people that boycott magic because it's not natural or whatever."

"But he's ridden in carriages with us," Ruth countered. "I don't know, maybe Rose is right and this guy is weird."

"Don't listen to anything Rose says," Milly urged. "Walking isn't weird, it's good exercise."

"Whatever," Ruth muttered as she tapped her foot impatiently. "Did you sign up for any events this morning?"

"All of my usual ones," Milly said. "I didn't want Elsif to walk by the list and get suspicious if my name wasn't on there."

"I don't think she'd notice your name among hundreds," Ruth commented. "I'm just going to sign up when we get back. Oh my gosh, can he take any longer?"

"He's almost here," Milly said. "Settle down."

After another ten minutes Will finally arrived on Merlin property. The girls walked up to him, and strolled with him to the front doors.

"You could have been here hours ago," Ruth said as the girls approached him.

"What?" Will asked in confusion as the girls fell into step on either side of him.

"Nothing," Milly said. "We don't have much time."

Will glanced at each girl with uncertainty. "Time for what?"

"We need a favor," Milly began.

"And before you say no," Ruth added. "You should know that we have the power to make Elsif break up with you."

"No we don't," Milly opposed.

Ruth nodded at Will. "Yes we do. It starts with a random comment. Like, hey Elsif, have you ever noticed that Will has a weird walk or is actually kind of ugly. Then a few days later say, hey Elsif, Will was kind of rude when we said this. Then the next day, hey do you remember when he proposed to you and you were super upset. Then eventually we'll twist everything you do into something bad and Elsif will never want to see you again."

"That's horrible," Milly argued. "We would never do that."

"I would," Ruth said with a smug smile. "And that's why you better stay on my good side."

"Ignore her," Milly assured. "She's joking."

Will looked from girl to girl, confused, and not sure who to believe. "What was the favor?" He asked with reservation.

"We want to go to Andorae tonight," Milly explained. "To find the power source."

"But Elsif is going to say no," Ruth added. "Because she's the worst."

"But we *need* to power the tracker," Milly insisted. "And she won't let us go alone. So she needs to come with us."

"And," Will said. "You want me to convince her."

Ruth shook her head, and gestured to herself and Milly. "No, *we'll* convince her. We need you to agree with whatever we say and tell her that it might be fun to go."

"Okay," Will nodded. "I think I can do that."

"Good," Ruth said.

"Thank you," Milly added as she crossed off the third task on her list. "Now we just need the gold."

"Gold?" Will asked.

"Yeah," Ruth confirmed. "We're going to steal some from the treasury."

"No we're not!" Milly snapped at Ruth. "We're going to leave an equal or greater amount of money in the treasury and exchange that for some gold because Andorae doesn't use regular money."

"I have gold," Will commented. Both the girls stopped in their tracks.

"No you don't," Ruth said with suspicious eyes.

Will reached into his bag and pulled out three small bars of gold. "It's yours if you want it."

Milly grabbed the gold from Will and immediately felt the heavy weight. "Why are you carrying around random gold?"

Will shrugged. "For fun?"

The girls shared a glance and decided to not ask any further questions. "Ok thanks," Ruth said as she grabbed Milly's arm and they ran off.

"We'll see you tonight!" Milly yelled back as they ran.

They were amazed at how well their plan was going and didn't want to stick around for it to go wrong.

*****

"I can't believe I let you two talk me into this," Elsif said with annoyance as the carriage began rolling to Andorae.

"I can't believe they didn't go with my suggestion of kidnapping," Rose mumbled. "So rude."

The plan went exactly as planned, and the whole gang was on their way to Andorae. The only hitch was that Elsif didn't know about the wyverns, yet...

The carriage ride was a total of twenty-one hours. They decided to go through Mirabilis and Animalium, which was nice because then they were able to see the mountains. It was about three in the afternoon when they arrived at the edge of Reuter.

Andorae was a beautiful region. There was a stark difference in the landscape from the neighboring regions of Stellae and Animalium. Stellae had large skyscrapers and advanced technology, and southern Animalium had a lot of desert plains. But Andorae was a vast, dense jungle. There was one road that led to Reuter and no side streets.

"Why is the road ending?" Elsif said as she looked out the window. "Are we there already?"

"Almost," Milly said, while trying not to sound suspicious. "We still have to travel a few miles."

"Are we walking?" Elsif asked.

"Nope," Ruth said with a smug expression.

"She's not going to make it," Juniper muttered beside Ruth.

"Just keep an open mind during this next part," Will suggested.

"And don't think about your imminent death," Rose added.

Jazzy patted Elsif's arm. "I heard they're very peaceful creatures in their native land."

"Creatures?" Elsif questioned. "Please tell me we aren't talking about wyverns?"

"Ding, ding, ding," Rose cheered as she opened the carriage door.

"No," Elsif said, following Rose out of the carriage. Immediately, screeches were heard from above, and Elsif had to cover her ears. The rest of the gang exited the carriage, grabbed the bags, and walked to a hollowed tree with a man with green tinted skin sitting in it.

"We'd like to rent some wyverns," Milly began negotiating with the man. He was clearly Vaniian with his dark green skin, curly dark green hair, and his towering height. Milly handed over a gold bar and he walked into the jungle, towards the screeching noises.

Everyone began to follow the Vaniian man, but Elsif jumped in front of them. "Do I have to remind everyone that Milly almost died riding one of these things?"

"But I didn't," Milly countered.

"Thanks to Juniper!" Ruth added.

Elsif clenched her fists. "Don't even, Ruth," She warned. "This wasn't part of the deal. I thought we were taking a *carriage*!"

"You don't have to come with us," Will said. "You could stay here and we'll be back in an hour. Two hours tops."

Elsif frowned at Will. "Since when did you join this coup?"

"I only found out yesterday," Will replied innocently. "But the girls have been planning this since April."

Rose grabbed Elsif by her wrists and began dragging her into the jungle. "Just get on a wyvern already. We all know you won't let us do dangerous things alone."

Though she protested, Elsif allowed Rose to drag her to where the Vaniian man had walked. They traversed through a dense jungle floor with lots of bushes and ferns, and eventually came to a small clearing with dozens of wyverns with harnesses.

"You don't have to do this," Will assured, even though Rose was still actively dragging Elsif.

"Well I'm not letting them go without me," Elsif said. "It can't be that bad."

It was *indeed* that bad.

The wyverns were relatively small creatures so each person had to ride their own. Some of the wyverns were nice and gentle, only flying in straight paths. Others decided to take detours. Only Vaniians were able to communicate with wyverns so the man told the wyverns where to go before take off, but once they were off the ground, some of them decided to take detours.

Elsif's wyvern decided he wanted to take a quick trip to the Nemoa Ocean. He soared above the water and dived through waves. Elsif was glad she insisted on being strapped in extra tight. Because of the detour, she was the last one to land in the center of Reuter.

"I'm walking back," Elsif declared, as soon as her feet hit the ground.

"I'll walk with you," Will said as he quickly joined Elsif's side.

The others had already dispersed through town to find someone selling the meliocordian. The heart of town was a little busier with a few people walking around or in the trees. Many of the shops were above the ground level, settled between the branches of the large trees. A couple shops were embedded in the trunk of the trees, and that's where Ruth, Juniper, and Jazzy started. But Rose and Milly began climbing.

After a few minutes, Ruth walked out of one of the shops and called for the others. Everyone met at the entrance of one particularly small shop that was farther away from the other businesses.

The shop was nothing more than a small hut, with sticks and moss covering the ceiling, and large leaves as the walls. There was one native Vaniian man who had a deep green complexion with a lot of scarring on his arms and face. He sat behind a small table and slowly sharpened a large stick with a knife. He did not look pleased to see the visitors outside his shop.

"I saw it in the corner there," Ruth pointed. "But I didn't stick around because the shop keeper didn't look particularly welcoming."

There were various items on shelves and tables, but in the far corner there was a small block that glowed.

"Maybe we should try somewhere else," Jazzy suggested.

"We didn't come all the way from Magicis, ride wyverns, and almost die to back down from a fight," Rose stated.

Milly looked into the store from where they stood outside. "Only a couple of us should go in so we don't crowd the place. It should be me and one other person."

"You should take Will," Elsif said. "I don't like the look of that spear."

"No," Ruth interjected. "Take Juniper, he's scarier."

Elsif huffed. "We don't need to be starting any fights."

"Juniper won't-" Ruth started but Milly cut her off.

"I'll take both guys," Milly said.

A moment later, Milly, Juniper, and Will walked inside the hut and straight to the meliocordian. Milly reached to pick it up but the Vaniian man stood up.

"Do not touch that," He warned, brandishing his spear-like stick. Milly's hand froze in midair.

"We'd like to buy it," Will explained.

The Vaniian sat back down and continued to sharpen his stick. "You are not welcome here."

"Isn't this a store?" Juniper questioned. "A place where people buy things?"

The Vaniian grunted. "It is not a store for people from Magicis. Your war isn't welcomed here."

"I'm from Navisia," Milly clarified. "And we aren't a part of any war. We just want to buy the meliocordian."

"I do not care," He warned in his low voice. "Get out!"

Milly took a step back while Will took a step forward. "We can pay you. Two gold bars."

The Vaniian paused his sharpening. "Let me see."

Milly quickly tossed her bag to Will, and he took out the last two bars. "Pristine condition," He said as he placed the bars on the counter in front of the Vaniian.

The Vaniian leaned over the counter to inspect the gold, and Juniper did the same from behind Will. There were several markings on the gold that the Vaniian ran his finger across.

"Take the meliocordian and leave," The Vaniian said, snatching the gold. "Take it and leave Reuter. Leave Andorae."

"Thank you," Milly said quickly as she grabbed the power source and ran out of the shop. Will and Juniper walked out behind her.

"Where did Milly get the gold?" Juniper asked Will.

"It's mine," Will replied. "I keep some on hand in case of emergencies." Juniper refrained from his other questions and saved the information floating around in his brain for later.

*****

The wyvern ride back was a lot smoother than the one before. No one got wet and no one went off route. Elsif almost enjoyed the ride but wouldn't admit it out loud.

Once they returned the wyverns, the girls were quite tired. It was around seven o'clock and they needed to find food and a place to sleep. They found a local inn that would take regular money, which was important because they didn't have any more gold.

Elsif wanted to get in the carriage and drive to Animalium to find a place to spend the night, but she was outvoted. The inn was called Stargazer's Tavern, which was a fitting name because their beds were under the stars. They ordered food and took it to their 'room' which was a bunch of hammocks throughout the branches of a tree.

As the sun slowly sunk, the gang ate their dinner in their hammocks and watched the jungle come to life. The plants around them began to glow in different colors, flowers bloomed, and creatures chattered. It was a different type of magic that the girls had never experienced before.

The most spectacular sight might have been the stars. They were the same ones as home, but they were far brighter in Andorae. Something so normal became so beautiful.

"I connected the power source to the tracker," Milly said as she climbed into her hammock.

"Cool," Rose replied. "Where's the Hat?"

"I read that the meliocordian takes a long time to power up," Milly said. "It might take a few weeks or maybe a month."

"In other news," Ruth changed the subject as she swung in her hammock. "Want to hear some gossip?"

"You shouldn't gossip," Elsif said. "But yes."

"If it's about how I am the new President of Currus," Rose mentioned. "Then you're a little behind on the times."

Ruth's hammock swung faster as she prepared to share the news. "Bernard got kicked out of school last month."

Several gasps were released once the news sunk in. The other girls bombarded Ruth with questions while Elsif remained quiet. Out of the corner of her eye, Elsif could see Juniper staring at her.

"I don't know what happened," Ruth explained. "But Juniper said he was just dragged out of his room early one morning. Completely randomly. He was shipped back to Versario within minutes."

"No way. No one heard anything else about it?" Milly asked while looking at the other girls. Everyone shook their heads except Elsif. "Elsif?" Milly continued. "Did you hear anything?"

Elsif wanted to say no. She almost said no. But she had a feeling Juniper would rat her out. On the other hand, lying was also wrong, and Elsif had to quit the habit.

"I might know what happened," Elsif said quietly.

"Tell us!" Ruth urged.

Silence fell over the group as they waited for Elsif's response.

"Well," Elsif began. "I might be the reason he got expelled." Elsif rushed through the story, telling the girls everything that had happened from the very beginning. Every time Elsif thought Bernard or the twins had followed her because of the Staff and the Hat.

Once Elsif was done, she waited patiently for a response.

"Good," Ruth finally said. "I'm glad he's gone."

"Major creep," Rose agreed.

"I'm sorry you had to go through that," Jazzy said.

Milly's mouth had fallen open the second Elsif admitted she had a hand in Bernard's expulsion. "Elsif," She said in disbelief. "That's horrible."

Elsif blinked. "What?"

"You got him *expelled*," Milly said, her voice troubled. "You might have ruined his life."

"He was following us," Elsif explained. "I had to protect us."

"But you didn't have proof," Milly argued. "It could have been a coincidence."

"Seeing Bernard in Struth and one of the twins in Silvia was a coincidence?"

"You didn't see a clear view of their faces," Milly stated. "If there's no proof then it's just conjecture. If anything you could have told the office the truth, but you made it sound so much worse than it was."

Ruth interjected, "Why are you taking his side? Bernard is the worst and Elsif is our cousin!"

"Our relationship to her doesn't stop her actions from being bad."

"It's a grey area," Ruth countered.

Milly scoffed as her anger grew. "There is no grey. There's good and bad and what Elsif did was bad. She didn't have enough evidence!"

"Juniper saw Bernard watching us too," Elsif said, gesturing to Juniper. "He knows how serious it was." Everyone turned to Juniper who wore his usual emotionless expression.

Juniper shook his head. "I don't know what you're talking about."

"You warned me-" Elsif said but Milly cut in.

"It doesn't matter if he saw or not," Milly stated. "It doesn't change the fact that you exaggerated everything to the administration and didn't have probable cause."

"Calm down," Elsif snapped. "I did what I had to."

"And you had to do something bad?" Milly retorted. "I've looked up to you my whole life, but right now I've lost a good amount of respect."

Elsif took a deep breath. "You don't have to agree with what I did," Elsif said in a solemn tone. "But everything I do is for this family."

Milly's head drooped. "You sound like Grandma Theadora when she kicked out Uncle Louis. It's always for the greater good, right?"

Ruth gulped loudly, and glanced at Jazzy. "Why are you mentioning Uncle Louis?"

"Because," Milly fumed. "I'm tired of everyone doing horrible things for the sake of our family. I'm tired of everyone acting like how we treated Uncle Louis was alright. It wasn't and I'm not going to sit around anymore and not say anything."

"Milly!" Elsif shouted. "It's done, there's nothing I can do now!"

Milly slumped down in her hammock, and ended the conversation. Elsif leaned back into her own hammock. Everyone else grew silent.

Elsif looked over at Rose. "Is this the first time you don't have anything to say?"

"I was enjoying the show," Rose said with a downcast smile.

The stars continued to shine above, but the magic had been drained from the sky.

Chapter 29: Choices Have Consequences

The carriage rolled into Merlin in the early morning two days later. The carriage ride had been quiet and awkward since the argument. Neither Elsif or Milly had brought up the subject during the ride.

Once the carriage had pulled into Merlin, several of the girls jumped out and ran to the dueling event in the gardens. Milly was running full speed to the other side of the school, and Rose was close behind her. Ruth grabbed Jazzy's hand and forced her to run to the games as well.

Juniper, Elsif, and Will stepped out of the carriage last. Juniper walked straight towards the school, while Elsif and Will loitered by the carriage.

As Elsif watched Juniper walk away, she was filled with rage. "Thanks for lying before!" Elsif called out.

Juniper turned around to face the accusation. "I never lied."

Elsif walked towards Juniper and Will followed. "Yes you did," She insisted. "You warned me that Bernard was following me last year. You were his roommate. You had to know."

"Keeping tabs on people isn't the same as stalking," Juniper stated bluntly. "You don't have proof that it was anything more and I don't weigh in on issues unless there's proof."

"So you're a coward?" Elsif asked in disbelief.

"No, I'm just smart," Juniper snapped. "And not a paranoid rat like you."

Will stepped forward. "Watch it."

"I'm not the one that started the attack," Juniper retorted towards Will. "And you're not going to be around much longer so I'd watch my tone if I was you."

Will frowned. "What's that supposed to mean?"

"I guess you'll find out."

"If you're willing to lie about Bernard," Elsif said harshly. "Then what else are you lying about?"

Juniper looked from Will to Elsif. "I'm not a liar."

"Don't play that game with me," Elsif warned. "I know exactly how much truth you can stretch without actually lying. I don't want you hanging around Ruth anymore."

"Good thing it's not up to you."

Elsif crossed her arms. "Be careful how you tread, Juniper. I'm sick of my cousins being tied up in this stupid Hat and Staff business and I think you might be the loose end that needs to be cut."

Juniper scoffed and shook his head. "I never thought I'd see the day where Elsif Menzie would be threatening me."

"Stay away from Ruth."

Juniper backed away and walked to the school. He retreated inside the front doors before Elsif or Will said a word.

"I don't know what to do," Elsif said out loud but the words were for herself.

Will looked at Elsif with a sober expression. "Did you really see Piper or Paisley in Silvia? You didn't say anything."

"I hardly knew you at the time," Elsif explained.

"But afterwards," Will continued. "You never mentioned that Bernard or the twins were following you around."

Elsif looked away from Will, her eyes downcast. "I thought I was crazy for a long time. I tried to convince myself it was a coincidence. But eventually I knew that they'd never leave us alone as long as they thought we were mixed up with the Hat and that stupid Staff. Do you-" Elsif hesitated, as she looked up at Will. "Do you think I did the wrong thing?"

"I don't know," admitted Will. "I didn't see everything you saw. I didn't experience what it was like to have people following me. But I trust your judgement."

Elsif bit the inside of her cheek. "I don't know if I do. I know I exaggerated what happened when I went to the office, but- I don't know. I wanted to protect my family. Is that a crime?"

"When you went to the office," Will began reluctantly. "Did you intend to get him expelled or were you trying to get help?"

The taste of blood burst into Elsif's mouth from where she chomped down on the inside of her cheek. "I should go," Elsif stumbled away from Will, while she touched her sore mouth. "I need to make sure my cousins aren't killing anyone in the event today."

"I didn't mean to upset y-"

"You didn't," Elsif stated apprehensively, while taking steps away from Will. "I just want to be done with the Hat and the Staff. I want to give the tracker back to Jerry and never think about it again. It's too much drama and talks of danger and stalking and I'm done with it all. I'm done. I want my old life back."

"Okay," Will said, watching Elsif leave. "Can I see you tomorrow?"

"Yeah," Elsif said, continuing to walk away. "See you tomorrow."

Elsif took several more steps before she heard Will call her name. "Elsif?"

She took several deep breaths and turned to face Will. "Yes?"

"You're not going to get Juniper expelled, are you?" He asked. "I know he's a jerk but I don't think he's a bad guy."

Elsif was surprised, and a little hurt by Will's question. "No, of course not. I'd never. I just don't want him talking to Ruth."

"Right," Will forced a smile. "I didn't think so, I just thought I'd ask."

Elsif turned from Will and walked to the school, her expression dropping. She went straight to her chambers and sat down at her desk. She stared at herself in the mirror as ideas and morals quarreled inside of her.

*****

"You didn't beat me," Milly insisted. "You cheated!"

"Fighting for survival isn't cheating!" Rose exclaimed as she twirled through the halls.

"I've never seen someone surrender in a duel before," Ruth said with a laugh. "Especially not before a sword was even swung."

"I don't like swords," Jazzy answered timidly.

The girls roared with laughter as they walked back to their chambers from the garden. Happiness consumed the four as they walked into their living quarters.

Ruth was met with a rude existential crisis when she stumbled into her bedroom. "Why are you staring at yourself in the mirror?" Ruth asked with a giggle as she plopped onto Elsif's lower bunk. "I never took you for the vain type?"

Elsif sighed as she continued to look at her reflection. "Do you ever look at yourself and not like the person you're becoming?"

"No," Ruth stated casually.

"I'm serious," Elsif said, looking back at Ruth.

"So am I," Ruth assured, sitting up. "If I didn't like who I was then I'd change. Simple as that."

Eyes downcast, Elsif replied, "I don't think it's that simple."

"Is this about what Milly said about Bernard?" Ruth asked with a roll of her eyes. "She's overreacting with her high and mighty morals. You know Mills, everything has to be for the good of humanity or whatever. Forget what she said. Bernard was the worst and deserved to be kicked out."

"But maybe he didn't deserve for me to orchestrate it?"

Ruth waved off Elsif's concern. "You think too much."

Elsif spun back towards the mirror. She saw herself, her eyes, her hair, and every imperfection that haunted her. Elsif feared that it may be worse than not liking who she saw in the mirror. Maybe the thing that irked her so much was the fact that she no longer recognized the person looking back.

She needed to go back. Find her love for history and Merlin again. Get away from treasure hunting and danger. Elsif hated not knowing who she was, and since she couldn't figure out the current version of herself, she needed to find the old one.

"Ruth, I need you to listen to me," Elsif said calmly.

"Girl, stop with the doom and gloom," Ruth said with exasperation. "You're fine!"

Elsif stood up and sat across from Ruth on the bed. "That's not what I'm talking about. You're not going to like what I have to say but you need to listen."

Ruth frowned but sat quietly. "Okay."

"You need to stop seeing Juniper."

"Not this again," Ruth said immediately, jumping to her feet, and waving her arms. "You can't keep going back and forth on him. He's alright, no actually he's a villain, eh I guess I won't fight it, well guess what- now I'm fighting it and I forbid you to see him even though you're not my mother and can't physically stop me!"

Elsif stood up as well and faced Ruth head on. "I'm done, Ruth! I'm done with the Staff and I'm done with the Hat!"

Ruth's arms fell to her side as she was overtaken by Elsif's harsh tone.

"I thought Jerry was crazy before," Elsif seethed, an anger evident in her that had never been seen. "But maybe he actually is caught up in some mobster, black mail, illegal rubbish that we don't need any part in. I'm done with it all and I don't want any association with it. As soon as we give back the tracker then we're done. We're severing ties with it all. That includes Juniper and his whole friend group. We're done!"

Ruth stood quietly as she absorbed all the words. "Are *you* done?" She eventually asked after a few seconds of silence.

Elsif deeply sighed, tired of her anger. "Yes."

"Good," Ruth said, and stomped out of the room. She walked straight to the front door of the chamber, and slammed it shut behind her.

Elsif walked into the living room and watched her leave. After the door was shut, she turned around to see three concerned audience members.

"You all heard that?" Elsif asked.

Milly, Rose, and Jazzy nodded.

"I'm serious," Elsif stated in a steady tone. "We're all done with the Staff, the Hat, Juniper, and Melissa. We're done." No one argued with Elsif's proclamation. "Okay," Elsif said in a lighter tone. "Then I'm going to go sign up for the advanced history program. I'll see you guys later."

Elsif left the chambers and left the three girls in awkward silence.

Rose's laugh broke the quiet. "We're not done."

"Not even close," Milly agreed.

Jazzy shifted in her seat, and wondered how she was going to keep her friendship with Melissa a secret.

*****

Elsif marched to the office on the first floor of Merlin. She was on a mission, and no one could distract her. Well, except the girl that started it all.

"Hey Elsif," Melissa said with her plastered smile front and center. "Could I talk to you real quick?"

"No," Elsif said, and continued walking.

"It's about Bernard," Melissa said as Elsif passed.

Reluctantly Elsif stopped and faced Melissa. "What?"

"I heard what happened," Melissa said sympathetically. "With Bernard, and I wanted to tell you how sorry I am about everything that happened."

"What?"

"I had no idea that Bernard was following you and your cousins around," Melissa continued. "Paisley admitted to me this morning about how obsessed he was with you because he thought you had something to do with that Staff or maybe it was the Hat. I don't know. But he had convinced Piper and Paisley to watch you guys once in a while and report back to him. So what I'm saying is that it was all *him*. Piper, Paisley, and I all know that you and your cousins have nothing to do with our situation, so we won't be bothering you again. I promise."

Elsif scrunched her eyebrows in confusion. "Are you admitting to something?"

"No," Melissa said nonchalantly. "I'm just letting you know that the three of us will never bother you or any of your cousins again. As long as you don't bother us, that is. The only person I can't speak for is Juniper. He does his own thing. But you probably already knew that."

"Okay," Elsif said, lacking better words.

"Okay," Melissa replied cheerily. "Bye. Good luck with your last month of classes."

Elsif continued on her way, more confused than ever. But at the end of the day, none of that mattered. Because she was done.

"Hi," Elsif greeted the secretary. "I'd like to sign up for advanced classes for history."

A form slid across the desk to Elsif. She grabbed a pen and hovered over where her signature belonged. All she had to do was sign the paper. One signature and her life would go back to normal.

"Elsif Menzie," a friendly voice greeted. "I've been meaning to meet with you."

Elsif looked up to see the President of Merlin looking at her from the doorway of his office. He was in a pressed suit with a black tie, and had more wrinkles than Elsif thought he would. It was odd to see him close up, a reminder that he was a real person, not just a figurehead giving speeches in the distance. His eyes were different then Elsif thought they would be, like they should be on someone else's face.

"Would you mind speaking to me in my office for a moment?" He asked with a wave of his hand.

Elsif looked around the office to make sure there wasn't another girl with a weird version of a common name from Gelida around. She was the only student in the room, so Elsif concluded that the President must be talking to her.

With bewildered footsteps, Elsif found herself seated in the President of Merlin's office. It was a fancy room with a fireplace and a mantel full of awards. Between the dauntingly black curtains, there was a beautiful view of the distant sea. Elsif's chair was uncomfortable, but that may have been from Elsif's own paranoia that imminent doom was looming over her.

"Do you know why I wished to speak with you, Ms. Menzie?" The President asked while leaning forward and holding his hands on the desk.

"Is it because I broke that globe?" Elsif asked in a meek voice

The President shook his head. "No, nothing like that. You're in no way in trouble, Ms. Menzie. Actually if I'm not mistaken you were top of your class here at Merlin when you were enrolled in the regular program, and now you're excelling in our advanced program. And did I hear correctly that you're about to sign up for our advanced history classes?"

"Yes sir," Elsif replied quietly.

"And I've heard from some faculty that you're planning to become Merlin's youngest professor," The President continued. "You know, it warms my heart to see such dedicated and loyal students following the right path here at Merlin. I commend you for your hard work and dedication during your time at Merlin."

"Thank you, sir."

The President smiled warmly and sat back in his chair. "And I personally want to offer you an internship here at Merlin Academy. I want you to be an aid for our history department while you complete your advanced degree. You'll be earning credit while doing this, of course, and there's a real good stipend that comes along with it. And I can't make any guarantees, but between you and me, this internship practically gives you a teaching position here at Merlin as soon as you graduate."

Elsif's mouth fully fell open and an overwhelming shock overtook her. Her dream since she was five years old was being served to her on a silver platter.

"I've, um," Elsif stumbled over her words. "I've never heard of this internship before."

The President released a friendly laugh. "That's because your professors and I created this position, just for you. You're a one-of-a-kind student Elsif, and we recognize that. We want you to know that you belong here. Merlin Academy wants you and your wonderful mind for the rest of your academic and professional career."

Elsif's hands began to tremble and her heart started to pound. "I don't know what to say."

"Yes would be a good start," The President teased. "But first I wanted to ask you a question, Ms. Menzie."

"Anything," Elsif said with an enthusiastic nod.

"Juniper Miller," The President stated. "What can you tell me about him?"

Elsif blinked several times before answering, giving her mind time to catch up. "What do you mean?"

"I'll be frank with you Elsif," The President said, his smile dropping and his tone changing to a serious one. "Merlin had an important relic go missing some time ago and we've been doing everything in our power to recover this item. Recently we have had intel that Juniper Miller may have been involved in the theft of this relic. We also noticed that recently he has been spending a great deal of time with your cousin Ruth, and in turn, you. So, I want to know, from the horse's mouth, if *you* think he was involved in the thievery of one of Merlin Academy's priceless and historic relics?"

Gears turned in Elsif's mind, but no concrete thoughts occurred. Jumbled notions bumped around in Elsif's brain, but the last twenty-four hours did not help Elsif think clearly.

But one idea reigned victorious in the battle of her mind. A little voice began to chant louder than the rest. She wanted to be done, and Juniper was the last straw.

Elsif's eyes moved downward, not able to meet the eyeline of the President. Her hands found each other and fiddled nervously. Suddenly her throat was tremendously dry and it was hard to swallow.

"Yes."

She heard the President's chair slide across the ground, signaling that he was standing up, but Elsif's eyes were still pinned to the ground.

"Thank you, Ms. Menzie." He must have been standing much closer to Elsif, because she could feel his breath on the top of her forehead. "You have been very helpful."

Elsif heard his footsteps leave the office and then she heard his voice at reception. "I need all available guards right away."

"Yes sir," the secretary replied.

More footsteps were heard moments later, and the President began addressing them. "We are taking Juniper Miller in for questioning. He's in chamber 2340."

Elsif looked up at the last second to see a dozen guards and the President walking out of the office. She sat there quietly for a moment, trying to push away every feeling in her body. Elsif didn't stand up until she knew she was fully numb.

"Are you ready to sign now?" The secretary asked when Elsif walked back up to the desk. "Also congratulations on your internship Ms. Menzie. I look forward to working with you in the future."

Elsif didn't respond because she was too busy staring at the form. Staring at the place her signature belonged. This was supposed to be the happiest moment of her life, but instead she was fighting the worst feelings of her life.

"Ms. Menzie?" The Secretary asked. "Did you hear me? I'm congratulating you."

"Do I have to sign this now?" Elsif asked with a tremor in her voice.

"Well, no," the Secretary said with a hint of confusion. "You don't have to sign until the night of the Felix Finis Ball, but there's no reason you can't sign now-"

Elsif grabbed the form and ran out of the office before she heard the secretary finish. She stuffed the form in her pocket, and ran the fastest she had ever run. She sprinted through the hallways and towards the gardens.

Elsif knew she hated the person she was becoming, and was going to take some advice from Ruth and change. She was going to change that second, and not a moment later. She knew what she did was wrong, and she had to rectify her choices.

The guards were heading to Juniper's chambers, but Elsif knew he wouldn't be there. He'd be with Ruth, because that's where he always was. And Ruth had a favorite place in the garden that she thought was a secret. But when you have three very close cousins, nothing is a secret.

Elsif raced through the back doors of Merlin and bounded to the fountain area of the garden. She bolted to that one stupid fountain that Ruth loved so much, and she found them. Juniper and Ruth sat together underneath the statue.

"Elsif, stop," Ruth said, standing up with crossed arms. "Whatever you're going to say, stop, because I won't be listening."

"They're coming for Juniper," Elsif said, completely out of breath. "I told them you stole Malum's Staff and now they're coming for you."

Ruth shook her head. "What are you talking about?"

Juniper shot to his feet. "When will they be here?"

"There at your chambers right now," Elsif said with worry in her voice. "I don't know how long until they're in the gardens."

"Who's coming to the gardens?" Ruth questioned.

"They'll be blocking the carriages," Juniper said, beginning to pace around. "And all the main roads out of Merlin."

"What is going on!" Ruth demanded.

Elsif's nerves were on edge and she ran her hands through her hair, wanting to pull every single strand out. "The President told the guards to bring in Juniper for questioning because I told them he had something to do with Malum's Staff."

Ruth's expression changed from bewildered to red hot rage in half a second. "Why did you do that!"

"Because I wanted Juniper to leave us alone!" Elsif yelled. "But I'm sorry! I'm so sorry! Juniper, *I'm sorry*!"

Ruth turned to Juniper. "We'll make a run for it. Go around the gardens and into the nearest town. We'll grab a random carriage and go far away."

"I'll make a run for it," Juniper corrected. "I can't use any carriages. Merlin will be able to control any carriage I get into. But I don't know if I can outrun the guards."

"We'll find horses," Ruth said. "Wait, there's horses in Merlin's sanctuary. We'll steal the horses and run away together!"

"You're not coming with me, Ruth!" Juniper snapped.

"Yes I am!" Ruth yelled back.

Juniper groaned. "You'll slow me down. You have to stay here."

"No," Ruth insisted. "You're not leaving without me."

Elsif saw a large group of men in the distance. "Guys. Guys they're here." Juniper turned and ran the opposite direction, leaving Ruth next to Elsif.

"Wait!" Ruth screamed after Juniper, but her short legs were much slower than him.

But it didn't matter anyway, Juniper was caught by a flying guard before he was able to run thirty yards. He came from above and tackled Juniper to the ground. Several more guards were by Juniper's side within seconds. They bound his hands and yanked him to his feet.

Elsif and Ruth watched from afar as Juniper was dragged inside Merlin by a dozen guards.

Chapter 30: Should've Left The Purse At Home pt. 1

"**I**'m tap dancing!" Rose exclaimed, as she practiced her dance moves for her first Felix Finis Ball. "Leave me alone!"

Milly groaned as she held the dud of a tracker in her lap. "I think we all have better things to do than to interrupt your dancing."

"Can you tap in your *own* room?" Elsif suggested gloomily.

"Or you can dance off the roof of Merlin," Ruth muttered, while staring out the balcony door.

Rose tapped her feet louder. "I like the sound of that second option." Silence filled the room instead of the normal laughter and even Rose could feel the difference. "Actually," Rose said, as her feet slowed down. "I think the acoustics *are* better in my room." She tapped backwards into her bedroom and swiftly shut the door.

Jazzy sat in a chair with her current sewing project in her hands. She shifted uncomfortably from side to side before asking, "Are we going to the Felix Finis Ball tonight?"

Elsif sighed silently as she prepared herself for the storm to return. It had been fifty-seven days since Juniper had been dragged out of the gardens. Since then Ruth had been glued to the window, watching for when Juniper was sent back to Versario. Except he never was.

Ruth refused to leave the windowsill. The cousins had to take turns watching the window to get her to sleep, eat, or go to the bathroom. She even faked being sick for most of her classes in July, so she could stay by the window. The classes she did attend, she hardly paid attention because her eyes were glued to the windows in the rooms.

Juniper was still inside Merlin Academy, but the girls had no idea where, and no idea why.

Ruth was completely overtaken by her anger. Anger that Juniper was gone, anger that Elsif had caused it, and anger that there was nothing she could do but sit by the window.

Milly was also having a dreadful month, because of the tracker. She sat on the couch most days, and did nothing but stare at the empty box. It had never turned on and there had been no word from Jerry. The Warlock's Hat journey seemed to be coming to an end, and Milly was not taking it well. Despair crept into her more each day as she held the useless tracker.

During the last fifty-seven days, Jazzy had also grown more quiet and spent more time by herself. She would often disappear into the gardens after classes and return with nothing to say to the girls.

Elsif had lived with her guilt, and struggled to know the right thing to do. She had also completely abandoned her previous claims from the night Juniper was taken. Instead she overcompensated for her mistakes. She encouraged Milly that the tracker would turn on soon. She went to the administration and told them she had misspoke before and Juniper had nothing to do with the missing relic. Though Elsif tried to right her wrongs, the tracker didn't work and Juniper wasn't released.

"Oh," Ruth said bitterly. "Is the ball tonight?"

Elsif leaned towards Jazzy and spoke in a quiet voice. "You should definitely go. You made that lovely purple gown."

"Are any of you going?" Jazzy asked.

"No," Milly groaned.

"Never in a million years," Ruth muttered.

Rose opened her door. "I'm going and nothing will keep my tapping toes away from my first ball!" She slammed the door behind her and the girls could hear Rose's feet stomp around her room.

Jazzy looked at Elsif. "Are you going?"

"Well," Elsif said hesitantly.

"You *should* go," Ruth interrupted. "Go and don't worry about how you ruined my life!"

"Juniper's life," Milly corrected.

Ruth glared at Milly. "*Our* life. It's a shared collective life!"

"Are you married?" Milly questioned with little patience.

"No," Ruth pouted. "Only because we're too young, but one day we will be, so Elsif preemptively ruined *our* life."

"It's legal in Koronia," Jazzy mentioned.

Elsif sighed. "Don't give her ideas, please."

"Yes Jazzy, don't give me any ideas of being happy," Ruth stated. "Elsif couldn't bear to see that."

Elsif walked over to Ruth and took a seat next to her. "What if you just popped into the ball tonight? I know it won't be the night you imagined but maybe it could be a good distraction. And you have the prettiest dress hanging in your closet. You picked it out a week after the last ball and the dress has been waiting to be worn all this time."

Ruth crossed her arms. "The dress *is* beautiful."

"It is," Elsif agreed. "And no one else could do the dress justice like you."

Ruth frowned. "Maybe."

"You should get ready," Elsif insisted. "I'll watch the window."

With little persuasion, Ruth dashed into her room and began pampering and primping herself. Jazzy smiled and left to get ready.

"Mills," Elsif mentioned. "You should go too. There's a low chance that the tracker will turn on tonight since it's been two months."

"But it could," Milly insisted. "And I need to know the second it shows the Hat's location."

"You could bring the tracker with you to the ball," Elsif suggested. "Ruth has a million purses. I'm sure one would work."

Milly debated her options inside her head for a moment before eventually agreeing. "Fine."

"Thanks," Elsif said. "Do you mind keeping an eye on the window for a little bit. I need to do something real quick."

"Sure," Milly shrugged. "Where are you going?"

Elsif stood up and walked towards the chamber door. "I have to run a quick errand. I'll be back soon." Elsif closed the door behind her and desperately hoped that she was telling the truth.

*****

"Are you sure about this Elsif?" Will asked somberly. "There's still time to reconsider."

Elsif reached into her pocket and unfolded the paper that had been weighing her down for too long. "I've made my choices," She said as she tore her application for the advanced history program. "And I'm not changing my mind this time."

"Okay," Will said resolutely. "I'll meet you on the other side."

Will walked away from Elsif, and headed to the east side of the school. Elsif stood in place for a moment and watched Will leave. He was already wearing his suit jacket for the evening, and his hair was a little longer than normal. Elsif wondered how she got so lucky, to have someone so willing to risk everything just to help her right her wrongs.

A single tear escaped Elsif's eyes as she watched him disappear from the gardens. Her life had been completely disrupted but somehow there was a glimmer of hope whenever Will was with her. She looked down at the torn pieces of paper again, and overwhelming clarity rushed through her mind. She dropped them and didn't look back.

Elsif walked away from her picture-perfect future at Merlin and marched toward her fate.

The hallways were quiet, since most students were getting ready for the ball and the staff was setting up the banquet hall. Everyone was busy that afternoon, and didn't have time to pay attention to out of character actions. Such as a quiet and studious girl who walked into the guards office and then out with a ring of keys.

Elsif made her way to the top floor of Merlin, and stood behind a corner that led to a long stretch of hallway. There were a dozen empty chambers with no one around, except one guard who stood in front of the last room.

Reaching into her bag, Elsif pulled out three of Rose's 'special' bombs. Elsif threw the bombs into the nearby stairwell and ran into a closet. She heard loud pops and saw flashes of light followed by colorful spiderwebs shooting from the stairwell.

After twenty seconds, Elsif saw from the crack in her door that the guard had run into the stairwell. Elsif sprinted from the closet and to the last chamber. She took out her recently acquired keys and began trying each one to unlock the door. The third key twisted and Elsif heard a click. She entered the chamber and shut the door behind her.

The chamber didn't look anything like Elsif's cozy home away from home. It was empty, completely barren. There was no furniture, no carpet, not even a light. All the doors had been bolted up with panels of wood, except one. Even the glass balcony door had a large lock and chain on it, which blocked most of the light.

The first room to the left was locked but not bolted. Elsif walked over and tried her keys again. The very last key turned and clicked just like the key before. Elsif slowly opened the door.

The room was also completely empty, no windows, no furniture, no light. The only thing the room contained was one chair and a boy who sat in it with shackles around his wrists and ankles, and a cloth in his mouth.

"Hi Juniper," Elsif said hesitantly, leaving the door open so light from the balcony could shine inside. "I'm really sorry."

He stared back with his usual expressionless facial features. Now that light had flooded the room, Elsif could see that Juniper still had the same clothes on as he did the night he was taken. The only difference was that they were wrinkled and tearing. There was also a large dark bruise on the left side of his face.

Elsif raised her hand to grab the cloth from his mouth, but at the last second she withdrew. "I need to tell you something."

With a large intake of breath, Elsif began, "I need you to understand why all this happened. I don't hate you for no reason. I have a very good reason. Well, I guess it's not exactly good, and it doesn't excuse my actions, but it's *a* reason."

Juniper rolled his eyes but in his condition he didn't have any other choice but to listen.

"My family is very close to each other, strangely close," Elsif continued. "We've always been a close family but we've been especially close ever since my grandparents found my Uncle Louis dead in a ditch on the edge of Stellae. He had gotten into an argument a few years prior with them, and the next time my grandparents saw him he was decaying on the side of the road.

"This all happened when I was really young, almost too young to remember. Almost. But once it happened Uncle Louis became a taboo subject. No one talked about him. It was like he never existed. But I remember he existed, because I couldn't forget what my mom told me the day she found out. She thought I would be too young and I would forget. But I didn't. She told me everything about Uncle Louis, his past, him getting expelled from Merlin, and his argument with my grandparents and especially my grandmother. But I will never forget what she said at the end. She said that Uncle Louis' death and life was all her fault because she was the eldest girl, and the eldest girl is always in charge of the family. I remembered that because, even at that age, I knew I was the eldest girl in the new generation and the new responsibility would be passed down to me.

"I am responsible for the life, happiness, and success of my cousins," Elsif stated, desperately hoping Juniper would understand even an ounce of the reason behind all of Elsif's actions. "I can't do much about the boys because they're older and do their own thing, but I always knew that I was going to do everything in my power to make sure my girls were taken care of. Put them on the right path, and have a chance to succeed at anything they want.

"For Rose it's having fun and being free. She's pretty good at that so all I have to worry about is keeping her alive. Milly wants to be a captain of a ship, and she's going to do it with my help or not. And now that I've practically adopted Jazzy, I'm going to do the same things for her as soon as I figure out what she wants in life. I haven't quite figured her out yet.

"But Ruth has always been the one I worry about. Because she doesn't want to succeed in school or have a good career. More than anything else in life, she wants to fall in love. She wants other things too, don't get me wrong, she's a well rounded girl, I've made sure of that. But deep down she's a hopeless romantic that wants the perfect love story. How am I supposed to give her that? Especially when she falls in love with every guy with a pulse who is semi-close to her age.

"She's probably going to kill me if she ever finds out I'm telling you these things but I need you to know," Elsif said steadily. "I need you to know all this because I'm trusting you with one of the most important things in my life, and I need you to not take that lightly. I love Ruth, and I can't see her get hurt.

"I'm sorry for everything that I've done. I shouldn't have been prejudiced against you or even Melissa. I shouldn't have gotten you or Bernard kicked out. I've lied more times than I can count, and I'm sorry for everything. But for all the wrongs that I have done and I am sorry for, please know at the bottom of it all, is a girl who loves her family. Please don't make me regret trusting you. Okay?"

Juniper's response was muffled, so Elsif finally took the cloth out of his mouth. "Are you going to unlock me now?" He asked dryly.

Elsif huffed. "I just poured out my heart to you and that's all you have to say?"

"It's sort of on my mind right now," Juniper stated.

Elsif crossed her arms. "I could leave you here."

"You're the reason I'm in here!" Juniper snapped.

Elsif rolled her eyes. "How did you get the bruise?"

"I tripped," Juniper said with sarcasm.

"Did you get it while trying to resist arrest?" Elsif asked, hoping it wasn't an alternative method.

"Something like that," Juniper muttered.

Elsif nodded. "Have they kept you in this room the whole time?"

"Yeah, it's been a lovely visit," Juniper mocked. "But if it's fine with you, I'd like to leave now."

"I'm literally rescuing you," Elsif said. "Can you not be rude for maybe two minutes."

"You haven't been rescuing me!" Juniper shouted. "You've been talking my ear off!"

"Shhh!" Elsif warned. "The guard might be back by now."

"Then how about," Juniper said quietly. "You take my shackles off?"

Elsif relented and began trying each key with the locks around Juniper's wrists and ankles. After a minute the locks came off and Juniper was free.

As soon as the last lock clicked, Juniper was on his feet and heading to the front door of the chambers. "Juniper wait," Elsif ran after him. "Wait, wait!"

He reached for the door knob, and Elsif had to push her shoulder into the door to stop him from opening it. "Juniper!" Elsif shouted in a whisper. "I have been planning this break out for fifty-seven days and you are going to get us caught in the first five minutes!"

"I've also been planning this break out for fifty-seven days and that includes knocking out the guard and anyone else that gets in my way," Juniper snapped.

"Good luck getting past the extra guards at every entrance and exit on the first floor," Elsif said.

"Do you have a better plan?" Juniper asked with doubt.

"Yes," Elsif insisted. "We're going to hide you in the gardens until midnight. After the Felix Finis Ball, there will be huge crowds leaving for August break. You and Will will walk to the nearby villages. You'll walk until you can buy some horses then you can go wherever you want. The important part of this plan is that you can't use any carriages. Merlin might find you then."

"Will?" Juniper questioned. "You're not serious-"

Juniper was cut off by a knock on the glass balcony door. Elsif and Juniper turned and saw Will waving from the balcony. "Seriously?" Juniper grumbled.

"He's going to help you climb down," Elsif said, walking over to the balcony, and unlocking the door.

"Hey," Will said once the door was open. "I made a good path down."

"This is a horrible plan," Juniper muttered.

Will tightened a rope that was tied to the balcony. "It's a great plan." Once the rope was secure, Will patted Juniper on the back. "You're up first. Stay close to where the tower and the wall meet so you'll stay out of the eyesight of anyone in the gardens."

Juniper shook his head. "Why don't you go first?"

"Because I have to untie the rope so we don't leave evidence behind," Will stated. "So I'm climbing down *last*."

"They'll see that I'm gone as soon as they see the open door," Juniper protested. "A rope won't matter at that point."

"I was going to close it and relock it," Elsif snapped. "If the guard decided to pop his head inside we don't want him seeing anything suspicious."

"And then they'll open up the room I was in and see I'm gone," Juniper complained. "We'll be saved a couple extra seconds."

Elsif threw her arms up in frustration. "You are the worst rescuee in the history of ever. Be quiet and let us save you," She said through gritted teeth.

Juniper rolled his eyes and climbed over the balcony railing. "I could have made a better plan."

"Next time we'll let you rot and find a way out yourself," Elsif muttered.

Will held the rope taut to keep it steady, as Juniper began his descent. "He's a real backseat rescuer."

Once Juniper made it to the ground, it was Elsif's turn. She climbed over the railing, and held onto the rope for dear life. Scaling down a wall was a difficult task, but somehow Elsif survived. Will untied the rope on the balcony, and made his way down to join Juniper and Elsif on the ground.

"You guys head to the gardens. I'll be back," Elsif said, while rushing back to her chamber. Glancing over her shoulder, Elsif saw the boys disappear.

Elsif felt good about her plan so far. As long as there were no flying guards they would be in the clear. Flying guards usually only came out after curfew and the Felix Finis Ball didn't have a curfew, so Elsif hoped they had the night off.

She ran all the way back to the chambers without breaking her stride, and burst into her bedroom. Ruth was sitting in front of the mirror in her beautiful pink mermaid-style dress. The bodice had a million tiny jewels with intricate flower designs, and the skirt had a dozen layers of different shades of pink. Her makeup was done and she was finishing her last curl when Elsif ran into the room.

"Ruth, I have to show you something!" Elsif said with a breathless smile. "We have to go to the gardens right now!"

Ruth finished her hair and turned towards Elsif in disgust. "You don't have your dress on. Or any makeup. And your hair looks terrible, worse than usual. Have you been standing in front of a fan?"

"None of that matters," Elsif insisted. "We have to go-"

Ruth stood up and forced Elsif into the chair. "Let me see if I can do something with this crow's nest. Do you own a comb?"

"Yes," Elsif retorted. "But I need to show you something in the garden!"

"Sit still!" Ruth rebuked. "The ball starts in fifteen minutes and instead of getting ready you've been gone for the last hour. Probably dawdling in the library."

"I had to run somewhere," Elsif stammered. "I asked Milly to look out the window."

"She is," Ruth said. "But I don't think they'll move him today. Too many people on the grounds and the guards will be too busy with the ball. I told her she could take a break to do something with her hair or- Fantasma forbid- put on some make up. But I guess getting her in that dress was a miracle in itself."

Elsif had rushed into her bedroom so quickly that she hadn't noticed if the other girls were ready for the ball. "Mills is going?" Elsif questioned.

"Please," Ruth said unimpressed. "You think I wouldn't drag her to the ball? I was about to drag you out of the library before you came back."

As Ruth pinned several of Elsif's curls up and tamed her frizz, Elsif was tempted to blurt out the great news. On one hand, Elsif wanted Ruth to go to the gardens as soon as possible so she could witness the great surprise before anyone was caught. But on the other hand, Elsif liked that Ruth had returned to her old self even before she heard the great news.

For a few minutes, Elsif enjoyed the moment. Ruth scolding Elsif about not caring about her appearance while fluffing her hair and forcing Elsif to apply a little make up. It was a wonderful few minutes before the girls returned to reality.

"That's the best I can do with limited time," Ruth said, taking a step back from Elsif. "Is Will meeting us here or at the ball?"

"At the ball," Elsif said offhandedly. "But we should go straight to the gardens first."

Ruth rolled her eyes. "We have to make our grand entrance at the ball, *then* we can go to the gardens if you want. But you have to get your dress on. We're leaving in three minutes!"

Elsif opened her mouth to argue, but decided to shut it and get her dress on. It would probably be quicker than arguing with Ruth. Elsif ran to her closet and brought out her ballgown.

It was a tradition at Merlin for advanced female students to wear white dresses at the ball. It was a sign of new beginnings and Elsif had always dreamed of her first Felix Finis Ball in her white gown. Elsif had picked it out when she was twelve years old at a local dress shop in Magicis, and bought it two and a half years ago. She had altered it in the last four months to make sure it was absolutely perfect.

Clothes normally weren't a big deal to Elsif, but this was the one exception. The ballgown fit like a glove, with its elegant silk material, simple design, and small puff sleeves that hung off the shoulder.

"Elsif, you look like a marshmallow," Rose said once Elsif had walked into the living room.

"And you look like a banana," Elsif retorted. Rose was wearing a golden yellow gown with long flowing sleeves that trailed behind her, and a spiky golden headband.

"Thank you," Rose replied smugly.

Jazzy walked out of her room. "Are we ready to go?" She was wearing her deep purple gown that she had sewn herself, with silver accessories.

"Yes," Ruth said, ushering everyone out the door. "Let's go or we'll be late. Milly let's go!"

Milly stood up from where she was looking out the window and walked towards the door while stuffing the tracker into a purse. She was wearing an a-line red gown with a full skirt. "Let's get this over with," she muttered.

The girls walked out of their chambers and down the stairs to the second level. While they were traveling, Elsif could no longer contain her information.

"Ruth," Elsif whispered while they walked. "I need to tell you something."

"Is it about how you really want to go to the gardens?" Ruth questioned. "Because I'm aware."

"Yes," Elsif began, while looking over both shoulders. "But I don't want to go for me. I want to go for you."

"I don't like the gardens anymore," Ruth muttered.

"You might now," Elsif said, lowering her voice. "Because there might be someone waiting for you."

Ruth stopped in her tracks. "You better not be messing with me," she warned Elsif. The other girls stopped as well and looked at Ruth and Elsif with confusion.

"I'm not," Elsif said sincerely. "Will and I broke him out. He's in the gardens right now."

A gasp escaped Ruth's mouth as she stared at Elsif in shock. Elsif eagerly nodded her head. "That's why we need to go to the gardens."

"I need my purse!" Ruth shouted, then frantically began waving her arms. "I forgot my purse! I need my purse!"

Elsif frowned. "What?"

"I have a purse that makes this outfit look absolutely perfect," Ruth replied desperately. "But I didn't bother finding it because the night was already not going to be perfect, so why bother? But now it is going to be perfect so now I am bothered!"

Jazzy stepped up to calm Ruth. "I'll go get your purse. I'll run right now and meet you in the garden."

"Okay," Ruth nodded as Jazzy ran off.

Milly and Rose rolled their eyes together. "Why would a purse matter when you have the love of your life?" Milly questioned.

"Who can explain the weird thought process of Ruth's head," Rose told Milly. "Let's go dance."

Rose grabbed Milly and they continued to walk into the ball.

Ruth punched Elsif's arm with excitement. "Ow," Elsif responded while holding her arm.

"I'm going," Ruth said while jumping even though she was in five inch heels. "See you later!"

"Bye!" Elsif called after Ruth. "Can you send Will back up to the ball?"

"Will do!" Ruth said as she ran to the garden.

Elsif smiled and entered the Felix Finis Ball, feeling good about herself for the first time in awhile. Who knew that moment wouldn't last for even half an hour.

*****

Jazzy looked through Ruth's closet and drawers trying to find the purse. She thought it would be obvious which purse was the perfect match to Ruth's gown, but it was harder than she expected. Most of the purses were either pink or beaded or both. Jazzy decided to look through all of Ruth's storage spaces just to make sure she didn't miss any purses that may have been *the* purse.

Underneath the bunkbeds Ruth had a bin of miscellaneous things. Jazzy didn't see any purses so she began to slide it back under the bed, but something caught her eye. It was a journal that Jazzy had never seen before with lots of pages sticking out.

Jazzy knew deep down, she shouldn't pry. It was Ruth's personal journal, and Jazzy had no business snooping. But unfortunately, Jazzy was a very curious person at heart. So could anyone really blame her for the mess that was about to ensue?

She grabbed the notebook and began flipping through the pages. That moment would be etched in the back of Jazzy's mind for the rest of her life

*****

The name Jasmine Arabella was announced by the master of ceremonies. A girl who was normally meek and reserved, stormed down the steps instead of gliding gracefully like the rest of the guests. She practically ran across the room to Elsif, who was standing with Will.

"I hope Ruth's finally happy," Elsif told Will, who had arrived back from the gardens. "And now hopefully everything will be alright."

"Yeah," Will said, his hand rubbing the back of his neck. "You know, I've been meaning to tell you something."

Elsif looked at Will intently. "What?"

"It's about my past," Will said. "I never meant to keep it from you this long. It was nice living a *normal* life, but you deserve to know. I'm-"

Jazzy ran up to the couple and interrupted Will. "Where's Ruth?"

"In the garden," Elsif said absentmindedly, not taking her eyes away from Will.

"By the fountain," Will added, looking back at Elsif.

Elsif cleared her throat. "Jazzy, could I catch up with you in a min-"

"Did you know?" Jazzy demanded, holding the journal in front of Elsif, so she was forced to avert her eyes from Will.

"What?" Elsif questioned, looking at the journal with confusion. "That's not mine." Elsif glanced at Jazzy and saw a foreign expression. A combination of anger, sadness, and disgust was mixed into one big pot that was spilled upon Jazzy's face. "What's wrong? Did you give Ruth her purse? Who's journal is this?"

Jazzy shook her head and backed away from Elsif.

"Jazzy?" Elsif questioned, not understanding the interaction. "Jazzy, what's wrong?"

Jazzy didn't answer but instead ran towards the balcony that led to the garden.

"What happened to her?" Will asked as he and Elsif watched Jazzy leave.

"I have no idea, but I-" Elsif stuttered, as she weighed her options. "I need to go after her." Elsif ran quickly after Jazzy.

"Elsif!" Will yelled, running after her. "Wait! I'll come!"

Elsif didn't wait, but instead ran faster. She sprinted out to the balcony and raced down the stairs that lead to the garden.

*****

"I need to tell you the most important thing you'll ever hear in your entire life," Ruth said, taking Juniper's hands in hers.

Juniper rolled his eyes but allowed Ruth to hold his hands.

"Are you going to tell me how to get off Merlin grounds alive?" Juniper said in a teasing manner. "Because that seems important right now."

"No," Ruth said, tilting her head and smiling up at Juniper. "Far more important than life or death. I need to tell you-" Ruth hesitated and looked up at the sky. A few seconds passed before fireworks began erupting. Ruth turned back to Juniper, who was staring down at her. "Juniper Miller, I'm in lo-"

Juniper dropped Ruth's hand, which made her lose her words. "What are you doing?" She asked, and he motioned to something behind her.

Ruth whirled around to see Jazzy coming straight towards them. "Jazzy, not the time," She said while waving her away, but Jazzy didn't listen. Instead she marched up to Ruth and held up the journal.

Annoyance drained out of Ruth, along with the color in her face. Horror rapidly filled her as words began sputtering out of her mouth.

"I was, I wanted to, it was never the time," Ruth scrambled for words, as Jazzy stood in front of her, hurt beyond imaginable measures. "I promise you Jazzy, I never meant to keep this from you. It was complicated and I'm not good with feelings and you were going to be upset and I don't know how to comfort crying people, but I couldn't find anyone else to comfort you without telling them and I knew I had to tell you first, and eventually so much time passed that the secret kind of went to the back of my mind and other things took precedence." Ruth spit out every word that came to her brain, as Jazzy stood in front of her. "Please say something."

Lowering the book, Jazzy's lips shook as she asked, "Was I some type of cruel joke? A pet for you to drag along. Or maybe I was entertainment? And everyone knows. And you- you all laugh at me when I'm not in the room? Share mocking looks when you see me be so naive?" Jazzy shook her head as her anger overtook her. "What did *I* ever do to *you*?"

Ruth shook her head desperately. "It's not like that at all! This is a big misunderstanding! Please, let me explain-"

"No," Jazzy said, backing away. "Don't," she warned. "Don't."

"Jazzy," Ruth pleaded, as Jazzy ran away and vanished into the garden. Ruth could hardly breathe as she stood in the grave she had dug for herself.

"Ruth," Juniper said. "What's going on?"

She was speechless and mortified when she looked at Juniper.

"Ruth!" Elsif yelled, running from the direction of the school. "What's going on? Is this about your purse?"

"No, it's about, uh," Ruth stuttered. Since no satisfactory answer came to Ruth's mind, she sprinted away instead.

"Why is everyone running?" Elsif complained as she tried to catch her breath.

"What's going on?" Juniper demanded.

Elsif shook her head. "I have no idea."

Will ran into the clearing. "Did I just see Ruth running away?"

"Yeah," Elsif said. "Apparently everyone is getting their exercise today. Juniper, what did Jazzy say to Ruth?"

"She just held up a book," he replied. "I need to find Ruth."

"Which way did Jazzy go?" Elsif asked.

"Towards the maze," Juniper said as he ran in the other direction.

Elsif and Will headed to the maze to find Jazzy.

Half an hour was spent in the maze without Elsif and Will coming across a single person. Apparently the maze was not a popular spot during the Felix Finis Ball.

Finally they found another person, but it wasn't who they were looking for.

"Juniper?" Will questioned with surprise .

"Where's Ruth?" Elsif asked.

"I'm looking," Juniper muttered with annoyance.

"She's not going to be in the maze," Elsif stated. "She doesn't like the maze that much."

Scoffing, Juniper whirled around. "I know she doesn't like the maze! She's told me a thousand times! But she's not anywhere else in the garden so she has to be in here!"

"Maybe she's back at the school," Will said, since it was the obvious answer." She's not," Juniper snapped and continued walking.

Elsif felt bad for Juniper. She knew that if Ruth wasn't in another part of the garden, then she would probably be inside the school, and in that case, Juniper wouldn't be able to find her. But it would be quite surprising if Ruth didn't want Juniper to find her. Whatever had happened between Ruth and Jazzy, it was bad enough that not even Juniper could comfort her.

"Where are you going?" Elsif asked. "It leads to a dead end over there."

"I know," Juniper huffed over his shoulder. "This is where Melissa disappeared. Ruth might be-" Juniper abruptly stopped when he turned the corner and saw Ruth wasn't there. "Nevermind."

"Maybe she's wandering," Elsif suggested.

Juniper ignored Elsif and began walking away.

"Hey," Will said. "This isn't a dead end."

Juniper whipped around. "What?"

Will gestured to the right wall where an opening in the maze could be seen. "Right there."

"Melissa's dead end must be somewhere else," Elsif said as Juniper marched past her and towards the opening. "Maybe Ruth *is* there," Elsif said encouragingly while Juniper walked into the opening.

"Ruth?" Juniper asked as he walked into the clearing, but then added in a confused tone, "Jazzy?"

"Jazzy?" Elsif echoed as she ran into the clearing, with Will behind her.

It was clear from the second Elsif passed over the threshold, that the place they had found was not a normal part of the maze. It wasn't a normal dead end, but instead a circular alcove with a covering over head, that blocked all light from the sky. It was so dark that Elsif could only see two other shadowy figures. But after a second, green fire began bursting around the clearing. Torches with green flames glowed one by one on the walls, and everything came to light.

In front of Elsif, Will, and Juniper, Jazzy stood with tears next to a statue. Elsif rushed to Jazzy's side but her words caught in her mouth when she saw the stone figure. Disgust crept across her face as she saw the glorification of Fantasma's most horrendous villain. It was sickening to think of all the blood Malum had shed and she was still allowed to exist peacefully in the garden at Merlin.

"Why can't you leave me alone," Jazzy whispered bitterly.

Elsif turned to Jazzy, and remembered the reason she was there. "Jazzy, tell me what's going on."

Taking slow steps back, Jazzy shook her head at Elsif. "That's why you asked me to sit next to you in the carriage. You knew all along and you've been toying with me ever since."

Jazzy continued to back up until she was on the other side of Juniper and Will. They both moved towards Elsif as Jazzy isolated herself.

"I don't know what you're talking about," Elsif stated plainly.

"Really?" Jazzy asked with angry disbelief. "You *happened* to befriend the one girl in all of Fantasma who *happened* to be your Uncle Louis' long lost daughter?"

Elsif didn't understand the words Jazzy said at first. Her brows were scrunched, her head was cocked, and her expression was tense. But slowly her facial muscles relaxed and her mouth fell open as Elsif recognized the familiar nose that had been hiding on Jazzy's face all along. It was plainly obvious now that Elsif saw it, and she couldn't believe she had never noticed before.

The Walker nose was strangely distinct, and only a few people in the family had it such as Milly, Max, Aunt Poppy, and Uncle Louis. But it was their great-grandfather's nose that could not be mistaken. It was smaller on Jazzy, the hook of the nose slightly less noticeable, but there was no doubt it was the Walker nose.

"You did know!" Jazzy accused as she watched Elsif's expression change.

"No!" Elsif pleaded. "Jazzy no, I don't, I didn't-"

"Go away!" Jazzy screamed, as the air became thick. "Leave me alone!"

Elsif called out to Jazzy again while green tinged smoke swirled from the ground. It filled the alcove quickly and condensed at the feet of Elsif, Will, and

Juniper. Without warning, the smoke created an opening in the ground, and three people disappeared in front of Jazzy's eyes.

Chapter 31: Should've Left The Purse At Home pt. 2

"I can promise you one thing," Rose warned Milly. "If you don't start dancing with me right now then the fireworks tonight will be pointed suspiciously close to your favorite ship."

Milly ignored Rose as she stared at the tracker. "Dance by yourself. I think the tracker is loading. It keeps flashing."

"Lame," Rose muttered. "I should have convinced Kfred to come. He wouldn't be staring at a box all night. Unless it was a sciencey shaped box. Then maybe he would."

"We all need to start worrying about you more," Milly muttered. "If you're going to create fake people then you need to give them more convincing names."

Rose crossed her arms in a huff. "Kfred is real! He can reach the top shelf in the magical herb closet and is related to a herd of pigs."

Milly rolled her eyes, when she spotted a disheveled Ruth walking in from the balcony. "What is Ruth doing here without Juniper?"

"More importantly," Rose stated. "Where's her purse?"

Ruth shuffled into the ball. The edges of her skirt were dirty and her make up was smudged. She looked around the ball with a downturned mouth and eyes that darted around the room. Eventually, she spotted Milly and Rose at an empty table in the corner, and trudged over to them.

She plopped down in a chair and laid her head down across her folded arms without saying a word.

"So," Rose broke the silence. "Where's the purse?"

"Shhh," Milly urged Rose. "Leave her alone."

"Fine. I'm guessing you don't want to dance either? And it's the Elven Waltz too! I'm bringing my other, cooler cousins next time."

"Your other cousins are twenty years older than you and they're too busy cooking pudding," Milly retorted.

"Puddingtry is a noble career in Mirabilis!" Rose exclaimed. "You puny Navisians would never understand!"

Milly shook her head with annoyance and looked back down at her tracker, when an enormous gasp escaped her through her mouth. "The tracker!" Milly bellowed as she jumped out of her seat. "I saw a map!"

Rose practically jumped on top of Milly to see the tracker, but all she saw was a blank screen. "There's nothing there," Rose complained as she tried to take the tracker from Milly.

Ruth even lifted her head and looked at the tracker from her seat.

"It was there!" Milly argued as she fought off Rose with one hand and clutched the tracker in the other. "There!"

"Where?" Rose questioned.

"It's flashing," Milly said, staring at the screen. "There it is again! It's flashing a map for a split second at a time!"

"I saw it!" Rose sang out as she jumped in excitement.

"Where is that?" Milly tried to memorize the map as it flashed every couple of moments. "I need a map. Rose! Get me a map of Fantasma! GO!"

Rose took off running, while Milly looked around frantically for something to write with. She grabbed a cloth napkin that was mostly clean, but couldn't find a pen.

"What are you doing?" Ruth asked with a raspy voice.

"I need to draw the map, in case the tracker dies," Milly answered as she looked under the table on her hands and knees.

Ruth searched her pockets. "Uh, I have a lip liner."

"That'll work," Milly leaped to her feet and grabbed the liner. She went to work on drawing the map from her memory and the short flashes from the tracker. All those years Milly's parents made her practice her cartography finally came in handy.

Within minutes, Rose was running back with a ten foot scroll of a map of Fantasma. "You don't want to know how I got this."

Milly and Rose quickly rolled the map across the table, and began scanning for the land mass that matched the tracker. Even Ruth stood up and helped look.

"I think it's Vulputate," Ruth said. "It looks like a town surrounded by forest."

"The town is too small to be Vulputate," Milly replied.

"It's Currus," Rose said, with her fourteenth guess.

"Currus is all factories," Milly argued. "And no woodland. Think with your brains people!"

"You're asking far too much from Rose," Ruth muttered.

"At least I remembered my purse," Rose snickered.

Ruth shot dangerous eyes at Rose. "I'm going to kill you."

As Ruth and Rose bickered, Milly exclaimed, "I found it! It's Humilis! Right there!" Milly excitedly pointed at a spot in Humilis about half a mile inland. "It matches perfectly! Look at the small river and the curve of the forest!"

"We found it!" Rose cheered, jumping around the table. "We found it! We found it!"

"When should we leave?" Ruth asked with anticipation. "I'll need to change. Pack my bag. Fix my makeup. But I could be ready in an hour or two."

"There's no time for any of that nonsense," Milly chided. "We have to leave right now- where's the tracker?" Milly looked around frantically, flipping over chairs, and folding the map in a million different ways.

"It was right there before we started looking at the map," Ruth said, gesturing to a chair. "I saw you put it down."

"Well, it's not there anymore!" Milly yelled with panic. "Rose I swear if you did anything with it!"

"I didn't!" Rose claimed. "I promise I didn't!"

Ruth grabbed Milly's arm. "Melissa stole it. She stole it and she's going to steal the Hat!"

"Not if we get there first," Milly said, before taking off running with her makeshift map and the map of Fantasma.

*****

"No." The words echoed through Jazzy's limp body as she watched the green smoke subside and the empty ground restored. Not a soul remained in the place where three figures stood merely seconds ago.

"No," Jazzy said louder as the passing moment had caught up to the present. Whatever had just happened, was a direct consequence of Jazzy's actions. She didn't know how or even what occurred, but something supernatural coursed through Jazzy's veins seconds ago, that was unmistakable.

"I didn't mean it," Jazzy said as she dropped to her knees, tears beginning to form. "I didn't mean those things. Come back!" Jazzy dug into the grass for any sign of hope but only came up with fistfuls of dirt.

"Well," a sly, familiar voice spooked Jazzy in her trembling state. "This has been an interesting turn of events."

Jazzy whipped her head around. "Melissa," She gasped as a sob overcame her. "Melissa, I need help. Elsif and, and, they've disappeared. I don't know where, they were just here-"

Melissa laid a hand on Jazzy's shoulder. "Shh, it's alright. Everything is happening as it should."

Jazzy shook her head in confusion. "What? We need to find a teacher or a shovel or something. They're in trouble!"

"They aren't our concern anymore," Melissa said sternly. "We have a much more important job."

"What are you talking about?" Jazzy uttered. "They could be dead, Melissa!"

"I'm talking about," Melissa began as she knelt beside Jazzy and took her hand. "Our destiny. Our future. Our purpose."

"But Elsif-"

"Forget about them!" Melissa interrupted harshly. "They don't matter! *We* matter, Jazzy, you and me. The future of the Mimpius is relying on *us*."

"You're speaking nonsense," Jazzy replied with fright.

"You need to understand," Melissa urged. "It wasn't a coincidence that you came to this school. It wasn't a coincidence that you found this place. And it's not a coincidence that we relate to one another. Our legacies have been intertwined and brought us back together even though our pasts have tried everything to rip us apart. Our legacy is to continue her legacy," Melissa glanced up at the statue. "As her rightful kin."

"I have no kin," Jazzy answered bitterly.

"But you do," Melissa continued. "I knew it as soon as I saw you on your first day at Merlin. I only caught a glance of you when those stupid girls dragged you into that hallway, but I instantly knew who you were. You're indistinguishable from her. Your eyes, your hair, your smile. I'd do anything to look like my mother."

Jazzy remained quiet, not fully understanding Melissa's words but beginning to piece together the confusing puzzle.

"I've snuck home a hundred times and have heard the story of your mother more than I can count," Melissa carried on with a distant gleam in her eyes. "Dia haunts Cent in a way that I never understood until I saw you. You're the reckoning between our mothers. The tie that'll bring not only our family back together, but the Mimpius name as well."

"Melissa," Jazzy interrupted. "There are more pressing matters-"

"Don't be so naive Jazzy!" Melissa shouted while dropping her hand and standing up. "You're the reason this has been set in motion. You are the reason I stole the Staff and you are the reason this war has begun."

Jazzy looked up at Melissa with dirt-covered hands and tear-stained cheeks. "Why would *I* be the reason?"

Melissa scoffed as she pulled out a piece of paper from her pocket. She dropped it on the ground where Jazzy kneeled. Jazzy picked it up and found a photo of two young girls. The younger one was a few years younger than Jazzy and had long dark hair and a slight green complexion that matched Melissa. But the older girl was almost a carbon copy of Jazzy, except for the nose and the fact that the girl's skin had the slightest shade of olive to it.

"I was told you were dead," Melissa said, her softer tone returning. "But I saw you that day at Merlin, and I knew it was a sign from fate that everything was different now. I'd been encouraged for years by my family to steal Malum's Staff because it was our birthright to have it. That Staff belongs to the Mimpius line, not some stuffy pompous school. But I didn't care about the Staff before. I didn't care about the Mimpius, or even my own family. My mother tried everything to convince me, even telling me about this place that can only be opened by Mimpius blood. Eventually, I relented and told my mother that I would steal the Staff and bring it to Versario, not for duty or responsibility, but because I wanted her off my back. But then I saw you, and everything was put into perspective.

"So I stole the Staff but I didn't leave and escape to Versario like I had originally planned. I stayed because I needed you. I wanted you to bring back the Mimpius name with me. Your appearance is the destiny I've been looking for my entire life. I've always known I was worth more than Versario or Merlin could ever give me, and now with the Staff and you, we can find that destiny together. So I stayed. I hid the Staff in a place I knew no one would find, and I attempted to pin the theft on Juniper."

Melissa laughed before continuing, "It's funny really, how it all worked out. Juniper had been a pain in my side for years. He's just not Versarian like Bernard, the girls, and I are. He actually *likes* Merlin. He wouldn't sneak home with us, and would hate it when we criticised the school. I knew I couldn't tell him about the Staff or any of the plans that were happening back home. So instead of just hiding the plans, I decided- last minute of course- to pin the theft of the Staff on him so I could stay and get to know you."

"I told Juniper about how I stole the Staff and how I was going to try to use the Staff that night. He- very predictably- came to my chambers that night to stop me. I snuck out first so that as soon as he was out of his room I could find the perfect place to hide the Staff's bag in *his* chambers. Bernard let me in and I pried up the floorboards and cleared out a perfect space for the bag. I had to do it myself, you see, because Bernard's an idiot and would have just put it under Juniper's bed or something. I needed the bag to be in the perfect place, not too obvious- like Juniper actually hid it himself- but in a place where eventually the guards would find it. But then your cousins found it! How funny is that?"

Melissa smiled when she saw the surprise register in Jazzy's expression. "Oh yeah, I know about that too. It was quite easy to figure out actually. Once I knew that I was going to hide the Staff and stay here for a while, I began crafting my plan to get to know you. I didn't want to walk up to you and explain everything right away. I wanted us to bond first. Understand each other and care about our purposes in life. I needed you to be as passionate as I was, so you had to go on your own discovery of self with finding your parents and all that nonsense. It didn't go exactly as planned because Dylan kept bailing last second every time I tried to get him to help. But I've learned my lesson with him. He's more unreliable than I thought. But that's besides the point.

"I needed to get to know you first," Melissa explained with her crazy smile growing larger and larger. "I was puzzled and a little stumped when you first arrived because you were encapsulated by this group of girls, and I had no idea why. You weren't making any other friends, hanging out with any other people, or even talking to anyone else. It was just this little core group of four, and five with you.

"There was something off about the whole thing, so I had Bernard, Paisley, and Piper follow them closely. I thought maybe you somehow knew them before coming to school here, but that wasn't the case. I learned that these four girls were cousins, and very close ones. But what confused me the most was this Elsif girl. She was the one that befriended you first and she seemed to be so protective of you. Then I learned that she had followed me that night when I tried to pin the bag on Juniper, and *then* Piper found out she left a letter to the President that told him *I* stole the Staff.

"So you can imagine how perplexed I was. Who was this girl? Why is she taking control of you? How does she know I stole the Staff? None of it made sense," Melissa paced slightly from side to side. "But then I did some digging on this girl and it all became clear. She was a Walker and that meant her weasley little uncle was Louis Walker. Your father and the man who took my aunt away and ruined her life.

"So of course it all made sense!" Melissa exclaimed with excitement. "She somehow got you to Merlin and wanted you all to herself. She knew that I was also your cousin so she was trying to get me kicked out. Elsif was trying to do the same thing as me, heal her insignificant family by introducing the lost cousin. So I, of course, couldn't follow you too closely with the Walkers around. I instead continued to have Bernard and the girls keep an eye on them.

"I don't know why all of you were so obsessed with finding the Hat at one point," Melissa added casually. "I assumed it was because the Walker family wanted some ancient relic for themselves like the Staff is for us, but it made my family back home happy for some reason. I've been sending concealed letters back home to keep them updated and once you all met with Joseph Ellison, they became very interested. So thanks for that, it was very helpful.

"I did underestimate Elsif though," Melissa admitted. "I can't believe she got Bernard expelled. I did not see that coming. I also am dying to know why she apparently got Juniper kicked out of school too, but then he was here with her tonight. That's actually how I found you. I saw Juniper, followed him, and he led me straight to you where you uncovered Malum's statue and Staff all by yourself. I also never understood why he was suddenly friends with all of you. I assumed it was just because he was mad at me for framing him and he wanted to hurt me by keeping you away from me. But we have the rest of our lives to tell each other all the fun details of the last two years. We should probably get going. I have a Versarian carriage waiting for us."

Melissa finally stopped talking and waited for Jazzy's response. Jazzy stared up at Melissa with her mouth open and eyes wide.

"How do we get them out?" Jazzy pleaded quietly while stroking the ground.

"Oh I have no idea," Melissa stated casually. "That must have been a secret of Malum's or something, and you must have unlocked it. Which only a true Mimpius could do. So good job, I'm proud of you. Now let's go. It's going to take a couple days to get back to Moorville."

Jazzy's breath was unsteady as she finally found the strength to stand up. "I'm not going anywhere with you."

"Excuse me?"

"I don't remember what a Mimpius is, I'm tired of being everyone's lost cousin, and I don't have a destiny or fate or perspective or whatever you're calling it," Jazzy spluttered out indignantly. "I just need a shovel so that I can save Elsif and the boys."

Melissa's face changed to a deep scowl. "They're gone. You're wasting your time. Come to Moorville with me and you'll become someone. Have importance and meaning in your life instead of the pathetic path you're going down."

"No," Jazzy said immediately with a shake of her head. "I'm saving them if it's the last thing I do."

Melissa stared blankly then shrugged. "Fine," She snapped, then grabbed the Staff that the statue of Malum was holding. "You'll regret this!" Melissa shouted angrily as she left the clearing.

Jazzy was once again alone.

*****

"Anyone got any cards?" Elsif asked. "We could play Cats and Goblins? Or Angry Elves Down the River? Oh, I learned a new game recently called Twelve Red Sostomi, that could be fun."

"Could you shut up," Juniper grumbled.

"You don't have to be a jerk," Will retorted.

The three had dropped through the ground into a circular room that was pitch dark. There was absolutely no light and no apparent way out. They spent the first twenty minutes or so yelling and feeling around the walls for a door or window.

Elsif and Will eventually became discouraged and sat down. Juniper continued to feel around for a way out, and was annoyed at the lack of effort from the others.

"And you two don't have to sit around, telling jokes, while I'm the only one doing anything," Juniper grumbled.

"I would expect you to be a little more grateful after we saved you today," Will snapped.

Elsif ignored the bickering as she laid her head back against the cool stone, and wondered how the evening could have gone so wrong.

"You're the one that should be grateful to me," Juniper fumed. "I haven't told anyone about your stupid secret yet and if you keep getting on my nerves then it's not going to stay that way."

"What secret?" Will demanded. "You don't know anything about me."

"I know everything," Juniper muttered. "And I'd shut up too if you don't want me telling Elsif."

Will rolled his eyes even though no one could see him. "Go ahead. Say whatever you want. You don't know anything."

"I know you're the prince and heir of Regium," Juniper snapped.

Silence followed in the pitch dark, until Elsif finally said, "What. What?" Blackness was Elsif's only response for half a minute.

"Was I right?" Juniper asked.

"How did you-" Will began to ask with exasperation. "How, in all of Fantasma, would you know that? No one outside of Koronia knows anything about the royal family."

Elsif shot up straight. "Is Juniper right? Are you the crown prince?"

"Eh," Will said with reluctance. "Not technically anymore."

"No way!" Elsif yelled while covering her mouth.

"So I was right," Juniper commented for clarification.

Elsif reached out into the dark until she found Will's arm. "Tell me you're joking. Are you actually a prince? Do you have a huge crown and a million servants who bring you gold and tea?"

"Yeah," Will agreed with a grumpy sarcasm. "That was my favorite breakfast."

"Why are you upset?" Elsif asked. "This is cool. I thought you were a murderer at one point. This is a major step up."

Will shuffled uncomfortably for a moment. "I'm not that person anymore, haven't been since I turned eighteen and left home. My younger brother's the heir now and I don't miss it. I liked being just Will without all the extra baggage."

"The extra baggage of gold?" Elsif teased, but no laugh came in response. "Will," Elsif said in a softer tone. "Being a prince or former heir doesn't change who you are."

"I was going to tell you at the ball tonight," Will explained. "I promise I was going to tell you. Everything, on my own terms. I just don't consider that part of me real anymore. I'm so sorry, love, I should have told you sooner."

"Or at all," Juniper muttered from across the room.

"How'd you figure it out?" Will snapped at Juniper.

"The gold you used in Andorae," Juniper said. "It had the royal family crest on it and Jazzy has a little trinket box that has the same crest. She told Ruth about it once and then Ruth told me one time. She mentioned something about the heir's name being William Woods."

Elsif could feel Will shaking his head. "I can't believe it."

"Do you think Jazzy knew?" Elsif wondered aloud. "I think she would have said something, but I'm definitely going to ask her if she had any suspicions-" Elsif trailed off, the previous events hitting her like a rock to the head.

"Jazzy will come around," Will insisted.

"Maybe," Elsif said with uncertainty.

"You really didn't know?" Juniper asked.

"No," Elsif replied honestly. "I didn't know until she said it. Then it seemed so obvious."

Silence once again filled the room. The darkness seemed to grow whenever there was a lack of words.

"I *am* really sorry Elsif," Will repeated. "I wanted to tell you myself. I almost told you so many times, but the words never seemed to come out."

"Will, I honestly don't care about your past," Elsif told him earnestly. "I know who you are and that's enough for me. I love who you are, not what your past was."

"You love me?"

Elsif smiled. "Of course I do."

Will reached his hand out to Elsif, and accidentally bumped into her glasses. Elsif laughed and took his hand and placed it gently on her cheek.

"I love you too," Will said.

Juniper grumbled from the other side of the room. "I swear if you guys kiss then I'm going to throw up. Then we're all going to decay in my rotting vomit."

They ignored Juniper's wishes.

"I don't appreciate how quiet it is over there," Juniper complained. "You know the only reason she's not mad is because you're a rich prince. If you were a poor simpleton this conversation would have gone very differently."

"Do you enjoy ruining everything?" Will asked with annoyance to Juniper.

"Hey, I didn't agree to be a part of your little lovefest," Juniper snapped. "If you guys stopped and- wait I found something. I think I have a door handle!"

"Seriously?" Will asked as he and Elsif jumped to their feet.

"Where is it?" Elsif asked, carefully making her way to the other side of the dark dwelling.

A couple thumps were heard before Juniper answered, "It's low to the grounds, maybe a foot or two above the floor. I think I'm feeling a door but it's only half the size of a regular door."

"Does it open?" Elsif asked as she reached her hands out to find the wall.

"No," Juniper said as he wiggled the doorhandle. "It's either locked or jammed. Will, we might have to push it down."

Will tried to walk over to the door, but ended up slamming his head into the wall instead. "Ow," He groaned. "Where are you?"

"Over here," Juniper called out. "Over here. Over here! Where are you?"

"I'm making my way over to you- oh there you are," Will suddenly said. "Where's the door?"

"Right here," Juniper said and guided Will. "I think the hinges are on the other side so we need to push through."

"Or Elsif could freeze the locks," Will suggested with a tease.

"Haha," Elsif replied dryly. "Maybe I did freeze that lock in Silvia? We'll never know."

Juniper sighed. "Can we stop wasting time and get this door open?"

It was awkward to break down the door, since the boys had to crouch and slam themselves into the wall at the same time. But after several attempts the rusty hinges flew off and the door slammed to the ground.

Green light flooded the room. It was dim but since they had been in the complete dark for so long, the light was still bright to them. Once their eyes adjusted they could see that there was a long hallway in front of them, lined with green torches every several yards.

Juniper grabbed the first torch from the wall. "Let's go."

The trio set off down the endless hallway. Will and Elsif both grabbed a torch for themselves and the green light filled their surroundings as they walked.

Elsif's white dress was completely tattered and muddy. It hardly resembled the dress that Elsif had once dreamed of. It was completely ruined and would never be the same again.

After a few minutes they came across several bars in the wall, and an empty space behind it. The boys paid little attention to it, but Elsif lingered a moment.

"What if it's a way out," Elsif said as she looked through the bars.

"The hallway is heading southeast, and that will take us straight to the school," Juniper stated.

"It looks like some kind of prison cell," Will mentioned over his shoulder. "It's probably left over from the Ancient Ages or something."

The boys continued to walk and discuss the differences between green fire and regular fire. Elsif remained for a few more seconds. The bars were just wide enough for her arm to fit through, so she stuck her torch inside the cell and took a quick look around. It was a large space that seemed similar to the place where the three of them were stuck minutes ago.

The only difference was this place had a couple pieces of furniture, like an old bed with ripped blankets, a wooden chair, and a small table with a million carvings in it. As she passed her torch's light over the room, she saw a lump in the corner. At first, she thought it was another piece of furniture but suddenly familiar eyes and pointed ears stared back at her.

Elsif screamed and fell backwards, dropping the torch beside her. Will and Juniper came running full speed back to her, and were at her side within seconds.

"What's wrong," Will asked with concern, crouching next to Elsif.

Juniper picked up Elsif's torch and examined both sides of the hallway hastily. "Did you see something? Is someone following us?"

"No," Elsif said, shaking her head, and trying to calm herself. "I saw-" Elsif's tongue caught in her mouth. What she saw was impossible. A cruel mind trick or her overactive imagination would be a thousand times more logical.

"I was spooked by a bat," Elsif finally spit out, not daring to reveal the true thing she had seen or imagined she saw. No, Elsif could not have seen what she saw. She had been reading too many books about old historians and magical creatures.

"A bat?" Juniper rolled his eyes.

"It got really close to me," Elsif said.

"They have exceptional sight," Juniper muttered as he continued to walk. "There's no way it would have touched you."

Will helped Elsif up, and she brushed herself off. "I hate that I know Ruth told you that."

"Are you okay?" Will asked, as they continued down the hallway.

Elsif took a deep breath and pushed that moment to the deepest crevice of her mind. "Yes, I'm fine."

*****

"Milly!" Ruth yelled as she and Rose ran behind Milly. "What's the plan! Where are we going?"

"To the docks!" Milly called back without slowing her pace. "We're going to get to Humilis first!"

"Wait!" Rose pleaded. "We need weapons!"

"And I need to change!" Ruth added.

Milly stopped in her tracks. "You're right," she said while turning to the others."

"Thank goodness," Ruth complained. "If I stay in these shoes and dress one more minute I'm going to collapse."

"No!" Milly chided. "We need weapons. If Melissa is on her way to Humilis then we might have to fight for the Hat!"

"You two can go get weapons," Ruth said. "I'm going to change."

Milly rolled her eyes but didn't have time to argue. "Fine, but meet us at the ship in ten minutes. If you're late, we're not waiting!" The pair ran off towards Rose's dungeon while Ruth scurried off to the chambers.

Milly and Rose quickly arrived at the closet, and climbed down into the dungeon. They grabbed every weapon they could carry, including three swords, a bow, several daggers, the chain whips, and miscellaneous bombs. They were about to climb back up, when suddenly a loud thud made the room shake. The girls hesitated a moment, and then realized the noise was coming from the mysterious door.

"That's not good," Milly commented. "We should get out of here."

"Or," Rose said mischievously while dropping her weapons, except for her beloved chain whips. "We can be polite and answer the door."

"Rose no!" Milly yelled but Rose had already unlocked the door and swung it open. To everyone's surprise the unexpected visitors on the other side were none other than Elsif, Will, and Juniper holding torches with a weird looking fire.

"Fancy meeting you two here," Will joked as he came through the door.

"Have you seen Jazzy?" Elsif asked frantically.

"What is this place?" Juniper asked in astonishment.

Milly shook her head. "No time! We have to get to the docks! Grab some weapons and we'll explain on the way!"

*****

After changing into her own clothes, Ruth stuffed a bag with a few extra shirts and pairs of pants for the other girls. She buttoned her bag and turned to leave when the door opened and Jazzy came crashing into the room.

For a moment the girls stared at each other, wordless panic spreading between them.

"Jazzy I'm so sorry-"

"Elsif, Will, and Juniper are stuck under the ground!" Jazzy said frantically. "We need a shovel or a spell or something. I don't know!"

A confused expression came over Ruth. "What? Are they hurt?"

"I don't know," Jazzy confessed in alarm. "But we need to dig them out."

"Okay, okay," Ruth said, looking around. "We don't have a shovel in here but Rose and Milly are at the docks with a bunch of weapons. Maybe we could use one of them to dig in the ground?"

Jazzy nodded her head, looking for any help possible, whether it was logical or not. "That might work."

"Let's go find them," Ruth said, putting an arm around Jazzy. "And we'll figure something out. Let's go."

Chapter 32: We're Just Kids

"How are we supposed to get to Humilis before Melissa if we're assuming she already took a carriage?" Elsif asked as they arrived at the ship. "They'll be going through Koronia *and* Navisa where there's no speed limit so they can go as fast as they want. I don't think a ship can go faster than a carriage at full speed."

Milly disappeared into the captain's quarters before quickly returning with a large conch shell. "It can when we have help."

The conch shell had a loud and low pitch. Seconds later the top of a large sea creature's head emerged beside the boat.

"Elwin," Milly called down. "I need you to take the boat to Humilis. Northwest, ninety knots." A splash rushed up the side of the boat and drenched Milly's front. "Elwin! I know it's the middle of the night but this is life or death. Life or death! You better take a two minute nap, because we're leaving in three!"

"Ruth's not here yet," Juniper stated. "We can't leave without her."

"If she's not here in three minutes then we'll have to," Milly stated. "Rose, help me prepare the sails."

Juniper opened his mouth to argue, but stopped mid word when Ruth and Jazzy were seen from the distance, coming out of the front doors. As they got closer Jazzy was shocked to see Elsif, Will, and Juniper safely on the ship. But when she saw them alive and well, she was able to breathe again.

"Let's go!" Milly urged Jazzy and Ruth as soon as they walked onto the docks. "We've got to go if we're going to beat Melissa."

"Melissa?" Jazzy questioned as she boarded the boat. "But she's in the garden."

"She stole our tracker!" Rose exclaimed. "Haven't you heard? We have to get to Humilis to get the Hat before she rules the world!"

"Oh," Jazzy said with a confused look.

"Where were you?" Juniper asked, meeting Ruth halfway up the ramp and walking with her onto the boat.

"I was, uh," Ruth hesitated. "Helping Milly. The tracker showed us the location and we had to find it on a map." Ruth then added in a teasing tone, "Why? Do you hate leaving my side for even a second?"

"I couldn't find you," Juniper stated solemnly.

Ruth found herself annoyed at Juniper's response. "Well, I was with the tracker." She walked away so the conversation couldn't continue.

Elsif ran over to Jazzy once she was on deck. "Jazzy, are you alright?"

"Yes," Jazzy said, taking a few steps away. "I'm glad you're not under the dirt anymore."

"I'm glad too," Elsif replied. "Can we talk about-"

Milly came onto the deck and began yelling and handing out rope, "We need to get this boat sailing people! Elwin can only do so much, the rest is up to us! If you're not doing something productive then you're doing something wrong!"

Everyone was given a task so there was no room for discussion to ease the awkward tension in the air. They were an odd looking crew, as they ran around the ship. Most of them had no idea what they were doing, but even their appearances looked funny. Milly, Ruth, and Rose had been given regular clothes to change into, but Jazzy and Elsif were still in their ballgowns. Will was in his suit, and Juniper was still in his clothes from months ago. Any passing boats would surely give them a funny look as they passed.

Eventually, the boat began moving once Elwin wrapped his large tentacles around the ship and the sails picked up wind.

*****

The ship sailed across the Dextram Sea in six hours, which was a complete and utter miracle according to Milly. The rest of the crew thought the journey was about five hours too long.

Humilis had the smallest port that Milly had ever tried to dock at. But luckily Elwin was able to help with the steering. Once Milly had secured the rope to the dock, she boarded the ship to give directions.

"If the Hat hasn't moved then we have to go half a mile northwest," Milly stated. "Our goal is to get in and get out as fast as possible. We want to be out of here and back at Merlin before Melissa or anyone else shows up. But if we do run into them, then we have our weapons as backups. Any questions?"

"Yes," Ruth stated. "Who put Margo in charge?"

"Elsif did," Milly retorted. Everyone turned to Elsif, who shrugged in response. "And it's Milly," she grumbled under her breath.

Juniper was the first to leave the huddle. He grabbed a sword and walked off the ship. "Instead of talking, how about we actually go get the Hat."

Ruth ran after Juniper with a bow in her hand (she still had no arrows). Milly and Rose quickly grabbed their weapons and ran off the ship as well, not wanting to be left behind. Rose had her chain whips in each hand, and Milly had her sword strapped to her left side and her dagger contraption on her right forearm.

Jazzy walked off the ship next, alone and with no weapons.

"Did you want your blaster?" Elsif offered. "It's the one we stole from the weaponry for you," She said with a small laugh.

Jazzy shook her head and continued down the ramp.

"I don't know why we need these stupid weapons," Elsif muttered, but tucked her fancy dagger into the pocket of her dress anyway. "Melissa won't be here for at least another eight hours."

"I guess it just makes everyone feel safer," Will said, while grabbing a sword.

"I suppose," Elsif said, as they left the boat behind. "But we better all run back to the ship at the first sign of danger."

"There won't be any danger," Will assured. "And then after we find the Hat and give it to Merlin, then it'll all be over. Just like you want."

Elsif smiled with a gleam of sorrow in the corner of her eyes. "I haven't known what I've wanted for quite some time."

*****

The finale of the adventurous treasure hunt of the Warlock's Hat ended in a way no one expected, and nobody wanted. There was no epic battle, no triumph of a new treasure found, and no hoorah echoing through the town. Where the long awaited Hat should have sat, a dead body laid instead.

The gang stood at the edge of a huge crater, exactly where the map showed the Hat to be as the sun first began to rise. It was about fifty feet in diameter and twenty feet deep. There was rock, dirt, and scattered lumps along the bottom, but no Hat.

"There must be a mistake," Milly said, looking at her handdrawn map. "Maybe we're in the wrong place, or the Hat moved in the last six hours."

A creaking door was heard behind the group. An old, hunched over woman with a scarf draped over her head walked out slowly. "It's gone," She croaked from her porch. "If you're looking for the Elven cap, it's gone."

Milly walked towards the woman and stopped in front of her house. "Are you talking about the Warlock's Hat? Do you mean someone already took it?"

"No," The woman shook her head sadly. "It's gone. Has been for a long time now."

"It's not gone ma'am," Elsif corrected. "We have a tracker for it, and it was here six hours ago."

The woman didn't change her downcast expression. "I've watched people come here for seventy years to find the cap, and I've told them all the same. This is where it was destroyed and this is where your search ends. My family has lived in this house since the Ancient days and they have seen hundreds of people just like you come. But it's gone. It's time Fantasma accepted that."

"It can't have been destroyed!" Milly replied. "We've been searching for it for two years."

The woman looked down at Milly with sympathy. "At least you found out now instead of wasting your whole life like the man down there. He spent his whole life searching for the cap, only to die where the cap died hundreds of years ago."

Everyone's heads turned towards the bottom of the crater, as realization sank in that the lump at the bottom was not a random lump, but a person.

Milly walked to the edge of the crater and looked intently at the body. "No," she muttered under her breath, before running down the rock wall.

"Milly what are you doing!" Rose called after her. "At least wait for me!" She jumped down the rocky slope and raced after her cousin.

"Guys stop!" Elsif yelled at them. "Come back!"

Ruth gagged. "Now they're going to smell like a dead body."

Jazzy turned to the old woman. "Who's going to take care of the person?"

The woman shook her head. "No one. We are a small village between two cities, and neither want to take responsibility for the ruckus that happens in this crater. In the past, I would bury them myself but I wouldn't make it back up now." The woman slowly walked to her door. "I am truly sorry for your disappointment," She said before disappearing inside her house.

"That's terrible," Elsif uttered with a shake in her voice. "The poor person."

Jazzy put a hand to her heart. "His poor family."

"The stupid towns," Ruth muttered. "Horrible people."

Juniper sighed with annoyance. "We should go."

"I'll go get Milly and Rose," Will volunteered, and made his way down the crater. He slid down the wall, and walked carefully over the millions of tiny rocks to find Rose and Milly arguing near the deceased body that lay in the middle. When Will walked up, instead of ushering the girls back, he stopped and stared at the body. He then looked back at the group that was still at the top of the crater, and then back at the body. He kept shifting his glances between the two, like he couldn't decide something.

"What is he doing?" Ruth questioned. "Get them away from the body before they start smelling."

"Can you have a little respect?" Elsif muttered.

"Sorry," Ruth grumbled. "But we have more pressing matters. Like getting out of here before Melissa gets here."

"I don't think Melissa is coming," Jazzy said quietly. "In the garden she said that she was going to Versario."

Ruth turned to Jazzy. "You saw Melissa in the garden?" When Jazzy nodded Ruth added, "Then who stole the tracker?"

"Why did Melissa tell you she was going to Versario?" Juniper questioned.

Jazzy looked down sheepishly. "It's a long story."

"Is Rose crying?" Elsif asked with concern. Milly and Rose's argument turned into a yelling match while Will wordlessly stood beside them. Rose seemed to be wiping away tears, and Will even put his arm around her for comfort.

Elsif took off down the hill with haste, because if Rose was letting Will comfort her, then something really bad happened. Ruth followed Elsif closely, and Juniper and Jazzy lagged behind them.

"Rose!" Elsif said, as she tried to run on the unsteady ground. "What's wrong?" She asked once she reached them.

Rose left Will's arms as soon as she saw Elsif, and buried her snotty face into her shoulder. "I want to leave!" Rose sobbed.

"Then let's go," Elsif said, completely flustered, while trying to calm Rose.

"No!" Milly insisted. "What about Jerry?"

"Jerry? What-" Elsif questioned as she laid eyes on the disfigured man that was just familiar enough to recognize. It was clear that Jerry did not die from natural causes. "Oh my-"

Milly crossed her arms. "We can't leave him here."

A whimper was heard from Jazzy who was standing behind Elsif, and a gag came from Ruth who moved to the side.

"I'm going to be sick," Ruth muttered as she held her stomach.

"Mil," Elsif said softly with a shaky voice, while her insides turned upside down. "There's nothing we can do. He's already gone."

"We can't leave him!" She repeated with a shout. "Will said the town won't do anything, so we have to!"

"What are we supposed to do?" Elsif asked in disbelief over the situation.

"Bury him," Milly stated. "We need to bury him. That's the least we could do."

"Milly we can't, we hardly knew him-"

"Yes we can!" Milly yelled. "We knew him enough for him to trust us with his greatest possession! His life's work was dependent on us! But now he's dead, and someone killed him! We should have been here to save him! We should have gotten here sooner! And we should have never let the tracker out of our sight! I let Melissa get the tracker! This is my fault!"

Elsif sighed, understanding Milly a little better now. "We don't know what happened. And we'll never know the millions of ways things could have gone differently." Elsif took a deep breath before continuing. "We're just kids, Mil. We could have never stopped this bigger mess that's surrounding us."

"I don't feel like a kid," Milly breathed. "Not anymore."

Milly dropped to her knees beside Jerry, and shot a dagger into her hand. She began digging at the rocks in a futile effort.

"What are you doing?" Rose complained between sniffles. "Let's go!"

"I'm not leaving until Jerry is buried in a proper grave," Milly stated.

Elsif was at a loss for words as she looked around at the group. Ruth looked nauseous, Rose and Jazzy were crying messes, Will was standing helplessly beside her, and Juniper turned to leave.

"Where are you going?" Ruth demanded, as she watched Juniper.

"To find a shovel," He said.

Elsif looked at Will. "I'm going to take the girls back to the ship."

Will nodded. "I'll help bury him."

Elsif had her arm around Rose as they walked out with Ruth and Jazzy closely behind them. As they climbed out of the crater, they saw Juniper walk out of the old woman's house with three shovels. The walk back to the ship was agonizing but waiting for the other three was even worse.

"Who would do this?" Jazzy muttered, as they sat on the swaying ship.

"Melissa would," Ruth muttered. "But at least they didn't get the Hat."

"But," Rose said, while wiping her face off with a rag. "They haven't used the Staff yet, so maybe they don't have it anymore or lost it or something."

Jazzy shook her head. "Melissa has it now, and she's taking it back to Versario."

Elsif looked at Jazzy with a confused expression. "How would you know that?"

"It's a long story," Jazzy repeated the phrase as she dropped her gaze.

Milly, Will, and Juniper arrived at the ship after some time had passed. The exact amount, no one could be sure. Time seemed to pass differently that day, as if it was frozen while it also flashed in a blink of an eye.

The journey back to Merlin was not as strenuous as the trip to Humilis. Milly didn't require anyone to do any specific jobs, and she didn't even steer the ship. They solely relied on Elwin.

The mysteries of the last twenty-four hours were revealed to everyone. Ruth shared what she had learned in Stellae. Jazzy shared how she found her father's journal in Ruth's drawer and about her meeting with Melissa in the garden. Elsif shared about her and the boy's time underground, except for one minor detail that she had buried in her mind. Milly shared about the tracker turning on and drawing the map with lip liner.

After they had shared extensively about the previous day, each member of the gang began to fall asleep. They were all tired, not just physically but emotionally as well, so it wasn't surprising that an hour into the journey there wasn't a single person awake. They all slept soundly, but not peacefully.

Chapter 33: Goodbye May Seem Like Forever

The ship arrived at Merlin in the mid afternoon. Jazzy was the first to wake and notice that they had arrived. She stood up silently, climbed off the boat, and walked alone to the only place she wanted to be.

Elsif woke a few minutes later and immediately noticed Jazzy's absence. She also knew the one place Jazzy would want to go, and went after her.

The maze had always been a tricky place for Elsif to navigate. It never changed but it was so large that Elsif was never able to get a proper handle on it. For people like Milly, who were good at memorization and direction, it was easy, but neither of those things had ever been Elsif's strong suits. But eventually, Elsif found the small opening that led to Malum's statue.

"Hey," Elsif said.

"Hello," Jazzy said with an unsteady breath.

Elsif slowly walked into the clearing, and stood beside Jazzy. The pair existed silently together in the alcove. Jazzy's eyes were on the statue, and Elsif's were everywhere but the figure in front of them.

"I don't understand magic," Jazzy said casually after several minutes. "I don't think I ever will."

Elsif teetered from foot to foot. "I'm starting to think I never will either," She said eventually, with a self-deprecating laugh. "But you know," Elsif added with a smile. "It's kind of cool to have your own hideout that only you have access to."

"And Melissa," Jazzy replied.

"Yeah," Elsif mumbled. "But it sounds like she's not coming back to Merlin, so I guess she's not our problem anymore."

Jazzy shifted uncomfortably as she stared at the statue of Malum. "I think I might want her to remain my problem."

"What do you mean?" Elsif asked.

"I don't know exactly," Jazzy admitted. "I'm not sure what family responsibilities should look like in this situation, but I can't forget about Melissa. I didn't understand most of what she told me about our family, or Mimpius, or Versario, but I want to know more. I want to know what she meant. But more importantly, if all of you are right and she's not going down a good path, then I want to stop her. Or help her? I don't know, I just feel the need to do something."

Elsif nodded. "Okay. What's the plan?"

"I think I'm going to Moorville," Jazzy said. "That's where Melissa said she was going. And that's where my mother grew up, so I want to go there too. I think I'm going to be there for a while."

"When do we leave?"

Jazzy shook her head. "You don't have to come. I'm leaving today, and I don't know when I'll be back. I'm probably not going to continue at Merlin in the advanced degree program. I know you won't approve but-"

"I don't care about Merlin!" Elsif blurted. "I don't care about advanced schooling anymore. And I don't even know if I can trust or believe anything they say anyway. Like Malum, who knows if she was truly a terrible person. I mean she probably was, there's a lot of evidence against her and the Mimpius, but in the end who knows! I didn't know her personally! How is anything in history supposed to be trusted! It's just a bunch of words on pages that we blindly put our faith in, and- I'm being really paranoid I know. But I'm just so confused, and I don't know what I believe, and therefore I don't know who I am! Sorry- I'm being dramatic, but all I'm trying to say Jazzy is that I don't care about Merlin. I care about you.

"I love you Jazzy," Elsif said earnestly. "I don't care if you're blood related to me or if we don't share even a drop of genetic heritage. You're my family Jazzy; you're more than my family. You're my *Yihov*. Have you ever heard of that word? It's from the Ancient Age. Actually it's far before the Ancient Age. A *Yihov* is the word that people used thousands of years ago for their chosen family. It loosely translates to 'brother' now, though it's really supposed to be a gender neutral term, but sibling is just too casual. It's supposed to be the closest bond you can form with someone. Closer than a brother because you chose them to be your brother, whether they're already your family or not.

"You're my *Yihov* Jazzy, and I'm going to go where you go. And I'm going to care about what you care about. I'm going to call home wherever you call home. I love you Jazzy, and I don't want you to ever feel like you're alone in anything ever again."

Elsif waited for Jazzy's response after she finished her long and confusing speech. A few agonizing seconds passed as Jazzy stared at Elsif wordlessly.

Jazzy was never good at expressing herself, and it would have been particularly hard through the incoming sob that was hidden behind her face. Instead she wrapped her arms around Elsif and embraced her.

"You're my *Yihov* too," Jazzy whimpered as she began to cry.

*****

"Should we be concerned that Jazzy and Elsif are gone?" Ruth asked casually in her sleepy state, as she rolled over on to her side.

Milly shot up. "What? Who's missing?"

"Good riddance," Rose mumbled, without opening her eyes.

"They probably went to their chambers to sleep in their actual beds," Juniper grumbled. "Better than the hardest deck known to man."

Will sat up. "Maybe one of you girls should check to make sure they're alright."

"Not me," Rose muttered as she used her arms as a pillow.

Ruth covered her eyes from the sun. "I'm asleep."

"I'm not leaving you guys unsupervised with my ship," Milly stated. "And shouldn't you be hiding?" Milly asked Juniper.

"It's Felix Finis weekend," Juniper replied. "No one was going to check on me until next week."

Rose sighed. "I love Felix Finis weekend. I can get away with so much."

Milly stood up, and grabbed a telescope from the captain's cabin. She began scanning the sea, and the surrounding area.

"You look ridiculous," Ruth said. "What are you doing?"

"I'm not leaving the boat," Milly answered. "But that doesn't mean I can't look for Elsif and Jazzy."

Rose laughed. "I'm pretty sure they didn't go for a swim."

"Can you check the window of your chambers?" Will asked.

Milly turned her telescope to the east side of the school. "Dark room and curtains are half shut. Just how we left it." Milly began scanning other windows and the lawn of Merlin. "Oh!" Milly exclaimed. "I think I found them! Yeah, they're walking on the west side of the building towards us. I think they're coming from the garden. Still in their ballgowns. I would think they'd want to change by now."

Twenty minutes later Elsif and Jazzy arrived at the ship with news. The girls were surprisingly receptive to the new plans, but only because of a small misunderstanding.

"So when do we leave?" Milly asked. "It'll take awhile for all of us to pack our stuff. Maybe tomorrow evening?"

"I need way more notice than tomorrow evening," Ruth argued. "Maybe I'll be ready by next week. But I have a *lot* of stuff."

"I can't wait to be in a region where daily massacres are the norm!" Rose bounced around excitedly. "I am going to thrive!"

"Rose, they still have common decency," Milly chided. "Even if it is a lawless land. I'm sure it will be a lot like Navisia, but maybe slightly worse."

"I'm going to need at least four carriages for all my stuff," Ruth added.

"No," Elsif tried to interrupt. "Guys no, you're not- guys, no, YOU'RE NOT COMING!" Elsif finally had to scream to be heard over the girl's chatter. They looked at Elsif with puzzled expressions.

"Who's not coming?" Milly asked.

"The three of you," Elsif clarified. "Jazzy and I are moving to Versario, no one else."

Disagreements erupted from each girl.

"You'll die without us!"

"That's not fair! We deserve to live in chaos too!"

"Why do you get to go and not us!"

"No!" Elsif repeated. "You all need to continue at Merlin Academy. Jazzy and I are both over eighteen and have degrees. You three don't have a choice. There's no discussion here."

Ruth left the ship and stormed off in the direction of the garden. Juniper walked off the boat soon after, and went after Ruth.

Rose crossed her arms. "Have fun leaving us behind," She grumbled as she left the ship and walked towards the school.

Milly shrugged. "I get it I guess." She walked sullenly to the captain's cabin and shut the door.

Jazzy tried to hide her discouraging look. "I'm going to go pack." She left the ship and walked towards the front door of the school.

Elsif sighed and turned to Will. "Could that have gone worse?"

"Yeah," Will replied. "Not much worse because that was pretty bad, but I'm sure somehow it could have been a little more unpleasant."

Elsif walked off the boat, and Will followed her. They walked along the shoreline in silence for a while.

"When do you leave?" Will asked.

"In a couple hours," Elsif said. "Most of my stuff is already packed, and Jazzy doesn't have much."

Will nodded. "Doesn't give me much time to pack, but I'll make it."

Elsif turned her head towards Will. "You want to come?"

"If you'll have me," Will said. "And I'll remind you that I am over eighteen and I do not attend Merlin."

"Of course I want you to come," Elsif smiled. "But I don't want to force you. I don't think Versario is going to be fun."

"I don't believe that," Will said. "Anywhere with you is guaranteed to feel like an adventure."

A warm feeling spread over Elsif. Even though she was in deep waters, she felt the courage to swim as long as Will was beside her. "Will, how do you feel about marriage these days?"

"I have a favorable attitude towards the concept," Will noted. "Why do you ask?"

"Because," Elsif began. "Maybe I have a favorable attitude towards it too. I don't know a lot these days, but I know that I want to be with you. For the journey to Versario and for the rest of my life." After a deep breath, Elsif asked, "William Woods, will you marry me?"

Will smiled wider than ever before. "I'd love to, love."

*****

"I can't believe Elsif!" Ruth shouted as she paced around the fountain. "The nerve she has is monumental! It's ridiculous!"

Juniper arrived at the fountain shortly after Ruth, but he wasn't able to contribute a word over Ruth's rant.

"And she won't let us come with her!" Ruth yelled. "The audacity! That's not her decision! She's always bossing us around and I'm sick of it! She's such a hypocrite! She's leaving Merlin! She's ruining her life! I have the right to ruin my own life! She's actually leaving us! Leaving me!"

"Ruth, I'm going with them," Juniper finally said when Ruth took a breath.

She stopped in her tracks. "What?"

"I'm going with them," Juniper repeated. "They don't know what they're getting into and they'll need someone from Versario to help them."

Ruth shook her head. "You wouldn't go without me."

"As much as it pains me, Elsif is right," Juniper said. "You're too young, you don't have a degree, and you need to stay here. I need to go back to Versario. To help them and for-" He hesitated. "For unfinished business."

"What about me?" Ruth questioned, her irritation growing. "You're leaving me!"

"It's not like I can go back to Merlin," Juniper argued.

"But you could stay in the region! In a nearby town or something!"

Juniper shook his head. "I need to go."

"No you don't! You need to stay here with me! If you leave then that's basically saying you don't care about me anymore!"

Juniper scoffed. "Ruth come on. That's ridiculous."

"Ridiculous?" Ruth asked in disbelief. She backed away from Juniper, separating herself in an attempt of protection. "We're done."

"What?"

"We're done," Ruth said in a deadly serious tone. "Whatever this was, it's done, and I never want to see you again."

"Ruth-"

"No!" Ruth exclaimed, and turned away from Juniper. "If we're not together then we might as well be done! Goodbye forever, you jerk!"

*****

Elsif, Jazzy, Will, and Juniper were packed and ready to leave for Moorville an hour and a half later. Most of the bags were in a carriage, and Ruth, Milly, and Rose were waiting to say their goodbyes.

Ruth avoided eye contact with Juniper, and stood with her arms crossed. Milly helped put the last of the bags in the carriage, while Rose was giving a million suggestions on how to fill their time in Versario. Once the carriage was fully packed, the final goodbyes began.

Milly gave a quick hug to Elsif and Jazzy, and a firm handshake for the boys. Rose hugged Jazzy then Elsif, but lingered for a few extra seconds on the second hug. After she let go, Rose proceeded to make jokes and pretend everything was normal.

Ruth walked up to Jazzy first, and embraced her. "Jazzy," Ruth whispered. "I didn't keep the secret from you because I was ashamed of you. I kept it a secret because I didn't know what to do and I'm bad at feelings and stuff. I'm just kind of an idiot, if you haven't noticed already."

"It's all in the past now," Jazzy said. "None of it matters anymore."

Ruth leaned back. "Still, I'm so incredibly sorry."

"All is forgiven," Jazzy smiled.

Ruth let go of Jazzy, and walked over to Elsif. Elsif nervously stood in front of her, until Ruth eventually hugged her. Pulling away, Ruth said in a whisper, "Can I please come?"

"I wish you could," Elsif said. "But this is for the best."

"Maybe I don't care about the best?"

Elsif smiled sympathetically. "But I do. Let's just wait until you're eighteen, have a degree, and maybe mature a little bit. Then we can talk."

Ruth didn't respond, but walked away with her head drooped as she joined Milly and Rose. They watched as the four deserters climbed into the carriage.

"We should get going before Merlin sees you," Will told Juniper.

"They won't stop me from going back to Versario," Juniper said. "That's the one thing I can be sure of."

The girls followed the boys' into the carriage, and they closed the door behind them. All too soon, it was rolling away and out of sight.

"Anyone want to get dinner?" Milly asked.

"I could eat," Rose answered and followed Milly to the school.

Ruth's feet stayed in place.

"So," Rose said as she and Milly walked to dinner. "What now?"

"I guess we go home tomorrow for August break," Milly said. "Do you want to come to Navisia with me?"

"No," Rose shook her head. "I want to go to Mirabilis. But do you want to meet up in Stellae half way through?"

"Sure," Milly agreed. "But I would like to point out that I'm having to make a much farther carriage ride than you."

"I'll get you a trophy," Rose teased.

"Should we invite Ruth?" Milly asked as the girls looked back to see her standing where the carriage once was.

"Later," Rose answered. "She's having one of her dramatic moments. Wouldn't want to interrupt."

Ruth stood in the same place for a while. Eventually she was accompanied by a little squawk.

"Hi Gertrude," Ruth mumbled, as a few tears fell down her cheeks.

"SQUAWK!" Gertrude cried, which Ruth understood as- *why are you crying?*

"Because someone really loved me, and I really love them too."

Epilogue: An Inevitable Aftermath

On October 5th in the year 4002 war broke out in Fantasma for the first time in over 600 years. Magicis sent troops to the border of Versario, and 1,200 miles of unquenchable fire was burned. Hundreds of buildings, homes, businesses, roads, and properties were destroyed. Magicis reported no casualties, and it was a necessary response to the war accusations.

Versario had a different view. Versario claimed that hundreds were killed and launched many attacks from that day forward. Word was heard every couple of weeks that a random town in Magicis was sieged, but that the attack was handled quickly and in Magicis' favor.

I didn't know what to believe at the time. Life was so different in those first three years. I was newly wed, a mother a year later, and trying to keep five people afloat. It didn't feel like a war zone, but I suppose my fear was the same as if it was. The first three years are a blur now, but sometimes I wish for those times. It was simple back then, or at least simpler. I guess it was the novelty of the situation that I miss. Everything was different but not bad different yet. The weight didn't begin to pull until the autumn of 4005. But you'll learn more about that time in my next correspondence.

I don't have many regrets from the two years that I have told you about. Well, regret probably isn't the right word. I suppose I have many regrets, but not many that I still think about. I've learned not to dwell on the past; it has never done me any good. It took me decades to learn that, but I've finally let go of my many mistakes. But there is one decision that I think of often. Too often. It haunts me to this day.

Those eyes. They were so familiar. The face that I had come to know from the hundreds of books I had read. The pointed ears that did not belong on the head that I knew so well. I forced that memory out of my mind for so long in fear I hallucinated or had a moment of insanity. But I never forgot. He showed up in my dreams. He forced himself into my mind during moments of weakness. I wish I could have had the courage to say something to someone. I don't know who that would have been, or who I could have trusted. But I so dearly wish I had done anything, besides the nothing I had chosen. Oh, how the world may have turned out so differently. Or maybe it would have been the same, but at least I wouldn't have to live with the guilt. He still haunts me. His eyes stare into my soul at night like when they stared at me for the first time at my final Felix Finis Ball.

Xen Siid, the warlock and owner of the famous Hat, is ever so present in my mind every day.

The End: The adventure will continue in book 2 of The Fantasma Series

Acknowledgements

First I want to thank my family. This book has been a crazy journey, and I appreciate all the support, love, and encouragement I have gotten from my family.

I want to specifically thank my mom, Karen Butenuth, for helping with initial edits of my book. You were able to help me tie down many confusing loose ends, so thank you!

I also want to thank my editors who have helped me with my terrible grammar. Thank you to Hannah Myrum, Rebecca Barak, Eden Myers, and again my wonderful mom. You made the book readable and everyone that has read to this point thanks you!

This book also wouldn't be what it is without the terrific inspirations from my younger cousins, Hannah Myrum, Emalie Myrum, and Abbey Myrum. Many of the scenes or plotlines are directly inspired by them. So thank you all for being entertaining during our family parties growing up.

I want to thank my co-author Tyler Cable, for being the first one to come up with the story of cousins going on crazy adventures. You reached out to your annoying little cousin years ago, and now this beautiful book has been written. Thank you Tyler for being the best eldest cousin and for showing me the world of writing.

But most of all, I would like to thank God. I had a very different life planned out for myself, that I don't think I would have enjoyed. God grabbed a hold of me, and showed me a passion that I had never thought possible. God took me down His path instead of mine, and because of His blessings I was able to write this book. I gave God Fantasma many years ago, before I had any wish to publish, and He did what only He could and made my dreams come to life. Thank you God, for blessing me beyond words. All glory goes to Him.

About the Authors

E.K. Butenuth (Ellie) is an indie author who has always loved a good story. She was born and raised in the best and most boring place in the world, the midwest. Ellie attended Trinity International University and then Olivet Nazarene University where she graduated with a psychology degree, and it is debated amongst many if it will ever be used. Ellie was raised in a wonderful family, who loved her along with Christ. Ellie loves everything Disney, Jane Austen, and Jesus.

Tyler Cable is an indie author who loved books, movies, and intense story building. He grew up going to Disney World, Door County, Devil's Lake, Brazil, and having many adventures of his own. His favorite books were Lord of the Rings, Harry Potter, Percy Jackson, and many other great stories. He had many journals filled with hundreds of different ideas for books, and wanted to write for a majority of his life. He spent the last few years of his life working for Disney World, where he witnessed magic and stories everyday.

***

In Ellie's 8th grade year, on a trip to Disney World, Ellie's older cousin Tyler suggested a wild idea. What if they wrote a story about Ellie and her crazy younger cousins going on adventures together? Ellie, who liked that her older cousin was giving her attention more than the idea of writing, agreed with excitement. Time passed and life got busy so the story was put on a back burner.

On February 23, 2020 Tyler unexpectedly went home to heaven at the age of twenty-six. Ellie missed her older cousin dearly, and began writing their story to remember him. While honoring Tyler, Ellie fell in love with writing. She developed the world of Fantasma and created a long series full of plotlists and interesting characters. In 2022 Ellie had the opportunity to publish Fantasma with a small Christian indie publishing company. After two years with this company, Ellie decided she wanted to rewrite some of the story and republish Fantasma with her own publishing company. So she did exactly that.

Fantasma would never have been possible without Tyler, and Ellie is extremely blessed that God chose her to be his annoying little cousin.

Introduction to Milk and Honey Publishing

Milk and Honey Publishing LLC was established in 2025 by E.K. Butenuth. Milk and Honey Publishing is an indie publishing company that publishes books of all genres written by Christian authors. Our mission statement is to honor God through written literature. 'The Adventure Begins In Fantasma' is the first book published through Milk and Honey Publishing and new books are coming out soon. Visit our website www.milkandhoneypublishing.net to see our newest releases and see what we are about!

Any inquiries about publishing should be directed to milkandhoneypub@gmail.com or at our website at www.milkandhoneypublishing.net

A Message of Hope

It's no secret that life is filled with hardship. The world can be a dark and weary place, and sometimes a good fantasy story offers the perfect escape. But when the story ends and reality returns, we're reminded that our own world still suffers. We live in a fallen world full of sin, death, and a desperate need for hope.

Yet, I'm here to tell you there *is* a glimmer of hope. But it's not a faint flicker, but instead it's the brightest light and our saving grace. Jesus Christ came to earth and willingly gave His life on the cross to save us from our sins. Because of Him, we have hope for tomorrow. He promises never to leave us, no matter how dark the night may seem. Through His sacrifice, He offers us the greatest gift of all, salvation.

When we accept this gift and believe that Jesus Christ died for our sins, we are restored to a relationship with God Himself. For no one comes to the Father except through Christ. Salvation through Jesus is the only path to eternal life. Our own goodness or good deeds can never earn it, but instead it's freely given by grace alone.

If you love stories of redemption, courage, and ultimate victory, then the greatest story ever told is waiting for you in the Holy Bible. The Gospels, Matthew, Mark, Luke, and John, are a beautiful place to begin, as they tell the story of Jesus' life, death, and resurrection. And remember, you can speak to God anytime, anywhere. Prayer is easy because God can always hear you.

Please know that you are deeply loved by Jesus Christ. He died for *you*. You are not alone. You are not beyond hope. You are seen, known, and loved beyond all measure.

With love and hope,

E.K. Butenuth

9 781970 544015